Dare moved to  **Carly about t unfortunately direction—an body was plast** ~~p~~ **against his.**

Right where he'd wanted her ever since he'd watched her sexy swaying in front of him in a little green skirt that had turned her eyes the same hue.

Neither one of them moved for a heartbeat. Two. And then they both took a step back. Her hand went to her hair, as if to straighten it, and a loose strand caught on the gloss of her lipstick. Dare nearly reached out to fix it himself, but shoved his hands in his pockets at the last minute.

Another blush rose up over her creamy cheekbones and her hand shook when she brought it back down to her side. 'This has to stop,' she muttered, frustration etched across her brow. 'I can't explain…'

She stopped abruptly and Dare picked up the thread. 'This thing between us?'

She shook her head in denial. 'There is no thing.'

Dare smile was slow in coming. 'Oh, there's *definitely* a thing.'

With two university degrees and a variety of false career starts under her belt, **Michelle Conder** decided to satisfy her lifelong desire to write and finally found her dream job. She currently lives in Melbourne, Australia, with one super-indulgent husband, three self-indulgent but exquisite children, a menagerie of over-indulged pets, and the intention of doing some form of exercise daily. She loves to hear from her readers at www.michelleconder.com.

Visit the Author Profile page at millsandboon.co.uk for more titles.

DEFYING THE BILLIONAIRE'S COMMAND

BY
MICHELLE CONDER

MILLS
BOON

First Published in Great Britain 2016
By Mills & Boon, an imprint of HarperCollins*Publishers*
1 London Bridge Street, London, SE1 9GF

© 2016 Michelle Conder

ISBN: 978-0-263-92130-4

Our policy is to use papers that are natural, renewable and recyclable
products and made from wood grown in sustainable forests. The logging
and manufacturing processes conform to the legal environmental
regulations of the country of origin.

Printed and bound in Spain
by CPI, Barcelona

DEFYING THE BILLIONAIRE'S COMMAND

To Mary, my mother.
Thanks for being the best mother a girl could ask for.

CHAPTER ONE

IT WAS OFTEN said that Dare James was a man who had everything, and most days he'd be hard-pressed to disagree. Blessed with bad-boy good looks, and the stamina and physique any star athlete would envy, he enjoyed expensive cars, even more expensive women, and homes that spanned the globe.

A self-made billionaire by the age of thirty, he had started with nothing and now, thanks to sheer hard work and old-fashioned grit and determination, he pretty much had anything a man could want.

What he didn't have was the ability to handle fools lightly, especially pompous, fat-cat fools who understood that the stock market went up and down as long as their own wealth wasn't affected.

Dare propped his feet on his desk and leaned back in his chair. 'I don't care if he thinks we should dump the stock,' he told his CFO over the phone. 'I'm telling you to hold it. If he wants to question my judgment again he can take his business elsewhere.'

Clicking off the call, he thumbed through to the next issue he had to deal with.

'Trouble?'

Dare glanced towards his office door to find his mother framed in it. She'd flown from North Carolina to London the previous night, stopping overnight at his before she headed to Southampton to visit an old friend.

Dare smiled and dropped his feet from his desk. 'What are you doing up this early, Ma? You should still be asleep.'

His mother strolled into his office and perched on one

of his sofas in the sitting area. 'I needed to talk to you before I head off today.'

Dare glanced at his watch. Business always came first in Dare's world, except when it came to his mother. 'Of course, what's up?'

If she wanted to borrow Mark, his driver, to take her to Southampton he'd already arranged it.

'I received an email from my father a month ago.'

Dare frowned, not sure he'd heard her right. 'Your father?'

'I know.' Her brow quirked. 'It was a surprise to me too.'

Dare wasn't sure what shocked him more, the fact that she'd received an email, or the fact that she'd taken so long to tell him about it. 'What does he want?'

'To see me.'

Her hands twisted together unconsciously in her lap and Dare's gut tightened. When a man who had kicked his daughter out of her home for marrying someone he didn't approve of contacted her thirty-three years later you could bet something was up. And Dare doubted it would be good.

'Bully for him,' he said without preamble.

'He invited me up to the house for lunch.'

The house being Rothmeyer House, a large stone mansion set on one hundred and twenty-seven acres of lush English countryside.

Dare made a derogatory sound in the back of his throat. 'Surely you're not considering it,' he dismissed. Because he couldn't think why she would. After the way the old man had hurt her, it was the last thing he deserved. And the last thing his mother should risk.

Unfortunately he could already tell that she was not only considering the invitation, but that she wanted to go.

'The man's done nothing for you,' he reminded her, 'and now he wants to see you?' Dare knew he sounded contemptuous on her behalf and he was. 'He has an ulterior motive. You know that, right? He either needs money or he's dying.'

'Dare!' his mother exclaimed. 'I didn't realise I'd raised such a cynic.'

'Not a cynic, Ma, a realist.' He softened his voice. 'And I don't want you getting your hopes up that he's suddenly regretting his decision to cut you off all those years ago. Because if he's not dying it will be some kind of power play, mark my words.'

Dare knew he sounded harsh but someone had to look out for his mother, and he'd been doing it for so long now it had become second nature.

'He's my father, Dare,' she said softly. 'And he's reached out.' Her hands lifted and then fell back into her lap. 'I can't explain it really but it just feels like something I should do.'

Dare was a man who dealt in facts, not feelings, and as far as he was concerned his grandfather, Benson Granger, Baron Rothmeyer, was offering far too little far too late.

His mother could have used his help years ago. She didn't need him now.

'He mentioned that he's tried to find me before,' she said.

'He couldn't have tried very hard. You didn't exactly hide out.'

'No, but I have a feeling your father might have had something to do with that.'

Dare's eyes narrowed. He hated thinking about his father, let alone talking about him. 'Why do you say that?'

'Once when you were young and I still believed in him he said he'd made sure my father would always understand what he'd lost. I didn't think much of it at the time but now I wonder what prompted him to say that. And you know my father had no idea that you even existed until I mentioned it.'

'Well, he'll know I exist if you decide to take up his invitation because you won't be going alone.'

'So you think I *should* go?'

'Hell no. I think you should delete the email and pretend you never received it.'

His mother sighed. 'You're one of his heirs, Dare.'

Dare scowled. 'I don't care about that. I have no interest in inheriting some old pile of rubble that probably costs more money to run than it's worth.'

'Rothmeyer House is very beautiful but...I can't help but think I made a mistake keeping you away from him after your father died. He is your only remaining relative on my side of the family besides your uncle, and your cousin, Beckett.'

Dare rounded the desk and took his mother's tightly clasped hands in his. 'Look at me, Ma.' He waited for her to raise her blue eyes to his. 'You did the right thing. I don't need him. I never did.'

'He changed after my mother died,' she said softly as if remembering something painful. 'He was never the most demonstrative man, but he became almost reclusive. Distant with everyone.'

Dare raised a brow. 'He sounds like a real gem.'

That brought a smile to his mother's lips, softening the deep lines on either side of her mouth and making her look more like her relaxed self. At fifty-four she was still a strikingly attractive woman, and finally seemed to have embraced life again and shaken off the many tough years she'd had to endure.

Which was one of the reasons Dare resented this communication from her estranged father now. His mother was happy and didn't need any reminders of the past; which was called the past for a reason.

'And our estrangement wasn't all his fault,' she continued softly. 'I was impetuous back then and…in the end he was right about your father and I was too proud to admit it.'

'You can't possibly blame yourself.' Dare frowned.

'No, I don't, but…' She looked up at him. 'You know, it's the strangest thing but right before he emailed me I started having dreams that I was back in the house. It's almost like a premonition, don't you think?'

Dare believed in premonitions about as much as he believed in fairytales.

'What I think is that you probably need closure. And I'll support you any way I can. Even going with you if that's what you want.'

She beamed him a smile. 'I was hoping you'd say that because after I mentioned you, he said he'd like to meet you.'

Great, Dare thought, just what he needed: a family reunion. 'When is this lunch?' he asked.

'Tomorrow.'

'Tomorrow!'

'Sorry, darling, I should have given you more warning, but I wasn't sure I was even going to accept until today.'

Dare still wished she hadn't, but his mind was already turning to the logistics. 'Who else will be there?'

'I don't know.'

'Has he remarried? Do you have a stepmother, by chance?' His lips twisted cynically.

'No, but he did say he had a guest staying with him.'

'A woman?'

His mother shrugged. 'He didn't say. Our communication has been a little formal up to this point.'

'It doesn't matter,' Dare dismissed. 'I'll have Nina rearrange my diary.' He frowned. 'We'll leave at—'

His mother shook her head. 'I promised Tammy I'd see her in Southampton later today and I can't cancel on her.

Why don't I meet you at Rothmeyer House tomorrow just before twelve?'

'If that's what you want.' He sat down at his desk. 'I've organised Mark to drive you today. I'll ask him to stay overnight to make things easier.'

'Thank you, Dare. You know I couldn't have asked for a better son, don't you?'

He stood up as she approached his desk and he enfolded her in his arms. 'And you know I'd do anything for you.'

'Yes, I know. And I appreciate it.'

Sensing a lingering sadness in her voice, Dare wondered if she was thinking about his father. Thinking about what a roller-coaster ride it had been with him right up until his death when Dare had just turned fifteen.

At best his father could be called a drifter chasing one dream after another in search of the big time, at worst he had been a conman with feet of clay. The only valuable lesson Dare had ever learnt from him was how to spot a con at fifty paces.

But it had been a good lesson that had helped Dare make more money than he could ever have imagined. And he had imagined a lot growing up in the poorest suburb in a small American town.

It had also stood him well when it came to relationships. For a while Dare had run with a rough crowd, but he'd soon learned that brothers were only brothers as long as you toed the line.

Since Dare didn't like toeing anyone else's line but his own, he kept to himself and trusted very few people.

Finding out when he was eighteen that his mother had an aristocratic lineage had only been interesting in that it had made Dare even more resentful of the family who had turned her away, thus forcing her to take three jobs just to make do. He'd never wanted to meet any of them and he still didn't.

But meet them he would and it wouldn't be tomorrow when his mother turned up for lunch. It would be today. This afternoon.

If Benson Granger thought he could insinuate himself into Dare's mother's life for any reason other than an altruistic one, he had another think coming.

And while it wasn't at all convenient to take a trip to Cornwall that afternoon, it would give him a chance to take his new toy out on the open roads.

Dare smiled, but it wasn't the charming, devil-may-care smile that made women swoon and men envious. It was a hunter-with-his-prey-in-his-sights smile, and for the first time since his mother had given him the disturbing news Dare thought he might actually enjoy setting his grandfather straight on a few things.

The locals at Rothmeyer village said that the summer they were having was the best in the last thirty years. Warm, balmy days, and light, breezy nights straight out of a Beatrix Potter fable.

Up at Rothmeyer House, the grand estate that bordered one side of the village, Carly Evans braced her spent arms on the edge of the deep blue swimming pool and hauled her tired body out of the water.

'Whoever said they got an endorphin rush out of exercise was either lying or dead,' she muttered to no one but the Baron's Pekinese, who snapped at passing insects as he lay like an untidy mop in the shade of the terrace.

Carly had been doing laps of the pool and jogging during her free time at Rothmeyer House since she'd arrived three weeks ago and she'd yet to feel anything other than exhausted and sore.

Not that she should be complaining on a day like today. Or any day. Working as the elderly Baron Rothmeyer's temporary doctor had been a real coup. Not only was the location spectacular, but, due to the Baron having to undergo a life-threatening operation in two weeks, it was also live-in. As in, living in the main house, live-in.

But the job would be over soon and she'd have to move on. Which was fine with Carly who, much to her parents' distress, had become something of a wandering gypsy this past year.

She pulled a face at the thought and squeezed water out of her long red hair, flicking it back over her shoulder. She was about as much like a gypsy as a nun was a circus performer, and up until a year ago she had led a very conventional life as a hard-working doctor in one of Liverpool's best hospitals.

That was until the bottom had fallen out of her world and ruined everything.

Grabbing a towel, Carly briskly swiped at her face and body. She grabbed her phone and settled onto a lounger, determined that with the Baron gone for another few hours she was not going to waste her free time thinking about the past.

'If you don't face things,' her father had said, 'they become mountains instead of molehills.'

As far as Carly was concerned hers had started out as a mountain and when it became a molehill she might consider returning home. Which was just as hard for her as it was her loving family because at heart Carly was a homebody who loved her parents. And her sister.

A familiar lump formed in her throat as the past lurched into her consciousness.

To distract herself she grabbed her cell phone. She had one new email from her parents, who would no doubt be subtly trying to find out if she really was okay, one from her old alma mater, and another from her temp agency, Travelling Angels.

Clicking to open her work email, she read that they had

another job lined up for her as soon as this one was finished and did she want it. Being one of only three fully qualified doctors on their roster, she had so far not been without work. Which was fine with Carly. Busy meant less time for contemplating past mistakes.

But she wasn't ready to think about her next move yet so she closed that email and tapped on the one from her parents. Yes, there it was, the question of when they would see her next, and whether she'd made any decisions about her future.

Carly sighed and closed that email as well.

A year ago her beautiful, kind and gregarious sister had died of a rare and aggressive form of leukaemia. To add insult to injury, Carly's über-successful boyfriend had been cheating on her instead of being by her side to support her.

Not that she'd really turned to Daniel for support during those months. Being an important cardiologist, he was generally busy and, if she was being honest with herself, their relationship had never been like that.

He had pursued her because he respected her and she had accepted his invitation to go out because she'd been flattered by his attention. Then Liv had become sick and everything had fallen apart. Daniel had become resentful of the time she spent with her sister, questioning her about her movements at every turn and accusing her of cheating on him and using her sister as a ruse.

No matter what she had said, he hadn't believed her and then she'd discovered that in fact he had been the one cheating on her. On top of all that, everyone at her hospital had known about it and no one had said a word to her. The whole experience had been mortifying.

Feeling the sun burning into her skin, Carly yanked on a pair of cut-off denim shorts, dislodging the slender black velvet jeweller's box that had arrived for her earlier that day.

Still not quite believing what was inside, she opened it and once more marvelled at the divinely expensive ruby necklace nestled against the royal blue silk lining.

'To match your hair,' the card had read, followed by a swirling signature that denoted the sense of importance Benson's grandson, Beckett Granger, cloaked himself in.

Carly shook her head as she took out the necklace. For a start her hair was more orange than ruby red so if Beckett had thought to impress her with his cleverness he'd be disappointed.

If he thought to impress her with the amount he must have spent on it he'd be disappointed as well. Carly was too practically minded for lavish jewellery and still wore the diamond stud earrings her parents had bought her ten years ago, much to Liv's disgust.

But she did have to give him points for his approach. The necklace was undoubtedly the most expensive attempt a man had ever made to get her attention and she'd had a few offers over the years. Some had been patients, or relatives of patients, others had been doctors—but Benson's pompous grandson had taken the cake.

Even if she weren't still getting over a bad relationship with a doctor with a God complex she would never have gone for Beckett. There was something a little bit slimy about the man. He also had a sense of entitlement a mile wide and at one point, when she'd declined yet another invitation to dinner, she'd been sure he'd been about to stamp his foot.

Since Benson didn't want anyone to know about his illness, Beckett believed her to be the daughter of an important friend of his grandfather's but that hadn't stopped him from cornering her one night when he'd been two drinks past his limit. His attempt at seducing her had been more a nuisance than anything else, and Carly felt sure he would have been embarrassed about it the following morning.

It also spoke volumes that Benson trusted his staff with the information about his illness, but not his own grandson.

Still, the man could have been a god amongst men and she wouldn't have accepted his attention. She hadn't exactly sworn off men for ever, but she couldn't think of anything worse than adding a man into her complicated life right now. Not with the poor judgment she'd shown in the past.

Her father assured her that all she needed was a plan to get her back on track, maybe finish her surgical studies, but Carly wasn't even sure she wanted to remain in the medical profession, let alone become a surgeon.

The ruby necklace lay heavy in her palm, the sun hot on her shoulders. She'd have to get it back to him as soon as possible, but, while Beckett had entrusted it to the postal service, Carly wasn't so trusting. She'd much rather hand it back in person.

Spying her cotton shirt under a nearby lounge chair, Carly was about to fetch it when Gregory started yapping as if the grim reaper were bearing down on him.

Carly frowned at the pretentious little dog. All her life she'd brought home orphaned children and injured animals to take care of, her mother even complaining that she would save a caterpillar from a broccoli stalk if she'd let her, but when it came to Benson's prized Pekinese she had to admit she struggled. The pampered pooch had more of a sense of entitlement than Beckett, but she supposed it wasn't entirely his fault. Not with the way Benson doted on him.

'Okay, Gregory,' she said to him, 'you're going to bring the fire brigade if you keep making that racket.' She frowned as he pulled against his leash. 'What's got you so riled up anyway, boy?'

He was looking off towards the forest and Carly made the mistake of following his gaze because while her gaze was averted he did his funny little twist manoeuvre she'd been warned about and slipped his collar.

'Gregory. No,' Carly called in frustration. 'I mean heel. Dammit,' she muttered as the dog tore off across the lime-green lawn, his caramel and black coat flying back in the breeze. 'Come back here!'

The last thing she needed was the Baron's beloved pet getting lost right before his operation. She'd never forgive herself.

Muttering a string of curse words, she shoved her feet into her flip-flops and took off after the cantankerous animal.

Halfway across the lawn she was glad she'd been exercising because she was gaining on him when he ducked through a border of shrubs and into the forested area. Cursing her bad luck, she vowed she'd give him to Mrs Carlisle to make potluck soup with when she got him.

The Baron would never complain about tofu again!

The thought made her smile. He'd been complaining about her menu plan ever since she'd arrived, trying to convince her that French fries and battered fish were fine in moderation for a man in his condition.

'Gregory, you little pain in the backside.' Carly shoved low-hanging branches aside and tried not to scratch her bare arms and legs any more than she had. 'If you get prickles in your coat I'll send you to that nasty dog groomer again! Gregory, dammit, come on, there's a good boy.' She tried to inject warmth into that last command but she wasn't sure he bought it.

A slight movement had her turning left and she stopped at the edge of a clearing. A family of rabbits lay sunning themselves on a small patch of grass as if they didn't have a care in the world. It was so lovely she forgot about Gregory until he burst out from behind an old oak tree like a bullet from a gun, scaring the daylights out of her and the unsuspecting rabbits.

'Gregory, no,' Carly shouted, rushing after him. The rabbits scattered, the largest—most likely the mother—dashing through the brush. Cursing the cranky dog for real now, Carly tried to keep pace with them. No way was he going to kill the mother rabbit on her watch.

In no mood to chase the Baron's insubordinate dog, Carly didn't hear the gunmetal-grey motorcycle bearing down on her around the bend in the driveway until it was too late. In what seemed like slow motion she realised that she wasn't going to be able to stop her forward momentum in time and, irrelevantly, that she was going to die with Beckett's silly necklace still gripped in her hand.

Half waiting for the sleek machine to barrel into her, Carly skidded on the gravel and landed on her bottom, rolling down the grassy embankment that ran alongside the road.

Winded, she lay unmoving, blinking dazedly up at the china-blue sky above.

She heard a choice curse word before a male head abruptly blocked out the light. The man was little more than a huge outline against the bright sun and then he went down on bended knee, leaning over her.

If she'd thought she was breathless before it was nothing compared to how she felt staring up into eyes so strikingly blue she could still have been staring at the sky. Combine those with chestnut hair that curled forward over his forehead, a square jaw, and strong nose and he had the kind of face Carly bemusedly thought she could look at for ever.

'Don't move.' He had quite the voice too. Deep and low with just the right amount of authority to it. Which surely explained why she did exactly as he bade.

It wasn't until his large hands ran down her arms and over her legs that she tore her eyes from the way his black leather jacket hugged his wide shoulders and impressive chest.

'What are you doing?' she asked.

'Checking if you've broken anything.' The cold censure in his voice immediately put her back up.

'Are you a doctor?'

'No.'

She hadn't really expected that he would be—she'd never met a doctor encased in black leather before. 'I'm fine,' she huffed, not really sure if she was but, heck, she *was* a doctor!

'Keep still,' he growled as she struggled up onto her elbows.

'I said I'm fine.' She pushed at his hand on her leg and he rocked back on his heels. Carly could feel her heart beating hard behind her chest as he silently surveyed her.

'Good,' he finally said, standing up so that he once again towered over her. 'Perhaps you can explain what the hell you were doing running across the road like that. You could have been killed.'

Carly glanced at the sleek motorcycle waiting in the middle of the road like something out of a Batman movie. A flash of the motorcycle skidding in a graceful arc right before hitting her made her stomach pitch. The man had been riding that thing as if he were in the Indie 1000—or whatever that silly race was called—and now he wanted to make it her fault?

'Really?' she murmured pleasantly. 'If *I* could have been killed it was only because *you* were driving like a maniac on a narrow, unpaved road.'

Dare gazed down at the redheaded goddess spitting fire at him from eyes that were too grey to be green and too green to be grey. Olive perhaps.

'I was hardly driving like a maniac.' He'd barely been pushing fifty.

'Yes, you were *and* you were also on your phone!'

She said the last with wide eyes as if he'd been traversing a high wire at the same time.

'Don't get hysterical,' he told her. 'I wasn't on the phone. I was checking my GPS.' And in complete control the whole time.

'You had a phone in your hand while you were on a motorcycle! That's illegal!'

'Calm down, would you? I handled it.'

'Only just. And it's still illegal!'

Dare glanced down at her skimpy attire, a smile entering his voice. 'So what are you going to do? Arrest me?'

She glared up at him as if she'd like to do exactly that but not in the way he'd just been imagining. 'Who are you anyway?' she said haughtily.

He felt like saying the big bad wolf, given her snooty tone, but a better question was who was she? He glanced again at her cut-off denims and bright pink swimsuit that should have clashed with her bright hair but somehow didn't, immediately dismissing the notion that she was his elderly grandfather's guest. She looked more like the pool girl. The very *hot* pool girl. 'Who's asking?'

Her lips pursed into a flat line. 'I am.' She went to push up to her feet and paused when Dare automatically stuck his hand out to assist her. It didn't surprise him when she tried to ignore his offer of help but Dare was in no mood to put up with some holier-than-thou woman who had just taken a few years off his life when she'd come flying out of the trees and into his path.

'Take it,' he growled, grabbing onto her elbow as she tried to avoid him.

The way she wrenched her arm out of his grip as soon as she was vertical made his teeth gnash together.

'I don't need your help.'

'Listen, lady, it's only thanks to my quick reflexes that you're still here at all. You could show a little gratitude.'

'Don't you "lady" me. It's thanks to your crappy driving that I now have a sore—' She stopped as his eyes followed her hands to her bottom as she brushed it off.

He arched a brow. 'Behind?'

'Never mind,' she said primly.

'How did you not hear the bike anyway?'

'This is a private lane and I was chasing after a dog.' She gave his bike a contemptible glance. 'I was hardly expecting Evel Knievel to come barrelling down the road.'

'A dog, huh?' Dare unzipped his jacket and planted his hands on his hips. 'What kind of dog?'

He noticed she was staring at his chest, then his flat abdomen, and finally his zipper and heat poured through him as if she'd actually touched him.

As if sensing his visceral reaction to her she started inching away from him as if he were some would-be rapist and he scowled.

'Yes.' Her voice had grown husky and she cleared it. 'A very big dog, if you must know.'

If she used her brain, Dare thought with rising annoyance, she'd realise that if he was going to grab her he wouldn't be standing around arguing with her.

But even as he thought it his eyes dropped to her high breasts pushing up against the straps of her one-piece suit and those long, lightly tanned legs shown to glorious perfection in cut-off denims. He'd seen many girls dressed similarly on a hot summer's day in his youth but he was quite sure he'd never seen legs as good as hers.

'What are you looking at?'

His eyes lifted to hers. Moss green, he decided, and full of awareness of how appreciative he had been of her figure.

'Your legs.' He smiled. 'You have them on display. You can hardly blame a man for looking.'

'Excuse me?' Her eyes shot daggers at him and he supposed he deserved it. He wasn't here to come on to the pool girl and he was hardly desperate for female company.

'Listen—'

'How dare you?' She stabbed a slender finger at his chest. 'I'm wearing a bathing suit because it's hot and I've just been for a swim.'

'And you were looking for a dog. I get it. But—'

'Not that I need to explain myself to the likes of you,' she vented.

Dare's eyes narrowed dangerously. 'The likes of me?'

'That's what I said. Are you hard of hearing? Oh, no!' She gave a cry of dismay. 'My necklace!' She turned quickly, her russet cloud of hair swinging around her shoulders. 'I can't have lost it.'

Dare sighed. He was tired after driving hours to get here on top of already putting in what felt like a full day at the office, and in no mood to be insulted by some sexy little shrew. 'What does it look like?'

'It's a ruby pendant, on a gold—'

'This it?'

He reached into the longer grass where it circled a bush. He'd noticed a glint of something before when he'd first rushed over to her and now held a very expensive little trinket in the palm of his hand. He let out a low whistle of appreciation. She definitely wasn't just the pool girl if this was hers.

Dare flashed a smile. 'A pretty piece. I'm not sure it goes with the outfit though.' She stiffened as he looked her over. 'Might I suggest a string bikini next time?'

'I wasn't wearing it,' she said hotly. 'It was a gift.'

Dare laughed. 'I hardly thought you paid for it yourself, baby.' In his experience no woman would.

She stared at him mouth agape and he supposed he had sounded a touch derogatory but...

'Did you really just call me *baby*?'

Yeah, he had. For some reason discovering the necklace had made his mood take another dive. 'Look—'

'Listen? Look?' Her finger stabbed in his direction again. 'You are one condescending piece of work, *darling*.' She stepped forward, her cheeks pink with annoyance. 'Give me that.' She reached for the necklace in his hand but Dare reacted instinctively and raised it above his head. She was medium to tall in height but there was no way she was close to his six feet four.

Realising it, she pulled up short, her hands flattening against his white T-shirt to stop herself from falling against him. Her eyes grew wide, her soft mouth forming a perfect 'O', and his eyes lingered before returning to hers.

Dare would have said the whole 'time standing still' thing was just hogwash, but right then he couldn't hear a leaf rustling, or a bird calling, his mind empty of everything that didn't include getting her naked and horizontal as soon as possible.

Instinctively his free hand came around to draw her closer when the sound of yapping at his feet broke the spell. Disconcerted, Dare looked down into the upturned face of an ugly little mutt the size of a cat with its tongue hanging out. He grinned. 'This the big dog you were chasing?'

The redhead stepped back and threw him a filthy look as she reached for the small dog that danced just out of her reach.

'Gregory,' she growled in a warning voice. 'Heel.'

Dare would have laughed at her futile attempts to stay the dog if he hadn't been feeling so out of sorts.

'Here.' He held the necklace out impatiently as she made to run after the dog. 'Don't forget your gift.'

Turning on him with a malevolent look, she snatched the necklace from his hand and took off after the mutt. He doubted he'd have cause to see her again but strangely he found he wanted to.

Shaking his head, he walked back to his bike and shoved his helmet on, dismissing the pool girl from his mind as he gunned the engine and headed to the main house.

CHAPTER TWO

DARE PACED BACK and forth in what he surmised was a parlour room inside the grand house. He'd never been particularly good at cooling his heels and finding his grandfather out when he'd first arrived had turned an already grim mood further south. Two hours later it was fair to say it had hit rock bottom. He wondered if it was a tactical move on his grandfather's behalf because Dare had presumed to turn up unannounced a day earlier than he was expected.

Glancing around the elegant room, he took in the heavily oak-panelled walls dating back to the sixteenth century. Like the bedroom he'd been shown to earlier to 'freshen up'—which had most likely been code for ditching his leathers—the antique furniture was graceful and well-appointed. Given the state of the rest of the house and grounds that Dare had seen, he surmised that money wasn't behind the old man's invitation to his mother. Which left the possibility that he was ill and/or dying.

The thought didn't stir an ounce of emotion in Dare at all. But the line of oil paintings mounted high on the walls? They were most likely his ancestors, he thought with distaste, and they gave him the creeps. He steeled himself against the unexpected need to search out a likeness. He was nothing like these people and never would be.

It was hard to imagine his mother running around here as a child. The place might be majestic and steeped in history, but it was completely devoid of laughter and lightness. And so alien to his own impoverished upbringing. Not that the wealth of the place bothered him. He could buy it a thousand times over if he wanted to.

He checked his watch, impatient to meet the old man

who had unsettled his mother's world once more. And his own, if the truth be told.

'I apologise for keeping you waiting, sir.' The butler who had shown him to his room earlier tipped his head as he stepped into the parlour.

Dare smiled at the man's cordiality, but it didn't reach his eyes. Fed up with waiting in his room like a good little schoolboy, Dare had prowled around the house on his own, finally being shown into this room by one of the servants.

'Forget it,' Dare said. His quarrel wasn't with the butler so why make his life harder by being a jerk?

'May I fix you a pre-dinner drink, sir?'

Dare turned away from a life-sized oil painting of a man in a bad wig. 'Scotch. Thank you.'

He had no intention of staying for dinner but the butler didn't need to know that either.

Dare gazed around at the book-lined walls, softly lit lamps, and matching damask sofas. A tartan throw rug caught his eye, the mix of autumn colours reminding him of the pool girl's glorious mane of hair. She'd been absolutely beautiful, wild and pagan with that long, unbound mane splayed out against the bright green grass, and then she'd opened her eyes and he'd been jolted by the greyish-green hue that reminded him of the Spanish moss that grew on many of the trees back home. The combination was startling. Then there was her skin that had been creamy and, oh, so inviting to touch.

She had reminded him of the angel he and his mother used to place on top of their Christmas tree when he was a child. Her temper, though, had definitely not been angelic and his lips quirked as he recalled how her eyes had shot sparks at him whenever he'd riled her.

Something about her had made him want to get her all hot and bothered, even when she'd insulted him. Not that he had any time for the pool girl, he reminded himself. But still…he had no doubt as to how good those sweet curves of hers would have felt in his arms.

Catching the ludicrousness of his thoughts, Dare gave himself a mental slap-down. He was thirty-two years old, long past the age of mentally drooling about how a woman would feel in his arms. How she would taste on his lips. How he might find her once this business with his grandfather was done.

He took a swig of his drink. He was long past the age of chasing after women as well. Not that he'd ever had to do much of that. He'd always been good with his hands and had a strong attention to detail and the women had loved him for it. True, they often complained that he put work ahead of them, but he'd never claimed to be perfect.

He wondered yet again who had given the pool girl the expensive bauble she'd been so afraid she'd lost. No doubt a lover, but who? His grandfather? He nearly sprayed his Scotch at the thought. As if a gorgeous woman like that would have anything to do with a decrepit, old man.

A light sound outside the door caught his attention and he looked up as a white-haired, elegantly dressed gentleman entered the room.

Finally…

Dare took his grandfather all in at once. The tall build and broad shoulders, the lined face that was both proud and strong. He'd somehow expected his grandfather to look frail and sick and the fact that he didn't was as irritating to him as his thoughts about the redhead.

Both men took a moment to appraise the other, Dare giving nothing away beneath the old man's regard.

Let him look, he thought, *and let him understand that I am not the weak man my father was. I don't run from my responsibilities.*

'Dare.' His grandfather said his name with an air of familiarity that rankled. 'I'm so very pleased to meet you at last. Please forgive my absence when you first arrived. I would have rearranged my afternoon plans had I known you were arriving earlier.'

Dare didn't respond. He had no intention of pretending any form of civility with this man who had thrown his mother out all those years ago.

His mouth tightened, his attention drawn to a subtle movement behind the old man. When he saw it was the pool girl it took all his effort to keep his expression implacable.

His eyes moved down the length of her. The wild, pagan angel was nowhere in sight. In her place stood a very regal, very sophisticated young woman in a simple knee-length black dress and high heels, her rich red hair swept back into a tight knot at the base of her skull. Not many women could wear a hairdo that severe. She could.

Her moss-green eyes returned his regard coolly and a muscle jumped in his jaw. She wasn't the pool girl, that was for sure, which left the only other conclusion he had arrived at front and centre in his mind.

But surely not...

His grandfather turned to acknowledge her presence, his hand hovering at the small of her back as he guided her forward. 'Please allow me to introduce you to Carly Evans. Carly, this is my grandson, Dare James.'

She gave his grandfather a quizzical glance and Dare's jaw clenched at the unspoken communication between the two.

But surely yes...

This was definitely his grandfather's mystery guest.

He could barely believe it was true. He was so caught off guard he nearly missed the way her eyes dropped nervously from his as she stepped forward to greet him. 'Mr James.' Her smile was a little tremulous and he was somehow gratified by her nervousness. He bet she wouldn't insult him now. 'I'm pleased to meet you.'

God, she really was stunning and he didn't like the jolt of adrenaline that coursed through his blood at the sight of her. 'Ms Evans, it's a delight to see you again.'

Her eyes cut back to his with surprise. So she hadn't told his grandfather about their meeting. How very interesting.

'You've already met?' Surprise crossed his grandfather's craggy features as well and Dare was glad he wasn't the only one in the room who was thrown off course here.

'We ah…met earlier,' the goddess hedged, her face blushing prettily. 'I didn't realise he was your grandson at the time. For some reason I thought he'd be younger. And English instead of American.'

There was only one reason a beautiful young woman would be sleeping with an old man like his grandfather and it left a sour taste in Dare's mouth.

He remembered one time at Harvard when a woman had been playing both he and his room-mate at the same time. They'd both ditched her as soon as they found out. Dare had laughed that she'd wanted Liam for his money and Dare for his sexual prowess. Then they'd spent hours over beers arguing the point and debating the morality of women on the make.

No need to debate this woman's morality. It was staring him in the face. Or rather gazing adoringly at his grandfather.

'Perhaps you would have been a little nicer if you had known who I was,' he suggested, wanting to ruffle her smooth feathers as she had ruffled his.

Her eyes narrowed. 'I wasn't rude.'

Dare's brow rose. 'You were hardly welcoming, if I recall.'

'You nearly ran me down.'

'Ran you down?' His grandfather's brow furrowed with concern.

'I got a fright when I didn't hear the motorcycle...it was nothing,' she assured him gently.

'Then why bring it up?' Dare asked pleasantly.

She frowned at him. 'I didn't. You did.'

'Carly, are you sure you're okay?' His grandfather's concern was like an annoying splinter under the skin.

'Absolutely. Gregory broke his leash again and when I went to get him I wasn't concentrating well enough.'

'A woman who admits fault; be still my beating heart,' Dare mocked softly.

She shot him a fiery look that left scorch marks across the silk rug between them. Dare smiled and watched, transfixed as she collected herself and reinstated her sophisticated façade. The transformation was quite something to behold.

'I apologise if you thought I was in any way rude, Mr James,' she said, as if a poker were rammed up her delectable backside. 'It was not my intention.'

Not now that she knew who he was, anyway. She wouldn't want to do anything to unsettle her gravy train.

'Is that right?' he said smoothly.

Her face coloured again and her little chin went up at the challenging note in his voice.

He trapped her gaze with his. *Don't mess with me, my little beauty*, he silently warned. *You'll lose.*

She blinked as if to say she had no idea what he was on about and he nearly applauded her for her acting skills.

Instead he dismissed her and set his chilly gaze on his grandfather. 'Why is she here?'

His grandfather shifted uncomfortably. 'Carly and I have taken to having a drink before dinner and as I wasn't expecting you until tomorrow I invited her to join us. I hope you don't mind.'

For reasons he didn't want to examine, Dare did. Very much. 'And if I do?' He asked, sipping his Scotch.

His deceptively amiable question froze the cool smile on Carly's face.

His grandfather frowned. 'Carly is…well, she's a guest of mine,' he finished lamely.

'How nice for you.' Dare ran his hand over the length of the tartan rug, noting the frown on Carly Evans's face as he did so.

'I can go.' She moistened her lips with a nervous flicker of her pink tongue. 'I don't mind, really—'

'Stay,' Dare said, rethinking his position. It might actually be better to have her around to get a full picture of what was going on.

Her eyes darkened infinitesimally at the command. She obviously liked to be the one in charge.

So did he.

His grandfather cleared his throat to cut through the awkward silence and Dare watched him move to the drinks trolley. 'Cointreau on ice, Carly?'

'No, thank you,' she husked, moving forward. 'I'll just have water but, here, let me get it. You sit down.'

The lady had expensive taste, Dare thought, but then he knew that from the ruby necklace, which was markedly absent. In fact she wasn't wearing any jewellery to speak of. Had she not had time to put it on?

He watched as she fixed her own drink and poured tonic water for Benson without having to ask what he would like. How very *comfortable* it all was. The nubile, young woman playing up to the doddery old rich fool no doubt hoping he'd kick the bucket soon. Dare couldn't help but acknowledge that he was disappointed. He'd somehow felt she had more substance to her.

Yeah, right. Substance. Was that what he was calling lust these days?

Nothing like a cold shot of reality to kill that bird dead.

He glanced at her ring finger. No diamond rock there. Obviously she still had some work to do yet.

He felt something primitive unfurl inside him. Something dark and dangerous. Disgust, he told himself. Every one of his senses had gone on high alert as soon as she had entered the room and he didn't like it that he was so aware of her as a woman. Not when she was screwing his grandfather.

Just the thought of the two of them intimate made his stomach turn. Could a man even get it up at that age? A cynical smile touched the corner of Dare's mouth. He certainly hoped so.

But he wasn't here to think about his grandfather's sordid sex life, he reminded himself. He was here to find out why Benson had contacted his mother, and he wouldn't let himself get sidetracked by this wide-eyed mistress again.

'As pleasant as this is,' Dare mocked, facing off against his grandfather, 'what I want to know is why you contacted my mother.'

A heavy silence followed his lethally soft words and it sent a chill down Carly's spine.

When Benson had informed her that his grandson would be joining them for drinks Carly had thought he had meant Beckett, and she'd been pleased that she would be able to return his necklace to him and not have to worry about losing it.

Now she wished that it *had* been Beckett, because she had no idea how to deal with this arrogant American's barely veiled hostility. She especially had no idea how to deal with the way her insides jolted with nervous heat every time he trained his piercing blue eyes on her.

The Baron inclined his head towards his grandson, a small sigh escaping past his lips. 'I didn't imagine this would be easy.'

Carly noted the aggressive stance in the younger man. He might now only be wearing faded denim jeans and a white T-shirt but he looked no less intimidating for it. In fact he looked even more so because now she could see that he was as leanly muscled as she had first imagined. And with black biker boots on his feet…

'What did you imagine it would be?' Dare asked the Baron with cold disdain.

'Difficult,' he acknowledged wryly.

'Glad to see you're a realist.' His gaze homed in on the Baron like a shooter lining up a clay pigeon. 'At first I thought you needed money but given the appearance of the place I've discounted that. Which leaves the possibility that you're sick or dying. Not that you look it.'

A gasp escaped Carly before she could contain it. 'That is so rude,' she admonished, welcoming the bite of her temper in replace of her previous uncertainty.

Dare's lethal gaze swung to hers, pinning her to the spot. 'I'm sorry,' he said softly, 'what made you think I was talking to you?'

Oh! Carly refused to let him intimidate her. The Baron was her patient and it was her job to make sure he was well enough to undergo surgery to remove a brain tumour the size of a golf ball in two weeks' time. He needed rest and relaxation, not animosity and outright aggression.

She would probably be able to add heart attack to his list of ailments if his grandson continued on in this vein.

'You shouldn't speak to anyone like that!' she reproved.

'It's all right, Carly.' The Baron patted her hand. 'Dare has a right to feel angry. And from what I understand my grandson has a reputation for being ruthless, powerful, and relentless when he wants something.' He listed the traits as if they were trophies to be shown off on a mantel, Carly thought with disgust. 'It actually pleases me that he feels the need to defend Rachel.'

Carly tried to accept the Baron's version of things. Rachel, she knew, was Dare's mother, but other than that she didn't know anything about their history.

Fortunately the butler chose that moment to enter quietly and announce that dinner was ready to be served.

'Very good, Roberts.' The Baron smiled, but Carly could see it was strained. 'Dare, I was hoping that you might join us for the evening meal.'

Carly couldn't believe he was extending an invitation, given the level of disrespect he had been shown.

'I hadn't intended to,' Dare said coldly, and Carly felt her shoulders relax slightly as he declined. 'But if it's okay with Miss Evans perhaps I will.'

If it was okay with her? Carly's spine snapped straight. *Why would he put this on her?*

'Of course it's all right with me,' she said, too brightly.

'Very good.' She felt the Baron's relief as he exhaled. 'Shall we adjourn to the dining room? I, for one, am very eager to find out what Mrs Carlisle has prepared in your honour, Dare, and I do so enjoy eating my food without indigestion. Roberts, if you would be so kind as to set another place at the table?'

'Very good, sir.'

For a moment Carly thought—*hoped*—that Dare was going to change his mind, but then he shrugged.

'I haven't eaten anything decent since breakfast. Lead the way, old man.'

She felt the Baron tense as he cupped her elbow and she wanted to strangle Dare James with her bare hands. She was quite sure that whatever bad blood was between these men it didn't warrant this level of disrespect.

Reminding herself that it really wasn't any of her business, and that she was here for the Baron and the Baron alone, Carly let him lead her out of the room, acutely aware of Dare's cold eyes on her as she moved past.

She was infinitely glad that she'd taken the time with her appearance before dinner. And she told herself that she hadn't done so on the off chance that she'd run into this horrible stranger again...she'd done it because...yes, okay, she had wondered if she'd run into him in passing and she'd somehow felt that she'd need armour if she did. Well, she'd certainly got that right. And she had no idea how she was going to make it through a whole dinner if the Baron's grandson didn't start playing nice.

'You've done well for yourself, Dare,' the Baron said as they were all seated at the large dining table.

'Unlike my loser father, you mean?'

The Baron sighed. 'I didn't mean to sound as if I was passing judgment.' He moved aside as a plate was placed in front of him. 'Though you do seem to have inherited your father's acerbic wit.'

Score one for the older gentleman, Carly thought, completely disconcerted when she glanced across the table to find Dare staring at her.

'That's not all I inherited,' Dare bit out tautly.

'Duck *à l'orange*,' the Baron said, inhaling the fragrance as the servant stepped back. 'My favourite.'

Carly gave him a secret smile. 'I do relent sometimes,' she teased.

'This is all very nice,' Dare bit out, not hiding the fact that he didn't think it was nice at all. 'But I didn't come here to discuss food or to make small talk.'

Tension crossed the table like laser beams.

'I can see that,' the Baron said. He put down his fork. 'What did you come for, Dare? To put me in my place?'

'It's no less than you deserve.'

'I'm not going to argue with you about that,' Benson said quietly, 'but you have to understand I've only recently become abridged of your father's death. And of the fact that Rachel must have struggled for years afterwards. That she even had a child. You!'

'And you think that entitles you to contact her?' Dare said with barely leashed fury. 'You rejected her. You kicked her out when she chose my father over your archaic expectations. But she doesn't need you now. She's doing fine.'

'Thanks to you,' Benson acknowledged softly.

'My mother is a strong woman with high morals. She would have made it fine without me.'

Completely shocked by Dare's revelations, Carly felt like an interloper with no idea how to ease the tension between the two men.

'Perhaps we should save this conversation for when we're alone.' The Baron touched Carly's hand as he spoke and she realised she had a forkful of food held halfway to her mouth. 'There's no need to ruin Carly's appetite, hmm?'

'But it was okay to ruin my mother's life?' Dare's gaze was harsh when it landed on her again and her heart thumped behind her breastbone. 'By all means.' He stabbed a morsel of food on his plate. 'Let's not upset the lovely Carly. Tell me, Miss Evans, how long have you known my grandfather?'

Clearing her throat, and glad for the opportunity to turn the conversation away from the Baron in case it ratcheted up his blood pressure, Carly smiled politely. 'A few months now.' She had met Benson at a nearby clinic when he'd first presented with breathing problems and when he'd learned she was temping he'd requested her services.

'And when did you move in?'

Distracted by his mesmerising blue eyes, she took a sip of her sparkling wine. 'Three weeks ago. I...' She stopped, realising that she was about to reveal the reason for her stay. 'I—'

'I know of Carly's family,' Benson cut in to save her. 'A

happy coincidence really. Our ancestors fought together against the Jacobite Rebellion in 1715. Carly is the relative of a famous viscount.'

Dare curled his lip as if he couldn't have cared if she were directly in line to the throne. And her heritage hardly counted when she was the distant cousin of a cousin, and her family had lived a very humble existence for well over a century now.

'Excuse me, sir,' Roberts said, approaching Benson. 'A phone call has come through. I think you'll want to take it.'

'Fine, Roberts. Thank you.'

Looking irritated at the interruption, Benson pushed to his feet and took the hands-free phone proffered by the butler. He frowned in Carly and Dare's direction. 'I apologise for this interruption.'

As soon as the door closed behind him Carly was acutely aware of the antique clock ticking away in the corner of the room and the lean, powerful male regarding her across the table.

Dare James was too big, too sure of himself, and too arrogant for her liking. Oh, he didn't exactly have Daniel's air of cultured superiority over others—something she hadn't noticed until Daniel had well and truly humiliated her—no, Dare's was more a latent power that drew the eye and let everyone around him know that he was in charge. Which was just as bad.

The T-shirt he wore did little to contain the bulge in his biceps and he looked as if he had the strength to rip a giant oak out of the ground and snap it in half. Right now he looked as if he wanted to snap her in half.

A shiver raced down her spine at the memory of those large hands skimming over her, leaving her hot and bothered. She'd attributed her earlier physical response to the heat of the day and her worry over Gregory muddling her senses. Now she knew that it was her feminine instincts signalling danger with capital letters and she was listening. This time, she was definitely listening.

'More wine, Miss Evans?'

Carly regarded him warily as he picked up the wine bottle. As tempted as she was to settle her sudden nervousness with more alcohol, Carly knew drinking any more would put her at a disadvantage with this man. 'No, thank you.' She cleared her throat, searching around her frazzled mind for something to say. 'So, is this your first time at Rothmeyer House?' she asked.

'You mean you don't know?'

'No,' she said politely, her mind still absorbing what she had heard about his family history. 'Should I?'

Dare watched her nibble on the corner of her lower lip and he almost felt sorry for her. Then he remembered why she was even here and felt like snarling. 'I would have thought so.'

'I can't imagine why.'

'So sweet,' he murmured, wondering if her lips would feel as soft as they looked.

She frowned. 'I can see that you're very upset with your grandfather but do you really think that coming over all macho and being aggressive is going to help the situation?'

'Oh, good,' he said. 'We finally get to the part of the evening where we give up pretending we have to be polite to each other.'

Carly stared at him in shocked silence and Dare nearly laughed. What did she expect? That he would welcome his grandfather's innocent little mistress into his life with open arms? Not likely.

'I wasn't aware that you had been polite,' she mocked. 'I must have missed that brief moment in time.'

Dare laughed. 'You've got guts, I'll give you that.'

She frowned at him. 'Is this because I ran out in front

of you on the road?' she asked. Her expression so sweetly confused he found himself wanting to be taken in by her.

'Try again,' he said, calling himself a fool.

'Try again?' She shook her head. 'I don't know what to try again. I have no idea why you're being so hostile towards me.'

'You think I'm hostile?'

He knew damned well he was being hostile, Carly thought. She took a deep breath and reminded herself that she was usually the doctor others called on to deal with belligerent patients. 'Yes, you're being hostile,' she said calmly.

'On the contrary, I don't think I've been hostile at all. But if it makes you feel better, then I'll try to fix it.'

Carly let out a relieved breath. 'Thank you.' She gave him a shaky smile. 'It's just that your grandfather is very... tired at the moment.'

'Oh, now that's just showing off, Red.'

Showing off? Red? Carly's teeth ground together at his mocking tone. 'It's a basic human kindness to be civil,' she reminded him. 'If he were a stranger on the street I'm sure you wouldn't say the things you have.'

'But he's not a stranger on the street. He's a wealthy old fool.' He smiled but it didn't reach his eyes. 'And while we're on the subject, I have to commend you on your fast work. You must have some very special attributes to get in here in under a month.'

Carly frowned. If this was him trying to be less hostile he needed to go see someone about it. 'What do you mean by fast work?'

'The innocent confusion is good,' he murmured. 'It's a real turn-on. But I'm quite sure you know that. Tell me, Miss Evans, do you like books?'

Carly blinked. 'Books?'

'Those things people used to read in print form, but now mostly download online.'

'I believe they still print books, Mr James,' she said, a glimmer of anger burning low in her stomach. 'But, yes, I like to read.'

'I'm being facetious, Red.' He smiled easily. 'I prefer non-fiction to fiction. You?'

Carly would prefer to be anywhere but having to look into his handsome face. 'Both are good,' she said warily, wondering where he was going with this.

'Personally I'm too straightforward for fiction. I don't like things that are made-up.'

'Well, it depends on the author's imagination,' Carly said, pushing a strand of hair that had come loose from her bun back behind her ear.

'Do you have a good one?' He ran the tip of his index finger along the long stem of his wineglass.

'Miss Evans?'

Carly blinked. 'Book?'

'Imagination?'

'I…I like to think so, but I'm not an author. I couldn't wri—'

'Helen Garner is an author I admire.'

'Who?'

'I wouldn't expect you to know who she is. She's Australian. Very literary. I lived in Australia for a while when I was young. Did you know that?'

'No.' Carly glanced at the door wishing the Baron would hurry up and return. 'Look, Mr James—'

'Call me Dare.'

Carly let out a breath. 'This is all very fascinating but—'

'My mother discovered Ms Garner's work first, but then I happened to study her at university.'

'University?' Her voice sounded shaky and she cleared it.

'Keep up, Red.' His smile was so phony she wouldn't be surprised if he pulled out a deck of tarot cards and started reading her fortune. 'A university is an institution one attends when they're looking to better themselves.'

'I know what a university is, Mr James,' she said from between her teeth. 'I'm just struggling to follow the conversation.'

'Don't worry your pretty little head about it. You have other great *qualities* that are far more important, but you know that, don't you?' His eyes held hers. 'Are you sure you won't have another drink? Benson's pulled out all stops with the wine.'

As she realised that he had only been amusing himself at her expense Carly's slowly simmering anger just met its point of ignition. 'I'm trying to be pleasant here,' she bit out.

Dare rose from his seat, wine bottle in hand. 'Believe me, Red, so am I.'

Like hell. She glared at him. 'Call me that name again and you won't like the consequences.'

Many children had tried while she'd been growing up and they'd got the wrong end of her temper every time.

'Is that a threat?' he mocked.

Carly took a deep breath and told herself not to let him get to her. Then she didn't care. 'I don't like what you've been implying,' she said, facing him squarely. 'Why not come right to the point if you're so straightforward?'

He rounded the table and prowled towards her. Carly had to fight every bone in her body not to get up and run.

'You picked up on that, huh?'

'On your veiled animosity?' She gave him a superior smile of her own. 'Even a small child would have found it hard to miss.'

'But then children are so perceptive. Do you want children, Red?'

He reached out and brushed the loose strand of her hair back behind her ear. Carly gasped, twisting in her seat to look up at him. 'You don't care if I want children or not,' she said, distracted by the way her skin tingled where his fingers had grazed it.

'Not really,' he agreed affably, leaning on the back of her chair. 'But if they're on your agenda you might want to consider Benson's age. He won't exactly be pitching a football with the youngster in the backyard. Not that the backyard isn't big enough. You made sure of that first, didn't you?'

Carly would speak but she wasn't sure she could pry her teeth apart to get words out.

If she wasn't mistaken this Neolithic fool had just accused her of being his grandfather's mistress. She wasn't sure what she thought was worse. The fact that he believed her to have been intimate with a man nearly three times her age, or that he thought her a gold-digger.

Incensed beyond all reason, Carly tried to shove her chair back but found she couldn't because he had effectively caged her by bracing his arms on either side of her chair, his palms flat on the tabletop.

'Temper, temper, Red.' His warm breath feathered across her ear. 'What will Benson think if he comes back and finds you all riled up?'

'Hopefully he'll kick you out!' She knew she'd said the wrong thing by the way his muscles bunched in his arms. Her earlier analogy with that tree came to mind and she swallowed heavily. But instead of breaking her in half he leaned closer.

'I wanted to kiss you today, Red.' She jumped as something gently brushed the side of her face. His nose? 'Out there on that hot, dusty road.'

Carly struggled to swallow. 'No,' she said automatically.
'Oh, yes.'

Carly jerked sideways as he inhaled her scent but that only pressed her up against the solid mass of his opposite shoulder, giving him access to the line of her neck. He was so close she felt enveloped by his heady, male warmth. 'And you wanted to kiss me too.'

'No!' she denied, pulling herself together. 'You're a bigger fool than I first thought if you believe that.' She gave a short, sharp laugh to reinforce her words.

He sniffed behind her ear. 'You smell sweet.'

Every part of Carly froze except her pulse, which was racing. Was he about to kiss her? If he was…if he was she would…stop breathing.

'I'm right is what I am,' he murmured. 'I think you'd like me to do it even now with the old man in the next room. Should we give him a show?'

Before she could pick up the water jug and dump its contents over his insolent head the door to the dining room swung open. Dare slowly straightened, picked up the wine bottle, and poured her wine as if that were all he'd been doing all along.

Hot colour swept over Carly's face and she forced a smile to her lips.

'So sorry for the interruption,' Benson said, resuming his seat. 'That was Beckett.'

'How is he?' Carly asked, her voice pitched just a little too high. Really she couldn't care less about Beckett, but he was a safer topic than the man slowly making his way back to his seat as if nothing had just happened between them.

And nothing had, she reminded herself. He was taunting her, that was all, because he was a rude, callous individual with no manners whatsoever. What she wouldn't give to wipe that superior smile off his face and tell him she'd rather kiss a snake. Only he was a snake, she thought venomously. It was unfair of him to include her in his bad feelings for his grandfather. Making assumptions about her out of hand.

If she had wanted to bring him down a peg or two earlier, she wanted to even more now. Especially as he sat slouched back in his chair, gazing at her as if he were the king of the world. Well, he wasn't king of her world, and, oh, how she'd like to wipe that crooked grin from his face. He was enjoying her discomfort, damn him.

But to correct his nefarious assumptions would be to disclose her real reason for being here and she'd assured the Baron that she'd keep his secret for as long as he wanted to. And although she felt sure that Benson would be horrified at the conclusions his grandson had drawn she wasn't going to bring them up now.

And perhaps it would be better to let the arrogant Dare James labour under his misapprehensions about her.

Let him hang himself with them. The embarrassment he would no doubt feel at being so wrong about her—and his grandfather—would keep a smile on her face for days.

Yes. She let out a slow breath. She was going to enjoy watching this arrogant stranger squirm when he found out that, not only was she not a greedy little gold-digger, but that she was probably more qualified than he was.

University... She raised her wineglass in the air and gave him a small toast. She knew all about university and before she was finished with him he would know that she was a woman to look out for. A woman who was not going to be cowed by a man like him ever again.

And as for wanting to kiss him? She couldn't think of anything more revolting than having his smug mouth on hers.

She brought her glass to her lips, pleased with how steady and cool she felt, how detached. But then his gaze dropped to her mouth and her equilibrium wavered, all but disintegrating when the tip of his tongue came out to touch his bottom lip as if he was thinking about how she would taste.

It was a brief, subtle move but it set every one of her nerves on edge.

She had to force the cool liquid down past the lump in her throat without choking but she did it, and was pleased with herself until she realised that he was deliberately trying to put her off stride again. And it had worked. She now felt as if she were burning up from the inside out.

Damn him.

The man was beyond evil. He was a demon. The devil himself.

Fortunately the Baron chose that moment to break into their silent stand-off with a comment about the meal, which Carly had completely forgotten about.

She pushed the last of it around her plate as if her appetite hadn't fled, but then she noticed how pale Benson looked and could have kicked herself.

Concerned, she forgot all about his obnoxious grandson and clasped Benson's wrist. He gave her a wan smile, knowing that she was surreptitiously taking his pulse. One forty over eighty, at a guess. Not critical, but definitely too high for a man in his condition.

She gave him a warning squeeze. 'I think you should call it a night,' she advised softly. And she definitely wanted to. Anything to get away from the pointed glare of the man opposite her.

Dare watched the intimate little tableau play out before his eyes. The woman had no shame. No shame whatsoever, and his increasingly bad mood had nothing to do with the fact that he would like those slender fingers wrapped around a certain part of his anatomy, and where he was imagining was a long way from his wrist.

He didn't know what had possessed him to taunt her the way that he had, but it had very nearly backfired when he'd got a whiff of her light scent.

He breathed in deeply. He was pretty sure it was only

shampoo he had smelt, shampoo and woman, and his recall was so strong she might as well have been sitting right
beside him. Or in his lap.

A muscle jumped in his jaw and he realised he was
clenching his teeth hard enough to break them. It pained
him greatly that his body hardened in anticipation every
time he looked at her. And when she spoke; that lilting
English accent…he'd lived on and off in the country for
about a year and never noticed what a turn-on it was.

At times she sounded exactly like a reprimanding English schoolmarm and at others as if she'd just climbed out
of bed after being satisfied over and over. Add in that fire-
cracker temper and haughty attitude and it was all he could
do not to haul her across the table and find out if all that
fire and ice translated to passion between the sheets. Or,
on the table, rather, given their location.

Dare wondered what his grandfather would think if he
told him it would take little more than the crook of his finger to have his mistress in his own bed.

The thought made him sick. He wasn't here for that.
And he certainly wasn't here to compete with the old man.
Let him make a fool of himself over a woman if that was
his wont. Dare never had before and he never would.

Especially not over a woman like this. One with such a
low moral compass. Which was probably why it bothered
him so much that he found her so attractive. He just didn't
understand it. He'd been exposed to a limitless amount
of beautiful women since he'd reached puberty and even
more since he'd made it rich. Women more beautiful than
Carly Evans, and yet all evening he'd struggled to take
his eyes off her.

Bottom line, he despised her for what she was and he
despised himself for wanting her regardless.

'Goodnight, Mr James.'

'It's Dare,' he reminded her, holding out his hand even

though he knew it would be a mistake to touch her again. He couldn't help himself it seemed, his legendary self-control a distant memory in her presence.

She hesitated, glancing at his hand, and he nearly smiled for real when good manners—of which, yes, his had been in short supply that evening—determined that she must.

Immediately he raised it to his lips. 'Sleep well.' *Or not*, his eyes said.

Hers widened as if she read him loud and clear before giving him a dismissive little smile.

'I'll see you later,' she murmured to Benson. 'Don't be too long.'

Eager little thing, Dare thought, his fist clenched beneath the tablecloth.

He watched her leave the room, the chandelier above the table lovingly catching the highlights in her hair, before he turned his gaze on the old man.

Benson raised a brow in question and Dare saw just how tired he looked. Whatever news he had just received on the phone it hadn't been good. Not that he felt sorry for the old fool. He'd made his bed years ago and he could lie in it.

'I'm glad you came a day earlier,' Benson said, and Dare was quite sure he wasn't glad at all. 'It has given us a chance to air some grievances.'

Dare hadn't even scratched the surface. 'I won't have my mother hurt.'

'I get that. And I want you to know it's not my intention to hurt her again.'

Dare didn't say anything, just waited for him to continue.

When his grandfather sighed heavily Dare almost felt sorry for him. Almost. 'Your mother is coming for lunch tomorrow. I take it that you're staying.'

'Will the lovely redhead be there?'

His grandfather frowned at his disparaging reference to his mistress. 'Carly is a very nice young woman, Dare, she—'

'Spare me your platitudes. I'm sure she's wonderful.'

'She is. And...yes, she'll be at lunch tomorrow. Is that a problem?'

'Not for me.'

Benson nodded. 'Then I hope you will also accept my hospitality and stay the night.'

'I hadn't planned to.' What he'd planned was to find a hotel room and get some distance from the claustrophobic element of this enormous place, check the Dow Jones, catch up on work, but... His eyes drifted unconsciously to the door Carly Evans had just disappeared through. Practically it made more sense to be on site.

'I'll stay,' he said gruffly.

'Good.' Benson stood up. 'Then, if you'll excuse me, I'll see you in the morning. Oh, and, Dare...' the old man stopped beside his chair '...I understand your concerns. I made grievous mistakes thirty-three years ago. Mistakes I want to rectify.'

'Why now?'

'I have my reasons, reasons I'll share with you when we have more time. For now just know that I'm not going to let my foolish pride stand in the way again.'

'Just remember that I'll be watching you every step of the way,' Dare said softly. 'And if you do anything to my mother to upset her, I'll ruin you.'

CHAPTER THREE

'YOU KNEW HE'D think that?' Carly paused in the act of placing her stethoscope's bell over the brachial artery in Benson's upper arm.

The Baron had the grace to look contrite. 'Not until I saw the way he was looking at you after my phone call, and then…it was sort of flattering.'

'Flattering?' Carly inflated the cuff. 'Flattering that your grandson thinks I'm your mistress?'

One thirty over eighty. Better.

She tore off the Velcro cuff more forcefully than she intended. 'Only a man would think that,' she griped. 'But he thinks I'm a gold-digger as well.'

'He's a virile male, Carly, and you're a beautiful young woman. His masculinity was dented, that's all.'

'Dented?'

'That you would choose an old codger like me over a young buck like him.'

Carly sighed. 'And men think women are hard to understand. I don't even *know* him!'

'Doesn't matter.' He grimaced. 'How's the blood pressure?'

'Still too high. You know, you don't need this extra stress right now.'

'Probably not.'

'Definitely not.'

But Carly knew what had made him bring it into his life. The operation he was due to undertake was dangerous. At his age it could be fatal. He was putting his affairs in order, although for the life of her she didn't understand how someone could be estranged from their own child for over thirty years!

Her parents would rather cut off an arm than be estranged from her and they still hadn't recovered from her sister's death.

Carly being away this past year was the longest she had ever gone without seeing them and she missed them as much as they missed her. She couldn't imagine not ever seeing them again.

A lump formed in her throat at the thought that none of them would ever see her sister again. It wasn't her fault and yet...

Don't go there, she advised herself. *Focus on your patient.*

'You know, Dare probably would have thought it even if he knew you were a doctor,' Benson said. 'Beckett thought it as well at first.'

Men, Carly thought. Perhaps she'd give up on them altogether! She didn't know which grandson she disliked more. Dare, probably.

'Perhaps you should just tell them both of your condition,' she suggested. 'Then they'll know why I'm really here.'

'I told Beckett tonight,' he said, moving to the bed. 'But I want to at least spend the weekend with Rachel and Dare before they find out how serious my situation is.'

Carly pulled the covers up over his legs and smoothed them out. 'I don't think Dare will care,' she said cautiously.

'The boy had it hard growing up. I'm only just realising how hard.'

Carly kept quiet. She didn't know the Baron well enough to be in the inner circle of his confidences but she could see that he needed to talk. She handed him his pre-op meds and a glass of water. He swallowed them in one and sighed. 'I really don't blame Dare for hating me.'

'But you'd rather he didn't.'

He smiled up at her. 'No, I'd rather he didn't.'

Carly returned his smile. She was a doctor. Doctors were trained to have good listening ears, although her mother had once claimed that she had always been a good listener as long as her temper wasn't piqued.

She put her stethoscope and sphygmomanometer back in her workbag, snapping the latch closed. 'Just so you know,' she said lightly, 'I'm not playing up to Dare's suspicions about me. I won't be a pawn in this power struggle between you.'

Benson had the grace to look sheepish. 'I know, my dear, and I'm sorry to have put you in such a position tonight. He's angry with me and you got caught in his cross-hairs. Both my grandsons could use a good talking-to. Would you mind passing me my phone on your way…?' He touched his forehead and Carly saw a flash of pain cross his weathered features.

'Benson?' She went to him, bending down to see if his pupils were dilated. 'Do you have a headache?'

'No, no…I just have a little business issue to sort out.'

Carly glowered at him. 'You're supposed to be resting.'

'I can rest when I'm dead,' he retorted. 'Especially when someone is meddling with the company my father created.'

'Meddling?' Carly frowned. 'What do you mean?'

'I've lost three pieces of key business lately because there are whispers in the market that someone is going to make a bid for my company.'

Carly frowned. 'Are the two issues linked?'

'I believe so, yes.'

'That sounds a bit underhanded,' she said, 'and not something you should be concerning yourself with right now.'

'I have to if I want BG to survive.'

'Who do you think is responsible?'

'I have my suspicions, but I'm hamstrung in finding out.'

'Dare,' Carly murmured half to herself. 'You think it's him?'

'I was hoping not but after tonight...' He stared past her and Carly felt a well of anger rise up at Dare James all over again.

'But I doubt it's him,' Benson continued. 'Not that I'll rule out the possibility until I've spoken with him in private. Who knows? Maybe he wants to buy BG and sell it off piece by piece. I can't half blame him if he does.'

'Can he afford to do that?' As far as Carly knew BG Textiles was one of the oldest and most successful companies in England.

'He can afford it ten times over.' Benson made a noise in his throat. 'He's more successful than I ever was.'

'But that's awful if he plans to do that,' Carly exclaimed. 'You don't deserve that.'

Benson gave her a weary look. 'I don't know if he does, but...it's partly my fault if you believe today's psychology. I worked too hard, especially after Pearl's death. I ignored both Rachel and her brother in their formative years.' He sighed. 'I lost my daughter as a consequence, and my son grew up lazy and entitled who spawned a son in his image.'

He coughed into his hand and Carly handed him a glass of water. 'Listen to me. An old man's lamenting. That's another terrible thing about old age. Apart from being that much closer to death you become full of remorse. You see things you never saw before and value things you hadn't even considered. When I was young I thought winning and success were all important. I had Pearl minding the home front and I didn't even know I was missing out on anything until she was gone. Dare, from what I can tell, lives the same way.'

'He's married!' Carly felt so shocked by the thought her heart stopped beating.

'No, no. As far as I know he's single.'

And now it was beating too fast. She had to stop dwelling on that horrible man. 'Well, I can't imagine a woman putting up with him,' she declared with feeling.

'Oh, they put up with him all right. They're banging down his door to get to him.'

'Aesthetically he's very pleasing,' Carly conceded grudgingly, 'but his personality could use some work.'

Benson chuckled. 'Maybe he just needs the love of a good woman.'

Carly glanced up sharply at his tone. 'Don't look at me when you say that,' she cautioned.

'Can you blame me?' He shifted against his pillows and Carly fluffed them. 'He already likes you and you'll make some man very happy one day, my dear.'

Carly felt a lump form in her throat and cleared it away. 'That's very nice of you to say but I'm probably more messed up than your grandson. And you couldn't be more wrong about him liking me. Now go to sleep. I'll see you in the morning.'

Just before she left, the Baron cleared his throat. 'Carly, there's one more thing.'

'Yes?'

'I was hoping you would join us for lunch tomorrow.'

'With Rachel?' Carly said, surprised.

'Yes. It might actually help keep the table balanced.'

What he meant, Carly suspected, was that he might need the moral support. After experiencing the full impact of Dare's calculated put-downs Carly wasn't surprised. Not that she couldn't handle men like Dare James. She'd learnt her lesson well at Daniel's cradle.

'I'd be happy to join you,' she said, and she was. Perhaps Benson would take the opportunity to tell them about his illness—and her real role in his life—and she would hate to miss seeing the shock on his grandson's horrible face.

'Thank you, Carly. You're a true angel.'

Carly gave him a pointed look. 'Call me that again and I'll have Mrs Carlisle serve you tofu for breakfast, lunch, and dinner.'

He chuckled. 'Pearl had your spirit.'

He heaved a sigh and didn't say any more. He didn't have to. He was a worried man who wanted to make amends. It quite broke Carly's heart to see it.

So much so that the following morning, while she tried to jog off her lack of sleep the previous night, she decided that no matter what happened at lunch she would remain completely civil to Dare.

She might not like the man at all, but then she didn't have to. He would be gone at the end of the day and, as she only had two weeks left at Rothmeyer House herself, the chances of seeing him again were slim to none.

Thinking about that reminded her of the email she'd received from her temping agency and had yet to respond to. The truth was she was a little tired of temping, but what would she do instead?

It was one year, three months and four days since they had lost Liv and she knew her parents wanted her home.

But was she ready for that? Ready to run into Daniel? Ready to face the memory of Liv's trusting face as she had held Carly's hand through every oncologist meeting?

The crunch of gravel under her feet soothed her troubled thoughts and she slowed up as the house came into sight. Maybe there was something to this exercise gig, after all, she mused, feeling better. Or was it that she was now anticipating her morning coffee instead?

A small smile lightened her face. Before becoming a doctor she had imagined they were all the epitome of healthiness but really...everyone had their vices and coffee was hers.

Using the bottom of her singlet top to wipe the sweat

from her brow, Carly climbed the stone steps that led to the rear balcony and outdoor breakfast table. It was too early for Benson to be up but she still needed to go over the day's menu plan with Mrs Carlisle and—

'Keeping your assets in shape, I see.'

That deep, modulated voice gave Carly a start, the mocking words threatening her earlier resolve to treat this man with distant courtesy and nothing more.

He was once again wearing his faded jeans that surely fitted just a little too snugly, but he'd paired them with a dark grey shirt worn out and rolled at the sleeves, and of course those boots again. The outfit should have looked too casual but on him it looked somehow right, drawing the eye to his wide shoulders and long legs, and Carly hated that her heart skipped a beat at the sight of him.

He gave her a lazy smile as if to say that he knew the effect he was having on her, but little did he know that blatant displays of masculinity had never impressed her overly much. She much preferred someone who displayed gentleness over toughness.

'Good morning, Mr James.' She continued up the steps as if her heart weren't jumping around inside her chest. 'I can recommend a stroll in the east garden this time of the morning. It has a lovely French feel about it.'

'I'm not one for feeling gardens, Miss Evans. French or otherwise.'

Annoyed at the twist he put on her words, Carly kept her back to him as she uncapped the water bottle she had left on the outdoor breakfast table before her run.

'I hope you slept well,' she finally said as he stopped beside her.

'Do you?'

Carly's eyes snapped to his as he leant against one of the teak chairs. 'Let's not start this again.'

'Start what?' he asked innocently.

'The cat-and-mouse game you played last night.' She eyed him balefully. 'I do so hope you enjoyed yourself.'

'Not half as much as I wanted to,' he said, gazing at her through heavily lidded eyes.

Carly was trying very hard to remain calm when he reached for her water bottle and plucked it from her suddenly nerveless fingers. Keeping eye contact, he took a healthy swallow before handing it back. 'Thanks.'

With narrow-eyed calm Carly set the bottle on the table. No way could she drink from it now and by his grin he had expected that reaction from her. Fuming that he should think her so predictable, she snatched the bottle back up and guzzled most of it down.

Unfortunately his deep, amused laugh made her spill some of it and she angrily swiped her mouth with the back of her hand.

'You missed some on your, ah, singlet,' he advised her helpfully.

'If you're looking for your grandfather he doesn't get up before eight-thirty,' she advised waspishly.

'I wasn't.'

'Then if you're heading out for a stroll, please don't let me detain you.'

'I'm not.'

'Then what do you want?' she snapped, raising her chin and wishing she hadn't when his eyes dropped to her mouth.

Her breath felt trapped in her lungs as her body responded to his sensual gaze with a mind of its own and she stood in appalled silence like a bystander observing a horror car smash.

She couldn't want him. It just wasn't possible and yet all the signs were there... She knew because she'd read about them. She'd just never experienced them before, not without being touched first, and never as strongly as this.

Carly swallowed, thankful that he couldn't possibly know what was going on inside her head, her body. She took a backward step away from him, reminding herself that his interest was no doubt a falsehood designed to give him some advantage over her. After all, he did think she was sleeping with his grandfather!

'I want lots of things,' he said pleasantly, 'but chiefly I'd like to send you packing.'

Carly squared her shoulders. He would not get the better of her this morning. 'Did you wake up on the wrong side of the bed, Mr James?' she said, walking past him.

Dare grabbed her wrist. 'Money-grabbing little tramps should not be left to take advantage of doddery old fools.'

'Really?' Carly glanced down at her wrist as if she couldn't care less that he was holding it. 'For your information your grandfather is not doddery at all. He's completely in charge of his faculties and if he wants to make a fool of himself I'd say that's his business, not yours. In fact, given your attitude, I don't know why you care. Unless it's self-interest.'

His gaze sharpened. 'You think I want you, is that it?'

Carly noticed the sting of colour that ran along the edge of his high cheekbones as his grip on her wrist tightened. He might want her to think he was completely in control but he was very far from it. Not that she cared. She was glad to be able to annoy him the way he did her.

'I meant,' she replied with relish as she peeled his fingers away from her skin, 'Rothmeyer House.'

Dare saw the light of victory in her eyes and could have cursed himself for revealing just how much he wanted this woman. Last night he'd brooded well into the early hours of the morning, imagining her with his grandfather. And since he'd already had his hands on her—albeit innocently—it was more than easy to picture her naked. Picture her breasts, high and round, falling into his hands as he cupped them and brought them to his lips, picture her thighs parting, the silky triangle of red-gold hair guarding her femininity from his gaze.

He had a violent urge to strip her running shorts down her long legs to find out if he was correct about her colouring, to press her up against the cement column behind her and wrap those long silky legs around his hips right before he pumped himself into her.

The image was so visceral he was already at full mast and he knew if she looked down she'd see it.

God, how he disliked this woman. Disliked her cool sensuality and greedy little heart. Disliked the fact that he wanted her to choose him over his grandfather.

What the...?

The wayward thought did nothing to tamp down the primal aggression running like a live wire inside him. He wasn't the possessive type. Not where women were concerned. In fact he couldn't think of anything worse than becoming so enamoured of a woman that he thought about her outside the bedroom, but this woman was like a nagging itch he couldn't scratch. Which was most likely the attraction. She was forbidden fruit.

Knowing it was a mistake but doing it anyway, Dare stepped into her personal space, forcing her to tilt her head back to look up at him. 'I don't need Rothmeyer House or any other of my grandfather's effects,' he snarled, 'but, mark my words, you won't get them either.'

She inhaled a sharp breath, the sound shooting along his nerve endings.

'Fortunately that won't be up to you,' she said, breathing fire. 'And if your grandfather has any sense he—'

Dare grabbed her by the shoulders, effectively cutting off her words. 'He'll what?' he rasped. 'Disown me?'

Carly's eyes widened in surprise before she could school

her features. 'Take your hands off me,' she ordered with icy precision.

A feral smile appeared on Dare's face, raising goose bumps along her skin. 'You don't look the worse for wear after last night. Sorry. Did I put my grandfather off his game?'

Carly held herself rigid. 'I said—'

'I noticed you have separate rooms, which tells me the old man can't want you that much.'

Carly sucked in a sharp breath, his words hurting, even though they were incongruous. 'Spying, Mr James?' she mocked.

'Call me Dare.'

'No.'

'Feisty.' His thumbs stroked her collarbones. 'Does my grandfather like that?'

Carly stiffened. 'Doesn't it bother you that you're so preoccupied with your grandfather's sex life?'

His gaze fell to her mouth. 'Maybe I'm preoccupied with yours.'

Ignore him, she told herself. *He's like a tomcat with a half-dead mouse. He wants you to react.*

'Nothing to say, Red?'

Oh, she had plenty to say. 'I'm not going to give you the pleasure,' she said archly.

'Is that right?' he drawled. 'Then maybe I should give you some.'

His hands moved to cup her face, holding her gently despite the hardness of his gaze. Carly couldn't move. If testosterone had a scent it would smell like Dare James, she thought mindlessly.

Dare's thumbs slowly, but inexorably, forced her gaze up to his.

'Aren't you tired of all that aging flesh over yours?' he

husked. 'Wouldn't you like to remember what it's like with someone young? Someone virile.'

Carly's hands came up to pry at his wrists, holding them instead. 'Sure,' she said coldly, 'let me know if you find someone who fits that description.'

Instead of being angered into letting her go, he laughed softly, moving so close she could feel the soft cotton of his T-shirt against her singlet. To her utter mortification her nipples peaked.

'Doesn't the old man like to hold you after sex?' he murmured.

Carly didn't know any man who liked to hold her after sex. Not that a grand total of two lovers could be considered vast enough experience. Nor would she tell him that the reason she slept so close to the Baron was in case of a medical emergency. 'How do you know it's what *he* wants?' she tossed at him. 'Maybe it's what *I* want.'

His mouth twisted into an amused smile and his nostrils flared. 'I doubt it. You have high maintenance stamped all over your beautiful little face. But it's clear that the old man isn't satisfying you. I can smell your arousal even now.'

Ignore him, ignore him.

'Fight it all you want,' he continued softly, 'but you can't hide what your body wants.'

Carly's eyes flew open. 'If you don't let me go immediately I'll scream.'

'I don't think so.' His head lowered slowly towards hers. 'If you were going to scream you would have done it already.' His lips grazed her lower jaw. 'But you don't want to scream, do you, Carly? You want me to kiss you.' His fingers flexed around her jaw. 'To touch you.'

'You think you have me all figured out, don't you?' Carly said, tugging uselessly at his hands.

'Not quite.' His eyes glittered like twin blue flames as they held hers. 'But this should answer a few questions.'

Then he shocked the life out of her and claimed her mouth with his.

Carly froze. She hadn't really believed he would kiss her, but now that he was she didn't know what to do.

Don't do anything, she told herself. *If you don't do anything he'll stop and be completely humiliated. He'll be... he'll be put off.*

She held herself rigidly in his arms as his masterful lips crushed hers, dominating her with angry insolence. She told herself she just had to withstand the pressure, the heat of him, for a moment more. She just had to hold out and he'd change the kiss. He'd...he'd soften his lips and nibble at hers instead of dominating them.

Carly made a small sound in the back of her throat. She could feel the control he exerted over himself in the bunched muscles of his arms, the hard press of his thighs. She never would have thought that physical power in a man was arousing but—

'Oh...' She let out a small breath as his tongue ran along the seam of her lips.

'Yes, that's it, Red. Open up for me,' he commanded gruffly. 'Let me in.'

Carly swayed. *Don't react, don't*— She sighed as Dare slid his hands into her hair and tugged on the band that held her ponytail in place, pulling it free.

The feel of her hair swinging loosely around her shoulders was an added stimulant to the gentle bite of his teeth as he took her lower lip into his mouth and sucked lightly.

Carly heard another soft sound, realised it was from her, and heard an answering one from him. Then she was opening for him, kissing him back with a hunger she didn't recognise.

He made a victorious groan in the back of his throat

but she didn't care because his tongue was in her mouth, his lips claiming hers with long practised strokes that had her melting against him.

She'd simply never been kissed like this before. Never been kissed with such skill and mastery, never felt a man's lips consume hers with such deep hungry pulls at her flesh, and she was powerless to do anything but give into him, her body arching closer to his to ease the ache that had risen up inside her. Nothing else mattered but assuaging that ache and she clung to his shoulders, her fingers tangling in the overlong hair at the nape of his neck. It was thicker than hers, slightly curly, but she couldn't really take it in with his mouth devouring hers so intensely.

His hands moulded her torso, running over her back and then finally cupping her bottom and lifting her into him.

His hungry groan reverberated throughout every cell in her body and his sinful mouth took everything she had to offer and demanded more. And Carly gave it without thinking, her legs giving out completely.

Dare held her tighter, his mouth forcing her head back on her shoulders, his hand rising to cup her breast, searching out the tip. Carly strained against him. Strained for the pleasure of that first contact...

With a feral sound Dare wrenched his mouth from hers and thrust her away from him, his breathing hard and fast. He stared at her as if what had just happened were her fault.

'No,' he scorned with a shaky laugh. 'Just no.'

Almost savagely he swung away from her and stormed inside the French doors, thankfully leaving her to pull herself together without him watching.

When she finally caught her breath, Carly didn't know who she was most angry with. Dare for grabbing her and kissing her or her for responding.

Flustered and furious, she stormed off towards the kitchen to speak with Mrs Carlisle about the lunch menu. She had a job to do, she reminded herself, and standing around arguing and kissing Dare James wouldn't get it done.

CHAPTER FOUR

'No, Nina, don't worry about forwarding the investor pro-
files to my handheld, have them delivered to my apartment.
I'll be back in London by…' Dare checked his watch. If he
left straight after lunch he should make it back by… 'Six,
six-thirty.' If he opened up the throttle maybe even five.

Shoving his phone back in his pocket, Dare leaned
against the balcony railing and took in the view. Green
lawns for as far as the eye could see bordered by manicured
hedges and a glassy pond set close to the house. A healthy
woodland stretched out beyond the house and behind that a
church spire pierced the clear blue sky. No, Benson wasn't
doing it tough, he thought cynically.

Unfortunately Dare had needed to tend to some issues
at his office all morning so he hadn't had a chance to corner Benson before his mother had arrived.

Then it had been too late. She'd been enveloped back
into her home almost as if she had never left. But she had
left, or rather she was forced to leave, and Dare sometimes
wondered why she had put up with his father for so many
years once it became clear that he wasn't the man she had
thought him to be.

Love, he supposed, with a twist to his lips. It didn't always come with hearts and flowers. Sometimes it came
with pain and desertion over and over and over.

And to think his mother had come from this genteel
society; it was difficult for him to grapple with when he
thought about how hard his mother had had it over the
years. His pride in her grew even more when he thought
about how easily she could have sold herself out and re-

turned to the lap of luxury. But she wasn't that kind of person. She hadn't had it easy just because she could.

His gut clenched.

There was no way the delectable Carly Evans would be duping his mother out of her inheritance if she decided she wanted it. And he hoped she realised by now that he was not a man to cross.

Of course, if his mother did decide she wanted nothing more to do with Rothmeyer House then the little gold-digger could have it and good luck to her. He supposed in her own way she was earning her money and he could hardly blame his grandfather for wanting to keep her. Hell, after that kiss this morning—

Dare stopped his thoughts dead in their tracks.

After that kiss this morning nothing. Why he'd even given into temptation was still eating away at him. It was something his fool father would have done. Gone after a magic moment and to hell with the consequences. And Dare knew Carly hadn't told his grandfather about it because the old man hadn't tried to take him out.

In some way he wished he had because the thought that he'd come on to his own grandfather's mistress made his stomach turn. Especially when he didn't even like her. In fact the only reason he'd even touched her was because she'd damned well goaded him into it.

Yeah, just like Jake Ryan forced you to steal a car when you were fifteen to take a joy-ride that could have ended a lot worse than a lecture from the local sheriff.

Dare sighed. Bottom line he'd wanted to kiss her and so what if it had driven him almost to the point of no return? His emotions were all over the place right now. Unusual, yes, but not unmanageable and certainly not worth thinking about. In a matter of hours she'd be history—at least for him—and he'd consign any memory of her to the bin. Where it belonged.

Hearing voices on the terrace below, he glanced over the wrought-iron railing. His mother was holding a bunch of flowers his grandfather had just given her.

Nice touch, he complimented cynically. His mother loved flowers.

Another voice joined theirs and Carly stepped into his view looking fresh and dazzling in white trousers and a striped T-shirt.

Scowling, he stepped back inside, changed into fresh jeans, a T-shirt and boots. It wasn't exactly garden-party attire, but then he hadn't brought garden-party clothing in the duffle that fitted beneath the seat of his bike. Nor was he in a garden-party frame of mind. And he certainly wasn't here to impress anyone.

He cast his helmet a pained glance. Two hours and he'd be on the open roads again.

'Walk to the village?' Carly repeated, not sure she'd heard right.

She had been counting the seconds until this torturous lunch would be over and now the Baron wanted her to extend it. And extend it with Dare of all people!

Oh, she knew why he had asked. He wanted some private time with Rachel without his odious grandson breathing down his neck and she couldn't say she blamed him. Sure, Dare hadn't been as hostile as he had been the previous evening, but he hadn't exactly been nice either. But take him on a walk to the village? That was definitely going above and beyond the call of duty. She was here to take care of Benson's *physical* health, not his *emotional* health.

'He'll be bored.'

'I'm game.'

Both she and Dare spoke at the same time and the older two at the table chuckled at them.

Carly's eyes cut to Dare's irritating blue ones, even more vibrant in the matching knit shirt.

He couldn't be serious. Why would he say that when it was clear to anyone watching that he wanted to monitor what went on between his mother and grandfather?

'It's quite a walk,' Carly muttered, hoping her intentions to put him off weren't too obvious.

She had liked Rachel on sight, finding Dare's attractive mother warm and down to earth, her tiny stature belying a woman with a core of steel. She also had a core of gentleness and evidently had a very close relationship with her son.

At first, Carly had wondered if Dare's posturing about protecting his mother hadn't come from some self-interested space, but she knew immediately she was wrong when she saw them together. These two people had a connection that reminded her of the love she shared with her own parents, and she'd felt a pang of homesickness as she'd taken her seat at the alfresco dining table.

'I'm young.' Dare smiled at her with only the slightest trace of mockery in his eyes. 'And fit. I'm sure I can make it.'

He had been polite to her all lunch and quite a few times Carly had longed to lash out at him and show his mother just how rude her son could be when she wasn't around to see it.

Especially when Gregory had scurried up to Dare and jumped up at him until Dare had reached down and placed the little mutt on his lap. As far as she was concerned the only reason the two of them got on so well was because they recognised each other as twin spirits of evil.

'He's really not that scary,' Dare had commented with an arched brow as he'd petted him.

Carly had offered a brief, forced smile, not wanting to find him the least bit amusing. As far as she was concerned he and the adoring dog deserved each other because it had been Gregory's fault she had nearly been run over by the man in the first place.

'A walk sounds lovely,' Rachel agreed, 'and I'm sure Dare won't be bored at all.'

Carly kept a smile on her face as she caught the Baron's pleading look. The man certainly knew how to tug at her heartstrings, that was for sure. And perhaps she could agree to escort Dare into the village and then kick him in the shins once they'd rounded the side of the house.

'Okay, fine,' she groused.

'Don't be too enthusiastic, Red. I might think you like me.'

She'd show him how much she liked him, she thought, right around the next corner.

Smiling pointedly at Benson, she took hold of his wrist. 'I'm sure you and Rachel have a lot of information to exchange.' And he'd better use this time to inform her of his illness or Carly would risk being fired and do it for him!

Satisfied that his pulse was fine, she stood up but not before she caught sight of Dare's narrowed eyes on her hand. She supposed to an outsider her casual touches could be construed as affection, but still… It was a big leap to go from affection to sleeping with someone and it certainly didn't excuse his rudeness towards her, or his grandfather.

Dare had been surprised Carly had not continued to try and wheedle out of their little walk to the village. He'd been surprised even more to find himself accepting the old man's suggestion even before he'd received his mother's not-so-subtle kick in the ankle beneath the table. She wanted time alone with her father. So, okay, he'd give it to her and accompany the little gold-digger into the village.

The little gold-digger who had played his mother like a finely tuned harp at lunch with her polite and surprisingly insightful views on current affairs and international issues. He'd even found himself agreeing with her at one point, but then he supposed if one aimed to become a trophy wife one needed to be able to converse with a variety of intelligent people. Perhaps Miss Carly Evans was just wilier than many of the women of her ilk.

'Okay, this is as far as we go,' she said coldly, stopping suddenly as soon as they were out of sight of the terrace.

Dare glanced at the ten-foot manicured hedges leading to what looked like a maze, and a set of well-kept clinker brick stables off to the left. 'Small village,' he offered.

'Don't be smart,' she snapped, giving him a look that could wipe ten percent off the Dow Jones in seconds. 'We're not going to the village.'

'And what will I tell old Benson when I return and he asks how I found it?'

'They've only thrown us together because they want time alone, you know?'

'I know that,' Dare drawled. 'I'm not an idiot.'

She gave him a look that said she disagreed and shrugged. 'So go polish your bike or something.'

Dare grinned. 'I think you like my bike. Go on, admit it.'

'That death trap?' Carly scoffed. 'Do you know how many emergency-department patients are injured on motorcycles every day?'

He pulled a face. 'I don't think I want to know.'

'Exactly,' Carly said. 'Next time take the bus.'

Dare laughed and she gave him a withering look.

When she made to continue past him he blocked her path. 'And where do you think you're going?'

'To the village.' Her little chin tilted up so high he wanted to nip it with his teeth. Nip it and continue down the long, slender column of her throat until he reached her collarbones and continued on to her sweetly rounded breasts.

'Great.' He cleared the gruffness from his throat and urged his body to settle down. This woman might affect him like no other but she was without morals and God only knew what else—panties, perhaps? 'Come on,' he growled. 'You don't want me telling Benson you're being stubborn.'

'I'm not stubborn.'

Dare took her elbow and laughed softly as she pulled it out of his grasp. 'As a mule.'

'I don't think you would tell him,' she challenged. 'I don't think you'd dare.'

'Try me.' His expression darkened. 'It might make him realise what a disloyal little gold-digger you are.'

'You were the one who kissed me,' she said, outraged colour winging into her cheeks.

'You kissed me back,' he pointed out, wanting to do nothing more than curl his hand around the nape of her neck and remind them both how good it had been. When she glared at him without responding he raised an eyebrow. 'You get points for not trying to deny it.'

'Why bother?' she tossed at him. 'Men like you do what you want anyway. You make your own rules.'

Something in her tone made his gaze sharpen. Rather than look like a woman on the make, she looked suddenly wistful and lost and innocently beautiful, like a woman he wanted to take to his bed and never let go.

And stupid thoughts like that were what had driven his father to follow one rainbow after another.

Scowling, he made an elaborate gesture in the direction of the village.

'Shall we?' he said tersely.

She looked as if she was about to tell him to go jump on his head but then she stuck her nose in the air and stalked off ahead of him.

Dare smiled grimly and set off after her.

They hadn't gone very far when Dare put his hand out in front of her body to stop her.

Startled, Carly threw him an annoyed look until he put his finger to his lips to keep her quiet and pointed into the bracken. A deer and two fawns were grazing on a patch of grass, their ears twitching. Dare could feel the heat of the sun on his shoulders, the soft breeze on his face, and was pleased to sense that Carly was as aware of the delicacy of the moment as he was. A bird called overhead and the deer all raised their heads.

He heard Carly's sharp intake of breath as the doe made eye contact. A moment later her nose twitched and she alerted her fawns before dancing off into the trees.

Dare smiled. He loved the outdoors and since starting his business ten years ago he hadn't had much time to commune with nature as he had done as a boy.

'Oh, my, that was beautiful,' Carly murmured.

'It reminds me of home.'

'Really?' She gazed up at him, wonder turning her gaze soft. 'How so?'

Dare swallowed. 'I grew up in a small town at the foot of the Smokies. Had plans to become a forest ranger at one point.'

Her eyes grew wide. 'What made you switch from forest ranger to finance whiz?'

'Whiz, huh?'

'Some media person's view, not mine.'

Dare shrugged. 'I was good with numbers. My math teacher saw it. He encouraged me, and I won a scholarship to Harvard.'

She nodded slowly. 'That's pretty impressive.'

'Yeah, I like what I do. I like investing in businesses and seeing what I can do with them. Seeing them come off. But living in cities doesn't leave much time to go round up deer.'

And what was he doing sharing his private thoughts with this woman? If he wasn't careful he'd tell her he sometimes felt lonely in those cities, living in large, empty apartments and never feeling settled.

'No deer in Liverpool.' She laughed. 'Our local wild-life consists of teens hanging out at train stations for all the wrong reasons.'

Disgruntled by how much he was enjoying her company, Dare scowled.

'Do you love him?'

She blinked up at him. 'Sorry?'

'The old man,' he rasped. 'Do you love him?'

A cold light entered her lovely eyes. 'Are we back to that?' She shook her head as if he had disappointed her in some way and his gut clenched. 'But he isn't "the old man", he's your grandfather.'

'And you're evading the question.'

'Because I don't want to ruin my walk any more than it already is.'

She marched away from him. 'Answer the question, Carly.' His long-legged stride easily matched hers.

'Or what?' She glared up at him. 'You'll make me?'

'Is that what you want?' His eyes bored into hers. 'Is the old man too soft for your liking?'

'Oh!' Carly tried to put distance between them but Dare grabbed her elbow and swung her around.

'You're disgusting!'

'You touch him like a lover and yet you're at least fifty years younger than he is. That's not natural.'

Actually she touched him like a doctor—or a friend, at most—but she knew Dare only saw what he wanted to see.

She shrugged off his touch and felt a pang of disappointment when he released her so easily. Incensed by a need she was hard-pressed to understand given her stance on casual intimacy in general, and men like this one in particular, Carly briefly closed her eyes. 'They say the mighty fall the hardest,' she said with a composure she had to fight hard to maintain. 'I so hope that's true.'

He scowled at her. 'If you're not his lover then what are you? Because I'm not buying the whole "friend of a friend" baloney.'

'Ask your grandfather.'

A beat passed between them before he nodded in agreement. 'I intend to.'

Realising that he might be going to do so now and ruin Benson's time alone with his daughter, Carly reached out and grabbed his forearm.

'The village is just over the next rise. I thought you wanted to see it.' She released him. 'Or was your accompanying me just a ruse to get information out of me?' She wouldn't have put it past him.

'Lead on,' he said hardly.

Both relieved and agitated, Carly continued on in silence but it wasn't the comfortable silence of before. Not even the view of the small village as they descended the slight incline onto the High Street was enough to elevate the tension between them.

Carly smiled at a few of the local folk walking by even though she'd never met them before. Which did make her feel better. In Liverpool most everyone kept to themselves in the city streets, hurrying about their business with grim determination. You hardly ever heard laughter in the streets, like here, where some sort of children's game was going on in the village square.

It was a children's birthday party and the game was dodge ball. By tacit agreement both she and Dare stopped to watch, Dare all brooding male energy with his hands shoved deep into his pockets, his shoulders slightly hunched as if he had the weight of the world on them.

If he did she had no doubt that he would come out the victor. Power and strength radiated from him. If this had been a couple of centuries earlier she had no doubt he would have been some kind of war chief with a thousand men at his back.

'I'm not in love with him.' The words were out before she even realised they were there to be said and the air between them pulled even tighter. 'I'm not in love with anyone.'

His eyes flicked to hers and she berated herself for the foolish comment. 'What I mean is…' she took a deep breath. 'You might want to cut your grandfather some slack.'

His eyes flicked to hers. 'Might I?'

Carly sighed. She would probably get more compassion out of a telephone poll. 'Forget I said anything,' she muttered.

The man was as hard as the sand rock used in the construction of the village buildings. Why she'd even said what she had she didn't know. The Baron's secrets were his own to disclose and it wasn't as if she wanted this man to like her, or think well of her. What would that accomplish?

'Then what is he to you?' he demanded, his keen gaze probing hers as if he were intent on learning all her secrets.

'I'd rather not talk about it.' He would find out soon enough and then it would be Carly's turn to have the last laugh. Until then she'd keep her mouth shut.

'You were the one who brought it up this time.'

'My mistake,' she said loftily over her shoulder, circling the small square as if she couldn't wait to see what was growing inside a potted plant across the way.

Dare shoved his hands into his pockets and watched her go. There was more to what was going on here and she held the key. But what was he missing? And why this constant nagging desire to take her into his arms and slay all her demons for her?

Because she had some; he'd sensed it a few times now. And while she might not love his grandfather, there was something between them. He felt it every time she stroked the old man's hand.

And why did seeing that irritate him so much?

Because you want her for yourself.

And he knew better than most that a life based on wanting was no life at all. Which was why he'd based his on action.

'I'm not in love with him. I'm not in love with anyone.'

Dare shook his head. She was doing a number on his head. But was it calculated, or just dumb luck?

He paced over to her, determined to get the truth from her once and for all. 'I know you're not in love with the old man, but you do care for him, don't you?' he demanded, his voice rough with unchecked emotion.

She heaved a laboured sigh as if he were an annoying insect she'd like to see the back of. Well, it was nothing compared to how he felt about her!

'Yes.'

Dare's gut tightened at the honest emotion behind that single word. What if there really was some genuine affection between this woman and his grandfather? What if she wasn't just after him for his money? It made what had happened between them on the terrace even uglier.

But what if she was only playing on his sympathies now? Trying to get him onside so that he didn't fight her for his grandfather's assets later?

Dare stared at the quaint row of shops lining one side of the square. He wasn't used to second-guessing himself all the time, but he'd been doing just that ever since he'd run into her.

Frustrated with his vacillating thoughts, Dare was almost relieved when a child cried out and a forgotten ball bounced past him. Without thinking too much about it he strode forward to where the kids had all clustered around a young girl who sat clutching her ankle, tears coursing down her face.

'Move back,' he said, going down on his haunches in front of the girl.

'Billie!' A woman's frantic voice made him look up as she jostled forward. 'Sweetie, are you okay? What happened?'

'My ankle hurts.'

'I told you not to play too rough. You have ballet tomorrow night—oh, darling, how badly does it hurt?'

'Why don't I carry her over to those seats?' Dare offered.

'No, you shouldn't move her just yet,' Carly interjected tersely.

Dare frowned at her and the woman's gaze flicked between them both before settling on his.

'Oh, well…' She blushed. 'That would be very helpful, thank you.'

Ignoring Carly's venomous glare, Dare lifted the girl into his arms.

'I think it's broken,' the child wailed as he placed her on a nearby bench.

'You'll be fine,' he assured her.

'Here, let me take a look.' Again Carly threw him a dark look and moved to the child's feet.

The mother shifted nervously, peering at Dare. 'Oh, do you think—?'

'I'm a doctor,' Carly said with a ring of authority. 'I can tell you if it's broken.'

'Oh, well, of course, I…'

Carly ignored the child's mother who, she noted cynically, hadn't been so distressed she had missed the bulge in Dare's biceps as he'd picked her daughter up off the ground.

It was pathetic, really, but she supposed if you liked the rugged type with an edge of arrogance and danger about him then this man would be appealing. Very appealing.

'Hi there.' She shoved thoughts of Dare's male appeal out of her mind and smiled at the worried girl, who must have been about ten years old. 'Billie, is it?'

The girl nodded.

'Okay, Billie, I'm just going to have a feel of your leg and you tell me when it hurts and how much, okay?'

Carly was aware the whole time of Dare's searing gaze on her and it took every ounce of professionalism to ignore it.

After a few minutes she announced that the ankle was probably only sprained, but, given the amount of bones in that area of the body combined with the girl's age, she should probably have it X-rayed. 'And in the meantime keep a bag of ice on it. That way you'll keep the swelling down, which will aid the healing process.'

'Oh, thank you, Doctor.' The mother smiled, but it wasn't at her. It was at Dare. No doubt she was still thinking about those broad shoulders and that scruff he hadn't bothered to shave off his horrible face that morning.

Disgusted with herself, Carly stood up and brushed herself off before finally looking at him, unconsciously setting her chin at a challenging angle. This wasn't the moment of victory she had anticipated and she knew Dare wasn't a stupid man. He'd guess straight away that his grandfather was ill.

'So you're a doctor?'

'Yes,' she said as if it were of no importance at all.

He scowled. 'And pretty pleased about it, by the look of you?'

'Why shouldn't I be?' Carly retorted, frowning into his angry face. 'I worked hard for my degree.'

His mouth tightened. 'I don't care if you got it from a paper bag.' He stared at her hard. 'What I want to know is whether you're tired of working so hard, or if the old man is sick and you're his attending physician.' His blue gaze pierced hers. 'Not that I've met too many doctors who live in.'

Okay, so maybe he wasn't that smart, Carly fumed, incensed that he was so determined to think ill of her.

'Unbelievable.' She shook her head. 'You have no shame, do you?'

'Not much. Which is it?'

'None of your business.' She stalked away from him but of course he followed.

'Are you saying that my grandfather's welfare is none of my business?' he asked silkily.

'I'm saying—' Carly stopped and whirled on him '—go take a hike. Off a high cliff preferably.'

Dare grabbed hold of her arm as she turned to walk off and swung her around to face him. 'What is your problem, lady?'

'I'm looking at it.'

'If you would just apply some logic—would you stand still? I'm the one who has a right to be angry here, not you.'

Carly slapped her hands on her hips. 'Of course you do,' Carly soothed with all the ice from the polar cap. 'And I suppose I should be the grateful little maiden on my knees apologising for making you feel that way?'

The air between them pulled taut.

Dare let out a slow breath. Talking to this woman was like trying to pull up weeds with a pair of tweezers. 'If you're on the straight and narrow, why all the cloak-and-dagger stuff?'

Aware of the small crowd still milling around, Carly

kept her voice low. 'As far as I'm concerned there is no cloak-and-dagger stuff. There's you jumping up and down drawing conclusions that belong in a Picasso painting and me caught in the crossfire.'

'Little Miss Innocent, is that it?' His lips twisted. 'Or should I say, *Dr* Innocent?'

If she had been expecting an apology—and she had been—she was sorely disappointed. 'Tell me, Mr James, do you have a low opinion of every woman you meet or is it just me?'

'I have a healthy disrespect for lying,' he ground out.

'I haven't lied to you.'

'You haven't been honest either.'

'Maybe it's just that you're so quick to pass judgment on everyone else's motives you don't ask the right questions.'

'If you think being a doctor somehow elevates you above gold-digger status, sweetheart, I have to tell you I've come across a lot of educated women who look at a rich man with dollar signs in their eyes.'

'Maybe women look at you that way because it's the only positive thing about you!' Carly turned and strode towards the path that led back to Rothmeyer House, disconcerted when he easily kept pace with her. 'I, on the other hand, have more sense.'

'Is that right?'

'Yes, that is right. But what's your excuse? Has a woman broken your heart in the past? Is that why you're being so horrible to me?'

'No woman has ever broken my heart.'

'Because you don't have one?' she asked sweetly.

Dare called for patience. 'Because no woman has ever gotten close enough.'

Her brow rose in surprise. 'And never will, by your tone.'

'Correct.'

'So you really have no excuse for making my life hell.'

'I have plenty.' Mainly that he wasn't going to be taken in by a sharp-tongued little witch only to find out later that he'd been played for a fool.

Still… He took a deep breath watching her disappear along the narrow walking path and around the first bend. He wasn't an unreasonable man. At least he never had been before. He frowned. He couldn't seem to get his thoughts straight where she was concerned and that temper of hers didn't help at all.

Scowling, he set off after her, his long strides eating up the distance to catch her up. If she were a new start-up he was interested in, he mused, he'd gather the facts first and then follow his instincts.

'Hold up,' he called when her bright hair came into view, his lips flat-lining when she ignored him. Oh, she was good at that. She'd pretty much pretended he hadn't existed all through lunch.

'I said hold up,' he growled, grabbing her elbow.

'And I said take a hike off a high cliff,' she panted, her eyes the colour of an incoming storm. 'But we don't always get what we want, do we?'

'Would you just listen for once? I want to clear this up and move on.'

She wrenched her arm out of his hold and moved away from him. 'This ought to be good.'

A muscle flexed in his jaw and he let out a slow breath. If she only knew how much he wanted to wrap his fingers around her slender throat and squeeze when she looked at him like that, she'd never do it again.

'So let me see if I've got this right,' he said calmly. 'You're saying there's absolutely nothing personal between you and my grandfather?'

He waited a beat, pleased with the reasonableness of his tone, when she started laughing.

'Oh, brother!' She tossed her hands up in the air as if he were a delinquent and right now he felt like one. This woman took his logical brain and turned it into a pretzel.

'You are unbelievable,' she stormed on. 'You can't even see what's right in front of your face.'

He took a step towards her, gratified when she involuntarily stepped back.

Oh, yes, my little beauty, you should be afraid if I find out this is all an act.

'I can see very clearly.'

Something in his tone alerted all Carly's feminine instincts that she was standing on rocky ground with a tornado bearing down fast. 'Really?' She felt suddenly breathless. 'And what do you see?'

Dammit. Carly knew her words were a challenge, one she hadn't meant to issue, and his slow smile said he knew it.

'Look, Mr James—'

'I am looking, Miss—sorry—*Dr* Evans, and I see something I like very much.' He took another step towards her, his eyes falling to the lips she'd just moistened. 'But I'm not telling you anything you don't know, am I? You know how desirable you are. How beautiful.'

The words were harsh, spoken more as an insult, but Carly felt her breathing quicken with pleasure at hearing them. A bird called out from somewhere high in the treetops; another answered. Instinct told her to run, while something much stronger kept her immobile.

Carly shook her head as Dare stalked towards her like a slow-moving lion whose prey was cornered.

'No…' A low-hanging branch brushed the back of her head and she swung around to move it. Before she could turn back Dare plastered his larger body along her back, his arms banded around her middle like a steel trap.

'Oh, yes.' His breath was hot against her neck and Carly's knees went weak. 'Your scent drives me crazy,' he growled, his mouth opening over the skin of her neck, his teeth biting down softly. Carly moaned, the back of her head hitting his shoulder.

His hands rose from her stomach to cup her breasts and a need rose up in Carly like never before. The urge to rub her bottom against him was overwhelming. It was like a fire in her blood, burning her up from the inside out.

Don't do it, don't—

Dare groaned deep in his throat. 'Do that again,' he ordered hungrily. A thrill raced through Carly at the naked need in his voice and she was powerless to resist, gasping with pleasure when he plumped her breasts in his hands and squeezed.

'Turn your head, Carly,' he growled against her ear, his fingers circling ever closer to the tight tips of her breasts. 'Kiss me.'

His voice was gruff and mindlessly Carly reached back, curling one of her arms behind her to cup his head and bring his mouth to hers. When their lips met she whimpered and he rewarded her by tweaking her nipples firmly through her clothing.

If Carly had ever felt anything so exquisite before she couldn't remember it. His mouth, those masterful fingers, that hard body covering hers from behind… Time ceased to exist and everything along with it.

Dare whispered her name and turned her in his arms.

Drugged.

He felt drugged as her tongue stroked along his, her mouth wide in an invitation he didn't need to receive twice. Self-control was a distant memory as Dare crushed her lush breasts against his chest. He felt a momentary relief at the contact but then it wasn't enough and he powered her back against the trunk of the hundred-year-old oak.

Her fingers delved into his hair to hold him closer and

his hands pushed beneath her T-shirt, shoving her bra higher so that she was completely exposed to him. He took his fill of those perfect orbs and pink-tipped nipples before lowering his head to take one into his mouth. Her taste, the texture of her skin was like ambrosia and he suckled her deeply, his mouth shifting between first one and then the other.

She gripped him tighter, her nails raking his shirt, her keening cries filling the air and he knew she would be wet for him. He knew that all he had to do was lower her to the ground, tug down her zipper and part her legs and she'd be his. All his.

And he nearly did exactly that before a modicum of sanity brought him back to where they were. On a public pathway in the middle of Rothmeyer Forest. Dare wrenched his mouth from her breasts, his eyes grim as they met glazed green ones. 'I'm not going to take you on the forest floor.'

Take her on the forest floor? Carly blinked a couple of times as if she'd just come out of a movie theatre in the middle of the day. Good God, she'd gone crazy!

She couldn't believe the way she'd opened her mouth wide and stroked her tongue along his, the way she'd wanted to strip the clothes from his body and touch him everywhere.

Realising that her bra was digging into her underarms, Carly yanked it back into place and straightened her T-shirt. 'Believe me, I don't want you to take me anywhere. I don't want you to touch me again. Ever!'

His eyes fell to her aroused breasts, her nipples like hard little diamonds against her clothes. 'I told you I don't like liars.'

'I'm not lying, I'm—' She broke off as his hand reached out and covered her breast, his gaze defying her to resist him. And she wanted to, she wanted to be completely unaffected by his touch, but she could feel the tension in her shoulders as she battled to stop her body from arching into his.

'If you'd been wearing a skirt you'd already be mine and you know it,' he said, his voice hoarse with unmet need.

'I would have stopped you before then,' Carly said with more bravado than she felt, flicking his hand from her breast.

'Would you?'

Dare looked at her mouth, swollen from where he'd ravished it, her cheeks still pink with a passion he'd invoked. She was beautiful. Perhaps the most beautiful woman he'd ever seen.

He rubbed at his chest. Even now the desire to take her in his arms was so strong he had to turn his back on her to prevent himself from doing it again.

How did he just switch it on and off? Carly wondered, still trembling from the force of the emotions he created in her. If he had a secret she wanted to know what it was because she'd use it to turn her reaction to him off permanently. It was almost as if her brain cells ceased to function when he reached for her.

'You enjoyed that, didn't you?' she accused hotly. 'Humiliating me like that.'

His heavy-lidded gaze met hers. 'On the contrary, I thought I was pleasuring you.'

Smug, condescending...

'I won't deny that you know what to do with your hands.' Her eyes dropped to his lips. 'Your mouth.' She raised her chin. 'But you need to know that there is nothing that would induce me to sleep with a man like you.'

A muscle ticked in his jaw. 'And what kind of man is that?'

'A rude, condescending player who takes what he wants and damn the consequences.'

Dare's brows rose. 'A player?'

'I looked you up online last night,' she said, tossing her hair back over her shoulder. 'And you've had more women than I've had patients!'

He cocked a slow grin. 'Considering I don't know how many patients you've had I can't really comment, but I am flattered you took the time to look me up.'

'Don't be,' she shot back. 'I was only interested in what kind of man would treat his own grandfather so callously. And now I know. A horrible one!'

It wasn't quite the put-down she'd been reaching for but Carly was too incensed to care. Straightening her spine she marched away from him, determined never to see him again.

CHAPTER FIVE

'DID YOU HAVE a nice walk, darling?' His mother smiled at Dare as he found her alone in a small, feminine sunroom at the back of the house. 'You know, I really liked Carly. She seems like an intelligent woman and so attractive, don't you think?'

It wasn't difficult to hear the hope in his mother's voice but he hadn't sought her out so she could wax lyrical about the most frustrating woman he had ever met. 'Don't matchmake, Mother, you know I don't like it.' And it was something she had tried more than once before. 'Mark has the car ready to leave when you are.'

'I was just expressing my opinion, Dare. No need to bite my head off.' She sniffed as if he had done her a great injury. 'I can't help it if Carly seemed entirely down to earth and...unpretentious. Normal, even.'

'Unlike the women I usually date.'

'Do you call it dating?' she asked innocently. 'I thought you young people called it hooking up when it only lasted a period of hours.'

Dare scowled. 'If you wanted grandchildren you should have remarried yourself and had more kids.' He felt like a jerk as soon as he saw her hurt face. He, more than anyone else, knew why she had never risked a relationship again. 'I'm sorry.' He ran a frustrated hand through his hair. 'That was uncalled for. But I don't want to talk about Carly. I want to know what happened with Benson after we left.'

She sighed. 'Why don't you come sit down? This used to be one of my favourite rooms when I was a child.'

By the looks of it, his mother had just finished a cup of tea. God, how he hated tea. 'Sorry. Again. I'm a little...'

He raked a hand through his hair and glanced around at the cushioned window seats and low side tables. 'How is it being back here?'

'Lovely, actually. In some ways it's almost as if I'm nineteen again. But you're a little what?'

Her parental radar had evidently picked up on his slight hesitation before but there was no way he was going to tell her that he was a little sexually frustrated. 'Nothing.' He smiled encouragingly. 'So what does Benson want?'

She looked as if she wanted to question him more but then she sighed. 'To reconnect. To get to know you. He's a big admirer of yours.'

Dare's eyes narrowed. 'Already?'

'Yes. He looked you up online.'

He was being checked up on a lot, it seemed. Had Carly and his grandfather looked into his past while in bed together? And why was he back to thinking about that when she'd denied sleeping with him?

No, actually, she had denied loving him—she had neatly avoided the whole topic of how deep her involvement with him was and Dare hadn't even noticed.

He frowned. 'That's it? That's all he said?'

'Well, now that you mention it he did ask if I would like to stay on for a few days.'

'What did you say?'

'I said yes.'

And she had a determined glint in her eye that said she wouldn't be swayed. Dare sighed. 'I need to be in the office Monday morning. I can't—'

'I'm not asking you to stay with me, darling, I know how busy you are. But once the two of us started really talking we realised that there's too much to be said in one day.'

Dare's frown deepened. He needed to talk to Benson himself and the sooner, the better.

'Dare, where are you going?'

'To see Benson.'

His mother sighed. 'Dare, be nice.'

He smiled at her. 'I'm always nice, Ma, you know that.'

After searching the downstairs area, Dare found his grand-father in his room with the lovely Dr Evans hovering over him.

'Dare.' The old man said his name with a touch of asperity. 'I'm glad you stopped by.'

He had known he would, Dare thought cynically, guessing by Carly's taut features that she had no doubt warned him that Dare would be on the warpath. Had she also shared anything else? Like those passionate kisses that had temporarily fried his brain?

Unbidden, his eyes shifted to the king-size bed that was—thankfully—without a wrinkle on it.

'We need to talk.'

'Yes,' Benson agreed.

Carly bent close to the old man's ear and murmured something that made him shake his head. A wave of possessiveness surged through Dare and he clenched his fists at his sides.

'It's not polite to whisper in front of others, Red,' he said. 'Didn't your mother ever teach you that?'

A blush rose up beneath the surface of her skin and all Dare could think about was heat. *Hot, she'd been hotter than the surface of the sun and sweeter than sugar.*

'I wasn't whispering.'

Benson touched the back of her hand reassuringly. 'I'll be all right.'

She clearly disbelieved that; her eyes chilled as they met Dare's.

'I'll see you later,' she murmured to Benson in a voice that, to Dare's ears, promised untold delights.

Benson watched appreciatively as she walked through the adjoining bedroom door before closing it behind her.

'Beautiful, isn't she?'

Dare didn't blink. 'Are you sleeping with her?'

'Direct, as usual,' Benson said dryly. 'I had heard that about you.'

Dare's patience was legendary. Right now it was also non-existent. 'In the States we appreciate directness. So much more effective than kissing someone's butt while waiting to get to the real issue. So, are you?'

Benson sighed. 'Carly is a lovely young woman but you give me far more credit than I deserve. And her far less.'

Dare's jaw clenched. 'A simple yes or no will suffice.'

'No, of course I'm not.'

Dare didn't think he'd felt this sense of relief when the first dot-com company he'd invested all his teenage savings in had been valued as a unicorn in its first year on the markets.

He swiped a hand through his hair. 'So how long do you have left?' Because if Benson wasn't sleeping with Carly Evans then he'd been right all along and the old guy was sick.

To his credit, his grandfather didn't pretend to misinterpret him. 'I don't know. I have a brain tumour they're hoping will shrink before they operate.'

A brain tumour? Hell. He almost felt guilty at his earlier cynicism that the old man was dying.

'And Carly is your oncologist?'

'No, Carly works for an agency I hired because apparently I need twenty-four-hour monitoring due to my diabetes. It's not a combination I recommend,' he said with a flair of black humour.

Dare frowned. 'Why haven't you given my mother this information?' Because he was pretty sure she would have mentioned it if he had.

'It's not public knowledge yet, and I wish for Rachel to want to spend time with me because she wants to, not because I'm gravely ill.'

'You want her forgiveness, you mean.'

'Yes, I want her forgiveness. I behaved badly all those years ago and I'm man enough to admit it.'

'You've had long enough to think about it.'

Benson acknowledged the comment with a rueful grimace. 'You don't pull your punches, do you?'

Dare had lived with a man who used manipulation as a hobby. He wasn't into games as an adult unless they were inside the bedroom and even then they had to be of the pleasurable variety.

'Here's the thing, old man—my mother suffered for years with my father and then for years working three jobs to give me the best start in life. At any time you could have thrown her a bone but you didn't. That makes you unforgivable in my book.'

His grandfather turned grey, but Dare refused to give a damn. If he wanted forgiveness he was barking up the wrong tree with him.

Finally Benson levered himself out of his chair and pulled an envelope out of his desk drawer.

Handing it to Dare, he sat down to wait. 'Read it,' he urged when Dare just stared at it. The postmark was Australia, where they had lived until Dare was six, at which time they had moved to America.

Knowing he wasn't going to like what was inside, he skimmed his father's handwriting, wincing internally at the shockingly angry letter that would have had the Pope thinking twice before reaching out again.

Then he saw the signature and swore; his startled gaze caught Benson's remote one. 'My mother didn't write this.'

'I know,' Benson said as if in pain. 'Now. I know that

now. When I received it twenty-seven years ago I was too proud to question it. And to my shame, I never tried again.' Silence filled the room as Dare stared at the nasty letter.

'And now you're dying and want to put everything right.'

'It's not exactly like that. Three months ago, before I knew my breathing issues were more serious than old age, I saw a photograph in a doctor's surgery. It was some society event in New York and I recognised Rachel straight away. I don't expect you to understand but after seeing her face again…nothing else mattered.'

Dare didn't say anything while he worked through what he'd just discovered. He couldn't imagine how he would respond if he had been in the same situation. Maybe he'd have done the same thing…

'Does my mother know about this letter?'

Benson shook his head. 'I haven't shown her yet.'

'Don't,' Dare decided. 'My father spun so many stories when I was younger I spent most of my youth believing he was a secret-service operative. He used to confide in me and tell me my mother didn't understand and it wasn't until his death that I realised he was just a low-level con-man with stars in his eyes.' Dare sighed and handed the letter back. 'And fortunately for you my mother won't need to see this to forgive you.'

'Unlike you.'

'Yeah, unlike me.' Though right now he couldn't say how he felt.

His grandfather sighed. 'A chip off the old block.'

Dare's eyes narrowed dangerously. 'That's the second time you've accused me of being like my father.'

'Actually, I was thinking that you reminded me of my-self.' He pulled a face. 'Bitterness burrows deep, Dare, like a tick, and eats away at you slowly, just like a parasite.'

'I have a great life. Nothing to be bitter about.'

'Yes, you've done well for yourself. It interests me that your company is a brokerage firm.'

'More hedge fund,' Dare corrected. 'I raise capital nowadays rather than trade stocks.'

'Capital you can use to buy companies to disband, perhaps?'

Dare shrugged. 'If the company warrants it. Not all companies can be turned around.'

'What about BG Textiles?'

'What about it?'

'We're experiencing some trouble.'

'So I've heard.'

'Heard, or helped create?'

Dare's eyes narrowed. 'What are you implying?'

Benson sighed. 'If I might borrow some of your directness, someone is stalking my company. Is it you?'

Dare laughed. 'Why would I want your company?'

'Perhaps to seek vengeance for the past.'

'If you were any younger, I'd deck you.'

'It would be a nice addition to your portfolio,' Benson persisted. 'And you did expand into the UK this year.'

'I opened an office in the UK because of opportunity, not vengeance. In fact I'd forgotten I even had European relatives until you contacted my mother. Whoever is after BG Textiles, it isn't me.'

Benson took a moment before nodding. 'I believe you.'

'I don't lie.'

'I get that. And to be honest I doubted you were the type who would work behind the scenes to bring the share price down, but I had to ask.'

Which was why his illness wasn't public knowledge, Dare guessed. If it were the share price of BG Textiles wouldn't just fall, it would crash. 'I hope you have some other ideas to follow up.'

'I have some, yes.'

And Dare had no doubt the wily old goat would attempt to get to the bottom of it when he should be resting in preparation for his operation. Not that it was any of Dare's business. If the old man wanted to kill himself sooner rather than later that was his concern.

'I'm sorry, Dare. If I had realised Rachel had reverted to Pearl's maiden name and that you were—'

'Stop there, Benson.' His grandfather's soft words struck like a sharp blade in Dare's chest. 'Shoulda, coulda, woulda—isn't that the expression?' he said stiffly.

Benson's shoulders dropped. 'Yes.'

A knock at the door broke the tension between them and Dare turned, half expecting to see Carly standing in the doorway.

It wasn't. It was the butler asking what time Benson would like Mrs Carlisle to serve dinner.

Once the elderly butler left Benson turned back to Dare. 'Will you stay another night with us, Dare?'

Dare looked at his grandfather's sagging shoulders. The stuffing seemed to have come out of him and he saw lines of strain on his face. He didn't want to stay, he really didn't, but the old man was getting to him, despite his best attempts not to let him.

Someone else was getting to him as well and she'd no doubt be coming down to dinner.

Dinner here, dinner in London… He needed to eat, didn't he? 'I'll stay,' he found himself saying impulsively.

But first he'd head out on his bike and get some fresh air.

And if there was a lightness to his step as he headed back to his room to put on his leathers, it was only because he was finally satisfied that Benson's intentions in communicating with his mother again were born from a genuine desire to make up for the past. It had nothing to do with the fact that his grandfather wasn't sleeping with the delectable Carly Evans. Nothing at all.

CHAPTER SIX

CARLY FELT A sense of relief as she checked her appearance in the mirror before heading down to dinner. She had heard Benson leave his room a few minutes earlier and had almost contemplated excusing herself to eat in her room because of a headache.

Then she'd remembered hearing Dare's death trap roar down the driveway so she knew he'd gone—without saying goodbye, *thank goodness*—so there was really no need to act like a coward. And she enjoyed dinner in the dining room.

Mrs Carlisle usually outdid herself with the evening meal and Carly had never eaten as well as she had since arriving at Rothmeyer House. Probably she never would again. Her beginnings, while not lacking by everyday standards, did not include household staff and a live-in cook! And Mrs Carlisle's cooking would definitely be something she missed when she moved on to her next job.

Something she was still putting off thinking about. She knew she had to go home at some point but...was she ready to return to Liverpool again? In many ways she had loved seeing parts of her country she never had before, but travelling had been Liv's dream and Carly sometimes wondered if she wasn't moving around a lot in an attempt to honour Liv more than herself.

Liv who would never get to travel, never get to fall in love... Carly's heart squeezed and for some reason Dare James's face swam into her consciousness. How on earth she could find a man like him attractive was beyond her.

Yes, he was good-looking...manly...fit...primal... She pulled a face. If you liked that kind of thing. He was also another version of the Daniels of the world. Full of himself, arrogant, rude…and that take-charge mentality? She shuddered.

Yes, it was definitely good that he hadn't bothered to say goodbye or try to apologise. She couldn't have been happier to have things back to normal. And right after dinner she'd set herself up with her computer and make some definite decisions about her life. Maybe she'd move to London and really live it up for once.

Liv would surely laugh at that. Her sister had always balanced her, pushing Carly out of the house and out of her studies, or work, to go to movies or a club, giving her fashion advice and turning her hair from a layered, carroty mess into the smoother style she wore it in today.

Feeling the sting of tears at the back of her throat, Carly twisted said carroty mess into a quick knot. Liv would have hated Dare James, she felt sure. She would have said he was overbearing and obnoxious and… Carly frowned. Actually, Liv probably would have found him funny and flirtatious. She definitely would have thought that his muscles were 'divine'—her favourite expression—and no doubt those rose-coloured glasses she'd viewed life through would have had her thinking him a hero always wanting to ride in and save the day.

Carly shook her head. Some hero coming over all macho and moving an injured child without first getting medical clearance. So, it was likely only a sprain. He hadn't known that, had he?

The man had heartbreak city written all over his horrible face and it was very lucky he'd gone without saying goodbye because she would have told him exactly what she thought of him. She would have told him… A hot flush rose up her neckline as she remembered the way she had wrapped herself around him in the forest like an anaconda in heat.

God, how embarrassing.

But she wouldn't think about that. The fact was he was gone and she needed to concentrate on her future. On a plan for her future. He could go jump on his white charger and choose some other woman's heart to stomp on. Some other woman to ruin. Her lips twisted into a brittle smile. She'd been in one disastrous relationship already and the old adage held true: once bitten twice shy.

And here she was thinking about him again.

Frustrated, she closed her bedroom door and headed down the hallway. It was just that, okay, she could see the appeal he held with his athletic build, and maybe that take-charge mentality meant that he did things exceptionally well when he did them. Like kiss.

The man knew what to do with his mouth, that was for sure. He'd kissed her as if he'd owned her and she'd loved it. An involuntary shudder raced through her. The truth was, being in Dare James's arms had made her feel incredibly soft and feminine, and, yes, if she was being honest, sexy. He'd made her feel so very sexy.

Her toes curled inside her heels at the thought. No amount of talking to herself late into the night had been able to reassure her that Daniel's constant cheating had been merely a reflection of who he was as a person, instead of who she was as a woman. Somehow she had still felt a small twinge of responsibility for his infidelities because she'd known his libido was a lot higher than hers. He'd told her often enough.

But with Dare…

Carly sighed when she realised where her thoughts were headed again. *He's gone*, she reminded herself briskly. And now she wouldn't be distracted in her care of the Baron, nor would she be constantly on edge, looking over her shoulder for when she might next run into him. He could go throw that swaggering grin and dimpled cheek at some other poor woman and see how she liked it.

A lot, probably. Especially if he kissed her as well. Carly swallowed heavily. If he touched her breasts and did that thing with his fingers—

'Mind if I accompany you down to dinner?'

Whirling around at the sound of his voice, Carly clapped her hand over heart as if that might stop it from flying out of her chest. Goddammit, where was a defib when you needed one?

She sucked in a lungful of air. 'What are you doing, creeping up on me like that?' she fumed. Her face bright red as much from the carnal thoughts she'd been having as the fright she'd just received.

Dare's brow rose questioningly. 'I don't believe I've ever crept anywhere.'

Carly's lips compressed together at his mocking tone. 'Stalking, then.'

He gave a short laugh. 'Not my style either. Maybe this is just a happy coincidence.'

Carly frowned. 'I thought you had left,' she said accusingly.

'Without saying goodbye?' His eyes moved lazily down her body, making her want to squirm. 'Are you really so eager to see the back of me, Red?'

Did he even need to ask? 'You were the one who said you were going,' she pointed out coolly. 'And I heard your raucous death trap take off down the driveway hours ago.'

He shrugged. 'I needed to go for a ride. Clear my thinking.'

God, did that mean he was staying?

He chuckled and she realised he'd read her expression perfectly. 'Don't look so worried, Red. I'm not insulted by your attitude.'

'That's because you have an ego the size of the Himalayas,' Carly griped.

'Maybe I'm just pleased to see you.'

A sharp sensation lodged inside her chest. 'Excuse me, I'm going to dinner.'

'Wait,' Dare said softly, gripping her arm. 'I have a couple of questions I want to ask you first.'

Schooling her features into a bland mask, Carly dislodged his disconcerting touch and looked up at him. 'Like what?'

Dare glanced along the corridor before leaning towards her to speak softly. 'Like how serious is Benson's condition?'

She grimaced. 'So he told you about his illness?'

He gave her a look. 'He told me everything.'

Dare knew she got the full import of his meaning because she blushed prettily.

'And now you're concerned?'

He frowned at her suspicious tone. 'I don't know what I am at this point. But I do want to know what his chances are.'

Carly debated what to tell him and why he wanted to know. Was he going to taunt his grandfather with the information? She really wouldn't put it past him.

'For God's sake, I'm not going to sell the information to the highest bidder, if that's what you're worried about.'

'I'm not worried about that.' She hadn't even considered that side of things. 'What I'm concerned with is what you're going to say to him. His blood pressure is all over the place, which isn't good for him. He needs to rest and not to be overstressed before the operation.'

'And you think I'm going to…what?' He frowned and stepped closer, towering over her. 'Make him feel worse?'

Carly shifted her weight to put some distance between

them. 'You were rude enough when you first arrived,' she pointed out

'Hell.' He ran a hand through his hair absently, drawing her attention to the way the caramel tresses drifted through his fingers and offset the strong bones of his face. 'I'm not that cruel. I'm not going to use it against him.'

He sounded genuine, she thought, and it wasn't as if she were giving away secrets anymore.

'Honestly I don't know. If the tumour shrinks enough that they can get it all and his diabetes doesn't complicate things, the prognosis is good that he'll survive the operation. After that it's a bit of a waiting game as to whether or not the cancer has spread. Now, if you'll—'

Dare moved to the left as he sensed Carly about to walk past him, but unfortunately she moved in the same direction and before he knew it her body was plastered up against his. Right where he'd wanted her ever since he'd watched her sexy butt swaying in front of him.

Neither one of them moved for a heartbeat. Two. And then they both took a step back. Her hand went to her hair as if to straighten it and a loose strand caught on the gloss of her lipstick. Dare nearly reached out to fix it himself but shoved his hands into his pockets at the last minute.

Another blush rose up over her creamy cheekbones and her hand shook when she brought it back down to her side. 'This has to stop,' she muttered, frustration etched across her brow. 'I can't explain…'

She stopped abruptly and Dare picked up the thread. 'This thing between us?'

She shook her head in denial. 'There is no thing.'

Dare's smile was slow in coming. 'Oh, there's definitely a thing.'

She let out an annoyed breath and her lips pursed. 'I'm sure it's entirely normal for you to feel this way about a woman but...' as if she'd said too much, her blush deepened, 'I don't like it.'

Nor did he. Not one little bit. And she was wrong about him feeling this way with every woman. He couldn't remember the last time he'd wanted a woman so much his body responded without his brain first giving the go-ahead.

His gaze dropped to her mouth, soft and pink and glossy. If he had met her under different circumstances and trusted her he might take things further. Take her to dinner. To bed. And while his body liked that idea a great deal, instinct told him that walking away was the sanest option. 'Then let's forget it.'

She blinked up at him.

'Just like that?' she blurted out, surprise ripe on her face.

'Absolutely.' Because once Dare made up his mind about something it was done. 'I'm staying one more night,' he said. 'You're here. Why don't we go down to dinner, make nice, then we'll both go to bed—separately, of course—and tomorrow morning I'll drive off into the sunset and it will be as if we never met.'

'Sunrise,' she corrected.

'Sunrise.'

'That sounds...' She squared her shoulders, pulling the silk of her blouse tight across her high breasts. 'That sounds like an excellent idea.'

Yes, it was.

'Shall we?' He directed her to precede him along the hallway. And he'd be fine as long as he didn't put his hands on her.

Which was a bit like telling a three-year-old to keep his fingers out of an open cookie jar, Dare thought ruefully two hours later as the dessert plates were cleared.

For the most part the evening had worked well. Benson was a consummate host and Dare found that he enjoyed hearing about the history of the local village and how it had changed. He especially enjoyed hearing stories about his mother as a child. It surprised him to hear that she had been a rebellious child with a wild streak, but it shouldn't have. It was that side of her, after all, that had seen her fall in love with his conman of a father, and also the side that had seen her knuckle down and go it alone instead of turning to her father for help.

Benson had openly admitted that he hadn't known how to handle either her, or her after their mother had died and for the first time Dare saw some value in revisiting the past.

But for all his focus on the conversation and enjoyment of the delicious food, nothing could dull his awareness of the slender redhead beside him. Every slide of her leg under the table, every tilt of her wineglass against her lips, every soft laugh as she joined in the conversation ratcheted up his desire to finish what they had started earlier.

It made a mockery of his confident assertion that he could forget the attraction between them *'just like that.'*

And now, with all the barriers to them being intimate effectively removed, Dare was having a hard time convincing himself that his promise to disappear from her life hadn't been just the teensiest bit impetuous.

And what would be wrong with spending a night or two with her? She was an adult, he was an adult…

'Sorry,' she murmured as her hand accidentally brushed his.

'No problem.' He cleared his throat. 'What were you after? The sugar?'

'Yes, thanks.'

Again their hands touched and again he felt an electrical current feather across his skin.

Carly stirred her coffee. Dare shifted in his seat. 'That'll keep you up tonight,' he pointed out softly.

'No, it won't.' She gave him a brief smile. 'You learn pretty quickly as a resident physician to sleep wherever you can, whenever you can, no matter what the circumstances.'

'Sounds hectic.'

'Oh, it is.' Her smoky green eyes were bright with pleasure. 'Emergency departments are busy, chaotic, orderly—which I know seems like a contradiction, but it's not—and really stressful.' Her smile grew. 'Coffee became my best friend during those years.'

'I know what you mean.'

'You do?'

'Sure. You don't put in an all-nighter at a gas station and then race back to campus to sit a three-hour exam after finishing up a paper on the history of economic rationalisation in the Eastern Bloc without a little caffeine hit on the side.'

Carly's eyes sparkled into his. 'Exactly.' Her smile grew. 'But you know the best coffee is the first coffee of the day, right? When it's nice and hot and the acidity just rolls across your tongue.' Her eyes turned heavenwards. 'It's sublime, isn't it?'

'The law of diminishing marginal returns,' he said gruffly.

Her eyebrow cocked. 'Say that again?'

Dare laughed. 'DMR, as I remembered it for the exam. It means that in all productive processes, adding more of one factor of production, while holding all others constant, will at some point yield lower incremental per unit returns.' He chuckled softly at her blank expression. 'In the case of coffee it means the more you drink, the less pleasure you get from it.'

'Oh, now I understand.' She laughed softly and Dare thought in the case of her smiles DMR didn't apply at all.

'What are you two grinning at?'

Grinning?

Dare frowned at his mother's smiling face. He wasn't traditionally a 'grinner.'

'Coffee,' Carly answered, her face carefully blank. 'And whether it keeps you up all night.' She shifted uncomfortably in her seat. 'And on that note I might go up to bed. I hope you don't think I'm rude if I call it a night?'

'Of course not,' Rachel said. 'All that walking today must have made you tired.'

'Yes.'

Carly smiled but it didn't reach her eyes and Dare had no idea what had just happened. One minute they were having a nice time together and the next she was giving him the cold shoulder and brushing him off. Acting as if he didn't exist.

Tension coiled through him tighter than the screws on his Kawasaki. 'Are you sure you're okay?'

'Perfectly fine,' she said briskly.

Dare gave himself a mental shake. If she wanted to go to bed when the night was only half over it was no skin off his nose. He had no hold on what she did. Certainly he had no cause to be irritated by it.

'Sweet dreams, Red,' he said, settling more comfortably in his chair. There was no way he was going to bed at ten o'clock. He wasn't a child.

He lifted the bottle of wine from the bucket. 'More wine, Mother? Benson?'

Carly felt infinitely better after brushing her hair and putting on her pyjamas but, good God, if Dare had touched her leg with his one more time she thought she might have attempted heart-removal surgery with her butter knife.

And not because he had been deliberately awful to her, but because he hadn't! Up until now she hadn't experienced a relaxed Dare and it only made it harder to remember how rude and egotistical he could be.

Her mother had always said that if a man was good to his mother he'd be good to his wife but she didn't want to think of Dare like that. She'd been obtuse in a relationship with a man once before, ergo she could easily fall into the same trap again.

Not happening, she told herself.

Once Dare left in the morning it would be as if they had never met; two strangers who had passed like ships in the night and destined to be nothing more.

A good thing, since she wasn't the casual-sex type and by his own admission he didn't let women get close to him.

And, yes, jumping into bed with Dare James might be utterly thrilling on one level, but what if he was just another mistake waiting to happen? Another bad judgment call? Hadn't she made enough of those already? And not just with men…

Frustrated with the way her thoughts kept veering back to all her failings, she grabbed her computer and placed it on her lap. She logged on and checked her emails. The one from her agency caught her attention and she reopened it.

The job they were offering her was in Kent where a small clinic needed a temporary doctor to fill in while someone went on maternity leave. Would she do it?

Carly bit her lip. A small clinic could be interesting but speaking with Dare tonight had reminded her how much she enjoyed working in a large, thriving hospital. And okay, they were often cesspits for gossip, but it wasn't as if she'd be fool enough to fall for one of the head doctors again.

The question was whether she wanted to re-enter that life again. And where? Then there was the question of her flat; the one she'd bought with Liv. She really needed to do something about that.

Oh, Liv, why couldn't I have saved you?

A fist felt as if it had just closed around her heart. What

good was a medical degree if you couldn't save people? Anger rose up inside her. Anger at herself. At life. Liv had trusted her and Carly had let her down.

Feeling the threat of tears clog the back of her throat, Carly fell back against her pillows and took her computer with her. Neither dwelling nor crying had ever brought Liv back to her so Carly didn't let herself do either now.

What she did do was click on a well-known job site and start scrolling down the entries under medical doctors. Don't make a mountain out of a molehill, she told herself.

Lost in thought as she was, she started when there was a thump on her door. She knew immediately who it would be. The Baron was much too circumspect to bang like that, and Rachel would bruise a knuckle if she knocked that hard.

Perhaps if she stayed completely still and pretended to be— 'I didn't tell you to come in,' she informed the man now framed in her open doorway. 'I could have been naked.'

Probably not the best thing to have said. What was wrong with her?

'You knew I'd come up here,' he said arrogantly.

Carly strove to remain calm. 'And why would I know that?'

'Because one minute you're all smiling and happy and the next you look like you'd seen a ghost.'

'You're exaggerating.'

'I don't think so. What's wrong?' he asked, closing the door and moving further into the room.

No way was Carly going to tell him that she'd just been overwhelmed by his presence. That she'd needed some space because he brought up so many painful memories from a past she'd prefer to forget.

That he made her want things she'd rather not want. Like a relationship. A connection. A place to call home.

'Nothing,' she said, trying to ignore the thudding of her heart. 'As you can see, I'm perfectly fine.'

His eyes drifted over her in response to her unintentional invitation. Carly held herself completely still under his steady gaze, conscious that all she was wearing was a cotton singlet and matching boxer shorts adorned with tiny red hearts.

'Perfectly.'

Carly smiled politely at his wry tone. 'Now you can go.'

She watched warily as, instead of doing as she requested, he stopped at the foot of her bed, his hands on his hips.

'Do you always ignore a woman's request?' she asked lightly.

'Was that what it was? It sounded more like an order.'

Unsure of his mood, Carly knew she was strung too tight to deal with him rationally. 'What do you want, Dare?'

His eyes ran over her again. 'Now there's a question.'

Knowing that he was being deliberately provocative, Carly took a deep breath and counted to ten. She had been a resident for three years at one of Liverpool's busiest hospitals having to face down more insolent men than this one. 'I thought you had forgotten all about that,' she challenged.

'Ah, so I did. The only problem is that attraction can be a pesky thing. It doesn't want to stay forgotten.'

'Try harder.' Because this would not end well, she knew it as surely as she knew her own name.

He laughed. 'Easy, Red. I only came to talk.'

Feigning a calm she didn't feel, Carly snatched up her silky robe from the nearby chair and pretended her legs weren't wobbling as she moved to one of the Queen Anne armchairs beside the fireplace.

In winter this would no doubt be a cosy place to hole up in with a good book. Or a lover.

Dare followed her and leant against the mantelpiece.

'I'm curious about something,' he said.

Carly rested back in the chair and curled her legs underneath her. 'Can't you satisfy it somewhere else?'

He laughed softly. 'Unfortunately not. Tell me, why does a highly qualified doctor take a lowly nursing position with an elderly man?'

Running was her first thought, hiding her second.

Unsettled by her reflections and the man making her face them, Carly glared up at him.

'First of all,' Carly began frostily, 'nurses are not *lowly* and second of all it's none of your damned business.'

She jumped to her feet and paced away from him.

His brows drew together. 'I didn't mean lowly, as in the profession. I meant as in below your professional capabilities. As I understand it there's a shortage of doctors all over the country.'

'So you're an expert on the medical profession now. Must be nice viewing the world from your lofty heights.'

'I didn't say that.'

'You didn't have to. You just stand there and pass judgment. It's what you do best.'

A muscle flicked in his jaw. 'I only asked a couple of questions.'

Carly took a deep breath. 'I've been at the end of some of your questions before and they're unpleasant to say the least.'

Dare shifted uncomfortably. 'Yeah, about that. I might have made a mistake.'

'One?' She arched a brow, her temper abating at his confession.

'One. Two...' He gave her a quick smile. 'What matters is that, yes, I owe you an apology.'

'Let's have it, then.'

Dare caught her small, slow grin and his deepened. 'You're enjoying yourself.'

'I'm enjoying finally seeing you squirm, yes.'

He tapped his fingers on his chest as if to say, *Who, me?* 'Who said I was squirming? I can admit when I've been wrong.'

'Happens often, does it?'

'No.' Usually he was bang on the money about people. It came from learning from the best shyster around.

'But it did happen this time. And I apologise for jumping to conclusions about your relationship with my grandfather.'

He watched her throat bob as she swallowed.

'It's fine. I might even have jumped to the same conclusions myself if our positions had been reversed.'

Dare gave a mock frown. 'You mean you would have thought *I* was sleeping with my grandfather?'

Carly's spontaneous burst of laughter made him grin.

'Okay, maybe not,' she conceded.

God, he wanted to kiss her. He'd lied when he'd said he'd stopped by only to talk. He'd stopped by because he'd wanted to see her. Needed to see her.

'Is that why you're really here?'

'What?'

'To apologise.'

Dare let out a slow breath. 'Maybe you intrigue me, Dr Evans. Maybe I just want to know your story,' he said softly.

She moved to stand behind the antique chair and all Dare could think about was shoving the chair aside and throwing her onto the waiting bed behind her.

'My story is boring.'

'Shouldn't I be the judge of that?'

That was just it. She didn't want him to judge her at all.

'If you must know, I had a very normal childhood, with

a sister and two parents, and…and I lived in Liverpool up until a year ago.'

'Don't give away too many details, Red.' He smiled. 'What happened a year ago?'

'Why does something have to have happened?'

He shrugged. 'You must have left for some reason.'

'I wanted to travel.'

'That's it?'

Carly narrowed her eyes. He was starting to sound a lot like Daniel during one of his interrogations. Should she tell him that? Tell him that she had been hurt and she should have known better? Tell him her sister had died and she…? Carly swallowed. No, he didn't need to know about Liv.

'I thought I was in love once,' she admitted. 'We dated, and he…cheated. End of story. Happy now?'

No, he wasn't happy to hear she had been in love with another man. Nor was he happy she had been hurt.

'So you left town because of him?'

Her eyes flashed in annoyance. 'Yes, and no, I…I don't want to talk about it.'

'Because you're still in love with him?'

'That's very personal.' Her eyes flicked away. 'But no, I'm not in love with Daniel.'

Daniel?

Dare hadn't wanted a name. He didn't want to be able to picture the idiot she'd been with. And now he was also wondering why she hadn't looked him in the eye when she'd answered him. Was she lying?

Agitated, he absently smoothed his hand along the mantelpiece, accidentally dislodging her handbag and spilling the contents in the process.

'Damn.' He glanced at the array of feminine-looking items scattered at his feet.

'It's okay.' She laughed, kneeling in front of him. 'I've got it.'

Feeling like a fool, Dare crouched down beside her. He handed over her purse and noticed a long velvet box beneath. Curious, he picked it up. 'May I?'

She glanced at the box and blushed. 'It's the necklace I nearly lost.'

So this was where it was.

Slowly opening the box, Dare stared down at the expensive little number twinkling up at him. This had certainly set someone back a pretty penny.

'Who gave you this? Your ex?'

She finished stuffing the things in her bag and straightened. 'No. It was…no one important.'

Dare knew an evasive answer when he heard one. His brow rose. 'Does he know that?'

'I'm sorry?'

'Does he know he's not important?'

Carly frowned, taking the box from his hand. 'Why are you using that tone again?'

Dare took a deep breath, wondering how it was that he could control a global corporation without batting an eye and yet one woman always seemed to have him on the back foot. Carly was a genuinely nice person—he knew that now. And not only that. She was smart and beautiful and he wanted her.

'Forget I said anything.'

Carly fidgeted with the box before placing it carefully in her bag. 'The person who gave me the necklace did so because he wanted to go out with me. There's nothing else to it.'

Dare doubted that. No man he knew gave a woman expensive jewellery because he wanted to go out with her. It was either a gift to show his appreciation or a parting one. Still…the guy was obviously history and that was all that mattered.

'You don't have to explain yourself to me,' he assured her.

'Good.' She stepped back from him. 'Because, frankly, I'm done with explaining myself to men. There's nothing more debilitating.'

'I agree,' he said, moving closer to her.

'What…? What…? Dare, what are you doing?'

'Taking you in my arms,' he murmured.

Carly flattened her hands against his chest to ward him off. 'Dare, I don't want this. I don't want *you*.'

Dare kissed her. Softly. Sweetly. Carly's breath hitched in her lungs.

'Yes, you do.'

'No.' She shook her head weakly. 'I don't. I…'

He kissed her again. This time it was more commanding. More urgent.

Carly melted. She didn't mean to, but she did. His touch, his scent, his heat—they all set off a minefield of emotions and sensations inside her that she just couldn't fight.

'Carly…'

Dare groaned her name and Carly clung to his broad shoulders. Maybe sleeping with him just once wouldn't be a mistake, she reasoned. Giving in to this desire between them that made her forget everything around her but him. That made her burn.

But then what? a little voice of sanity asked. *Then he leaves and you're left once again to pick up the pieces? Alone this time.*

Carly moaned in denial even as she kissed him. The voice was right. And yet… And yet… She couldn't seem to say no to him.

'Dare, I—'

A beeping sound cut off her weak attempt at resistance and Carly pulled her mouth from his. 'My beeper.'

'Ignore it.' Dare buried his hands in her hair and brought her mouth back to his.

'No. I can't.' Carly pushed at him again. 'It's Benson. I need to give him his medication.'

Dare groaned, loosening his grip with obvious reluctance, and Carly moved out of the circle of his arms, walking like an automaton to her bedside table to silence the beeper.

Dare's heavy breaths filled the room, but Carly kept her back to him. She knew he was waiting for her but she couldn't do this. She felt frozen. Frozen by her own unbidden desires and the mistakes she had made in the past.

'I think it's best if you go,' she said quietly.

She felt his hard, heated stare before he crossed to her. When he stopped beside her she was almost afraid to look up at him. Afraid she'd back down and tell him she didn't want him to go at all. That she wanted him to love her.

Oh God, that wasn't what she wanted at all. 'Why?' he asked tightly.

Carly shook her head, deeply held fears governing her words. 'I just don't want this.'

'You did a minute ago,' Dare said, a hardness creeping into his voice. 'I felt it. I felt your response.'

'Physically, yes.' She gripped her hands together. 'You're a virile man—I won't deny that—but that's all it is and…and it's not enough.'

Dare stared at her for long seconds. 'I think you're afraid,' he said.

'Afraid?'

'Afraid of the way I make you feel.'

Carly forced out a laugh as his words hit a little too close to the bone. 'And I think you're arrogant and full of yourself.'

Time slowed as his eyes scanned her face, and it was all she could do not to crumple and ask him to hold her.

'As long as we're clear,' he said coldly.

Carly tilted her chin up. 'I am. I hope you are too.'

His jaw clenched. 'As crystal,' he snarled, before stalking from the room.

Carly held herself perfectly still until he'd slammed the door behind him. Then she sank onto the bed, buried her head in her hands, and wondered if she hadn't just made the biggest mistake of them all.

CHAPTER SEVEN

'YOU'RE AWFULLY QUIET TONIGHT, Dare. The exhibition not to your liking?'

Dare glanced at the blonde by his side, who was now studying him and not the artwork in front of her. Lucy was a woman he had met a few years ago in New York and they sometimes caught up when they found themselves in the same city, like now.

Apparently she'd come to London to visit a client and since he was still here he'd said yes to her invitation and here he was in a warehouse-sized loft in Whitechapel where Jack the Ripper had carried out his horrifying work.

By the look of the life-size canvases splattered with paint and what looked like debris from the city's gutters, the artist prancing around the room was channelling Jacky boy's macabre energy. Dare wasn't sure he'd seen art that was so gratuitously self-absorbed.

On top of that the beer was flat and the wine tasted terrible.

'The exhibition's fine.' And why spend time explaining his view when Lucy would likely only agree anyway?

Normally at this point he would suggest they call his driver and head back to her hotel. Normally he would already be anticipating the night ahead.

'Well, something is bothering you,' she murmured.

'Nothing of any importance.'

'Anything I can help you with?'

God, he hoped so. It was the other reason he'd said yes when she'd called. He'd hoped very much that she could alleviate the funk he'd been in since he'd driven away from Rothmeyer House in a cloud of dust a week ago.

Nothing seemed to have been the same since then. By rights he should already be back in the States but his meetings were taking longer than they should and his mother was still at Rothmeyer House.

She'd sounded so happy to be extending her stay and spending time with her father and he was, surprisingly, genuinely happy for her. So happy he had agreed to help Benson find out who was behind the leaking of secrets at BG Textiles.

'What do you think of the artist's use of red in this one?' Lucy asked, hooking her arm through his.

Dare glanced at the enormous canvas in front of him. It looked as if the artist had met a shrewish redhead and decided to decapitate her.

His smile was all teeth. 'I like it. It has a certain…something, don't you think?'

'Hmm, I suppose you could be right,' Lucy purred, tilting her head so her hair fell just so across her shoulders.

Carly Evans could learn a thing or two from Lucy about how to attract a man's attention, he thought sourly. Then he scowled. He was tired of thinking about Carly Evans at the most inopportune times. He'd already decided to walk away from her so why bother?

Unfortunately she had burrowed inside his head like a debilitating tick…and his grandfather had been right: they ate away at you with sharp little teeth.

Perhaps she was on his mind so much because he intended to call Benson the following morning and report his findings about BG Textiles.

His *grim* findings.

It was a conversation Dare wasn't looking forward to. How did you tell an old man who was likely dying that his only other grandchild was selling secrets to a company competitor to fund a crappy investment decision he'd made months ago and couldn't repay? From what Dare had found out about Beckett, his fool cousin probably wasn't even aware of how seriously he was putting the company at risk.

And if the information wasn't what Benson was expecting the old man might keel over on the spot and then Dare would have another thing on his conscience. Should he drive down instead? Tell him in person? If he did that he'd likely run into Carly Evans and he could only imagine the type of greeting she'd give him.

But if something did happen to his grandfather after he heard the news the good doctor would surely blame him for it, regardless.

God, she made him mad.

That disapproving little chin of hers would no doubt go up when he arrived, just as it had the morning he'd left. Not that she'd come down to see him off, but he'd seen her, making sure he left from her balcony window.

And that was fine with him. He'd told himself all along not to touch her and nothing good came from not following sound advice.

Finally sick of trying to convince himself that the wine was drinkable, Dare dumped his glass on a nearby table.

'Ah, Dare, I think that's part of the exhibition,' Lucy said.

Dare glanced back at the tall white column and noticed the small card halfway down the side.

'Now it's also useful,' he said. 'Are you ready to leave?'

Lucy curled into his side. 'Whenever you are, lover.'

Yeah, Carly Evans should definitely be here right now taking notes.

He thought about the ruby necklace in her handbag. She'd said no one important had given it to her but the poor shmuck must have been at some point.

But why was he back to thinking about her?

She was history and the lovely Lucy was not.

He smiled at Lucy and fitted his arm around her slender

waist, guiding her through the throng of fancy-dressed art lovers. Or art haters, if they liked this showing.

Or was that him being judgmental again?

Him? Judgmental?

After living with a father like his Dare knew things were rarely as they seemed, which was why he was such a good analyst. He usually *reserved* his judgment until all the facts were in.

'Dare? Dare?'

Dare glanced down at Lucy. 'What?'

She gave a small laugh. 'Nothing…you just stopped. I wondered if you wanted something.'

'An exorcist?'

'Sorry?' Her laugh this time was tinged with nerves. She drew her blood-red fingernails down the lapel of his jacket. 'I don't know any of those offhand.'

What had Carly's fingernails been like? He hadn't paid any attention to that detail, too busy taking in other parts of her. The graceful arc of her neck, the gentle swell of her small breasts, those long, long legs.

He looked at Lucy. 'It was a joke.'

'Oh!' she murmured. 'You're in a strange mood tonight.'

'Tell me about it.'

He sidestepped a cluster of yuppies and finally spotted the main door.

Thank God for small mercies.

Short. Her fingernails had been short. He remembered the way they'd felt when she'd stroked the nape of his neck and then—he swore softly.

Lucy looked at him as if he'd suddenly morphed into an alien being.

Making a decision, he directed her outside, surprising Mark in the process, who scrambled to open the passenger door for him. Dare waved him off and placed Lucy inside. He couldn't do it. He couldn't be with one woman while he was still thinking about another.

'A change of plans,' he said apologetically. 'I'll have Mark drop you home—or somewhere else, if you prefer.'

Lucy bestowed him with a benevolent smile. 'What's her name?'

'Whose name?'

'The woman you've been thinking about all night.'

Dare hacked out a laugh. 'It's just work.'

Lucy all but rolled her eyes. 'I've known you for three years now and work has never put a frown on your face before.'

'I've had bad days,' he defended. How could she know him that well when he struggled to remember her surname?

She shook her head. 'You thrive on bad days. This is something else.' She shrugged. 'A woman was my first guess.'

Dare grunted. It pained him to admit that she was right. 'I'll call you,' he said instead.

She sighed and leaned back against the upholstery. 'I won't hold my breath.'

Dare tapped the roof of the car and Mark shot away from the kerb, leaving Dare to either catch a cab or walk home.

He glanced at the sky and turned towards the river. It couldn't be that far to Eaton Square on foot.

An hour later and Dare was reconsidering his decision. His feet hurt and his hair was plastered to his head from the rain that had come out of nowhere. Grimacing, he gave up the ghost and ducked into a small café that was still open.

'Long black,' he said to the pierced barista behind the counter. He could already feel the buzz of caffeine as the youth prepared it and he knew it would be a lot better than the coffee he'd picked up at that grungy gas station he'd worked at during university.

'Thanks. Keep the change.'

He took his coffee to the window and savoured that first sip.

'But you know the best coffee is the first coffee of the day, right? When it's nice and hot and the acidity just rolls across your tongue. It's sublime, isn't it?'

Yes, it was sublime and finally Dare knew what he had to do.

He wouldn't call Benson and give him the news about Beckett over the phone. He'd ride down to Rothmeyer House first thing tomorrow and deliver the bad news in person. Then he'd—no, he wouldn't ride all that way; it would take too long. Instead he'd take the chopper—except the chopper was in for repairs. Damn. So, okay, back to plan A. He'd take the H2 out first thing in the morning and speak to Benson. See if he wanted some advice, given that he was a week out from his operation. Then he'd talk to Carly.

She'd either be happy to see him, or not, and being a man who played the odds he'd put money on not, but either way he wouldn't have these lingering thoughts of *what if?* circling his brain at the most inopportune times. Like yesterday when he'd had to decide if an alarm clock shaped like a pig that was programmed to fry bacon as well was something that was going to take off in the market or tank.

He blew out a slow breath. She'd wanted him as much as he wanted her even if she claimed otherwise.

And if her beeper hadn't gone off he wouldn't still be wondering what it would be like to make love to Carly Evans, he'd know.

Or would he?

Dammit, all these questions were doing his head in. He was a man who dealt in facts, though right now he was behaving like an old woman in a knitting circle.

Well, time would tell. She'd either be amenable to his

visit or not and right now he didn't much care which. If she didn't want him he'd walk away and forget her. If she did…if she did he'd tell her it was senseless to fight it. Sex was sex. Why complicate it by abstaining, or over-thinking things?

Stepping outside the café, he walked to the corner and hailed a cab. He settled back against the leather seat, gave the driver his address and glanced out of the window. He felt like a general who had just made the decision to send his troops into battle, his heart thudding so loudly it drowned out the rain on the cab roof.

Carly pulled herself out of the swimming pool and leant back in the sunshine. The weather had been a little cooler this week but the sky was mostly clear and honeybees still hovered over the last of the summer flowers.

Benson's vital signs were all looking good for his operation and she was hopeful that his prognosis would be positive. Especially since he'd developed a real spring in his step with Rachel staying on. It was nice to see them playing bridge together and strolling around the gardens.

Their successful reunion had made her realise how disillusioned she'd become with her own life. Somewhere along the line she'd grown into a non-trusting person—exactly like Daniel, and that was no way to live.

Which was why she'd called her parents. They'd been so happy when she'd called and even said she sounded more like her old self. It had made her feel teary. Without realising it she'd closed herself off from everyone so effectively she'd had no idea just how worried her parents and friends had been about her.

But things would be different from now on. She'd promised to visit when she finished up with the Baron and she'd decided to take some time to figure things out.

And as for Dare James… She was just happy she'd never

have to see him again. Her attraction for him had been a complication she hadn't foreseen and most likely hadn't handled that well.

A frown scrunched her brow. If her beeper hadn't gone off she wouldn't have spent the week wondering what it would be like to make love to him—she was quite sure she'd know.

Because he had been right. She *had* wanted him. And it scared her how quickly she'd succumbed to the feelings he'd ignited inside her. How quickly she'd succumbed to his touch, his scent. Pheromones really were powerful aphrodisiacs when it came down to it.

Her hair drifted down her back as she shook her head. At least she could be happy that she had saved herself the ultimate humiliation by not sleeping with him. But what was it he had said? *'I think you're afraid of the way I make you feel.'*

Carly swallowed. He was right, but what did that matter now? When he'd walked out she had known that he wasn't coming back. Which was what she wanted.

'Oh, cut it out, Gregory,' she hollered as the wretched little dog who had been yapping nonstop for the last two minutes kept at it. 'I'm not in the mood!'

When he didn't stop she turned her head to locate what had agitated him—a butterfly flapping its wings perhaps—and caught sight of the recalcitrant little dog, which had seemed to be pining all week, dash across the lawn and round the side of the house.

Great, he'd managed to manoeuvre out of his new collar, the long leash he'd been tethered to lying uselessly on the lawn. Sighing heavily, Carly debated whether to let him go, but then her conscience got the better of her and she deftly rolled to her feet.

Picking her way gingerly across the pebbled walkway

with her bare feet, she cursed the little dog the whole time until the unexpected roar of an engine brought her head up.

Like some avenging conqueror from the future, Dare James came tearing along the main drive, kicking up dust in his wake.

He pulled the bike up to within an inch of the portico steps and slowly swung his leg over the side.

Mouth dry, Carly watched him pull the black helmet from his head and shake out his hair. Her heart stopped, and then restarted again at twice the speed.

Gregory spotted him at the same time and ran to him, long silky hair blowing back as he launched himself at the man.

Carly's heart beat double-time as Dare grabbed the dog and ruffled his fur, his eyes on her the whole time. 'Gregory, my old friend.' A slow smile spread across his face. 'What have you brought me?'

Heat suffused Carly's face as she realised she was standing before him in a new emerald-green bikini she had impetuously bought in the village a few days ago. The sales girl had done a number on her and raved about how the colour made her eyes pop.

'I always thought that dog had no sense,' she said waspishly, struggling to contend with the fact that he was standing in front of her, not least of all her embarrassment in being caught at such a disadvantage. 'Now he's confirmed it.'

Dare had the gall to laugh at her discomfort and a shiver went through her at the determined glint in his eyes. Placing Gregory on the ground, he pulled off his gloves and stuffed them inside his helmet. 'It's nice to see you too, Red.'

'Stop calling me that ridiculous name.' It made her want to throw herself into his arms like that wretched, deliriously happy dog had just done.

'It suits you.'

Carly tossed her hair back, telling herself that the safest course of action was to walk away. 'You know that leather get-up and hunk of metal behind you are attention-seeking devices?'

He gave her a slow grin. 'How have you been, Carly?'

'Perfectly fine.' Carly's brow arched at the seductive tilt of his mouth. *Walk away*, she told herself again. 'What do you want, Dare?' she snapped.

'I need to see Benson.'

It took a moment for his words to penetrate the story Carly had unknowingly begun to fabricate in her head that started with Dare telling her he'd missed her and ended with her in his arms.

Mortified by her own insidious attraction for this man, Carly finally took her own advice and whirled away from him, heading back in the direction that she had come. Benson and Rachel were out visiting friends, but Dare could find that out by knocking at the main door.

Unfortunately she'd barely made it two steps before she stood on something sharp and let out a gasp of pain.

'Dammit!' She lifted her foot up to investigate what she might have stood on and lost her balance and landed on her bottom.

Determined to ignore the man who had closed the distance between them, Carly prodded the ball of her foot and noticed what looked like a dried rose thorn marring her skin.

'Need a doctor?'

'No.'

He laughed softly at her snippy tone, unzipped his jacket, and crouched down beside her. 'This is becoming a habit.'

'Not a good one,' she said tersely.

She felt like a fool sitting on a gravel driveway in a tiny

bikini while this man was encased in black leather like some marauding invader. 'I can do it,' she insisted when he went to examine her foot.

'I'm sure you can.' He ignored her and wrapped his hand around her ankle, igniting every one of her raw nerve endings in his wake.

And of course he noted her shiver, his brilliant blue eyes searching out hers.

Carly kept her head down and winced when he gently brushed his thumb over the ball of her foot.

'Hold still,' he murmured before squeezing hard.

'Ouch!' Carly jerked her foot clean out of his hold. She knew she was being a baby but being a doctor didn't mean she was able to cope with pain any better than anyone else. In fact she was the ultimate wuss, if the truth be told.

Dare's soft chuckle washed over her and made her shiver again. He reached for her foot, moistened the pad of his thumb with his tongue and then pressed it against her skin. 'Does that hurt?'

Not trusting herself to speak, Carly shook her head and he lowered her foot to the ground but didn't let go of her ankle.

'It should be fine now,' he said, 'and it's not bleeding.'

Carly knew her cheeks must be flushed because her whole body felt hot as she half sat, half sprawled in front of him, but she couldn't move.

She was also aware of how she must look in her nearly nude state. Her chest heaving and her legs splayed apart.

A deep longing rolled through her and she willed Dare to get up. To release her and pretend the chemistry between them didn't exist.

'Carly?'

His fingers flexed around her ankle and Carly shuddered. 'Benson's not here,' she said hoarsely.

She'd meant to say the words to let him know he had

wasted his trip, but as soon as she spoke she knew why she had said them. She wanted him. It didn't make sense but what was the point in denying it to herself?

And by the heated glitter in Dare's eyes he knew it too.

Rocks bit into her bottom and a flight of swallows conversed in a nearby hedge, but all Carly could focus on was the frantic beating of her own heart and Dare's darkening eyes. 'Dare, I—'

She stopped as he planted his hands one either side of her waist and leaned over her. Heat suffused the surface of her skin and she breathed in his scent, her tongue coming out to moisten her lips in readiness—

'Damn,' he swore softly and yanked her to her feet.

Her senses scattered to the wind, Carly blinked up at him until the sound of an approaching car finally penetrated the fog of her brain.

'To be continued...' Dare drawled as Benson's Rolls Royce pulled up beside his bike.

'Dare!'

Dare scratched his jaw. *Of all the rotten luck in the world...*

'Benson. Ma.'

'You didn't call and tell me you were coming,' his mother admonished.

'I wanted to surprise you.'

'Well, you certainly did that. Carly, how was the pool?'

'Fine.'

Dare cast her a sideways look. Her lovely mouth was set in a firm line, her body as stiff as a post. So maybe what had nearly happened would not be continued...

He let out a sigh and looked at Benson. 'I have information for you.' And they might as well get that part of his visit over with and move on to more palatable topics. Maybe he might see if he could entice the good doctor back into the pool...

'Okay.' His grandfather nodded tersely. He seemed incredibly frail and Dare realised he really had been blinkered by anger a week ago to have not picked up on the fact that he was not a well man. Had he really grown that cynical?

'Shall we head to the library?' Benson offered.

Dare cast Carly a quick glance but she wasn't looking at him. He'd wanted to check if her foot was all right but she'd likely say yes, and it had only been a small splinter.

'I'll follow you,' Dare said.

'Benson, I should check your pulse first,' Carly called after him.

'How long will this take, Dare?' Benson asked.

'Not long?'

'Can it wait, my dear?'

Carly gave Benson a frustrated look.

'I'll take care of him,' Dare said and got a flash of disgust from her moss-green eyes for his efforts.

Rachel touched Carly's arm. 'Why don't we have tea in the sunroom? I can show you what I bought at the market.'

Carly hesitated. 'Okay, but...I need to change first,' she said, skipping up the front steps and disappearing into the house.

'Nice wheels,' Benson noted, gazing at Dare's bike.

Dare grinned. 'She does a hundred kilometres an hour in two point six seconds.'

'If only I were younger,' Benson bemoaned, climbing the steps.

Dare followed him and five minutes later yelled for Roberts to bring Carly as quickly as possible.

Dressed in white jeans and a simple green T-shirt, Carly knelt beside the sofa, her black leather bag at her side.

'What happened?'

'I don't know.' Dare's heart thundered inside his chest. 'We were talking and then he collapsed.'

Carly listened to his heartbeat.

'Was he agitated? Upset?'

'No.'

His grandfather had obviously been expecting news that Beckett was somehow involved in his company's problems and, while disappointed, had seemed to take it in stride. He stabbed a hand through his hair. 'But he wasn't completely happy either.'

'We need to get him to a hospital. In London,' Carly said.

'I'll call triple nine.'

CHAPTER EIGHT

HOURS LATER, CARLY stared tight-lipped at the white double doors leading to the operating theatre. Benson had been in there for four hours now, add that to the two-hour flight and it was going to be tough for a patient of his advanced years to survive.

It left Carly feeling quite emotional because the reclusive old guy had grown on her these past weeks, and she hated to see his time with his daughter cut short.

Carly had done everything she could to ensure that didn't happen and she had to admit her job had been made easier by Dare's calm competence at her side. He'd done everything she'd asked of him without question and even organised the best surgeon in London to be on hand when the helicopter flew in.

At one point she was sure he would have put Benson on the back of his superbike if he'd been able to.

Carly knew he'd done it all for his mother, but he'd been slightly grey when Carly had entered the library back at Rothmeyer House and she wondered if there wasn't some level of caring for his grandfather involved deep down.

Regardless, she was glad Dare was on hand because the press were already hounding the hospital to get a story on what had happened to the figurehead of BG Textiles. Not that there was anything anyone could tell them. It was a waiting game from here on in.

'I don't understand why it has to take so long,' Rachel complained.

Carly glanced at the clock on the wall. 'He should be out soon,' she murmured.

Dare looked into the bottom of his coffee cup. 'Who wants coffee?' he asked grimly.

Carly grimaced. Even she couldn't stomach any more hospital-grade coffee. 'No, thanks.'

'Me either, darling,' his mother said.

'DMR,' Dare said.

Rachel blinked up at him. 'Sorry, Dare, what did you say?'

Carly gave him a wan smile. He returned it.

'Nothing, Ma.'

Rachel heaved another long sigh. 'I'd just like news,' she said softly, standing to stare out of the window at the building opposite.

Dare went and put his arm around her, swamping her small stature with his height and the width of his broad shoulders.

'I'm taking my mother for a walk,' he directed at Carly. 'Will you be okay here?'

Carly nodded. 'I'll call if I hear anything.'

Dare thanked her and directed his protesting mother out of the door, grateful that Carly had stayed but not sure if she had done so because it was her job or...or what? Because he liked having her there?

Not likely. She owed him nothing and the way he'd gone at her when he'd spotted her in that bikini... He sighed.

'He'll be okay,' his mother reassured him, misinterpreting his heavy mood. Which was a good thing because he wasn't about to spill his guts about his feelings for Carly Evans. Especially when he had no idea what they were.

The call came through that Benson was out of surgery just as Dare led his mother back into the waiting room.

Carly looked up and gave them a small smile. 'The surgeon was just here and Benson survived the operation.'

'Oh, thank heavens.' Rachel held her hand over her heart.

'He's in a medically induced coma now, but Dr Lindeman feels confident that he got the tumour. If Benson makes it through the night he should survive the operation.'

Rachel frowned. 'A medically induced coma? I've never understood that.'

'It happens with most critically ill patients who need artificial ventilation to breathe,' Carly explained. 'It doesn't mean anything dire,' she assured her. 'So don't worry overly much. But he will be hooked up to a number of machines, so don't panic when you first see him.'

'Benson's a hard nut,' Dare said gruffly. 'He'll pull through.'

'I hope so.' Rachel buried her face against her son's chest. Carly turned away. Now she could add a caring Dare to his list of attributes, which didn't make her any more comfortable than before.

In fact, she should probably leave mother and son to it as soon as she'd checked in on Benson. It wasn't as if she had to hang around for any personal reasons, was it?

'Rachel James?' The surgeon stopped in the doorway. 'I can take you to see your father now.'

'Really, I can see him?'

The surgeon nodded, directing Dare's mother down the hallway.

Silence filled the small waiting area once they had left and Dare was acutely aware of Carly on the other side of the room.

'Thank you for everything you did today,' he said gruffly.

'It's what I was paid to do. I just wish I'd checked him over before he spoke with you. I might have been able to prevent his collapse.'

'If anyone is to blame, it's me,' he said tersely.

Her startled eyes flew to his. 'No, it's not—I was the one responsible for him. It was my job.'

There was a brittleness to her tone he couldn't place and it made him want to go to her and wrap his arms around her. Unfortunately the icy cloak she had enveloped herself in since they had arrived ensured that he didn't. 'It's been a long day.' She sighed. 'The operation took a lot longer than I expected.'

Dare frowned. 'Is that good or bad?'

'It's neither one way nor the other. It just is,' she said. 'The important thing is that the surgeon seemed pleased. That's definitely a good sign.'

'I figure doctors are like real estate agents,' he said wryly. 'They say what they think you want to hear.'

Carly gave a small smile. 'That might be considered a touch unethical.'

Dare shoved his hands in his pockets. 'Thanks for staying... It means a lot to my mother. To me.'

She paused, her eyes full of questions he didn't have any immediate answers to. 'I'm...I've grown fond of Benson these past few weeks. He's...' She cut him a brief look. 'He's not as bad as you think he is.'

Dare didn't think he was that bad at all anymore. In fact he'd grown quite fond of the old goat. 'You still think me an utter bastard, don't you?' he rasped out.

Carly looked up at him in surprise. 'No, I don't think that.' She paused. 'I think...I think...'

She stopped, glanced at the floor.

Dare felt his gut clench. He wanted to hold her. Kiss her. 'Red, I—'

'He's alive,' Rachel said with enthusiasm as she flopped down in the visitor's chair again. She gave them a relieved smile. 'But he looks so frail. When will he wake up?' she directed at Carly. 'The surgeon wouldn't give me a straight answer.'

'Without seeing his report I can't answer that, but he's in the best of care here.'

'I know. Thank you for everything you did on the way here. I'm sure he wouldn't have survived without you.'

Carly's sense of relief was immense and she felt immeasurably lighter for it.

'You look tired, Ma,' Dare said. 'Why don't I take you home to rest?'

'I'm not going home tonight. I'm staying here.'

'Don't be ridiculous—you need sleep, and Carly said they're unlikely to wake him up anytime soon.'

'That doesn't matter. I can still talk to him. He'll know I'm here, won't he, Carly?'

Carly gave Dare a rueful glance before responding. 'There is evidence to suggest that coma patients can still hear,' she said carefully. 'But they may not remember anything when they wake up. That being said, some appear to.'

'Then I'm staying.'

Dare scowled at his mother. 'I'll stay with him. You and Carly need to rest.'

'Huff and puff all you like, Dare. My mind is made up.'

Carly watched mother and son face off with amusement.

'Fine.' He turned to Carly. 'What about you?'

Startled to have those sky-blue eyes directed at her once more, Carly swallowed hard. 'What about me?'

'Do you have a place to stay tonight?'

Carly hadn't even turned her mind to where she was going to stay. 'I'll be fine,' she said briskly.

'Yes or no?' Dare growled.

'I said—'

'That's a no,' he decided. 'So you can stay at my apartment. And I know you have to be hungry as well as tired because you didn't eat anything earlier, so don't argue.'

Carly blinked at him. Was he serious? There was no way she could stay in his home. She'd go to a hotel for the night. Because while she did know a couple of people who lived in London she wasn't close enough to any of them to turn up on their doorstep at nine o'clock at night. 'I'll be fine,' she reiterated firmly.

'Dare has an amazing apartment, Carly, and plenty of room. You'll be more than comfortable staying with him.'

As soon as Rachel weighed in on Dare's side Carly knew this was a battle she wouldn't win. Rachel, she had learned, was as formidable as her son.

'My mother's hard to resist,' Dare murmured as he held the waiting room door open for her to precede him.

'Let's just say I now know where you get your hard-headedness from,' Carly murmured ruefully.

Dare laughed. 'Now I'm really insulted. There's no way I'm as bad as my mother.'

Carly hid a grin and slipped into Dare's waiting limousine. Fortunately traffic was light, either that or they had avoided the main thoroughfares, because they arrived at Dare's Regency apartment block in no time at all.

Dare greeted the smartly dressed doorman and punched the elevator button.

'Top floor?' she asked, her nerves strung tight at the prospect of spending time alone with him.

'Top two.'

'For one person?' Carly stared at him. 'Or is this where you tell me you have sixteen children?'

'I have about sixteen chickens on a small farm back home, does that count?'

'Not quite.'

Carly's lips quirked as she swept past him into the opulent foyer and living room beyond. 'Oh, my,' she murmured. The room seemed to stretch on for a mile of polished wood floors, coffee-coloured walls with white trim, floor-to-ceiling windows framed by silk curtains, and cream inlaid shelving and bookcases along each wall. 'This is magnificent.'

Dare tossed his keys and wallet into a ceramic bowl

that sat beside a vase of flowers on a circular table in the centre of the foyer.

'It serves a purpose.'

'Yes,' Carly mused half to herself. 'In some interior magazine.' She walked through to the other room and was almost too scared to step on the cream rugs with her shoes on. The apartment almost put Rothmeyer House to shame.

'There's nothing out of place here. Not even a remote control on the sofa,' she said, following him through to a beautifully appointed kitchen.

'I have a housekeeper when I'm here,' he said, opening the fridge.

'Where's home?'

'Mostly New York. Sometimes San Francisco. Bridget has left chicken pie and salad. I know it's late but I'm starving.'

'And Bridget is?'

His eyes lifted to hers over the door of the fridge. 'Not the mother of my sixteen children,' he said deadpan. 'She's my housekeeper. My elderly housekeeper.'

'Did I ask?'

'You didn't have to. Your face is very expressive.'

God, she hoped not because if it was he'd know…he'd know…

'You look about as exhausted as I feel,' he said softly.

Carly stared at him and blinked. So okay, he didn't have a clue how much she wanted to go into his arms right now. This was a good thing.

'That bad,' she said, grimacing.

Dare chuckled. 'You're still beautiful, Red. You just look like you flew in an emergency chopper from Cornwall to London about eight hundred hours ago—oh, wait. You did.'

Carly gave him a reluctant smile. 'So did you.' And yet he seemed no worse for wear at all. Still gorgeous and powerful and so potently male.

Not even fossicking around in a refrigerator could deter his appeal—if anything it made it worse. Daniel had always put himself above such duties, claiming that his hands were too precious to risk injuring them. And why did she feel the need to constantly compare the two men? It wasn't as if anything was going to happen between Dare and she.

'Do you want a shower?'

Carly nearly let out a low moan at the thought. She would love a shower but just the thought of getting naked with Dare in the apartment was enough to send her mind into a flap. Then there was the small issue that she had nothing clean to change into. Which more or less defeated the purpose of having one. 'I'm good,' she said stoically.

'You sure?' He set a dish on the counter top. 'I can lend you something of mine to wear if you don't want to put those clothes back on.'

'Yours?'

'I'd offer you something of my mother's but she's shorter than you and I had her suitcases delivered to Rothmeyer House last week.'

'I'm happy to sleep in my clothes.'

'Whatever you want.' His expression said she was mad and that was pretty much how she felt. But then he shrugged and went back to the fridge. 'It's just that I could have them laundered and ready for you in the morning.'

The fact that he was being so reasonable about the whole thing made her feel silly.

'And I suppose you have a laundry service that runs twenty-four-seven at your fingertips?' she quipped.

'Yeah, as a matter of fact I do.' He smiled. 'It's called Dare-o-mat and it's through that door back there.'

A laugh escaped Carly's lips at his unexpected humour and he gave her that grin that set off his dimple.

She couldn't take a breath as she read the way he looked at her. It was the way he'd looked at her so many times before. Right before he kissed her.

Anticipation coursed through her and then her stomach saved her from doing something she'd later regret by grumbling loudly.

'Or perhaps you'd like to eat first.'

Carly blinked as if that might clear her head. 'No, a shower…a shower would be great. Exceptional even.' At the very least it would give her some space to sort her head out.

'Follow me.'

He led her back through the main room to a spiral staircase she hadn't noticed.

She followed him up and when he stopped outside a door she was looking around so much that she nearly ran into him.

Her breath caught. 'Sorry.'

'No.' He cleared his throat. 'That was my fault.' He stepped away from her. Opened the door. 'You can have this room. Bathroom is through the other door. Leave your clothes on the bed and I'll exchange them for a set of mine.'

Carly gripped her bag tighter. 'Your clothes will be too big for me.'

His gaze was hooded when it meshed with hers. 'I'll find something.'

He gave her a brief nod and then closed the door after him. Carly leant against it and let out a pent-up breath. Coming here had been a bad idea, she thought, closing her eyes; a really bad idea.

Dare stopped at the end of the hallway and tipped his head back against the wall. Bringing her here was a bad idea, a really bad idea.

He liked to think that he'd made the offer for her to stay as a good Samaritan, not to jump her bones, but, hell… how much could one man take?

He pushed open his bedroom door and stood inside his walk-in robe. If he just concentrated on the basics maybe he'd be able to find his self-control and put it to good use.

Because he was not going to be such a jerk as to try and sleep with a woman after his grandfather had nearly died. What kind of callous idiot would do that?

So, sweats or shorts? Which would she prefer? And long or short-sleeved shirt? He didn't—

'For God's sake, man, she's not going to a fashion show,' he growled, yanking sweats and a T-shirt off the shelf. He glanced up and caught sight of himself in the mirror. 'You'll eat and go to bed. Alone. God knows, looking at you right now you'd be lucky to ever get laid again.'

Deciding to take a quick shower himself, he changed, and dropped the folded clothes on her bed. Then he snatched hers up, ignoring her floral scent as it rose to his nose, and the sound of the shower through the door, and went to check on dinner.

When it was almost ready he turned and found her standing in the doorway.

Dare looked at her. As she had warned, his clothes were much too big. His T-shirt drooped off one delicate shoulder and reached past her thighs even though he'd pulled out the smallest one, and the sweats… She must have rolled them at her waist but even so he could tell they hung low on her hips and brushed her heels when she walked.

She'd finished by pulling her hair into a rough topknot as if she was showing him that she hadn't made any special attempt to impress him. So different from the other women he had dated who usually took great pains with their appearance.

His fingers tightened around the wooden spoon he held. 'Hungry?'

Because he was famished. And not for Bridget's famed pie.

'Very.'

And there went that fantasy of having her walk up to him and whisper how much she'd like him to lift her onto the benchtop and rip his sweats down her long legs.

'Sit.' He gestured towards the small breakfast nook, wishing he'd worn denim instead of soft cotton.

'So why medicine?' he asked as he shovelled food into his mouth.

'My grandfather was a doctor and I used to be fascinated by his little black bag and everything in it when I was young.'

Dare smiled. He could just imagine her with her red hair in pigtails and freckles on her nose. 'Did you have freckles?'

Her eyes met his. 'Because of my red hair?'

'Sure. What else?'

She gave him a pained look. 'Yes, I did. My mother always said they would fade because I had Nordic blood and fortunately she was right.'

'So who was the Viking?'

'My father. And he'd love that description. He thinks he's invincible and not at all like your typical academic.' She grinned. 'But he is.'

Dare stared, transfixed by her avid face as she spoke of her parent. 'So you come from a smart family?'

'I suppose so. My mother is a teacher as well, and…'

She stopped and Dare studied the way she stared at her plate as if she'd just discovered a fly on it. 'And…' he prompted lightly.

'And nothing.'

'You know, Red, talking to you sometimes is like trying to get blood from a stone.'

A hesitant smile tugged her lips upwards and Dare felt an inexplicable urge to reach across and—oh, hell—before he could control it he caught her chin between his thumb and index finger, leaned across the table, and kissed her lips softly. Good God, that felt good, and all he wanted to do was sink into her softness again.

Slowly, reluctantly, he drew back. She blinked her eyes open and looked at him, her gaze smoky green.

'Why did you do that?'

'You looked sad.'

She bit into her lower lip and worried at it. Dare was quite sure she wasn't aware of the action, or what it did to him.

'I was going to say my sister was a social worker.'

'Was?'

'She died a year ago.'

Dare grabbed hold of Carly's restless fingers on the tabletop. 'I'm sorry, Red. How did she die?'

'A rare form of leukaemia.'

Her gaze flitted away again and he paused. Dare felt his heart go out to her. 'That's gotta be hard,' he said softly. 'You want to talk about it?'

'No. Thanks, I...' Carly rubbed at the space between her brows. The fingers of her other hand flexed around his and she stared at where their hands were joined on the table. 'Everything happened so suddenly. One day Liv was well and healthy and helping kids in need and the next she was gone.' Her throat bobbed as she swallowed. 'The doctors tried but...' She grimaced. 'They couldn't do anything and as much as I searched...' She took a deep breath, her gaze miles away.

'You couldn't save her either,' he said quietly.

Carly looked up as if startled that he had understood

her so well. But it wasn't hard. Not when she fascinated him so much.

'No,' she said, the word coming out gruff. 'And now I don't know what to do.' She gave a self-deprecating smile. 'I've thought about giving up on medicine but something stops me. Years of study probably.'

'Why would you give up on medicine?' He frowned. 'Because you feel like you failed your sister?'

'I did fail her,' she said in a pained whisper. 'When she said that she wanted to try some alternative medicines I encouraged her not to. I told her to trust her doctor. I told her that he would know best.' She pulled her hand from his, tucked it into her lap. 'If I hadn't intervened…'

'If you hadn't intervened, what?' Dare asked softly. 'She would have lived?'

'Yes!' Carly exclaimed. 'Maybe…' she added as he continued to look at her.

'Is that what the doctors believe or what *you* believe?'

Carly buried her face in her hands. 'I know it's not logical.'

'Emotion rarely is,' he said wryly. 'But I doubt your sister would want you to give up medicine, Carly. The fact is, not every person can be saved.'

'I know that too. I know…' She unconsciously lowered her hands into the prayer position. 'I miss her so much.'

Dare took her hands in his. Judging by her response, he doubted she had ever opened up about the responsibility she had erroneously taken on with regard to her sister's death.

'Come here.'

When she didn't move Dare stood up and came around to her. 'Dare, I don't—'

Ignoring her, he slowly drew her to her feet and, like a small stream bubbling over smooth rocks, Carly flowed towards him.

'Dare—'

He drew her closer. 'I just want to hold you.'

An odd tightness gripped Carly's chest. 'I don't need anyone to hold me, I'm—'

'Perfectly fine.' He pulled her in against his chest anyway. 'Humour me, hmm? Hell, after listening to that I need a hug.'

Carly felt a wave of tenderness envelop her. He didn't really need a hug, he was only trying to be nice, but, oh, how wonderful it felt to lean against him. To soak up some of his warmth. His strength. His *hardness*.

She breathed in deeply and felt his arms tighten around her like soothing bands. Taking away that lost feeling she'd carried around with her for so long and replacing it with comfort and heat.

She wasn't sure when she felt the change come over her but within a heartbeat comfort and soothing became something else entirely. Carly froze and tried to fight the urge to shift against him to assuage just a little of the ache building inside her.

Dare felt her subtle movements and swallowed heavily. He shouldn't have touched her. Even though he'd only been offering comfort, he'd known that wasn't all he wanted to do. He wanted her so badly he'd had to force himself not to grab her all night and now she was in his arms, her soft breasts pressed against his chest. Her hot breath like a flame against his throat.

Dare stifled a groan. To make a move on her now when she was vulnerable from the events of the day and her memories of the past would put him squarely in that bastard category she'd assigned him to a week ago. Now he had the chance to confirm that, or he could—

'Carly? Carly, baby, don't...just keep still.'

Dare loosened his grip a little when she squirmed again.

He half expected her to pull back and when she didn't he looked down into her upturned face.

The lighting wasn't overly bright in the room but it was bright enough that he saw the flush on her cheeks and the darkened pupils, the way her eyes were fixed on his mouth. He felt her muscles tense and his body read the meaning even before his brain had fully engaged with the idea.

Oh, who was he kidding? His brain, his body, his very being was invested in this and he was done trying to pretend that it wasn't.

'Carly.' His voice was deep and gravelly and he felt her tremble in response.

Dare set his hands to her hips. He wanted to take this slow and easy. He'd dreamt of having her beneath him ever since he'd met her and—

'Dare?'

Her gaze rose from his lips to his eyes and that was all it took to cement their destiny. His mouth swooped to hers, devouring her without any regard for finesse or seduction. He was hungry, ravenous, and she was exactly what he wanted to eat.

She opened wide to him and Dare groaned, one hand buried in her hair to hold her exactly where he wanted her and the other pressing her against his erection.

She made a soft, kittenish sound that drove him wild, and her hands kneaded his shirt, her teeth biting at his lower lip as if she was as hungry as he was.

'If you don't want this, Carly,' he rasped against the delicate shell of her ear, 'then stop me now.'

She gave him one of those exquisite little shivers, her body arching almost involuntarily towards his. 'I want it.' She forked her own hand into his hair and dragged his mouth back to hers. 'I want you to make love to me. I *need* you to make love to me.'

Dare understood exactly what she meant. This feeling

between them was a celebration of life and loss and for some reason he needed it just as much as he sensed she did.

Her heartbeat thundered against his, although it could have just been his own, and Dare lifted her up as if she weighed little more than a feather.

'Legs, around my waist,' he croaked, already moving in the direction of his bedroom. His blood was storming through his veins and his mind was consumed with the smell and feel of her, his body throbbing to just throw her down on the floor right now.

'Damn.' He groaned as she squeezed her ankles over his backside. He could feel her hot core through their layers of soft cotton and he gripped the staircase to steady himself.

He'd never had to navigate his spiral stairs with an armload of woman before and he laughed softly as she clung on like a spider monkey, attacking his neck with her sharp little teeth and lathing him with her tongue.

Dare very nearly disgraced himself and then, thank God, the bed was in front of him and he dropped her onto it and yanked the sweats down her long legs.

Slow down, buddy, his mind warned, but Dare was caught in a fever trap of desire he'd never experienced before and the need to make her his beat out his conscience.

He pulled his own clothes off and grabbed her ankles, spreading her wide.

'Condom,' she breathed, bringing him back from the hazy edge of insanity.

'Damn.' He dragged his gaze from the heart of her body to her face and tried to rein himself in. This was too much. Way too much…

He gazed into her eyes that were overbright with a lust that matched his own and he knew he wasn't strong enough to heed the distant warning bell in his head.

Swearing as he hadn't since he was a teenager, he

stormed into his bathroom and grabbed condoms. Since he didn't ever bring women back to his sanctuary he didn't have any by the bed. He would now.

Rolling one on, he returned moments later to find Carly leaning up on her elbows, her vivid hair falling to the pale bedclothes behind her. There was a sense of wariness in her eyes and she looked as if she was trying to regulate her breathing.

'Second thoughts?' he asked gruffly, praying to God she said no.

Her eyes flared wide as she took him in, her gaze hot as it skated down his chest and lingered on his shaft. He knew what she saw. He wasn't a small man by any means and he was so hard the tip was resting against his belly.

His eyes narrowed in on her reaction to the sight of him and if possible he went even harder as her legs shifted restlessly on the mattress, her lips parting as she breathed shallowly.

Goddamn, she was beautiful.

'No.'

Dare's breathing stopped. 'No?' he got out hoarsely.

'Yes, I mean no...' She shifted again as if she was aching for his possession. 'No second thoughts.'

Thank God.

Dare grabbed her ankles again and slid his hands to her knees, only mildly less rough than before as he urged them to part. She was still wearing his T-shirt, her breasts thrusting against the fabric.

'Take the shirt off,' he growled.

His heart felt as if it were trying to work its way out of his chest as she struggled to get the fabric over her head. When she was free of it she tossed it to the side and looked up at him.

Dare's gaze roamed over her pert breasts, her coral-coloured nipples standing to attention, her narrow waist and flared hips. 'Holy, sweet mother of... Tell me you're ready for me, Red.'

'I am. I—'

He glanced down at the dewy entrance to her body and fitted himself against her. She was so wet he slid in easily but he stopped part way, giving her body time to expand around him.

He held himself still, sweat turning his skin slick, until he felt her tight inner walls clench and release and then he thrust forward in one powerful motion, coming over the top of her, his hands on either side of her head.

She groaned when he fully seated himself inside her and, worried that he'd hurt her, he paused again. She whimpered and raised her hips, sliding her inner thighs along the outside of his and shattering his self-control in the process. 'Oh, yeah, Red, grip me tight.'

Dare powered into her, angling his hands beneath her bottom so that he hit the sweet spot that made her gasp and rub herself against him. He knew what she needed and, holding on by a thread, he thrust into her over and over until he felt her body stiffen right before it fluttered and rippled around him, signalling her climax and drawing him in deep; sending him spinning on his own powerful vortex of completion.

Nothing, nothing had ever felt this good. He was sure of it and he only raised his sweat-soaked body from hers when he felt her stir beneath him.

Good, she wasn't dead, was his first thought. Good, he wasn't either, was his second. Or if he was they were dead together and it didn't matter.

'Are you okay?'

'I'm not sure,' she panted, her arms lax above her head. 'I may never move again but if that's normal, then yes, I'm okay.'

Dare chuckled and eased out of her. Nothing about what

had just happened was normal but his brain was too stupefied to analyse it. 'I'm sorry…'

'Why?'

'I came at you like an animal.'

'We are animals.'

He gave a soft laugh. 'Only a doctor would say that.'

With strength returning to his limbs, he levered himself off the bed and went to dispose of the condom. When he returned she was sitting up in bed and looked delightfully rumpled. She also looked as comfortable as a cat on a hot tin roof.

Dare didn't know what to think, actually he still wasn't thinking, so he acted on instinct instead, bending to her and cupping her face in his hands. When her lips softened after a momentary resistance he stroked her tongue with his, feeling himself hardening all over again.

She made a little moaning sound and he nudged her backwards onto the bed.

'Dare?'

'Shh…' he murmured. 'Let me love you properly.'

'I'm not—oh!' She stilled as he licked across the tip of her breast, her small nipple tightening in response.

'I didn't get to say hi to these guys,' he said.

Her soft laugh turned into a small whimper as he tongued her and drew her nipple into his mouth, suckling deeply.

'Damn, you taste good, Red.' And he needed to explore her. Explore every inch of her to find out what she liked and what she didn't.

Like this little pressure point in the bend in her elbow that made her gasp when he licked it, and the soft skin at the base of her throat that made her arch upwards, begging him to feast on her breasts again. And, oh, yeah, she really liked that.

'Dare, I don't think we should do this again.' She shoved

her hands in his hair as he flicked her nipple with his tongue but instead of pushing him away she held him closer, making sweet little female sounds that had that primal part of him wanting to ditch the foreplay and move right on to the mating.

But he wasn't going to do that this time because he was enjoying himself too much. It was as if no man had ever taken the time to give her pleasure and those sweet little keening sounds were turning him inside out.

God, she was hot. So hot. 'Open your legs for me,' he murmured, nuzzling the undersides of her breasts and working his way south over the smooth skin of her belly.

'Dare.'

He shifted so he lay flat between her soft thighs, his chin resting on the golden red curls hiding her moist heat. 'You know that ex of yours was the biggest loser letting you go, don't you?'

She arched her head back as he parted her with his tongue.

'He never...I didn't...'

'Go down on you? Love you with his mouth? Taste your sweet, womanly essence?'

He punctuated each sentence with light, playful flicks of his skilful tongue, honing her senses to the point where nothing else existed but him. And her. And this.

'Oh, God, I never thought I'd find talking in bed such a turn-on.' She gripped his head in her hands. 'Please, don't stop,' she begged.

Dare chuckled and blew a breath over her femininity. 'Don't stop what?' he teased. 'Talking? Or don't stop this.' He licked her again, more firmly this time.

'That.' She twisted against him. 'Don't stop that. Don't stop anything. It's so sexy.'

'You're the sexy one, Red. Sweet and sexy. Like your scent.'

'Oh! God, I'm going to come.' She made to pull away from him as sensation overwhelmed her but Dare held her hips tight until they shuddered with pleasure as she came against his mouth.

'Dare… Dare…' She chanted his name, reaching for him blindly, her fingernails digging into his shoulders, his hair. 'I need you. Please, take me.'

Not forgetting a condom this time, Dare rolled a rubber down his rigid length and rolled on top of her. This time when he entered her he did so slowly, savouring the exquisite warmth of her body closing around his.

He groaned, determined to make it last, thrusting into her with firm, measured strokes until he couldn't take any more. Until he felt the soft pulsing of her body and that little hitch in her voice that told him she was on the edge. Then, only then, did he completely let himself fall over the cliff with her and down the other side.

What could have been hours, or only minutes, later Dare woke to find Carly sleeping beside him. He gently moved a strand of her hair to the side, gathered her against him and fell back to sleep with a satisfied smile on his face.

CHAPTER NINE

CARLY WOKE SLOWLY to the sound of a ringing phone. She moaned softly as her body ached in places it hadn't before and then she blushed as memory returned full force.

At the sound of Dare's deep voice she scrambled for the sheet and pulled it up over herself. Seconds later Dare walked out of the bathroom with a towel slung low around his lean hips, his chest and arms rippling with lean, hard muscle.

Oh, my God, she thought, *he is a demigod. A bronzed demigod who belongs in the V&A.*

'Benson is awake,' he said, tossing the phone onto the side table.

Okay, so they were going to play this completely normal. Good to know. 'What did the surgeon say?'

'It was my mother and she sounded very optimistic.' Which told Carly nothing at all. Family of critically ill patients always veered towards the bright side in these situations.

'Your clothes are dry,' Dare continued. 'I was planning to visit him. Do you want to come?'

'Of course.' Benson was still her patient—sort of—and even though she wouldn't be his attending physician post-op, she would have hung around to make sure he was all right, regardless.

They were both quiet on the drive to the hospital. On Carly's part she was still sorting through what had happened the previous night. It still stunned her that she had opened up about Liv the way that she had. Not so much that she'd told him, but more that she'd expressed her anger. Her bitter disappointment with herself. And Dare was right:

Liv wouldn't want her to give up medicine. Nor would she want her to run and cut everyone off the way that she had. It had all seemed so hopeless a year ago. But in Dare's arms...when he'd held her and soothed her...

Carly swallowed heavily. And the way he'd made love to her.

She released a slow breath, hoping he was so engrossed in returning work emails he wouldn't notice.

At least, she presumed he was returning work emails. For all she knew he could be lining up his next woman.

And when had she become so insecure?

She sighed again. She was not going to blow this out of proportion. It had happened and it had been wonderful. More wonderful than she could have ever imagined. She made a face. She had thought she'd reached orgasm before but apparently she'd been wrong.

But sex—no matter how earth-shattering—was not grounds to start measuring up white picket fences or planting fruit trees that took years to bear produce. She'd learned that lesson the hard way. And it wasn't as if she had fallen in love with him. That would be...

Carly's hand squeezed her throat.

Love? Who mentioned love?

She swallowed. Tried to breathe.

She wasn't in love with him. She wouldn't be that foolishly stupid. That brainless to fall for a man so much more potent than Daniel he might break her completely if she let him.

'That's a lot of sighing going on over there. You okay?'

Startled, Carly glanced at him. 'Fine.'

His smile cocked a little. 'You sure?'

He reached out and entwined his fingers with hers.

Carly's heart kicked against her rib cage. God, the man was lethal.

'Absolutely.' Absently, Carly wondered if she could add

acting to her résumé. But this was important. She needed
to keep things in perspective. Dare wasn't interested in
long-term relationships and neither was she. 'But I was
thinking,' she continued, 'that it would be best not to let
anyone know what happened last night.'

Dare frowned. 'Because?'

'Well, because I don't want to lose my job with the
agency for sleeping with a client's son, if it's all the same
to you, and I'm worried that Rachel and Benson might
read more into it than they should.'

'Don't go getting your knickers in a twist,' he said easily. 'I was only asking.'

She hadn't realised she'd been holding her breath until
his cavalier response, and then she felt silly. 'God, you're
arrogant,' she said, her temper directed mainly at herself.

She was doing it again—making mountains where there
should have been molehills.

He grinned at her. 'Next time I'm making you a morning coffee whether you think we have time or not.'

Next time? Carly's heart gave another jolt. She let out a
breath. What was wrong with her this morning? 'Sorry,'
she grumbled. 'I'm worried about Benson.' Which wasn't
untrue, she thought. She *was* worried about him.

'Forget it.'

Dare rubbed her fingers almost absently.

He'd woken up this morning to his ringing phone and
hadn't had time to think about much between then and
now. Which meant that he hadn't thought about how he
was going to play this thing with Carly in front of Benson and his mother.

And it irked him a little that she had because he was
usually on top of these things. And it irked him more that
she was right.

If his mother knew he had taken Carly to his bed the
previous night she'd be matchmaking within minutes.

Actually she probably already was. It was as inevitable as breathing really. She wanted grandkids and short of adopting a set for him she saw potential in every woman he went out with.

Well, almost every woman. Okay, so she hadn't seen potential in any woman he'd dated so far, but that didn't stop her from wanting him to meet someone and fall in love. And Carly was a perfect candidate. Smart, sweet-natured, beautiful, sexy.

Man, was she ever sexy. If his mother knew how compatible they were between the sheets she'd be asking what jeweller he was going to.

Probably Tiffany's. He'd purchase one of those diamond rocks as big as his fist. He smiled as he thought of how his ring would look on her long, slender fingers. Maybe he'd get one a little smaller than his fist, he decided, but it would be as perfect as her smile.

He frowned, then let go of her hand to fiddle with his phone.

His heart felt as if it had relocated into his throat and he took a deep breath.

What the hell had just happened? One minute he was thinking about sex and the next thing he was mentally shopping for rings? Okay, so it had been the best sex he'd ever had, but a ring?

He chuckled, and reached for her hand again. She looked at him questioningly and he kissed the backs of her fingers. Smiled. For a minute there he'd nearly lost his head.

Benson was awake when they got to the room, but barely. He was still heavily sedated. Dare leant against the small window and watched Carly going over the doctor's notes on his chart. His mother also watched her, waiting for her verdict that the other doctors hadn't been feeding her false hope.

'It all looks good.' She smiled at his mother. 'Of course, we won't know the results of the tumour for a couple of days but he's responding really well to the post-op meds.'

'That's a relief.' Dare's mother gripped his grandfather's hand in hers.

Before Carly could say anything more the door opened and his cousin, Beckett, swaggered in unannounced. Dare had never met him before and he remained completely unmoved as the younger man's eyes briefly narrowed in on him.

So far Dare had dug up quite a bit on his privileged cousin and he'd found that if stupidity and sleaziness were a crime Beckett would be in jail for life. Perhaps if good looks were a crime he'd be there even longer because even Dare could see that his cousin had been genetically blessed in that department.

'I came as soon as I heard,' Beckett gushed.

Dare stared at him. He'd like to know who had told him about Benson's condition, but kept silent.

'You must be my aunt Rachel,' Beckett said, as smooth as a snake gliding over sand. 'It's a pleasure to meet you at last.' He took her hand and kissed the back of it before turning to Dare. 'And you, cousin Dare.'

Dare folded his arms and tucked his thumbs beneath his armpits. 'Beckett.'

Beckett acknowledged the rebuff with a small smile and turned to Carly.

'Carly.' He said her name on a sigh and Dare's senses sharpened. 'It's good to see you again.'

'Beckett, how are you?'

'Better for knowing that my grandfather has survived his operation.' He smiled down at her, squeezing her shoulder. 'And for seeing you again. But I am a little miffed at you—' he pouted '—for not letting on about my grandfather's condition.'

'It wasn't my place to mention it,' Carly said, moving away to replace the clipboard at the end of Benson's bed. Which was fortunate for his cousin, Dare brooded, because he'd been about to rip his arm from its socket.

When the clipboard wouldn't catch Dare stepped between the two of them. 'Here, let me help you, Red,' he murmured softly.

Beckett ignored him, his gaze lingering on Carly a little longer. 'And how is he?'

Dare listened while Carly filled his cousin in. Beckett showed genuine concern for his grandfather, but Dare's hackles were raised. Fortunately his cousin had enough sense to pick up on Dare's cool regard and didn't prolong his visit. Which was a good thing. Dare didn't trust him, and he definitely didn't like the familiar way he had touched Carly.

His lover.

He pushed away from the windowsill. He wanted nothing more than to take Carly away from here and sweep her into his arms again. He wanted to kiss her long and hard and deep and feel her melt against him. Hear her make those breathy little moans he was rapidly becoming addicted to and smell her woman's smell. Taste her again. And if some small part of his logical side found that a bit disturbing, well, he would deal with that later.

He slung his arm around his mother's shoulders and dropped a kiss on her head, asked her how she was. He felt good. Really good. Why deny it?

Carly watched mother and son converse and she knew she'd lied to herself in the car. Somewhere in amongst the arguing and the accusations, the tenderness and the desire, she had fallen in love with him. Completely and stupidly in love with the arrogant, the self-assured Dare James.

The feeling was so different from how she had felt about Daniel that she finally recognised that there was some truth to her father's assessment that she had fallen for Daniel to help her deal with Liv's diagnosis. She hadn't wanted to face that because she'd needed a better reason than that as to why she had let him treat her so badly. It made her feel as if she had a terrible weakness inside herself that would allow any man she became involved with to walk all over her if he pleased.

Like this man.

Carly's breathing bottomed out as a slow panic set in like molasses sliding down the tip of a spoon. Before she knew it she was at the door and pulling it open.

'Carly?'

Schooling her features, she pinned a smile on her face before turning back to the occupants in the room. 'I'm just heading out.' And never coming back. 'Give you all some time together.'

She pulled the door firmly closed and barely registered the nurses' station as she strode past.

'Carly!'

Dare caught up with her just outside the lifts.

Carly stabbed at the button.

'Where are you going?'

Carly stared at the lift doors, willing them to open. 'I need to find a hotel for the night and—'

'What are you talking about?' he asked gruffly. 'You're staying with me.'

She heard the frown in his voice and made the mistake of glancing up at him. 'Dare, I—'

'Unless you're going to say last night was a one-night stand.'

'No, I—'

'That I took advantage of your vulnerable state.'

'I would never say that,' Carly said hotly.

'Good.' He looked altogether too satisfied with himself and Carly's temper spiked. 'Then we're decided.'

'You might be,' Carly snapped, 'but I'm not. And I'm tired of you pushing your way arou—'

'Carly?' He said her name softly, a burning intensity entering his blue eyes as he stared down at her. 'Stay with me.'

His earnest request was such a shock Carly's anger dissipated as quickly as it had arisen. Then she shook her head. Staying would be emotional suicide. 'Why?'

He frowned. 'Because something is going on here.' He placed his hands on her hips and a shiver raced through her. 'Between us. I know you feel it. Damn, after last night... I'm not ready to let it go.'

'Something?' she asked, holding her breath.

He leant his forehead against hers. 'I don't have a label for it, but—' he exhaled '—I can't explain it except to say that I've never wanted a woman as much as I want you.' He leaned back to look down at her. 'Spend the day with me.'

Carly searched his gaze and felt that same surge of love she'd felt well up inside her when she'd stared at him before. And something else, besides. *Hope?* Was it possible he felt the same as she did but didn't know it yet?

'Don't you have to work?'

He smiled down at her. 'At this rate I'll have meetings banked up until Christmas but I don't care.'

He bent his head and kissed her softly. She moaned against his mouth, rose up onto her toes to kiss him back. The lift door pinged its arrival and they ignored it.

When a couple of the occupants tried to manoeuvre past, Dare shifted them both to the side without breaking their embrace.

Carly released a nervous laugh.

'I want you.' He clasped her face in his hands, his blue eyes intense. 'All of you. Every bit of you.'

Every word was tautly spoken, his broad shoulders stiff with tension, as if he were the one standing on the edge of a cliff top wondering whether to go over. But that was only her, wasn't it?

She looked up at him and said the only thing that she could. 'Yes.'

CHAPTER TEN

DESPITE THE OVERHANGING grey clouds and constant threat of humid rain they had a glorious day. They walked along the Thames, had lunch in a tiny French bistro, and came across that horrendous art exhibition Dare had attended with Lucy. He had nearly groaned when Carly wanted to take a look inside, having the good sense not to mention that he'd already been.

'It looks like the artist really disliked his last girlfriend,' she mused. 'Or boyfriend.'

Dare laughed and asked her what she thought of the white column thing that still looked like a table to him.

After that they talked about everything from politics to Hollywood movies and which was better, *Thor* or *Iron Man*. She waxed lyrical over Chris Hemsworth; he might have mentioned Charlize Theron once or twice.

'Charlize, huh?'

'She's a fine actress,' he explained with a straight face. 'She's won awards.'

'Yes, but I bet it's not her awards you picture when you think of her,' she teased.

No, he didn't, but for some reason with Carly standing in front of him with shafts of sunlight striking her hair he couldn't bring any other woman to mind.

'You think?' he said.

She laughed and Dare grabbed her and dragged her up onto her toes in the middle of a busy street, forked his hands in her hair and kissed her.

After that they headed to his apartment. Made love.

He couldn't get enough of her and if he had enough brain cells left in his head he'd probably be worried about that.

'How can you have black coffee when you have this wicked-looking machine that can probably grow the beans, collect them, and roast them at the same time?' she asked.

She was wearing one of his T-shirts and he'd bet nothing underneath. He loved it when she did that.

'I like top-shelf stuff,' he said, thinking of her.

She perched on the edge of a stool. 'Because you never had it growing up?'

They'd talked a bit about his childhood. Nothing too drastic, just where he'd gone to school, how he'd had to work hard to put himself through college, his first car—a 1990 Mazda RX-7 he'd been so proud of at the time. But things he'd never discussed with anyone before.

'Yeah, I suppose so.' He gave her a quick smile. 'You might not believe this but I was a scrawny kid when I was younger, always coming from the bottom.'

'Oh, I bet you liked that!' She laughed.

He grinned. 'I might have gotten my head punched in a few times when guys tried to push me around about it.'

'What did your dad say? Did he step in and threaten to do the same to them?'

Dare's grin slipped a notch. 'My father wasn't around much.'

'Why not?'

'He was a dreamer.'

'A dreamer?'

Dare nearly laughed. Saying his father was a dreamer was putting it mildly. And part of him wanted to tell her everything. Tell her how he had looked up to his father, believing in him right up until his death, tell her how he had defended his father in the schoolyard, tell her how bitterly disappointed he was to find out that he was just a liar. But the words stuck like a block of cement in his throat.

And why sully the moment by rehashing the past? Especially when she was looking at him the way she was. All big-eyed and soft-mouthed.

'He's not worth talking about,' he said, pouring the coffee.

'Is he still alive?'

'No. He died when I was fifteen. Here,' he announced with a masculine flourish. 'One girlie coffee for your tasting pleasure. Tell me that isn't the best coffee you've ever tasted in your life.'

Carly knew Dare was deliberately changing the subject and she told herself it didn't mean anything.

Giving him a quick smile, she forced herself to sip the warm liquid. It really was good. She blinked up at him, wondering if there was anything he couldn't do well. 'Mmm...' She rolled her lips together, savouring the taste. 'You're right, it is good. But the best...' She took another sip. Licked her lips again.

Dare stared at her mouth. 'Now you've done it,' he said, coming around to her side of the counter.

'Done what?' Carly asked innocently.

'Gone and made something hard,' he growled, lifting her onto the benchtop. 'And seeing as how you're a doctor and all, you might like to take a look. Give me your professional opinion.'

'My professional opinion, huh?' Carly reached down and cupped him in her hand. Dare groaned.

She frowned at him. 'Hmm, my professional opinion is that you really should do something about that.' She tapped her finger to her lips. 'I'm just not sure what.'

Dare lifted his shirt to her waist. 'Here, I have an idea.'

A faint stream of early morning sunlight woke her and once more Carly's internal muscles cramped pleasurably as she moved. This time, however, instead of waking alone she found Dare still with her, sprawled out on his back, one arm flung over his head, the other curled beneath her neck.

Carefully, so she didn't wake him, Carly rose up on her elbow and looked down at him.

He was magnificent. His dark beard growth making his jaw appear even squarer, his dark lashes creating a thick curve on his cheekbones.

Last night he had been both passionate and gentle. Powerful and tender. And completely insatiable. *She* had been completely insatiable. Waking in the early hours of the morning to find his mouth on her as he drew her from sleep in the most delicious way imaginable.

But it wasn't just the way he made her feel that mesmerised her. It was the man himself. He was so strong, so sure of himself and, yes, controlling, but that was somehow part of his appeal, much as she never thought she'd ever say such a thing!

'What are you looking at?' he rumbled without opening his eyes.

Carly grinned. God, she loved him, and her heart felt as if it were glowing inside her chest.

'You,' she said, leaning down to gently kiss his jaw.

The arm beneath her came around her shoulders and he lazily caressed her spine.

'A little less looking and a lot more action would be preferable,' he advised with drowsy appreciation.

Carly laughed. 'You're insatiable.'

'Hmm.' He gripped the nape of her neck and encouraged her head to bend to his. 'I am where you're concerned.'

Carly stroked his chest. 'We should check how Benson is doing.'

'I already did.'

'You did?'

'I woke up earlier and called the hospital. They're thinking of moving him out of ICU later today.'

'Oh, that's fantastic news.' She smiled at him, drawing slow circles on the sprinkling of hair on his chest. 'That was nice of you to check. I think "the old man" is growing on you,' she teased.

Dare grunted and she hid a smile against his shoulder. He came over all cold and tough, but deep down he wasn't. Deep down he was the man of her dreams.

'Are you accusing me of going soft?' he murmured suggestively.

'Never!'

She squealed as he rolled her onto her back and held her hands above her head. 'Let me up,' she said breathlessly.

His eyes drifted over her naked breasts. 'Make me.'

Carly reviewed her options and her stomach chose that moment to growl loudly.

Dare's eyebrows rose in alarm. 'Okay, I give up.'

Carly laughed at his antics. 'I haven't eaten for hours,' she defended.

'Then I'd better feed you.' He rolled away from her. 'How does an American omelette sound?'

'Great, but what's the difference between an American omelette and our omelettes?'

He dropped a kiss on her mouth. 'We *cook* ours.'

Carly grinned, watching him tug on his jeans, leaving the top button undone, with the casual disregard of a confident male.

A surge of emotion shook her out of her happy delirium as it struck her that maybe she needed to pull back a little.

'Why don't you have a shower while I cook?'

She swallowed heavily and shook off the maudlin thought. Dare wasn't a mistake. How could he be when it felt so good?

'Sounds like a plan.' She smiled.

'Oh, I have plans for you, Red. I'm just building your stamina first.'

'Promises, promises.' Carly laughed and she headed for the shower.

Dare pulled a carton of eggs and a block of cheese from the fridge, a frying pan from the cupboard.

He was humming, he realised, and grinned. He couldn't remember a time he'd felt this good. This amped. Maybe when he'd seen his risky stock options turn him from a possible contender on the financial markets to a man everyone respected. And maybe when he was speeding along an open road. But never with a woman before.

He glanced at the day outside the window. It wasn't raining so maybe he'd try and get his doc to set aside her reservations and hop on the back of his death trap with him.

He frowned.

His doc?

She wasn't his anything. She was very definitely her own woman and he could only imagine her temper taking hold if he suggested anything else.

He cracked eggs, ground pepper and salt into a bowl, and grinned.

That ex of hers had really done him a favour, he thought, cheating on her. The guy must have been a moron. It was the only explanation Dare could come up with because Carly was magnificent. Everything a man could ever want in a woman.

He stopped stirring. What was he thinking? *That he was going to keep her?*

His heart found its way into his throat. Was that what he wanted?

He stared into space.

Yes, the answer came back, yes, *he did want her*, and that was when he knew that he could no longer avoid the truth. Somehow, some time, he'd fallen in love with the lovely, the beautiful Dr Evans. And he wasn't even worried about it. The fact was he'd never met a woman like her. So open and honest, so genuine and giving. And, man, was she ever giving. Last night—

The buzzer sounded on his intercom and almost bemusedly he pressed the button.

If someone had told him a week ago he'd fall in love with a feisty redhead he would have laughed. Deep down he'd believed love wasn't something he'd ever want or something he would ever need.

'What's up, George?'

'Sir, a Mr Beckett Granger is here to see you.'

Dare frowned and almost told him to tell Beckett to take a hike, to use one of Carly's expressions.

Then he thought better of it. Better to talk to Beckett here than at the hospital.

'Send him up, George.'

And what about Carly? he wondered. Was she falling in love with him too?

He recalled the breathy little sighs she made when he touched her, the way she moaned his name, the smile she'd given him when he'd woken up this morning that had nearly blinded him. Was that just lust or was it—?

'What the hell are you playing at?'

Distracted as he was, Dare wasn't even aware that he'd opened his front door until a very angry Beckett dressed in a pinstripe suit and smelling like a men's fragrance counter pushed past him into his home.

Dare swore under his breath and caught up with him in two strides but by then he was already in his open-plan living room.

'What do you want, Beckett?'

Beckett swung round. 'Nice digs. Glad someone can afford them.'

Dare stared at him. 'I repeat, what do you want?'

Beckett took his time answering. 'So I tried to log in to my computer this morning only to find that I've been banned from accessing certain parts of the business.'

'I hope you didn't bother Benson with that,' Dare snarled, knowing their grandfather wasn't fit for that kind of discussion just yet.

'I wasn't allowed because his *watchdog* said he was sleeping. But I figured you'd know all about it. And I'm right, aren't I?'

'We can discuss this later. At my office. If you call my PA she'll make an appointment for you.' And if he ever called his mother a watchdog again, Dare would deck him.

'I don't want to make an appointment. I want an explanation. Now.'

'I'm not prepared to discuss it,' Dare said.

Not until he'd spoken to Benson to see how his grandfather wanted to play things. This wasn't Dare's issue and, while he'd followed Benson's instructions to have BG's second-in-command take over as acting CEO, he wasn't about to further isolate Beckett without first knowing what damage he could do. 'And now you can—'

'Why, Dr Evans,' Beckett simpered as he glanced behind Dare. 'How very…unexpected.'

'Beckett? What are you doing here?'

Having heard voices, Carly had come to investigate and now wished she had taken the time to dress in more than one of Dare's T-shirts because Beckett was openly staring at her legs. And her breasts.

Carly folded her arms across her chest, gazing from one man to the other, and wondering if she shouldn't make herself scarce.

'It would seem that we have the same taste in women,' Beckett murmured and Carly very definitely thought about making herself scarce.

'Excuse me?' Dare's quiet question was lethal.

Beckett paused before smiling. 'I have dibs.'

Carly frowned. 'Don't be rude, Beckett,' she said sharply, remembering that she still had his necklace in her handbag.

Beckett ignored her in favour of Dare. 'Or is Grandfather just up to his old matchmaking tricks again? He really fell for our doctor here,' he informed Dare. 'I suppose he doesn't care which grandson ends up with her.'

Carly felt herself blush. Beckett was being a complete plonker. 'There was never anything between us, Beckett,' she said coldly.

'Oh Carly.' Beckett thumped his chest with his fist. 'You wound me.'

'Just because you're angry about what's happened at BG Textiles doesn't mean you have to make this personal,' Dare bit out.

Carly smiled. His defence of her warmed her heart.

'Besides,' Dare continued, 'I think we have more important things to discuss. Like your insider-trading efforts.'

Insider trading?

Carly's eyes flew to Beckett's. If Dare was right, then Beckett could be in a lot of trouble.

Beckett's face took on a mottled hue. 'Don't you dare try to tarnish my name to get the inheritance for yourself,' Beckett spat.

'As you so rightly pointed out when you walked in, I don't need Benson's inheritance. Nor do I need to try and tarnish your name. You're doing a good job of that all by yourself.'

'Sometimes I wish I had been born two centuries ago,' Beckett spat, 'because then I'd call you out for that slur.'

Dare gave him a bored look. 'Don't fret it. You would have lost.'

'You absolute, utter—'

'I suggest you leave without saying another word, cousin,' Dare broke in softly.

'Or what?' Beckett seethed. 'You'll take something else from me? Or hit me, perhaps? Go on, I dare you.'

Dare yawned.

Carly planted her hands on her hips. 'If he doesn't I might,' she warned. 'There's absolutely no need for any of this, Beckett.'

Beckett turned to her, his expression tenderly forlorn.

'Allow a man to express a little outraged jealousy, *Red*. I did find you first.'

Red!

He had never called her that before.

Carly noticed Dare take a step in Beckett's direction and shot forward. 'Wait.' She held her hand up to Dare and turned to Beckett. 'Don't move and don't say another word,' she instructed. Then she rushed from the room and pulled the velvet box out of her bag, wishing she'd remembered it at the hospital the previous day.

'This is yours,' she said, pushing the velvet box into his hand. Her eyes flashed to Dare as he stood by the front door, unconsciously noting his lethal stillness.

'I gave it to you.' Beckett glared down at her and Carly wondered how she had ever thought he was handsome.

'I don't want it.'

Beckett sneered at her. 'Not now that you've snared the bigger fish.'

'Get out, Beckett,' Dare said with icy fury.

Beckett had given her the necklace! Dare could barely believe it. His senses reeled, his mind shrouded in a red haze so thick he could barely see through it.

He could feel adrenaline coursing through his system like in the old days when kids used to laugh about his loser father.

He took a deep breath and did his best to ignore the

beating of his blood that wanted him to beat the crap out
of his insolent cousin. If Beckett didn't leave by the door
soon, he'd find himself using the window; a much quicker
way to the sidewalk.

'Goodbye, my lovely Carly. It seems I'm being asked
to leave.'

Beckett strolled towards Dare, a swagger in his step.
He stopped and shook his head at Dare as if he felt sorry
for him.

'Come in, spinner,' he said softly, laughing when Dare
slammed the door in his face.

Taking a deep breath, Dare turned towards Carly. She
looked beautiful and shaken standing in his living room
wearing only his shirt.

He frowned. Hadn't she heard their voices? Didn't she
know better than to come into a room wearing only a
T-shirt?

He glanced at his well-stocked bar and wondered if it
was too early in the day to have a drink.

'I never liked him,' Carly said, hugging her arms around
her waist.

Dare looked at her. Why had she felt the need to tell
him that? Was she feeling guilty about something? Like
sleeping with his cousin right before moving on to him?

Had she lied to him?

The adrenaline hadn't left his body and he felt edgy and
unsatisfied. Maybe he should have hit his cousin after all.

'Come in, spinner.'

Beckett's mocking words knocked around inside his
head as if they had been shot out of a pinball machine.

Was Carly really duping him as Beckett had implied?
He didn't want to believe it, but he couldn't deny the sick
feeling in the pit of his stomach.

'You liked him well enough to take the necklace,' he
said easily. Too easily.

'Sorry?' Carly blinked at him and then her brows drew together. 'Would you mind repeating that?'

Dare paced away from her. Maybe that hadn't been the best thing to say given how tightly he was strung. 'I need some time to think.'

'About what?' She wet her lips as if she was nervous. But what did she have to be nervous about?

Red. Beckett had called her Red.

Dare's teeth ground together. Had he called her that in bed? But no, Carly had claimed that she hadn't slept with him.

'Why are you looking at me like that?' she asked carefully. 'You don't actually believe there was something between me and your cousin do you?'

Dare rubbed a hand across his forehead, tried to collect his thoughts. Unfortunately they were scattered like freshly fallen leaves. 'I don't know what to believe.'

Carly stared at him. 'I already told you that Beckett gave me the necklace because he wanted me to go out with him.'

Dare stared at her. Rubbed his forehead again. 'Did my grandfather mention that he wanted us to get together?'

Carly flushed and Dare knew that he had.

'Not really.'

His eyes homed in on her like a heat-seeking missile locking onto a target. 'But he did mention it.'

'It was a joke.'

'Not one I find funny,' Dare said softly.

'You can't seriously be giving Beckett's hateful comments any credence,' Carly said incredulously. 'Dare, he was trying to get a rise out of you.'

Dare turned to her. He wasn't. He wasn't at all, but... 'What I'm struggling to understand is why a man who is in so much debt he'd throw his grandfather's company to the wolves, would then go and give a woman a necklace worth a small fortune.'

Carly felt a cold sensation slither into her stomach. 'What you mean is,' she said woodenly, 'why does a man give a woman he's *not sleeping with* a necklace worth a small fortune?'

A muscle ticked in his jaw. 'So why does he?'

Carly felt so sick she could barely breathe. 'I already explained it to you once,' she said slowly. 'He asked me out. I said no. The necklace was… I don't know…some sort of enticement, I suppose. I never asked him.'

Dare's gaze wouldn't meet hers and Carly knew then that he didn't love her. Because how could you love someone you didn't know? Someone you didn't trust?

Carly was just about at the bedroom door when Dare grabbed her arm and swung her towards him.

'Where are you going?

'I'm leaving.'

'We're having a conversation.'

'No, we're not,' she fumed. 'You're conducting an investigation.'

'I asked *one* question,' he said, as calmly as possible. 'Which apparently you don't want to answer.'

'I did answer it.' She tipped her chin up. 'Tell me you believe me.'

A heavy silence followed her request and Carly had her answer. How, she wondered, had she ever imagined she was in love with this man who was exactly like her ex?

A sob caught in her throat and she quickly stifled it.

'*Now* where are you going?' he asked irritably.

'I told you… I'm leaving. Do you need me to repeat that as well?'

Dare ran a hand through his hair. 'I just want the facts, Carly. Is that too much to ask?'

Carly clenched her teeth. 'How many times?'

'How many times what?'

'How many times do you want your precious facts until

you believe them? Because once wasn't enough. Will twice do? Maybe three times. A hundred?'

Dare swore under his breath. 'Look,' he began reasonably. 'I could have made a mistake.'

Carly shook her head. This time she wouldn't be cowed by a man. 'Well, while you *could* have made a mistake, I *did*.'

Dare watched her storm into his bedroom and he headed for the balcony. He looked down at the garden below. Breathed deeply. Tried to get his head together. It didn't work; if anything he felt more confused. Was she telling the truth or was she lying because she thought it was what he wanted to hear?

When he heard his front door slam that old sick sensation from his childhood returned and he gripped the balustrade in front of him and told himself that he'd done nothing wrong.

CHAPTER ELEVEN

THAT WAS SOMETHING he was convinced of right up until he'd snatched up his helmet and straddled his bike, intending to hit the open roads. Which was when the sick feeling was replaced with a sense of hollowness.

She'd left him. She'd really walked out. And why? Because she had an unreasonable temper. No man in his right mind would want to put up with that. And what had she expected him to say after he'd seen her return Beckett's necklace? After the way Beckett had smiled at her? The way his cousin had laughed at him?

All Dare had wanted was the facts. What the hell was wrong with that? Nothing—that was what.

Except obviously there was, or he wouldn't be feeling this hollow. This empty. Nor would he be sitting on his stationary bike, breathing in petrol fumes in his underground garage.

Dare grimaced. From the moment he'd met her Carly Evans had twisted him up and turned him inside out until he hadn't known which way was up. But not anymore. If she didn't want him then he didn't want her either. Only he did...

He shook his head. He needed to get home. Home to the Smokies. Whenever his father had gone off chasing rainbows Dare had usually spent a couple of days camping amongst the raccoons and bears. Not that he'd ever seen a bear. Much as he'd tried. Sometimes he'd been so hurt he'd wanted to fight one with nothing but his bare hands. During those times he'd felt as if he could have ripped a bear's head off.

But why couldn't he take what she said at face value? He

knew the answer: people often said one thing and meant another. His father was a case in point, but there had been others. Other women who had said they loved him, but really they had loved his money and status.

But how would he know if Carly had told him the truth? The fact was a man could only really ever rely on himself. He knew that.

He shoved the helmet on his head and kicked the stand up. First he'd go for a ride to clear his head, and then he'd stop off at the hospital before heading to the office. God knew his PA didn't know what to make of all this time he was having off. Then he'd think about what to do about Carly.

Right now though, right now he was too humiliated to contemplate it. And why wouldn't he be? If their situation had been reversed, if she'd discovered a woman's earring, or say a pair of panties wedged down the side of his sofa he wouldn't mind if she gave him the third degree. In fact, he'd expect it!

Not that he'd probably see her all that often. Not once he returned to the States next week. Because all that baloney about loving her? It was called hot sex. Hot sex that had fried his brain and had him building castles in his head, not unlike his father had done with his scams.

Dare shook his head at his own gullibility. Then he pulled out his phone and punched in her number. When she didn't answer he gritted his teeth and left a message, ending with instructions to call him.

Shoving the phone back in his pocket, he roared out of the garage and headed for the hospital.

Unfortunately his mood hadn't improved much by the time he pulled up. When he didn't find a missed call from her it turned a little more grim.

He barely took any notice of the hospital staff and visitors who scrambled to get out of his way as he stalked through the hospital corridors. Then he wondered if she would be waiting for him in Benson's room, to apologise to him for being so unreasonable.

That made him smile. If you could call the twist of his lips a smile.

He paused outside his grandfather's room, took a breath and pushed open the door.

Other than his grandfather, reclining in bed watching the TV, the room was empty.

As soon as he saw him, Benson clicked off the TV.

'Dare.' The old man's eyes watered and he brusquely cleared his throat. 'It's good to see you.'

'And you,' Dare said. 'How are you?'

'As good as can be expected.'

Dare let out a slow breath ignoring the way his gut felt like it was full of rocks. 'So what do the doctors say?'

'They don't know a lot yet,' Benson said. 'The biopsy results still have to come through.'

The conversation moved on to how annoying it was sleeping in a hospital what with the nurses coming in every fifteen minutes to check his vital signs and on to the lunch menu until Dare couldn't stand it anymore.

'Have you seen Carly today? Is she with my mother?'

Benson blinked and Dare realised he'd spoken over top of him. 'Sorry. I just… I need to speak to her.'

'Your mother has gone shopping and Carly stopped by a short time ago, but now she's gone.'

'I can see that.' Dare smiled with the patience of Job. 'But where? And when will she be back? Her cell phone is switched off.' He said the last as if that explained everything. Really it only explained that she didn't want to talk to anyone. Or her battery had run flat.

'She's not coming back,' Benson said.

Dare frowned. 'But she still has a week to work out her contract.'

'Her contract was only until my operation.'

'But surely you'll need post-op care or whatever they call it?'

'Yes, but Carly is a highly trained doctor. I could hardly be lucky enough to get her to extend her services.'

'So that's it? You'll never see her again.'

'I hope not. She's a lovely young woman. I've grown fond of her.'

Dare frowned. 'How fond?'

Benson's eyebrows shot up. 'What do you mean?'

Dare shook his head. He no longer cared if his grandfather had tried to implement some Machiavellian plan to set him up with Carly. 'Never mind,' Dare said, irritated with himself. 'You were about to say something.'

'Only that I believe Carly already has a new job to go to. And speaking of work issues, I've been meaning to ask your advice about how to handle the whole Beckett situation.'

'I've got my PR people working with yours,' Dare said distractedly. 'Did you know that Beckett gave Carly a necklace?'

'What? Another one?'

Dare turned back to find his grandfather frowning. 'How many did he give her?'

'I know he gave her one with a large ruby in it.'

'That's the one I'm talking about.'

Benson shook his head. 'That boy doesn't know the value of money. What fool gives a woman a precious necklace to try and entice her to go out with him?'

Dare swallowed. 'So she never went out with him?'

Benson laughed. 'Of course not.'

Heart beating too fast, Dare saw his life flash before his eyes. 'Many women would consider it a sizable inducement.' But even as the words left his mouth he knew that Carly wasn't one of them.

'Not a woman like Carly.'

No, Dare thought, shoving his shaking hands into his pockets, *not a woman like Carly.*

He'd been wrong. *Again.*

And suddenly his smug message replayed in his head. He was a bigger fool than he'd given himself credit for. A stupid, hard-headed fool.

He pinched the bridge of his nose. If she hadn't hated him before, she no doubt would after listening to that.

'Dare, are you quite all right?'

Dare nearly choked on his own stupidity, and knew he had no one to blame for his mistrust but himself. Beckett might have infected him with his venomous words, but Dare had made it easy for him, hadn't he? Because, as much as he'd tried to deny it, he hadn't trusted her; she'd been right about that. What she *didn't* know was that he didn't trust anyone.

'Dare, you've gone very pale.'

Dare stared at his grandfather without really seeing him. Being pale was the least of his concerns. How he was going to win back the only woman he had ever loved was much more important.

'I'm in love with Carly.'

Benson beamed. 'That's fantastic.'

'No, it's not,' Dare said tonelessly. 'I stuffed up.'

'What did you do?'

'I basically accused her of sleeping with Beckett.'

Silence fell between them.

Benson cleared his throat. 'That wouldn't have gone down very well.'

'It didn't.'

'What are you going to do about it?'

Dare looked at him bleakly. 'The hell if I know.'

'Want my advice?'

'Please.'

'Tell her how you feel. We all make mistakes, Dare. You're not perfect. And neither is she.'

Dare stared at him. 'You make it sound so simple.'

'Simple it's not,' Benson said. 'But it's a lot harder living without love. Trust me, I tried.'

Dare reached out and clasped his grandfather's shoulder. 'I'm glad you contacted my mother.'

'Best thing I did. Now go get your girl.'

Not knowing where to start, Dare did the only thing he could think of.

He called her again and told her he loved her. He poured his heart out to her message bank and admitted that he'd been wrong and hoped she'd forgive him because she was the most important person in his life. Then he called again and told her he wanted to marry her.

By the third day when he hadn't heard from her Dare felt as if he were going mad. No one knew where she was. She hadn't been back to Rothmeyer House to collect her things, and she'd quit her job with the agency.

He'd even called her parents in Liverpool. Her polite mother had said that Carly wasn't there. When he'd called again her polite father had confirmed her polite mother's words. They hadn't seen her. And then her father had graciously advised him to never call again.

Dare stared out of his office window.

Her father, the Viking, protecting his little girl. He would have smiled if he didn't feel so, so— Dare's eyes narrowed. Why would Carly's father need to protect his daughter if he hadn't seen her?

Dare closed his eyes and when he opened them he searched the room for his helmet.

Carly glanced at her cell phone and saw another voice mail message from Dare. Without even thinking about it she deleted it. After that first message she'd had from him she'd deleted every single one since without listening to them.

What woman in her right mind would do any differently after that first pompous message about panties?

Panties?

Carly hadn't known whether to laugh or cry.

'What was that, honey?'

She glanced up from her cell phone to where her mother was making tea for them both in the family kitchen.

As it was past ten o'clock her father had bid them goodnight hours ago, but, since she had arrived home three days ago, Carly and her mother had taken to staying up late into the night talking.

And it had been so cathartic to finally confront those things that had hurt her the most and face them head-on. She'd even told her parents how responsible she had felt over Liv's death and a weight of guilt had finally lifted from her heavy shoulders. Then last night she and her mother had cried themselves dry over photo album after photo album; remembering Liv, crying for Liv and loving Liv all over again.

And as for Daniel, well, she'd finally admitted that he'd dented her pride and not her heart and that if she ever saw him in the street again she wouldn't hang her head in shame. She'd likely walk up and give him a piece of her mind.

The one person she hadn't mentioned was Dare. And it wasn't because she was trying to avoid thinking about him. It was just that her mistake over him was still too new. Too raw. Because while Daniel had only dented her pride, Dare had torn it in half, making her feel like a fool for loving him so completely so quickly.

Now she just longed for the day that she didn't wake up thinking about him. When she didn't go to bed seeing his face in her mind.

'Carly?' Her mother set tea down in front of her. 'Did you say something?'

'No,' Carly laughed reassuringly at her mother. She hadn't realised she'd spoken out loud. At the time she'd heard the message she'd replayed it twice over. She shook her head. If she had found a pair of women's underwear anywhere near his sofa she wouldn't have bothered telling him to find a high cliff, she'd have driven him to it and pushed him off it herself.

'I thought you said panties,' her mother said, setting the tea down.

'No, I said…I said…*tanties*. As in tantrums.'

Her mother made a face. 'Why would you say that?'

'I was just remembering a message I received the other day. It was nothing.'

'Was it from that man? The one with the deep voice.'

'No,' she lied.

Apparently Dare had called the house a couple of times looking for her. She'd told her parents to act nonchalant and tell him they hadn't seen her. When they had given her that worried look she'd told them he was Benson's grandson who had thought she was a gold-digger and been horrible to her.

That had been all it had taken for her father's spine to stiffen.

'Oh, well.' Her mother sipped her tea. 'He certainly has the looks to back up the voice, but what did you say he was?'

'An obstinate, hard-headed—' Carly stopped, eyeballed her mother. 'How do you know what he looks like? Did you see his picture in the paper or something?'

Her mother cupped her teacup in her hands and looked flustered. 'Not exactly.'

'On the Internet?'

'He was here.'

'In Liverpool?' Carly's heart jumped into her mouth.

'He said he was in the neighbourhood.'

'Liverpool is not his neighbourhood, Mum.'

'I'm sorry, honey. I didn't confirm you were here, if that's what you're worried about.'

Carly relaxed. Slightly.

'If he's stalking you—if he hurt you—'

Carly shook her head. 'He's not the stalking kind.'

'Then why was he here?'

'I'm sure I don't want to know.' She frowned. Checked her phone in case she'd missed a call from the Baron or Travelling Angels. She'd resigned from there as soon as she'd left London so she wasn't expecting a call but if something had happened to Benson she knew they'd inform her.

But there were no messages.

'Carly, honey, what happened with this Mr James?'

Carly felt her throat close over. When she felt she could talk again she said the first thing that came into her head. 'I was a fool.' And then she burst into tears.

'Oh, honey, I hate to see you cry.'

'I know...I'm sorry. I just...I have terrible taste in men.'

She swiped at her eyes and grabbed a tissue from the nearby box. Then she told her mother what had happened. How she had tried to resist him but he'd been...

'The kind of man to make a woman swoon?' her mother offered.

Carly grimaced. 'He took my breath away from the first moment I saw him, only he isn't the kind of man who is interested in long-term relationships and...even worse, he was the same as Daniel.'

'He cheated on you!'

'No...I meant...' Carly swallowed. 'He didn't love me either.'

'Oh, Carly.'

'It's okay.' Carly hiccupped. 'He isn't worth it.'

And one day she hoped she'd believe that. She wadded the tissue into a ball and aimed it at the kitchen sink as she and Liv had done as kids.

'Carly—' Her mother's familiar reprimand was cut short by a loud knock at the front door.

Carly glanced at her mother. 'Are you expecting anyone?'

'No.'

Her mother got up to go to the door before Carly thought to tell her to ignore it.

Then she heard Dare's voice and immediately swiped at her eyes and straightened her shoulders.

When he walked in she caught her breath. Once again he was dressed in head-to-toe black leather so she knew he'd ridden his bike up from London, but gone was the cocky charmer who had nearly run her down and in his place was a man who looked as if he'd forgotten how to shave or sleep.

A deep yearning careened around inside her chest and it took all Carly's effort not to act like Benson's ratty little dog and bound into his arms. Especially when she no doubt looked just like Gregory with her unkempt hair and her mother's thirty-year-old dressing gown over her old pyjamas. Why was it that she had a cupboard full of nice clothes but this man never caught her wearing anything *decent*?

He looked her up and down. 'You've been crying,' he said softly.

'No, I haven't. I have hay fever.'

His brows rose. 'At the end of summer?'

'All year round.' Her heart was kicking inside her chest like a racehorse trying to break out of its barrier but she'd be damned if she'd let him see her so vulnerable.

'Would you like a cup of tea, Mr James?'

'Dare doesn't drink tea, Mother,' she said stiffly.

'I didn't think you did either,' he said gruffly.

Carly wasn't about to explain that this was her and her mother's special thing. 'What are you doing here? I thought I told you not to come near me again.'

His nostrils flared at her frosty tone. 'I needed to make sure you got my messages.'

'I got the one about the panties,' Carly scoffed. 'That was enough.'

'I think I might leave you two to talk,' her mother said softly.

Carly glanced up and saw her mother's flushed face. 'Thanks, Mum.' She had been so intent on Dare she had forgotten her mother was even in the room. By the look on his face, Dare had too.

'About that message.' He tugged at the collar on his jacket. 'I wasn't exactly thinking straight when I left it.'

'You don't say.'

He ignored her sarcasm and raked a hand through his hair. 'But I was referring to my other messages.'

'I don't care about your other messages. I want you to leave.'

Dare stared at her beautiful, defiant face. Was that it? Was that all she was going to say after he'd poured his heart out to her? After the things he'd told her?

Yes, it seemed so.

He sucked in a steadying breath. 'There's nothing you want to add?'

'If I'd had something to add I would have called you, wouldn't I?'

'Of course.' Dare zipped up his jacket, swallowed heavily. 'I'm sorry I disturbed you.'

'I'm sorry I ever met you.'

She said it under her breath but Dare rounded on her.

'You know, when a man pours his heart out to you, you might want to think about being a little nicer about it.'

'Pours his heart out?' Carly gave a harsh laugh. 'That's rich,' she said thickly. 'You talk about women's underwear and demand that I call you—as if *I'm* the one at fault—and you call that pouring your heart out?'

'I never said you were at fault. If anyone is at fault I am.'

'Well, finally we agree on something,' she fumed. 'Now you can go.'

That last word came out as a sob, and Carly dashed the back of her hand against her mouth to try and contain it. Dammit, she didn't want to cry in front of him.

'Carly, I'm sorry. I didn't mean to hurt you.'

He took her face between his hands and kissed her. It was meant to be a goodbye kiss. Short and sweet. But her lips clung to his and he groaned her name and gathered her closer.

'I want you to know that I meant everything I said,' he told her gruffly. 'And if you change your mind I'll...' He took a deep breath. 'My feelings won't ever change.'

'What are you talking about?' Carly looked up at him. 'What feelings?'

Dare stared at her to the point where she became uncomfortable. Then his eyes narrowed. 'Did you even listen to my other messages?'

Carly sniffed and wiped her nose. 'One was enough.' She lifted her chin. 'I deleted the others. I didn't want to—why are you laughing?' She frowned. 'This is hardly funny.'

She tried to pull away but Dare clasped her shoulders, preventing her.

'Carly?' Dare began softly. 'Those messages you deleted.' He cleared his throat. 'They said that I love you.'

'They said…' She shrugged out of his hold and wrapped her arms around her waist. 'They said what?'

'That I love you.'

Carly shook her head. 'You can't love me—you don't trust me.'

'You're right, I didn't trust you, but I need to explain that.'

And he did. He told her about his father and how his actions had made Dare grow jaded and cynical. How he'd grown up prepared to take risks with everything other than his heart. 'With you, I couldn't seem to stop myself. Every time I tried to back off you were there, inside my head. Inside my heart.'

Carly stared at him. She wanted to believe him. She was *desperate* to believe him but something still held her back. 'What happens when another Beckett comes along? When—?'

Dare reached for her again. 'There won't be another Beckett because this time I'm giving all of myself to you just as you gave all of yourself to me the other night. Tell me it's not too late. Tell me you'll give me another chance.'

Carly looked up at him. 'But I didn't give all of myself to you,' she murmured, looking up at him. Because even though she'd thought she had, she hadn't taken the ultimate step. She hadn't told him she loved him.

'The truth is that I thought I was in love with Daniel and he used to accuse me of sleeping with other men and it was horrible.'

Dare frowned. 'You told me he had been the one to cheat.'

'He was. He did, but then he'd belittle me and I felt stupid and—'

'And I came along and did the same thing.' His arms tightened around her waist. 'I'm sorry, Carly, please forgive me. I've been a bigger fool than I first thought. That was what was on some of my other messages.' He looked down at her imploringly. 'A fool who was so afraid of getting hurt it was easier to let you walk away. It won't happen again.'

'I was afraid too,' she admitted. 'Afraid of making another mistake but I could have stayed. I could have made you listen.'

Dare shook his head. 'That wouldn't have worked because all I wanted was the facts.'

'And now?'

'And now I know that facts are well and good but they don't tell the whole story.' He leaned down and kissed her softly. 'Now I know I should have listened to what was inside my heart, not my head.'

'Oh Dare, I'm guilty of the same thing. After Liv died I felt so frozen inside by my sense of guilt and loss, at the fact that I was alive when she wasn't...even now I wish she could experience what I have right now. With you.'

'She'll always be in your heart, Red. And if you want we'll open a hospital wing in her name.'

'For kids?'

'For the whole world if you'll agree to be my wife.'

'Your wife?'

'What did you think this was? A one-night stand proposition?'

'No, I just...I thought you didn't want a long-term relationship.'

'I didn't. I didn't believe I needed love. Then you came along.'

Carly's smile was watery. 'You know, I love you so much I just want to shout it from the rooftops.'

Dare ran his hands over her arms, then cupped her face. 'Why don't you just tell me?'

'How many times?' Carly teased.

His grin was slow, but it showed that dimple she loved so much. He tugged her closer. 'Until I'm satisfied.'

'That could take a really long time.'

'It's going to take for ever, Red. For ever in my arms.'

'Yes,' Carly said, linking her arms around his neck. 'For ever sounds perfect.'

EPILOGUE

THEY WERE MARRIED the following month at Rothmeyer House, with Carly's parents and Dare's mother in attendance, along with the Baron and Gregory. Gregory got the best-man position, although Carly had already warned him that if he ran off she would not be chasing after him this time.

Mrs Carlisle cooked up a feast with tofu well and truly disguised in the mix, and Roberts was their celebrant.

Fortunately the summer days had continued into an Indian summer and the breeze was light with the perfume of late-summer blooms.

Benson's medical results had been the best anyone could have asked for and all of them hoped for many more years to make up for those that had been lost.

As for Beckett, he had apologised to both Carly and his grandfather but had yet to speak to Dare. A man had a point of pride, apparently, and fronting up to Dare and admitting he was a jerk was his.

But that was okay with Dare. He'd paid off his cousin's debt and helped BG Textiles weather the storm caused by his cousin's desperation. Because none of it mattered now that he had the one thing he'd always longed for—a family he could rely on and give his heart to.

Especially his beautiful wife-to-be who was walking towards him down the short aisle that had been laid out in the rose garden.

Both Rachel and Beth, Carly's mother, pulled out hankies, but Dare's eyes were totally focused on the gorgeous redhead in the long white sheath.

Just as she got to him Dare reached out his hand to take

her from her father's arm when Gregory shot up like a rocket and started yapping for all he was worth.

'It's okay, buddy,' Dare said. 'We've got her now.'

The little dog cocked his head, yawned, and then dropped immediately at Dare's feet, his nose in his paws.

Carly shook her head, laughing. 'For all the time I've walked him and petted him he has never once done anything I've asked him to do.'

'Don't sweat it, Red,' Dare said, smoothing a wisp of her hair back beneath her veil. 'I'll do anything you ask me to for the rest of our lives.'

Carly gazed at her husband-to-be and glanced at the large photo of Liv on a nearby stand. Yes, her sister would have adored this man and, fighting back tears, she gave Liv a small smile, silently telling her sister that she wished she were here to share in this grand occasion. Then she laid her hand in Dare's and turned to face the future with the man she loved with all her heart.

* * * * *

If you enjoyed this story,
check out these other great reads from
Michelle Conder
HIDDEN IN THE SHEIKH'S HAREM
RUSSIAN'S RUTHLESS DEMAND
PRINCE NADIR'S SECRET HEIR
THE MOST EXPENSIVE LIE OF ALL
DUTY AT WHAT COST?
Available now!

'You're untemptable, right? Your absolute rejection of any physical intimacy is cowardly.'

'In what way?' Antonio asked icily, his words sharply enunciated. 'Doesn't it denote self-control?'

Something burned in his eyes now, but Bella was too hurt to take heed and too hurt to stop herself lashing out. 'Maybe you're afraid that once you start you won't be able to stop.'

Silence strained for two beats, before he broke it with a soft-spoken, hard-hitting whisper. 'You want me to prove it?'

He didn't move a muscle, but somehow he made the room smaller. The subtlest change in his tone, the darkening in his eyes put her senses on alert. He'd gone from angered to something else altogether. Something more dangerous.

Goosebumps rose on her skin, but deep down satisfaction flickered. 'You don't have to prove anything to me.'

He walked closer, until he loomed in front of her. She held her ground and watched.

Dared.

These powerful princes request your presence before

The Throne of San Felipe

Destined for the crown, tempted to rebel!

Crown Prince Antonio and his wayward brother Prince Eduardo have grown up in the shadow of the San Felipe throne. Now, with their royal destinies fast approaching, the rebel Princes must choose their path.

They've always resisted expectation, so the kingdom waits with bated breath to discover if the San Felipe heirs will be dictated to by duty or ruled by desire…

The Secret That Shocked De Santis
The Mistress That Tamed De Santis

Available now from Mills & Boon Modern Romance

THE MISTRESS
THAT TAMED
DE SANTIS

BY
NATALIE ANDERSON

Published in Great Britain 2016
By Mills & Boon, an imprint of HarperCollins*Publishers*
1 London Bridge Street, London, SE1 9GF

© 2016 Natalie Anderson

ISBN: 978-0-263-92130-4

Printed and bound in Spain
by CPI, Barcelona

Natalie Anderson adores a happy ending—which is why she always reads the back of a book first. Just to be sure. So you can be sure you've got a happy ending in your hands right now—because she promises nothing less. Along with happy endings she loves peppermint-filled dark chocolate, pineapple juice and extremely long showers. Not to mention spending hours teasing her imaginary friends with dating dilemmas. She tends to torment them before eventually relenting and offering—you guessed it—a happy ending. She lives in Christchurch, New Zealand, with her gorgeous husband and four fabulous children.

If, like her, you love a happy ending, be sure to come and say hi on facebook.com/authornataliea, follow @authornataliea on Twitter, or visit her website/blog: natalie-anderson.com.

Books by Natalie Anderson

Mills & Boon Modern Romance

Tycoon's Terms of Engagement
Whose Bed Is It Anyway?
The Right Mr Wrong
Blame It on the Bikini
Waking Up in the Wrong Bed
First Time Lucky?

The Throne of San Felipe

The Secret That Shocked De Santis

Visit the Author Profile page at millsandboon.co.uk for more titles.

For my husband and family,
and for the laughter we share.

CHAPTER ONE

CROWN PRINCE ANTONIO DE SANTIS strolled along the dark street, savouring the stolen moment of freedom as he walked off the burn from the last eighty minutes in the palace gym.

Silence. Solitude. Darkness. Peace.

He checked the hood of his sweatshirt still hid most of his face. He'd soon have to turn back. In less than an hour this road would be crawling with workers frantically finishing preparations and testing the barricades they'd installed over the last day. The crowds would gather early too. San Felipe's car rally was prestigious, hotly contested and the starting gun for the annual carnival, which meant Antonio's next couple of weeks were even more packed than usual. State balls, trade meetings, society events, the carnival celebrations required a round-the-clock royal presence as the world's wealthy and glamorous came to indulge and experience his country's beauty. And with his younger brother away, Crown Prince Antonio was the only royalty on offer.

He'd do it all anyway; he always did.

He approached an intersection. The road to the left headed into the heart of the city and was the enter-

tainment 'strip'—lined with restaurants and bars that
would soon be packed for race action. He glanced up
at the ornate exterior of the former firehouse on the
corner—the latest building to have been reclaimed
and refurbished into a hot night spot. But after only
a week of business, the city's residents were debating the merits of this particular establishment more
than any other.

BURN.

The four bronze letters bolted to the wall screamed
both defiance and demand. He read it as a blatant statement of intent—she was here, she didn't care, and she
didn't intend to hide.

Antonio frowned. Suddenly the window just ahead
was flung wide open. The shutter banged on the wall
right beside him. If he'd been one pace on, he'd have
been knocked out cold on the pavement.

He halted. Even with the relaxed rules in carnival
season, the club ought to be closed at this hour. He
glanced into the open window, expecting to see a few
intoxicated patrons still partying, but no noise streamed
out. No endless thud, thud, thud of drum and bass. No
high-pitched giggles, loud laughs or low murmurs. It
seemed there was no one in the vast room—until something white silently flashed in the deep recesses. He
looked closer, tracking the fast-moving creature as the
white flashed again. The woman wore a loose white
top and…nothing else? The most basic instinct had
him locking on her legs—unbelievably long legs that
right now were moving unbelievably fast.

Pyjamas. *Short* pyjamas.

His suddenly slushy brain slowly reached a conclusion. She opened another window down the side of the

room and turned again. She wore ballet flats on her feet, not for fashion, but for function, dancing across the floor—spinning so quickly her auburn hair swirled in a curling ribbon behind her. She leapt and landed near the window on the opposite side of the room and opened that one with another dramatic, effervescent gesture before turning yet again. That was when he saw her face properly for the first time.

She was smiling. Not one of the usual sorts of smiles Antonio received—not awed or nervous or curious or come-hitherish… This smile was so full of raw joy it made him feel he should step back into the darkness, but he couldn't find the will to turn away.

Heat kicked hard in his gut.

Anger. Not lust. *Never* lust.

He'd have to have spent the last six months living under a rock not to know she'd moved to San Felipe. Given he ruled the island principality, he knew exactly who she was and why she was here. And he didn't give a damn that she was even more stunning in real life than in any of the pictures saturating the Internet. Bella Sanchez was here to cause trouble. And Antonio didn't want trouble in San Felipe.

Nor did he want Bella Sanchez.

He didn't want anyone.

Yet here he was with his feet glued to the pavement, watching her whirl her way round the room with glorious abandon, from one window to the next in flying leaps until she'd opened them all.

She executed another series of dizzying spins across the floor, and suddenly stopped—positioned smack bang in the centre of the window frame he was looking through.

'Enjoying the view?' Her smile had vanished and her voice dripped with sarcasm.

When he didn't move, she glided closer, her feline green eyes like lasers. She wasn't even breathless as she stared him down like a Fury about to wreak revenge on a miscreant.

Antonio's reflexes snapped. She thought she could shame him into scuttling away? Another hit of heat made him clench his muscles. He pushed back the hood of his sweatshirt and coolly gazed back up at her, grimly anticipating her recognition of him.

Her eyes widened instantly but she quickly schooled the shock from her face—her expression smoothing until she became inscrutable. Somehow she stood taller. She had the straightest back of anyone he'd ever seen.

'Your Highness,' she said crisply. 'May I help you with something?'

Unfortunately he couldn't reply; his tongue was cleaved to the roof of his mouth. How could she look this radiant so early in the morning? She had to have had an extremely late night and yet here she was without a scrap of make-up on, looking intolerably beautiful.

Antonio actively avoided being alone with women—especially models, actresses and socialites—but, given his single status and Crown Prince title, they littered his path and made their play nonetheless. Over the past few years he'd met hundreds, if not thousands, of stunning, willing women. He'd refused every single one.

But none had ever looked as gorgeous as Bella Sanchez did right now. And none had looked as haughty.

At his continued silence, she stepped closer. 'You were spying on me?'

His anger sharpened. He'd avoided meeting *her* most of all and now she made him sound like a peeping Tom. No matter that in part he felt like one.

'It is past closing hours,' he said stiffly.

'You're policing me?' As she stared down at him that haughty barrier locked fully into place, leaching the last of the vitality in her eyes. 'The club is closed.'

Her English accent was muddied. He figured it was from the years she'd spent abroad and the mix of people in her life.

'I'm merely ventilating the rooms,' she explained.

'Getting rid of suspicious smells?' He'd heard the rumours and he wasn't going to ignore them.

A small smile emerged, nothing like the earlier one. 'This is a non-smoking venue, not some den of iniquity.'

'There are other vices,' he replied with calm consideration. 'Salvatore Accardi warned me this operation was going to bring San Felipe nothing but trouble.'

'He would know all about trouble.'

She didn't so much as blink as she snapped back her answer.

He'd wanted to see her reaction to his reference to Accardi—but he'd got almost none.

Salvatore Accardi, former Italian politician, had taken up permanent residence in his San Felipe holiday home. And Salvatore Accardi was reputedly Bella Sanchez's father.

Twenty-odd years ago she'd been born of scandal, supposedly the love child of the married Salvatore and his sex-symbol mistress. Their affair had been splashed across all the newspapers of the day. But Salvatore had never acknowledged Bella as his baby. He'd refused to undergo paternity testing. He'd stayed with his long-suffering wife, pregnant at the time, and raised their daughter, who'd been born a mere three months before Bella.

Bella had been raised in the public eye, eventually dancing professionally before becoming chatelaine of this party house in the heart of Antonio's principality. And according to Salvatore Accardi now, her presence would attract nothing but sleaze to San Felipe.

'Is it so terrible to provide a place for people to have fun?' Bella asked, shrugging one of her delicate shoulders. She looked slender, but strong.

Antonio frowned at the direction—distraction—of his thoughts.

'This isn't about that,' he said coldly. 'This is revenge. This is setting up so you're right in Accardi's face.'

'Is that what he told you?' Her poise cracked briefly as anger flashed. 'Do you honestly think you can believe everything—or *any*thing—he says?'

At a gut level Antonio had never much liked Salvatore Accardi, but nothing had ever been proven. All those rumours of corporate and political corruption had remained only rumours. And if the man had the personal morals of an alley cat, that was his own business. He'd owned property in San Felipe for too long for Antonio to find reason to require him to leave.

Just as there'd been no reason to refuse a work permit and residency to Bella Sanchez.

And didn't everyone have the right to be believed innocent until proven guilty?

In her white short pyjamas Bella looked both innocent and unbearably sensual, because that white cotton was thin and she wore nothing beneath it. And when she moved? He could see the outline of her slim waist and generous curves.

'I'm not sure a venue like this suits San Felipe,' he said tightly.

'As if there aren't other clubs?' she questioned softly but her gaze was sharp. She almost leaned out of the window frame, making him acutely aware of her unfettered breasts. 'This isn't a sex club. There are no pole dancers or strippers.' She lingered over her quiet words, but then her eyes glinted. 'Definitely no drugs in dodgy back-room deals.'

Her voice shook with fierceness. He knew her mother, Madeline Sanchez, one of the world's greatest 'mistresses' in a time when such things had been scandalous, had overdosed more than a year ago in a Parisian apartment. Everybody knew all there was to know about Bella Sanchez.

'This is a legitimate bar and dance floor,' she added more calmly. 'And I'm a responsible club owner.'

'You're young and inexperienced.' He paused pointedly. 'In managing a commercial enterprise, that is.'

Her eyes widened, for a split second she looked furious. But he watched the change as she controlled her emotions once more—the stiffening of that already ramrod-straight spine, her smile so different from the one earlier, the hint of calculation as she glanced at his casual attire.

He braced. She was sizing him up and about to fire her own shot. And oddly, he was looking forward to it.

She swept her arm across her body in a dramatic gesture, drawing his attention to her attributes once more. 'Why don't you come in and find out for yourself?' she invited in a sultry tone. 'Come inside and see if you can find anything wrong with my club.'

It was a blatant dare—she'd switched into 'Bella Sanchez, Sex Symbol' without skipping a beat.

But it wasn't *that* challenge that did it for him. Not that coy smile of sophisticated amusement. It was the emotion lurking in the backs of her eyes. The anger she was trying hard to control—that slight tremor in her fingers before she curled them into a fist.

'Yes.'

He said it because she didn't expect him to.

She thought he'd politely and coldly refuse, smile distantly and retreat, like the conservative Crown Prince he was. She'd called his bluff.

So he'd called hers. Because at this moment, he damn well felt like doing the last thing anyone—least of all her—expected.

And she hadn't expected it. Her shock flashed for one satisfying second.

He waited while she unbolted the heavy door, opened it and stepped aside for him to enter. He paused just inside the room, watching as she closed the door and marched around him to lead the way.

'No suspicious smells, see,' she said pointedly. 'Nothing illegal.'

The ground-floor space was sleek and smelled clean, not yet permeated with the lingering, less than fragrant scent of five hundred sweaty clubbers dancing there night after night.

He glanced up—away from the back view of her never-ending legs—and saw the decadent wallpaper and the wrought-iron railings protecting patrons who wanted to party on the mezzanine floor. The chandeliers gleamed even this early in the morning. He hadn't been in a nightclub in a decade. He'd been crowned in his early twenties, but had been aware of the restraints on his behaviour for years before that. He'd always been dutiful. He'd had to be.

Only now he felt the stirrings of a desire he'd buried deep all those years ago. When *had* he last danced?

'You'll want to see the liquor licence.' She stalked over to the main bar. 'And there it is, exactly where it should be. The emergency exits are well marked,' she added, all officiousness. 'It was formerly a fire station, you know.'

He did know. But there'd be no putting out the fire in her eyes.

'The rest of the paperwork is upstairs,' she said defiantly, turning to face him.

'So lead the way,' he answered bluntly. He was committed now.

For a split second her shock was visible again.

Yes, Crown Prince Antonio would never ordinarily go up into the back room of a notorious nightclub in the sole company of a supposedly scandalous siren… but he felt like doing it just to see that reaction again.

He suppressed a smile as he followed her to one of the winding staircases that were like pillars at each side of the room. But as he climbed behind her his amusement faded.

He hadn't been so alone with a woman so barely attired in years. And it shouldn't have been a problem now. Except her legs went on for ever. He tried to tear his attention from them. Failed. Was relieved when they reached the mezzanine and she darted ahead to open another window. She then headed to a small alcove that hid a door marked 'Private'.

Another flight of stairs.

This time he gave in to the temptation to look. She would never know. But there was the faintest flush on her porcelain cheeks as she waited for him to walk into her office.

The top floor was clearly her private space and very different from the dark and sensual decor of the club downstairs. This room was lighter, with white walls and a cream rug covering the floorboards. A large desk dominated the room. A laptop sat open on it, paper files spread beside it. A filing cabinet was behind the desk, while a couple of chairs sat at angles in front of it. But Antonio remained standing because there was another door—open—through which he could see a small kitchenette. And given she was wearing pyjamas, he figured it was safe to assume there was a bed in there too. Tension hit. This had been a mistake. And Antonio couldn't afford any mistakes.

Bella stared. Crown Prince Antonio De Santis had accepted her challenge and was standing in her small office. She'd thought he'd decline, all unbending regal politeness. But it seemed he really had chosen this morning to inspect her business—obscenely early, name-dropping the man who refused to acknowledge her and dressed like *that*.

She'd recognised him the second he'd pulled back the hood of his sweatshirt but he looked nothing like the austere Crown Prince she'd seen on screens and in magazines. That man was tall and broad-shouldered, with not a hair out of place and almost always dressed in an immaculate midnight-blue suit. Perfect for the reserved, always polite but distant Prince.

The man in front of her now hadn't shaved. His hair was mussed. He must have been out running or something what with the old sweatshirt, track pants and trainers he was wearing. And the edge she'd glimpsed in his eyes? She never would have expected that. Nor would she have expected to feel breathless and hot in his company. Not so hyper-aware.

She never felt that around any guy.

'You'll find everything is in there.' She opened the file and turned it so he could read it, reading it upside down herself. She wanted him to see every single piece of paper and be satisfied and leave as soon as possible. She wasn't going down without a fight. She'd prove to all her doubters that she could manage this club. She'd prove it to *him*.

So never mind that she was in her shortie pyjamas, her top slightly too loose and with no bra beneath, because she couldn't be embarrassed. Never mind that she'd only managed two hours' sleep because she had so much to do. The club had been open only a week and, while it looked promising, she had a long, long way to go before it could be declared a success and she could sell up and start up the business of her heart.

But he didn't say anything about the paperwork. She glanced up and caught him staring at her. Again.

She was used to men looking. They all wanted the same thing, right? They all thought they knew everything there was to know about her. But the ice in this man's eyes was something else. It burned.

He stood silent. Guarded. *Judging*.

She'd not expected that from San Felipe's broken,

beloved Prince. Wasn't he supposed to hide a wounded heart? Wasn't he supposed to be kind and benevolent under the weight of all that duty?

Everyone knew his story. His 'One True Love' had tragically died of cancer barely two months after his coronation and the accident that had claimed the lives of both his parents. He'd not been linked to another woman since. The Prince had buried his heart with his girlfriend. And, according to the glossy mags, the nation believed only the love of a pure and perfect woman could heal him and bring him happiness...

That woman clearly wasn't her given he was looking at her like *that*.

Forbidding. Disapproving.

Thrown off balance, she felt goaded into provoking a reaction from him. Beneath the fifty feet of ice he hid behind, it had to be there—emotion of *some* kind.

She should have been intimidated. She should have remained polite. She should have respected the power he held. But she was too tired. And too hurt.

'Why are you staring at me like I've forgotten something?' She stepped out from her desk. 'Should I have curtseyed as you walked in?' She lifted her chin at his utter impassivity. 'Should I get on my knees before you?'

She regretted the sultry taunt the second she'd uttered it.

Because there was no reaction. He didn't move a muscle. Didn't speak a word. Just kept, ever so coolly, regarding her.

Her cheeks burned as shame grew. She'd been everything the world expected her to be—a scandalous, tarty temptress. But she was a big fat faker.

And he wasn't. He really was as frozen-hearted as they said. And every bit as breathtaking.

'You're going to have to do better than that,' he finally said. 'Do you think you're the first woman to try seducing me by stripping and dancing in front of me?'

His words hit like hailstones.

'I didn't strip.'

'Only because you didn't bother getting dressed properly.'

'And I didn't dance for you.' She ignored his interruption. 'I was just warming up alone. You're the one who stopped to watch. You could have kept walking, Tony.'

For a split second she got a reaction—his jaw dropped. Before he snapped it shut and then shot his words like bullets.

'What did you just call me?'

'Tony,' she repeated, refusing to back down. 'Crown Prince Antonio is too much of a mouthful.'

There was a pause, then his gaze skittered down her body—so deliberately. 'Too much of a mouthful,' he echoed slowly.

This time *Bella's* jaw dropped. Did he say that while scoping out her breasts? Which, yes, were on the fuller side. Especially for a dancer.

Crossing his arms, he continued to regard her, making her feel uncharacteristically vulnerable. His complete attention wasn't like any ordinary audience of thousands. His scrutiny was way more intense.

'I've seen it all, every artifice, every attempt to attract me,' he muttered. 'It won't work.'

'Because we're all out to entrap you?' she asked, shocked at his direct approach. 'You think I'm trying to use my feminine wiles to draw you in? Because you're the biggest prize?'

'Aren't you?' he answered, cocking his head. 'Or are you just trying to provoke me? You want to win a reaction from "the Ice Prince",' he mocked. 'Because you're all about getting the reaction.'

She drew breath at the accuracy of his hit.

'I've had every kind of play,' he continued with a quietness that belied the edge to his words. 'The sympathy, simpering agreement and the bitchy comebacks of the treat-me-mean kind…there's nothing I haven't seen or heard, so don't bother.'

Anger rushed along her veins, scalding her skin. 'You think I want you anywhere near me?'

His lips twisted in a coolly mocking look and he didn't bother to answer.

'You're unbelievably arrogant,' she said.

'You think?'

Yes, she did. But swirling beneath the frost-covered atmosphere was elemental attraction at its most basic. He was appallingly attractive—her body yearned to get closer to his. And when he didn't back away from her challenge?

Primitive instinct could be a powerful thing. But she had more of a brain than that. So her basic instinct could go bury itself back in the cave it had been dwelling in for the last three years.

'I have no desire to attract you,' she declared passionately. Totally meaning every word. 'This isn't some *ploy* with which I hope to gain your grace or favour or sexual interest. You do not interest me in the least.'

'You interest me,' he said softly, slicing the ground from under her.

Sensual awareness feathered over her skin.

'Why San Felipe?' He stepped closer. 'Why now?'

Her heart stopped beating as she looked up into his blue eyes. For a second he actually looked human— as if he actually cared. And for a second she longed to open up and just be honest.

But as if she could ever tell him. When he'd so arrogantly assumed she wanted to land herself a princely lover? When he chose to listen to the father who'd always refused to recognise her?

He'd be just another man who denied her.

She wanted him to leave but she couldn't tear her gaze from his. She'd thought she could handle anything. But she wasn't sure she could handle him.

He reached out as if to take her hand. 'Why now, Bella?'

Abruptly she turned to avoid his touch.

'Careful—'

His warning came too late. As she whirled to escape her weak ankle went and she stumbled, catching her thigh on the corner of her desk.

Antonio winced at the grimace of pain on Bella's face as she grabbed the desk to stop herself falling down. She'd gashed her leg, just above her knee. As he looked close he saw a long, jagged scar running in a wonky line up her shin.

She paled, her lips pressed together to mute any sound of pain.

It had been so long since he'd had any kind of physical comfort. Or offered any. He'd almost forgotten how. 'Bella?'

'It's fine.' She straightened and drew in a deep breath.

'I'm sure,' he replied, but he knew it wasn't.

'Wouldn't want you thinking this was another ploy.'

'It is my fault you fell,' he said stiffly, his hands at his side, wanting to help her yet feeling oddly impotent.

'You feel responsible? Rest easy, I won't sue you.' Her lips compressed. 'It's no more damaged than it already was.'

'It still needs dressing.' Blood was already oozing from the small wound. 'You have a first-aid kit?'

'Of course.' She didn't move.

He sighed at her reluctance. 'I need to see it. Or I'll revoke your operating licence.'

She gritted her teeth and limped behind her desk. His irritation smouldered. She really didn't want him to help. Was that because he'd really offended her or because he'd struck too close to the mark?

She *had* been trying to get a rise out of him, but she hadn't meant the vampish 'on her knees' offer—not when she'd jumped to get away from him.

She clutched the small container but he held out his hand. Sending him a death look, she passed it to him. Antonio bit back the smile of satisfaction and opened the lid.

'Lean on the desk,' he told her.

'This isn't necessary.'

He wasn't used to repeating instructions. He glanced up and her stormy expression clashed with his. 'Lean on the desk.'

Slowly, stiffly, she rested her body back.

'Thank you,' he said, ultra-politely.

He knelt at her feet, inwardly grimacing at the irony given her provocative remark only moments ago.

He knew an injury had ended her professional career. In the last decade Antonio had attended the ballet only out of duty but he could appreciate the strength and commitment it would have taken Bella to reach the level she had.

Her body was still incredibly athletic. This close he could smell her light, floral scent. It made him think of summer sun, not endless nights in a darkened dance club. In his mind's eye he saw her on the floor, bumping and grinding up close to her patrons. He gritted his teeth. Not jealous. And *not* aroused.

He was *not* aroused by her.

He wasn't like all the other red-blooded men in the world. He didn't have time to be. He didn't have the right. But just at this moment, he was every *inch* a mere man.

'Do you dance your way through all your tasks?' he asked, trying to distract himself from her sweet scent and delicate skin. He dabbed the blood and prepped a plaster as quickly as he could, not touching any part of her beyond necessary.

'Is that a serious question?' she mumbled.

'Yes.' Satisfied with how the plaster neatly covered the gash, he glanced up to read her expression. She was sitting unnaturally still—apparently holding her breath.

She met his gaze with those deep green eyes that were now almost liquid. 'You want to know if I dance while brushing my teeth?'

He inwardly smiled at the image. 'I bet you brush in time to the music playing in your head.'

Her eyes widened and *her* smile broke free—her

full mouth softened and her eyes sparkled. She looked fresh and beautiful and bright.

Heat flared from flicker to flame, urging him to touch those lush curving lips—

He jerked to his feet and stepped away before he did something colossally stupid.

'Have you been out drinking?'

He turned at the bitterness in her tone and saw her smile had vanished.

'I don't drink,' he said simply.

'No vices at all?' she mocked. 'No sex, right?'

That speculation was correct. It had been years since he'd had a lover. He was only about duty: to serve his country and to protect his people. *All* of them—dead and alive. That was his penance.

'And no drinking,' she added. 'I guess that just leaves drugs.'

'None of those either.'

'Fast cars?'

He shook his head. 'The Crown Prince cannot be injured or killed in a car accident. That can't happen in San Felipe again.' His parents' tragedy had cut the nation too deeply.

'So you're reduced to *watching*.' Storms gathered in her eyes.

'If you wanted privacy you would have kept your curtains closed,' he answered abruptly. 'But you didn't, because you like to be watched. You've made a career out of it.'

Anger flashed in her face. Before she could reply a short melody burst through the charged atmosphere. Then again. And again. His damn cell phone.

'Are you going to answer that or would you like me

to?' Those temptress tones returned—but so shaky this time.

She was trying to goad him again, using her voice, her eyes, her femininity to bring a man to his knees.

Not this man. He wasn't that weak.

Yet she knew that already. And that was the twist. She expected him to pull away—she wanted to drive him further back because she didn't want him too close. Because *his* nearness bothered *her*.

That realisation shocked him. His body had already betrayed him. She was so damn beautiful, for the first time in years his desire was stirred.

'It's my security team.' He cleared the frog from his throat and ignored the call.

'I'm amazed they let you wander the streets alone,' she said dryly.

'They know exactly where I am.'

Her eyebrows lifted. 'You told them you were coming here?'

'GPS.' His watch was tracked. It even had a silent emergency alarm button. Very spy film but he'd had to agree to it to get his morning walks alone.

'Your every movement is accounted for? So you're like a prisoner on electronic monitoring?'

'The concept is not dissimilar. They're concerned because I've not returned to the palace by my usual time.' He pulled the phone from his pocket as it began to ring again. If he didn't reply to this next call, a security team would be on its way in seconds.

'A change in the usual routine,' she drawled. 'Heaven forbid.'

'Yet here you are, doing the same warm-up dance routine you've been doing for years,' he answered blandly. 'We are creatures of habit, just doing what we usually do.'

Like falling back on old defences.

But as he read the message from his security chief he tensed. He double-checked the time on the screen— how had twenty minutes passed so quickly? He crossed the room to glance out of the window. In the space of a few minutes, the world had changed.

Outside people were lining the barricaded street, already standing two to three deep. He'd been so engrossed in dealing with Bella he hadn't heard the crowds gathering.

Swiftly he stepped back. To be seen inside Bella Sanchez's apartment at this hour of the morning would be unacceptable. But to be seen leaving it even worse. Especially given his unshaven, dishevelled appearance. The world would think he'd had another kind of workout altogether.

His gut burned.

Was this *want*? It had been so damn long since he'd wanted any woman. Clenching the phone in his fist, he faced her. She'd stilled, listening to the rising clamour outside. Given the way her features had tightened, the realisation the world had woken wasn't good news for her either.

'It seems it is your lucky day,' he muttered, feeling like provoking her the way she had him. 'I will have to remain here.'

Her eyes widened. 'For how long?'

Until his team could work out a subtle extraction plan. 'Until they've all gone home.'

'But that race won't finish for another six hours!'

Her obvious discomfort gave him a macabre pleasure. That she didn't want him near echoed his own unwanted feelings.

But he looked at her, outwardly unmoved. 'What do you suggest we do to pass the time?'

CHAPTER TWO

BELLA STARED. HE was joking, wasn't he? But Prince Antonio never joked; he looked as straight up serious and remote as ever. Worse, if anything.

'Why can't you leave now?' She still didn't understand why he was here at all.

He stepped further from the window, looking at his phone as it buzzed again. 'The crowds outside are already too big.'

'They love their Crown Prince. They'll be happy to see you.' He could do no wrong in his people's eyes.

'I'm not prepared for a meet and greet at this point in time.' He quickly sent a text.

'Because you're not in one of your navy suits? The track pants aren't all bad…' In the baggy hoodie he looked younger and more approachable than in any of the stills she'd seen. In fact dressed like this he looked alarmingly attractive. 'A prince at leisure—'

He glanced up and her words died in her throat. It finally dawned on her why he refused to leave.

'You don't want them to see you here,' she said. 'With me.'

He didn't answer. Didn't need to. She could see it all over his icy expression.

He was loath to be seen anywhere near her. Why? Did he think she could taint him in some way?

That hurt where she was most vulnerable. No one—not her old dance company, not her ex-boyfriend, not even her own *father*—wanted to claim a personal connection to her. Only those wanting instant Internet fame wanted to be caught near her. And as if that were what he wanted. Like her, Crown Prince Antonio De Santis had been born famous, but he was legitimately so—whereas she?

He steadily held her gaze. That unnerving reserve made her too aware of him, but she refused to let him silence her with little more than a stare. Not now or ever.

'You think it would damage your reputation to be seen exiting my club at this hour of the morning?' Her voice shook and she drew in a sharp breath. 'Maybe it would *enhance* it.'

He still didn't answer but his demeanour changed. He might be wearing worn workout gear, but now he looked every inch the powerful 'Head of State'. Clothes made no difference. Nothing could pierce that princely aura. Bella's anger flared. He was so protected, whereas she?

'No one would believe anything "untoward" of you. But me?' She laughed bitterly. 'I'm the vixen, right? But surely not even wicked little Bella Sanchez could trap Prince Antonio with her wiles…'

It was what he'd accused her of attempting only moments before. And he was right, it was laughable. Scathing, she stepped closer; her words tumbled unchecked, unthinking.

'I don't know why you're so worried,' she snarled.

'You're untemptable, right? You're the frigid Prince.'
She took no notice of his sudden frown or the muscle
jerking in his jaw; his wordless judgment had unleashed
the banked-up bitterness of so many betrayals. 'Your
absolute rejection of any physical intimacy is cowardly.'

Just as hiding here for hours would be cowardly.

And dangerous for her.

'In what way?' he asked icily, his words sharply
enunciated. 'Doesn't it denote self-control?'

Something burned in his eyes now, but she was too
hurt to take heed and too hurt to stop herself lashing
out. 'Maybe you're afraid that once you start, you won't
be able to stop.'

He said nothing. He didn't need to. His rigidity
screamed irritation and arrogance.

'Everyone loses control some time,' she taunted.
She'd seen it every night since she'd opened the club.
People got carried away. Just as she was now. But she
didn't care.

'Not me,' he finally countered.

'Because you're a robot?' she scoffed. 'You're just a
prince—that doesn't give you super powers.'

Silence strained for two beats before he broke it
with a soft-spoken, hard-hitting whisper. 'You want
me to prove it?'

He didn't move a muscle, but somehow he made
the room smaller. The subtlest change in his tone, the
darkening in his eyes put her senses on alert. He'd gone
from angered, to something else altogether. Something
more dangerous.

Goosebumps rose on her skin, but deep down satisfaction flickered. 'You don't have to prove anything
to me.'

'Don't I? When you've taken it upon yourself to judge me so completely?'

'You'd judged me before you even crossed my threshold,' she pointed out with relish. 'And you collude with other people's judgments when you react with concern about being seen in my company.'

'You're mistaken in many ways.' He frowned. 'I'm not a robot. And no, I don't have super powers. But I don't lose control, Bella.'

He walked closer, until he loomed in front of her. She held her ground and watched. *Dared.*

'I can start,' he promised with wintry imperiousness. 'And then stop.'

'Start what?' she taunted again.

'You're Bella Sanchez,' he murmured. 'You live for kisses and adoration.'

That stung. Her mother's reputation had stained her own from the start. Men assumed that as she'd inherited her mother's figure, she'd have her 'skills' too. But her mother had been discarded by every one of her many lovers. Which was partly why Bella was *not* the lover of anyone bold enough to make a move. And the truth was she was unmoved. Always.

She should shake him off with some glib retort and a smile and make her escape from a situation like this the way she'd done many times before. Or she should tell him exactly where to go and why.

'What if I don't want you to kiss me?' she asked, determinedly standing in place despite the adrenalin rush urging her to run.

'Don't you?' He laughed then. A low, sexy, mocking laugh.

That he'd laughed at all was a shock, but that he

laughed like that? She just gazed at him, stunned by this glimpse of someone else altogether—a gorgeous virile man.

His smile disappeared as he neared, but there was still that glimpse of human behind the pale blue. 'You are beautiful.'

Beneath that clinical assessment she heard huskiness. Heat washed over her, confusing her more.

'Beauty isn't everything,' she pointed out.

Glossy magazines and plastic surgeons would argue otherwise, but Bella knew the truth. Beauty faded. Beauty depended on who was looking. Beauty didn't count for anything at the end of the day.

'No,' he agreed softly.

The atmosphere thickened, building the tension both within her and between them. She wanted to duck and run. She already knew she wouldn't feel anything if he kissed her. She never felt anything. That was the point. She'd tried but she wasn't the hedonist the world wanted her to be. In ten seconds it would be obvious who the frigid one was. He'd know her secret. She gritted her teeth, angered by that old humiliation.

'Go on, then,' she finally snapped. 'Try it and see what happens.'

'Such an invitation,' he mocked.

'You're hardly bounding over with unbridled lust.'

'I don't do unbridled lust, remember?' He regarded her intently. 'You're not going to drive me crazy.'

It was almost as if he was challenging himself. Not her.

'I don't want to drive anyone crazy,' she retorted. 'People ought to take responsibility for their own actions.'

She just wanted to do her own thing. She hadn't asked to be raised in the glare of paparazzi flashes. Yes, she'd chosen the ballet stage, but it wasn't supposed to have intruded into her personal life as much. And now she did all that Internet sharing only to build something for the future—funding her escape route.

'Indeed they should.' He gripped her waist, his hands not too high or too low or too tight. He didn't step closer so there was a clear two inches between them. He held her in the position perfect for a formal dance. But they weren't in a ballroom. They were yards from her tiny bedroom.

Heart thudding, Bella fisted her hands and held them to her stomach, but she couldn't bring herself to say *stop*. Instinctively she knew that if she did, he would. But she was curious to see how far perfect Prince Antonio would take this. She kept her eyes open, focusing intently on him. It was a trick she'd learned when amorous dates had moved closer than she'd wanted. Guys didn't like to think they weren't wowing a woman with their sensual prowess.

But Antonio kept his eyes open too. As he inclined his head she found herself sinking into their surprising depths—they were such a pale blue, but there was an echo of that smile glinting in the backs of them. That smile was what she really wanted more of.

He pressed his lips to hers in the lightest caress, offering less than a heartbeat of touch. But it delivered a lightning flash of heat. Bella froze, teetering on the edge of something unknown, so tempted to tumble over—but he didn't take her there. He didn't touch her again.

He remained a breath away but she couldn't fathom his feelings in his unreadable eyes.

Finally it dawned on her that he had no feelings. He'd been teasing her. He'd intended to give her nothing but that chaste peck all along. Perfectly, bloodlessly executed. Any second now he'd step back and say, 'I told you so'. He was utterly in control at all times.

Disappointment spilled into that vast, empty space in her chest. She really shouldn't feel it, she really shouldn't care, she should concede his victory with laughing grace and push him away.

But she'd felt a glimmer of what might have been— a sliver of heat that had stunned her with its strength.

So she could only stay still, unable to move for thinking—for *feeling*. His eyes were so damn mesmerising but now she couldn't bear to look into them any more. Yet when she dropped her gaze, she saw his sensual mouth and his chiselled jaw roughened with morning stubble. He was picture-postcard perfect and it was so unfair because for one millisecond she'd actually *wanted*—

His fingers tightened, pinching her waist. She looked up in surprise but before she could speak his lips brushed hers again. Another soft, too brief—tantalising—caress. She got the smallest glimpse into his eyes before he bent to her again. His reserve crumbled as intensity flared. Her heart stopped at that flash of emotion.

When he kissed her that third time, he lingered. She lifted her chin, meeting him, her body instinctively yearning for him to stay. She wanted more—a *real* kiss. She wanted him to release the energy she sensed building within him and ease the need starting to ache within her. She wanted more of the magic she'd tasted in that first swift touch. She wanted more than disillusionment and emptiness and abandonment all over again. She just wanted *more*.

For the first time in her life, she *really* wanted it.

He didn't disappoint her this time. He stayed. He held. He kissed. His lips moved from gentle, to more insistent, to finally demanding. As she acquiesced, parting her mouth, his demands grew greater still. His hands shifted, shaping her curves and then possessively pulling her closer. Her heart struck up again, sprinting to a frantic tempo—in shock. In passion. She wriggled her hands from where they'd been squashed between them and reached up to his shoulders so she could literally hang on as he bent her backwards and kissed her more thoroughly still.

Oh, he kissed her. Her eyes drifted shut as she focused on the pressure of his lips—the teasing pleasure. His kiss lightened and she gripped his shoulders more tightly, afraid he was about to pull away. But he kissed her again and again in a series that mimicked that first—softly stirring desire, building her frustration until she couldn't control the small moan that escaped. Then he kissed her hard and long again. And he repeated the pattern—unpredictable, maddening. Delicious.

She'd never have expected Prince Antonio to be as playful. Or as skilled. But what did it matter when he made her feel like *this*?

She moaned in pleasure as he kissed her deeply again. It was as if all the empty places within her were

being filled and heated and the sensation was so addictive. There was pure pleasure to be had in his arms.
The kind she'd never experienced with anyone else.

Breathless, she wanted to say something, but
couldn't. She didn't want to break the magic—uncaring
of any consequences, of how crazy this had suddenly
become. She just wanted to feel it—all of him—all of
the gratification she could get. Instinctively she moved,
circling her hips. His hand slid, pressing over the curve
of her bottom and pulling her harder against the heat
of his pelvis. Feeling how aroused he was made her
melt all the more into his embrace.

His arms tightened around her but she didn't resist
as he walked her backwards and then pushed her back
against the desk. She couldn't remain standing anyway
and she had no desire to stop. She only wanted more.
Just here. Now. In this white-hot moment.

He shoved the files behind her to the floor with a
sweep of his arm, pushed her back until she lay on the
hard wood, and followed her down.

He kissed down the side of her neck, burying his
mouth in that sensitive spot where her neck met her
shoulders. His hand slid beneath her light pyjama top.
The sensation of skin on skin made her arch involuntarily. His hand was heavy, then light, teasing as he
traced small circles over her abdomen, up to her ribs,
then higher still. She shivered as he neared the hard
peak of her breast. He lifted his head from hers, breaking the kiss to look into her eyes. He didn't look down
as he lifted her top to expose her breasts. She felt the
cool air, felt her nipples tighten more—until they were
almost painful. She licked her dried lips as she waited,

splayed on the desk beneath him, until he looked down at her partially naked body.

A groan ripped from him when he finally looked. She looked down too, saw how her breasts thrust up towards him, her nipples tight and needy and erect—begging for more than his visual attention. They wanted touch. He muttered something unintelligible. Before she could ask him what he'd said he bent his head and took her nipple in the hot cavern of his mouth. Her breathing came quick and erratic as she watched him take pleasure in her body—in pleasuring *her*.

She closed her eyes, sprawled back on the desk, basking in the sensations as he explored her more fully. He pushed between her legs, grinding against her, and cupped her other breast in his hand, his fingers teasing that taut peak. When he pushed her full breasts together to lave both nipples with his tongue, she almost arched off the wood completely. All her restraints were now off, her need unleashed. She bucked, thrusting her hips against his, wanting him to strip her, touch her and kiss her where she was hot and wet and so, so ready.

Never had she been ready for a man the way she was for him. Never had a man made her feel this aroused. The ache between her legs burned, her blood ran faster in a quickening beat of need. She reached out, wanting to explore him too. His skin was hot to the touch. His jaw bristled but it was so good as it gently abraded her tender skin. She raked her hands across his back, the heat of him burning through his sweatshirt.

His muscularity surprised her. He was only ever pictured in suits so she'd never have guessed he'd be this defined. Granite muscles like these meant he worked out—regularly and hard. She wanted to see them. Wanted to touch. But he pressed down, smothering her attempts to pull his sweatshirt up, distracting her from that goal by simply kissing her again and again and again while running his hands over her bared breasts with wicked skill.

And she couldn't resist succumbing to the pleasure of it.

That it could be this man who pulled this feeling from her? This unadulterated *lust*. He left no room for regret or reason. There was only this, only now. His breathing roughened but he said nothing more. He kissed down her neck, then lower to tease with fiery touches across her quivering belly, then back up to her breasts. But his hand worked lower, slipping beneath the waistband of her flimsy short pyjama bottoms. She parted her legs further without thinking about it, aching for him to touch her there. He growled guttural approval as his fingers cupped her intimately. She shuddered at the intensity of desire that consumed her as he gently stroked. She was so close. The pleasure built so shockingly quickly. She'd never been so close with anyone.

'Antonio…' She breathed the quietest plea as she arched against him, right on the edge.

He froze, then glanced up to look into her eyes for a heartbeat. Dazed, she didn't register his tormented expression. But then he pulled away from her, his face now utterly impassive.

'You're stopping?' She gasped in disbelief. *'Now?'*

His lips twisted but he didn't reply. Running his hand through his hair, he huffed out a harsh breath and stepped back from her.

Astonished, she stared, realising what he'd done. He'd done this to prove a petty point. And he'd proved it already. But it was also a punishment. He was putting her in her place in a humiliating show of power—he could have her any way he wanted, however he chose.

But now he chose not to.

That he'd use his sensual dominance over her this way was most especially cruel because she'd never felt anything like this. No man had made her *want* in this way and this one time she'd almost felt pure, sensual pleasure, it had been snatched from her. She swept her hand over her belly, as if she could press away the ache deep inside.

'I don't need you,' she muttered angrily. So hurt. 'I don't need *any* man.' She didn't need any *one*.

He turned back, his gaze smouldering. Her legs were still splayed. She was so exposed, half-stripped and spread on her own damn desk for him to toy with but she refused to cover up and show how shamed she felt.

'What are you doing?' His words sounded raw and accusing.

She realised he was staring at her hand pressed low on her belly. Bitterness rose in her throat. Because yes, the only way she'd ever experienced an orgasm was by her own action. But as if she'd do that now?

Heat burned in his narrowed eyes. Outrage burned in her. She wasn't giving him the pleasure of *watching*. She curled her fingers into a fist, her vision swimming with acidic tears.

She heard his groan and a muttered word, but she didn't know what he said because suddenly he was there. Back where she needed him. Bending between her parted thighs, his spread hand raking up her body.

'It wouldn't be as good,' he muttered, leaning close, catching her gaze with his.

She tried to turn her head away but he moved too fast, holding her chin with a firm grip. He almost smiled as he moved closer.

This kiss was cautious and tender.

She didn't close her eyes and when he drew back a fraction to gauge her response, she kept glaring at him. But then he kissed one eyelid. Then the other. Making her close her eyes. Then he caught her mouth with his again. Not cautious at all. Not holding anything back. Just that passionate teasing, stirring her to react again. To want.

And heaven help her she did. So quickly she was there again, lost in the lust he roused within her. She couldn't wriggle away from him. Couldn't break the kiss. Rather she moaned in his mouth—a mixture of hurt and want and pleading.

In answer he slid his hand firmly over her stomach, wrapped his broad palm around her fist and lifted her arm, pressing it back on the desk beside her, clearing his path down her body. He cupped her breast, then teased his way lower again, to where she was still wet and hot and wanting. All the while his lips were sealed to hers, his tongue stroking and teasing and claiming her the way the rest of her wanted to be claimed.

She moaned again, nothing but want this time. She wanted him naked, wanted to touch him everywhere, wanted him to thrust deep inside her and ease this hellish ache. He didn't. He just teased—decadently, mercilessly until she was sweat-slicked and shivering and mindless.

She bucked against his hand—wanting faster,

deeper, more. He groaned in approval, kissing her harder, letting her feel more of his weight. She wanted to take it all. Her hips rocked, undulating in an increasing rhythm, matching the stroke of his fingers and tongue. She wanted to force him to break free of his control. She wanted him to stop holding back. She wanted him to just take her.

But he didn't relinquish his restraint for one second. He kept kissing her. Kept touching her where she needed him most. Stirring, rousing, until she was almost out of her mind with desire, until she was moaning a song of need into his mouth, her body trembling beneath his, her nails clawing into his skin as she hurtled towards the peak. Finally he broke the passionate kiss, letting her gasp as the rest of her arched, utterly rigid in that unbearable moment before release. Oh, it was here. He'd pulled her through the burn and made her feel it. Her eyes closed, she cried out as the wave of pleasure hit, sweeping her away in that powerful turbulent crest. She clutched him fiercely as the sensations tumbled within her, drowning her in almost unendurable bliss. He pressed hard against her as she convulsed, not letting her pull back from the intensity he'd stirred. His fingers rubbed relentlessly, ensuring she received every last spasm of pleasure from her orgasm.

Finally she fell back on the desk, limp as the warmth spread along her veins, sending her into a lax, dazed state. Raggedly she gasped, trying to recover her mind, but it was impossible to catch her breath. Impossible to wipe the smile from her face. Impossible to believe what had just happened.

Never had a man made her feel so good. It wasn't

just the orgasm, it was the heat and vitality he'd seemed to pour into her. He'd made her feel wholly alive, here and now. Twin tears escaped her closed eyes before she had the chance to brush them away but she was smiling at the same time, because it was so good and such a surprise and she was so happy.

Yet even now, despite that mind-blowing pleasure, the ache within burned anew. Suddenly she felt empty even with that elation still zinging around her. She wanted all of him. And she wanted him now.

Shocked at her surging hunger, she opened her eyes and looked into his.

'Antonio,' she whispered, shocked when she read what was so obvious in his unguarded expression. Torment—desolation and desperation. Feelings she understood all too well.

'Please.' She reached out to cup him—to make him feel as good as he'd made her feel. But he gripped her wrist and stopped her, his hand painfully tight.

'Don't touch me,' he ordered through clenched teeth.

His words hit like physical blows. It was utter, raw rejection.

She closed her eyes but his spurn had already slammed the lingering sense of pleasure from her. Emptiness ripped her open. Now their imbalance struck her forcefully. She was almost naked. He was fully clothed. She was vulnerable and exposed. He was sealed and silent.

But they were both angry.

He released her wrist, pulling away to put three feet of distance between them. He stopped and stood with his back to her, his hands on his hips, his head bowed. She could see the exertion in his breathing, as if he'd run a race to the death. He was trying to slow it, regulate it and recover his equilibrium. Well, so was she. But she was failing.

She sat up, yanking her top down to cover herself, confused and lonelier than ever. 'Maybe it's time—'

'I behaved like—' he interrupted her harshly, then broke off. He twisted to face her. Tall and proud and formal. Icy again. 'I behaved inexcusably,' he said in those remote, clipped tones. He bowed stiffly. 'I apologise.'

For a long moment she couldn't speak. Couldn't believe he'd become this remote statesman again. Did he feel guilty? Was he upset that he'd sullied the memory of his dead lover because he'd felt up the tart from the nightclub? Was that what this was?

Fury burned but oddly pity was entwined with it. She felt sorry for herself. Sorry for him. Sorry this whole moment had started.

But she only had to look at him to know any attempt at conversation would be futile. He'd scorched any sense of connection or compassion. There was simply nothing left. Yet he remained standing like a statue in the middle of her room, staring at her with that damned unreadable expression.

In the end she could only whisper, 'You behaved like a human.'

His nostrils flared but he didn't reply. He swiftly turned and strode to the door.

'You didn't want to be seen,' she called scornfully as this next rejection scalded her all over again.

He still didn't hesitate. He just walked out without a word, rapidly descending the stairs.

Bella closed her eyes until the sound of his footsteps receded completely. She understood anyway. He'd rather risk being seen leaving her club than staying another second in her company.

He didn't want to be near her ever again.

CHAPTER THREE

CARS ROARED: a relentless mass of humming metal and fuel. Distracted, Antonio almost forgot to applaud when the first passed the chequered flag. He'd not been looking at the finish line because she was down with the winning team's pit crew, and she was dressed not to be seen, but to stun.

Photographers called and clicked constantly, like seagulls incessantly circling a kid with an ice-cream cone. Bella paused long enough to send them a glittering smile, then turned to snap a selfie with the winner of the race. Doubtless she'd upload it once she'd filtered it to her satisfaction.

I don't need any man.

Her vehement denial replayed in his mind, but the vulnerability that the harsh-edged words revealed echoed loudest of all. Those tears after she'd come apart in his arms haunted him. He'd broken past that slick, sophisticated façade and found her to be tender and he'd been a jerk. Because he hadn't reciprocated. He hadn't been as honest with her as she'd been with him. And she'd been mortified.

But now, only hours later, her façade was back—beautiful and bulletproof. Grimly he fought the urge to take her somewhere isolated and break her walls down to get to that genuine, emotional response again. As if she'd allow him to now.

While he'd returned to the palace without detection that morning he was in no way pleased. He was a leader of not just an army, but a nation, and he never ran from a situation. Yet he'd run from the desire she'd aroused in him. Now regret and anger burned alongside it.

For the best part of a decade he'd staved off sexual want, using extreme exercise to gain self-control; his honed physique was a by-product of that intense discipline. Because he refused to hurt anyone the way he had Alessia and he refused to use women to satisfy purely physical desires. Discipline had become habit. It had almost become easy.

Until today.

Maybe his apparently uncontrollable desire for Bella had been a reaction to tiredness and stress. Or maybe it was because it had been so long since lust had burned him, it had been able to slip his leash like quicksilver…

He could come up with reasons, but they still didn't excuse his actions. And they didn't explain why he was unable to look away from her now.

She was ravishing, putting on a performance for more than the thousands in this crowd and her online audience of millions. This fortnight on San Felipe was packed with festivities and events, ones he had to attend while sandwiching in the vital trade talks and tax-exemption debates with the foreign politicians who'd come to work during the day and party at night.

Bella would use this fortnight to build her brand and define her club as the most 'it' venue on the island—

if not the world. This was the reason for the glamour, the smiles and selfie-central behaviour. All those society events that he had to attend, she would be present at too. There would be no avoiding her. Not in the immediate future.

His jaw ached with the effort of holding back his frustration.

As soon as the race formalities had concluded, he returned to his large office in the palace. He listened to the requests of his aides, read through the official papers in the scarlet box on his desk and braced himself for the celebration reception that evening.

As he'd figured, she was there, draped in an emerald-green silk dress that skimmed her curves before falling in a dramatic swathe to the floor. He was even less talkative than usual, preferring not to circulate at all. It would hammer home his icy reputation even more, but so be it. If only Eduardo weren't away—his brother had more social patience. Antonio just wanted to get back to the paperwork and the important decisions.

Except that wasn't quite all he wanted.

He endured her presence three more times over the next two days. At a charity brunch, at the unveiling of the plans to redevelop the marina, at the opening night of the new exhibition in the national art gallery...

Every time he saw her, the craving bit harder.

He avoided speaking directly to her, but more than once he met her gaze. Across the crowd in the gallery, during speeches, every glance seared, stopping that breach in his armour from sealing shut again.

Three days since that morning in her office, he seethed at his inability to wrest back his self-control.

His mind wandered every chance it got. When he should be focused, when he should be listening to someone else, when he should be thinking about things so much more important than himself, he thought about what he'd do to make her writhe in his arms until he heard her soft cry of release again.

That cry had made him harder and more wanting, yet more satisfied than he'd ever been in his life. He'd revelled in it for one incredible moment. Then he'd remembered. He couldn't have any kind of relationship.

Then he'd run.

But that cry had tormented his dreams day and night since. Now it was all he could think of.

He glanced at the valet pointlessly polishing Antonio's already buffed-to-brilliant shoes. He had a performance at the opera house to attend tonight and there was no way Bella Sanchez wouldn't be there.

'Leave me.' Abruptly he dismissed the man.

'Sir?' The servant looked nonplussed at the sudden command.

Varying from his schedule was impossible, given how crammed it was, but Antonio needed to pull himself together and cool this burn with a reality check. He needed to see *through* Bella Sanchez and remind himself she was merely a woman. And he'd refused hundreds, if not thousands of women. It was in their best interests that he had.

'I need ten minutes alone,' Antonio ordered.

His valet swiftly bowed and left. Antonio picked up the tablet he used to scan newspaper headlines. With a couple of swipes he opened up a video channel. The simplest of searches retrieved an endless list of clips. He clicked on the first. Lifted from a performance at one of the US's most prestigious ballet theatres, it had been viewed millions of times.

Bella Sanchez dancing the title role of Carmen. In this scene she was seducing a soldier to get him to do her bidding. Antonio watched, his gut tightening, as Bella sent the man a smouldering look over her shoulder—alluring, enthralling, *practised*. It was a move she performed on stage night after night after night, yet she made it utterly convincing. At the end of her solo the audience exploded, chanting her name over and over, stomping their feet, delaying the rest of the performance for a full five minutes while they called for encores. He stared at the screen, as spellbound as everyone in the audience had been, watching as she didn't break character for even a second. Haughtily she waited, accepting the adulation and keeping them in her sexual thrall as if it was only to be expected.

But when she'd lain before him, warm and exposed, she'd not been at all practised or polished. She'd been unrehearsed and real and what had happened had taken her by surprise as much as it had him. And the raw emotion in her eyes when he'd pulled away from her?

He'd hurt her. He regretted that. He regretted touching her.

Yet all he wanted was to do it again.

He tossed the tablet back onto the desk. Reduced to *watching* her like this, like some unbalanced stalker, was no way to find relief.

Why couldn't he end this aching awareness of her? The slow burn threatened to send him insane. He'd resisted already, hadn't he? He'd stopped before taking the pleasure he'd wanted so badly. He'd proven himself.

But he was tired of having to prove himself, tired of

devoting every minute of his life to his crown. Maybe resisting had been the wrong action.

Why shouldn't he have something for himself for once? He'd been restrained for so long. Every other damn prince took lovers. His younger brother had been a total playboy. In other countries princes, politicians, people with power and wealth indulged their desires. Ordinary people did too. It was *normal*.

But not for Antonio.

Not when he knew the heartache the inevitable intense media coverage would cause. Nausea churned in his gut from guilt as he remembered. He was sure Alessia's parents knew the truth of what he'd done to their daughter. They never discussed it, but they knew. So the least he could do was protect and honour both them and the memory of her. It was his duty. Having a public affair with a woman like Bella Sanchez would destroy everything he'd worked so hard to maintain. And an affair *would* become public.

Slaking this haunting lust was impossible.

But still his blood burned.

At the theatre he saw her immediately. She'd made that unavoidable. A scarlet petal in a sea of black suits, she wore the colour of seduction and vampishness, unapologetically sensual and attention stealing and a bold choice given the red highlights in her hair. Held up by thin straps, her dress was cut low over her generous breasts, their size and shape accentuated by her slender waist. Her strappy sandals made her almost tall enough to look him in the eye. Except tonight she refused to look at him at all.

Her shoulders were very square, her spine ramrod straight, her chin lifted. She knew every single man in the audience was salivating over her. That was the point, was it not?

She was here to be noticed, coveted, prized, but not claimed. This was a costume. Which was the real Bella Sanchez—the cotton-pyjama-clad woman stretching before six in the morning, or this carefully made-up temptress?

His heart drummed a fast, heavy beat. He kept his hands at his sides and didn't even try to smile. Unfortunately she was seated in the box to the left of the stage. Of course she was—it meant everyone in the audience could see her. As the royal box was in the centre of the dress circle, he could still see her even as he stared hard at the stage.

A violinist performed a haunting adagio, a choir sang, a soprano dazzled. But it was when a couple performed a *pas de deux* in the first half that he caught the first reaction in Bella. He studied her closer and saw the heartache in her expression as she watched them dance—was that the sheen of tears glistening in those blue-green eyes?

The downturn of her mouth arrested his heart. He gripped the armrests of his seat. He would not stand and go to her. He would not press his lips to hers. He couldn't let lust ignite again. But his imagination danced on, teasing him with the fantasy of her beneath him, smiling now as she looked up at him. How hot she'd feel, how she'd drink him in—

He gritted his teeth and glared back at the stage.

By the time the house lights came on for the interval she'd composed herself and was smiling again as she engaged with the city councillors she was seated with. The look she'd just sent one of them was straight from the stage. Antonio had seen it on that video clip only a couple of hours ago. It made sense. She'd spent most of her life studying how to entrance and entice and tell stories and emotions with her body. Her appearance tonight in the audience was just as much of a performance as any she'd done on stage. Just as he was performing as 'Prince Antonio' and masking the unruly battle swirling within.

He paced ahead of his aides, desperate to burn the energy building up inside, glancing at some of the other women present. They were as beautifully attired, but he felt nothing. It wasn't clothes, jewels, hair or make-up attracting him. It was that indefinable, unique essence. *Lust.* He grimaced. Why couldn't he just shake it off?

A throng waited for him to receive them during the interval. He listened and asked a few courteous questions. He'd got through five guests when Bella walked in alone. A murmur rippled across the room as people reacted. The crowd parted, giving her a halo effect as she moved into the middle of it. She didn't look to where he stood at the farthest end, but he was certain she knew exactly where he was. Her 'not looking' was too deliberate.

Now the crowd's attention was divided—half watched him, half watched her. The flamboyant Spanish entrepreneur who'd financed her club scurried over to speak with her. But it was the wolfish man trying to manoeuvre his way towards Bella who snagged Antonio's full attention—and animosity. Jean Luc Giraud was a predator out to amass as much money, and seduce as many women, as possible. But the man barely got five paces before his path was stopped by another, equally predatory-looking male.

Antonio stilled and watched closely. The ability to communicate was vital to his work and long ago he'd learned to lip-read. It was a useful skill, never more so than now.

'Don't even bother.' The taller man blocked Jean Luc's path.

Antonio couldn't see Jean Luc's response, but the blocker was facing him, and every word was clearly drawled with arrogant laziness as he answered.

'She won't give you what you want.'

Antonio's gut clenched. He waited while Jean Luc responded. The blocker shook his head in mock pity.

'Go ahead and try. She'll flirt, but won't follow through.'

Jean Luc turned, enabling Antonio to see the last of his response.

'...a tease.'

'Exactly. Looks hot, but is colder than an icicle. When you get her alone she drops the act and refuses. She's a fake. Like her injury was fake. She couldn't handle the demands of the company. The second she got hurt she was out of there so she could become the club queen.'

Red mist momentarily fogged Antonio's vision, blinding him to whatever the asshole said next. That this fool had been lucky to kiss Bella and made such a muff of it that she'd shut down? That he'd not treated her how she ought to have been?

Once more he remembered her look of surprise when that passion exploded between them. How often had she *not* got the pleasure she should have?

Compassion burned at the injustice. Just because he didn't indulge didn't mean he thought others shouldn't, but it should *always* be good. Wasn't that the point? And if it wasn't any good, then of course she was going to say no. And the jerk here should just—

'Your Highness?'

He turned to the man beside him, forcing on a polite smile. 'Forgive me, I was thinking of something else.' He drew in a breath when he realised who had stepped up to speak with him. 'Salvatore.' He inclined his head, making a conscious effort to unclench his fists.

'You're enjoying the show?' Salvatore Accardi asked with an obsequious bow.

'It is nice to see families out enjoying themselves together celebrating the island.' Antonio faintly underlined the word *families*. 'I enjoy San Felipe's festival season very much.'

'As do I.' Salvatore smiled. 'I'm sure you remember my daughter Francesca.'

His *other* daughter. The legitimate one who was a few months older than Bella.

Antonio turned slightly. Francesca Accardi was taller than Bella, her hair a glossy brunette, her slim figure beautifully dressed. 'Of course.'

'It is an honour to be here tonight, Your Highness.' She smiled brightly. 'The performances have been amazing and I'm sure the rest of the concert will be as incredible.'

'I'm glad you are enjoying it.' Antonio bowed, about to step away.

But Francesca suddenly spoke again. 'My father's new boat came into the marina after the unveiling of the new plans this morning.'

'Francesca is a designer specialising in marine interiors,' Salvatore chimed. 'Graduated top in her year.'

'Congratulations,' Antonio replied with a nod to Francesca.

'You might like to see our latest beauty,' Salvatore added. 'Her work is very unique.'

'I'm sure it is spectacular,' Antonio answered guardedly.

Everyone knew he liked his boats—thought they were his one indulgence. But the truth was he liked them because he could work in peace without interruption.

'I thought the plans for the marina expansion were very interesting,' Francesca said. 'Overcrowding is a problem of course, but I've had some thoughts as to how it could be made more efficient...' She trailed off and smiled up at him.

Was this politicising or flirting?

Antonio figured boldness was a family trait, but he felt none of the stirring he felt in the presence of her fiery half-sister. He couldn't resist glancing over at Bella to see if the wolf jerk had made his way to her. But she stood alone, looking right back at him, her green eyes stormy and accusing, watching him talk pleasantries with the man who denied that her existence was his responsibility. As his gaze clashed with hers, she lifted her chin and she looked away without so much as a blink.

Anger bubbled. She'd deliberately blanked him. He wanted her to look at him, needing to understand that emotion in her eyes. Instead he wrenched his attention back to the woman beside him. Bella's supposed half-sister Francesca Accardi was watching him too closely. He flicked his fingers and the aide hovering nearby stepped up.

'This is Matteo,' he introduced him briefly. 'Matteo, I believe Ms Accardi has some interesting ideas on the marina development. I would like you to meet with her to discuss them.'

There was no mistaking the disappointment in Salvatore's eyes as Antonio stepped back, leaving Matteo to arrange an appointment with Francesca. But Antonio was too used to people trying to make time with him, especially when accompanied by their single daughters. He turned back to spot Bella, but she'd vanished.

Bella sat in the plush seat in the exclusive box, one of the first to return for the second half of the variety performance. She'd intended to be one of the last—to maximise her exposure. As much as she loathed the tricks, she'd learned well from her mother. But her knees were now too wobbly to make that late entrance, her nerves too shredded from seeing Prince Antonio schmooze her father. The thing was, it was seeing Antonio that hurt more than Salvatore Accardi's customary rudeness.

Was she so stupidly weak she trembled at the mere sight of him?

Tonight she'd dressed with as much care as if she were still stepping onto a stage in front of thousands. She'd no shortage of glamorous dresses—people paid for her to wear their designs as long as she put her picture on social media. Getting the right look took longer than imaginable but it was a necessary part of the mystique and the 'lifestyle' her club was selling. Having lost her ballet career, she'd no other qualifications—*yet*—to call on. For all their fabulousness free dresses couldn't be eaten and she couldn't sell them for cash.

If she ever did clear her wardrobe it could only be to raise money for charity.

So if she wanted to eat, she needed to earn real money from a real job, study on the side and eventually save enough to move on to what she really wanted to do. And as much as she hated her inherited 'notoriety', she needed it, because without it she'd have absolutely nothing and she had to work it hard now because it wasn't going to last—some other model or actress or lifestyle blogger would be the new flavour soon enough.

She had to be seen. Flirt if necessary. Dance in her own club. But most importantly she had to avoid the heartless Prince who'd judged and punished her so personally.

But deep down she knew she'd dressed tonight with him in mind. She'd felt his gaze on her at those other events since that morning and his attention—his disapproval—stung. She'd tried not to care that he'd left her so abruptly but she did. Too much.

She'd wanted more but he'd reacted with such fury when she'd reached for him, he couldn't have made it clearer—she was so far beneath him.

And he was the ultimate jerk.

For a moment she'd actually thought they'd had a real kind of connection. He'd made her feel so good, then snatched it all away. She didn't know why but that one betrayal bit deeper than all the others she'd faced in her life.

She didn't enjoy the rest of the performance. She wanted to go and hide but she had to appear at the after-party backstage to show she wasn't down and out, had to smile at those she'd once danced alongside, knowing how they'd talked about her, and then had to go to her club and tirelessly work it up.

When the curtain finally fell she escaped her local council companions, telling them she'd meet them at the party shortly, but it was to the now empty stage she went rather than the powder room. Even with the curtain down, that vast black expanse felt like home to her, the one place she'd felt she truly belonged. Loneliness surged and she quickly ducked back into the wings before anyone saw her.

Pull it together.

She had her new kind of show to put on tonight.

'Bella?'

She whirled at the low whisper, blinking to get rid of the impending tears. How had he found her? Why was he alone?

'You're distressed.' Antonio stood stiffly at a short distance from her. In his black tuxedo he almost disappeared into the dark wings.

'I'm fine.' She tried to answer evenly, never wanting him to know how much she still hurt from his behaviour.

'Do not lie to me,' he said, very quiet and formal. 'Did somebody say something to upset you?'

'No one here could say anything to upset me,' she muttered, wishing it were true.

'No?' He held her captive with a mere look. 'I just told you not to lie to me.'

'Nobody has said anything to upset me. *Yet,*' she elaborated pointedly.

The scepticism remained in his eyes. 'Then what is it?'

She didn't answer—couldn't. He had no right to pry

and he couldn't expect her to open up to him now just because he was asking in that gentle tone.

'Bella?' He remained standing so restrained a few paces from her, yet there was that huskiness in his voice.

'I miss it,' she replied quickly, as hushed as he, because it was easier to talk about her ballet than what was really upsetting her. 'I miss the moment when I'm waiting in the wings and I take a last deep breath and step forward.'

'You miss the applause?'

She sighed inwardly at that edge. Of *course* she damn well did. She'd been seeking approval from someone—*anyone*—all her life. And she'd never got it from those supposed to love her, so yes, she'd sought it from the masses. She loved that applause and she'd worked so hard to earn it. But she heard criticism in his voice and knew he'd never understand.

'I miss the freedom.' The stage was where she'd felt most comfortable. 'The feeling of being in control.'

'Control of what?'

'Myself. Knowing I can move the way I need to... That I'm as strong and as fast... That I've done the work and the world is at my feet.' She stiffened at the look in his eyes.

'So you're the one who doesn't like to lose control,' he said softly. 'And yet you did.'

Anger burned—swift and uncontrollable. 'And isn't that just what you wanted?' she snapped. 'To make a fool of me.' His rejection had been her ultimate humiliation.

And she wasn't letting it happen again.

She pulled up and tried to speak calmly. 'You'd better go before someone comes looking and sees you talking to me.'

But he walked towards her, not away. 'I want to talk to you.'

'You want to gloat? To crow over your victory?'

He halted barely an inch away. 'I don't feel like a winner.'

'You started. You stopped. You wanted to prove your power—'

'I wanted to please you. I wanted to see you pleasured,' he interrupted in a rough whisper. 'That is *all* I wanted. I wasn't thinking of anything else.'

The words, the way he said them, silenced her. A trickle of warmth worked down her spine. He'd *wanted* to please her? It hadn't been about making her pay?

Confused, she gazed at him. Passion smouldered in the backs of his eyes, but the way he stood so still was so *controlled*. Was that because his emotions were awry? Was that because he didn't trust himself?

'Don't you think I might have wanted to do the same?' she whispered, unable to hold back even when she knew she ought.

'I *can't*.' The words were wrenched from him. His sharply drawn breath sliced into her.

'So you can give me pleasure but you can't receive it?' she asked, somehow feeling even more hurt than before. 'You punish yourself that much?'

A wild look flared in his expression. Her heart thundered but she refused to run; instead she stepped that last inch closer to stand toe to toe with him.

'That isn't it,' he muttered harshly.

'Then what is it?' she whispered, all caution lost. 'You don't like sex? Or just sex with me?'

She never talked back this way. She worked to keep men at arm's length, smiling and dancing but maintaining distance in a finely balanced art. But with Antonio she'd lost all that ability. For the first time in her life, she wanted a man to come closer.

He gripped her shoulders, leaning in to answer her. 'I haven't had sex in a long time. Thanks to you, it is all I can think of now.'

Satisfaction poured into her. Raw, feminine, sensual satisfaction. 'Then what stopped you?'

Why had he rejected her so brutally?

He didn't answer. He just looked at her. They both knew she would have let him do anything. She'd almost begged. And he'd jerked away. That memory burned. She wanted him to burn too.

'You're scared you won't be any good after so long?' she taunted.

His laugh was short and unamused. 'Don't try to provoke me into proving everything to you again. It isn't necessary.'

He gazed into her eyes, then his focus lowered to her mouth. Her limbs weakened with that languorous feeling. The low ache that had been with her for days now sharpened. She wanted a kiss. Then she wanted *complete* satisfaction. It was only a millimetre away. One tiny decision.

'This situation is intolerable,' he snapped, pulling her flush against his lean, hard frame. 'We have to—'

'Bella? Is that you?'

She jumped, stepping back as Antonio released her at the exact same time. A quick glance at him showed sharp cheekbones and a clamped jaw.

Erik, her former ballet partner, stood just to the side

of the wings. He was someone she counted as a friend, but he was the biggest gossip in the company. And with him—watching with eagle eyes?

Sebastian. Her blood iced. Of all the creeps she'd met in the world, Sebastian was one of the worst.

'I thought that was your dress…' Erik paused as he looked past her and saw who she was with. 'I'm awfully sorry. Are we interrupting?'

'Not at all. Ms Sanchez was kind enough to show me the stage on the way to the celebration,' Antonio answered with his customary quelling reserve, deflecting any suggestion of impropriety by demeanour alone.

For a split second Bella just gazed at him, amazed at his ability to revert to his formal 'prince' façade so quickly. And she now realised it *was* a façade. Why did he need such a remote, cold veneer? Did he never let anyone in?

He glanced at her, and she was shocked again to see that the heat had completely vanished from his eyes. A different expectation was within them now.

'Crown Prince Antonio, may I introduce you to Erik Lansing? He was the lead dancer tonight.' Bella obeyed Antonio's implicit order and acted as if nothing had happened. 'And this is Sebastian, the company's artistic director.'

Instinctively she straightened her spine as she faced her old boss. Sebastian had decided which ballerina got which part in each production. He was the man who'd assumed she'd be happy to become his lover, who'd been angered when she'd said no. She'd had to dance better than ever to prove her worth—to make it impossible for him to deny her the parts. But she could never shake that smoke of suspicion and innuendo amongst the other dancers. Sebastian had liked to let that smoke hang in the air, refusing to have it known she'd rejected him.

'I enjoyed your performance tonight.' Antonio grimly acknowledged the two men who'd almost caught him in a clinch with Bella.

He'd been a breath from kissing her. And if he had, he wouldn't have been stopping any time soon. Because she'd wanted it too. They'd have ignited the attraction sizzling between them and neither could have stopped until it had been fully assuaged.

He never should have followed her to the stage. But his curiosity—and desire—had been too strong. She fascinated him and he'd felt compelled to apologise and explain himself at least in part to her. Something he never did in a personal situation, because there *were* no personal situations. Until now.

But now he stood face to face with the 'blocker' who'd warned Jean Luc off Bella. This Sebastian slimeball was her old company's artistic director? That title meant power—over a ballerina in the company. Presumably he could offer promotion, or he could pass her over and give a prized part to another, more willing woman. Yet Bella hadn't given him what he'd wanted. And she stood straight, head held high, bracing herself in defiance in front of them all.

Antonio had known she had strength. Now he knew she had integrity too.

'Thank you.' Erik half bowed. 'I miss Bella though. I don't dance anywhere near as well with anyone else.'

He'd been Bella's ballet partner? Antonio watched as Erik slung his arm along her shoulders. Bella smiled at Erik but the look in her eyes wasn't the same as when she looked at Antonio. There was no desire, no anger, no passion. There was only a sorrow-tinged amusement. She didn't want the same thing from Erik as she wanted from him.

Even so, Antonio's stomach tightened. The jealousy was ridiculous. He was no better than any of the other predators in suits, sniffing around her.

'I must return to the other guests,' he clipped, his jaw aching. 'Excuse me.'

'Of course,' Bella murmured.

'We have to stay at this thing for at least twenty minutes, right? Then we're hitting your club.' Erik's voice carried as Antonio strode away. 'I hear it's full of beautiful young things.'

'Absolutely. Wait 'til you see my star barman.' Bella's laughter bubbled as she went back to her performance.

During the reception in the backstage lounge Antonio watched her execute those choreographed moves in real life again. But his bitterness receded when he saw that blankness in her eyes. It told him everything. This was an astute businesswoman doing what she deemed necessary to make her work a success. Beneath that determination, she had needs and desires that weren't being met.

So, thanks to her, did he.

An affair was impossible. But he wanted just one taste of the forbidden.

No one could know. And for that to happen, it could only happen the once.

Clandestine. Discreet. Finite.

There'd be no power games, threats or sleazy rewards. They would just be two people working out an intense attraction on their own terms and in private.

Five minutes later he watched her leave with her entourage of dancers. She was deliberately breaking royal protocol and leaving the reception before he, the Crown Prince, did. Showing him she didn't give a damn.

Which might be true.

But she still wanted him.

CHAPTER FOUR

BELLA RECOGNISED THE man immediately. Prince Antonio's aide might be immaculately and discreetly attired, but he still didn't fit in. His expression was as austere as his employer's and he clearly wasn't at her club to dance.

She wasn't dancing either. She was playing the 'exclusive VIP room' card, trying to let Erik distract her, but not even his endless talk could keep her thoughts from one tall, dark and handsome prince for long. And now here was Antonio's errand boy at almost three in the morning looking as if he was on a mission. Her pulse sprinted, swiftly overtaking the fast-thudding beat of the club anthem blaring from the state-of-the-art speakers.

From her seat on the mezzanine floor she saw him identify her bar manager. She immediately rose, discreetly radioing for that manager to escort the aide to the small private office at the back of the bar. She went down via the curling steps in the main dance space, taking her time to smile with some of her guests so no one could suspect how on edge she'd suddenly become. There were too many people and every single one of them had a smart phone with a camera app.

After another few minutes working her way past the bar, she entered the small private room. He stood waiting in the middle of it.

'Ms Sanchez, my name is Matteo. I am Prince Antonio's assistant.' He half bowed as soon as she'd closed the door behind her. 'The Prince requests your company.' He held a thick white envelope out to her.

Her name was on the front, inked in a scrawling hand and underlined with a couple of heavy pressed lines that suggested urgency. Demand.

Bella.

Her blood ran faster. She could hear his voice, whispering her name as he touched her, devastating her defences until she'd melted in his arms. But he wasn't here now. He'd sent a messenger in the middle of the night. Had he even written her name himself?

'He requests my company right now?' she asked Matteo carefully.

'Apparently an issue has arisen,' Matteo answered, still offering the envelope.

Bella stared, unable to be sure that she'd heard innuendo in his tone or not, but his face was a blank mask. He'd learned from his master well.

'And this issue can't wait until morning?' she asked.

'If you would take the envelope, Ms Sanchez.'

She took it from him and turned it over, breaking the seal on the back. She drew out the single thick card and, with a cool glance at Matteo, turned away to read the note. But the card bore only two lines of that harsh writing.

We need to talk.

The bald statement was followed by a number and an address—she recognised it as an apartment building near her club and her pulse was *not* accelerating, but her breathing quickened. Her nerves tightened.

'I will escort you there now,' Matteo said, as if he were offering her the greatest service ever.

'That won't be necessary.' She put the card back into the envelope with care. 'I can't go there now.'

The surprise that flashed on his face gave her an inordinate sense of satisfaction.

'Prince Antonio requests your company,' Matteo repeated.

'So you said,' she answered, determined to stay cool. 'And I will get there when I can.'

'You don't understand—'

'I understand perfectly.' She smiled at him though her mouth felt dry as dust. 'You're the one who doesn't understand and nor does he, obviously. I have a business to run. So you can tell him that I'll get there if and when I can.'

Matteo didn't reply but she wasn't bothered by his scrutiny. She wasn't afraid of him. But she was wary of how Antonio made her feel—and how much she wanted him.

'If you'll excuse me, I need to get back to my guests.' She clutched the envelope and left him to find his own way out.

But she didn't return to her guests. She climbed all the way to her own tiny apartment at the top. She put the card on her desk—the one he'd kissed her on— and stared at it.

Was this how a prince made a booty call? With just her name, an address and a lame 'we need to talk'? Did

he do this all the time? Send his aide to set up shag-
a-thons for him in a private apartment in town so no
one would ever know?

So much for the myth of heartbroken, isolated
Prince Antonio. Turned out the supposedly heroic,
self-sacrificing Prince of the People had feet of clay.
He just wanted it like any other guy. On the side when
it convenienced him.

She was livid. And she was ignoring him.

She went back down to the dance floor. She wasn't
going to drop everything at his beck and call. But she
couldn't concentrate properly. Time crawled. It felt like
hours until four a.m. finally struck—yet it was only
forty-five minutes since Matteo had left.

It was another hour before her staff had gone and
she'd locked up and could shower. The cascading hot
water didn't ease her tension any. Sleep wasn't happening. So she dressed in skinny jeans, a light tee and
ballet flats on her feet.

It was five-thirty in the morning when she finally
made her move. She'd go and see him and tell him to
his face.

No.

She wouldn't be his latest secret lover.

She walked out of the side door, ensuring the alarm
was enabled, and saw Matteo leaning against the doorway of the building opposite. He crossed the street to
where she stood.

'I will escort you there now,' he said.

'Have you been waiting here all this time?'

He nodded and turned in the direction of the apartment.

'You don't need to—' She started to argue but realised the poor man was only following orders. She was better to save her fight for facing Antonio. She started walking, pretending not to care that Matteo remained a half pace behind her the entire way. Clearly he *was* used to doing this kind of errand for his boss.

Fury pushed her faster.

At the apartment building the security guard wordlessly opened the door, not looking Bella in the eye. Matteo stepped in front and led her to the elevator.

Yeah, he'd definitely done this many times before.

He entered the lift only long enough to punch in a code at the keypad. It whooshed up swiftly, leaving her feeling as if her stomach were still on the ground. Ruefully she reckoned her brain was back at her club.

When the elevator stopped on the top floor she stepped out. The heavy door on the small landing was open. Antonio stood, resting a shoulder against the frame, staring at her. He still wore the jet-black tux, the jacket immaculate and tie neatly fastened; only the hint of shadow on his chiselled jaw gave away the passage of time—that and his glare. Serious, handsome, smouldering, he said so much in silence.

Too bad. She lifted her chin, because his rejection still *hurt*. 'You summoned. I came.'

She walked past him into the apartment, commanding the centre space.

'What do you want from me?' Years of training stood her in good stead; she knew how to fake confidence 'til she made it.

Antonio quietly closed the door, taking a moment to temper his response. She'd kept him waiting, he'd had zero sleep, and he didn't have the patience for endless debating. This was one situation in which action would speak louder than words.

But he needed the words because they meant he'd retain control. Of himself, of what was to happen, of how this would end.

And he wanted to hear her speak too. He liked her challenging edge, as if she wasn't going to agree to everything he had to say. At least, not immediately.

'Would you like to sit down?' He gestured to the plush armchair rather than the wide sofa. Enforcing social niceties at this moment would help keep him civilised.

'I'm not going to jump just because you said to.'

Her reply shredded the remnants of all polite pretence, exposing the sensual tension. Combustion was a breath away.

He gave up on civility and crossed the room to tower over her. 'And yet here you are.'

He'd known sending Matteo had been a mistake. His brother Eduardo had relied on Matteo for his discretion and reliability. Antonio had never had cause to before and should've known it would be better to do a job himself. He should've waited until later and gone to her club alone. Yet he liked this look in her eyes—baleful anger bubbling over sensual awareness.

'What do you want from me?' she repeated unevenly. 'You want me to dance for you?' She rolled her shoulders and took a half-step to the side.

It was barely a dance, more a suggestive movement, but Antonio was unable to answer. Another emotion entered her eye—determination, then *calculation*.

She moved ever so slightly while her gaze remained locked on his. There wasn't the freedom he'd seen when she'd not known he was watching her alone in the club. She looked every bit as beautiful, but he saw her self-awareness, her moves made for their intended effect on her audience.

On *him*.

'No,' he snapped.

Instantly she stopped. Her sultry mask fell, revealing her anger in full, making her all the more stunning.

'Not like that,' he added. 'I don't want to *watch*. I don't want a *performance* from you.'

'Then what do you want?' she flared. 'To humiliate me again?'

'Humiliate you?' His own anger ignited. He'd never intended to do that and he was furious he had. He grabbed her hips and hauled her against him. 'I want what we had. I want the real thing.'

He crushed her mouth under his, unable to contain himself a second longer. Energy radiated from her—resistance, anger, but most of all desire. In the next moment she melted, opening, pressing closer. Then she kissed him back—*hard*.

This was what he wanted. Her unrestrained reaction to him—negative and positive and the total eroticism that burst to life the second they touched. All the resistance within her transformed to passion. She burrowed closer, angrily clutching his jacket.

He lost his head in her heat. He ached to rip them free of their clothing. Have her exactly as he wanted—bared and welcoming with that fire-gilded hair tumbling free about her shoulders and her body hot and slick.

But he pulled away, brutally breaking the kiss because he had to put restraints around this. And he was damn well ensuring she had more than a quick, angry orgasm this time. He'd see her fully sated. Fully his.

Breathing hard, he held her at a distance, taking primitive pleasure in how long it took for her to regain her balance and stand on her own.

'This cannot go on.' He'd give in to lust, but only once.

'What?' she asked. Fury combusting, she shoved his hands from her shoulders.

'It only worsens with time,' he said quickly, before she continued to think he didn't want to resolve this in a way they'd both appreciate. He could hardly bear to look at the luminescent need in her gleaming green eyes; he couldn't resist her ferocity. 'We have to work this out.'

It had only been a few days, but Bella knew what he meant. The hunger, desire, and the *frustration*. The emotions he roused in her were the most intense of her life.

'So you sent your errand boy to make your booty call.' It was anger and arousal coursing through her veins now, a heady combination that made it almost impossible to think. She *felt* too much.

'I didn't want to attract attention,' he explained crisply. 'It wouldn't be good for either of us.'

'The publicity would be good for me,' she argued hotly, pushing forward what she knew would be his greatest objection to anything happening between them. Just because she could. 'Make my club even more popular. I could do with that success.'

'They would drag *you* through the mud and you know it. Don't act vapid. I know you care more than that.'

'Do you?' How could he really know anything about her?

He cupped her chin and tilted her face to his, capturing her gaze in his steely one again. 'I saw you. I felt you. You're more vulnerable than you wish to admit.'

Ever so lightly he touched the tips of his fingers to the pulse beating frantically just below her jaw. Not a threat, but a caress of concern.

Her heart stuttered. 'I don't need your protection. I can handle anything.' She jerked her head, forcing him to release her. 'It's your name you're worried about. Having an affair with me would ruin perfect Prince Antonio's holier-than-thou reputation.'

'I don't care what others think about me,' he said softly. 'But there are other people who would be hurt by my personal life becoming public. Discretion is necessary because it is kind.'

Silenced, she gazed up at him, her heart melting. He wanted to be kind? He wanted to protect people other than the two of them. She couldn't help but wonder who they were.

'And you do not want to be hunted any more than you already are.' His gaze narrowed, penetrating. 'You do not want to be treated the way your mother was. You do not want to have every detail of your life reported on. Invented. You do not want to have your ex-lovers paid fortunes to tell your sexual secrets. They would stop at nothing to get that information should you be known to be my lover.'

He hit precisely where she was most vulnerable. She never wanted to live the way her mother had. And yes, while she courted publicity now, it was one thing to manage her own media relations and give them enough to keep them interested but not have them hound her completely. But the way they would pry if they knew she was having an affair with Prince Antonio?

It would be unbearable.

'Yet you're still willing to take the risk?' she asked.

'I am talking only one night.'

Just once.

So this would never become an affair. It would be nothing more than a one-night stand. And there wasn't even much of this night left.

'I don't want to fight it any more,' he said ruefully. 'The last few days have been hell.'

That he felt as intensely as she did soothed her some.

'No one will ever know,' he added.

'Except you sent your man to fetch me at three in the morning in a club full of people,' she pointed out.

'I trust him with my life,' Antonio said.

'Because he's done this for you so many times before?' Maybe that shouldn't bother her, but it did.

'Never for me,' Antonio answered solemnly. 'But I cannot answer for my brother.'

Relief seeped into her stiffness. Prince Eduardo had been 'the Playboy Prince'. Of course.

'You do not need a man. A husband. A hero,' Antonio said quietly continuing his persuasion. 'You are determined to be independent. I respect that. But you want…' He paused. 'I have duty and obligations. I will never marry because I can never give a woman all she deserves. But I, too, want…'

'Do you?' She was somehow hurt, despite knowing everything that he said was true. 'But you don't have lovers. Or is that just the publicity line?'

'It's not just a line,' he said quietly.

She rested her palm on his chest, daring to intrude where she really had no right. Just to see if he could be honest with her. If he could share when only a few days ago he couldn't share anything. 'How long?'

'A long, long time. I've been busy. After a while it wasn't something that was important to me.' A glimmer of laughter suddenly lit his face. 'But don't worry, it won't be over too quickly.'

His ability to pleasure her was the last thing she was worried about. He'd already given her the best orgasm of her life, and proven his personal restraint at the same time. 'Why now, why me?'

That serious, brooding look returned. 'Because I can't think of anything *but* you. Because I'm tired of trying to fight it already. I know it's the same for you. I come near and your body reacts. You can't help the way you respond to me.' Unflinching, he demanded equal honesty from her. 'Do you have a lover currently?'

'Do you think I would be here if I did?'

'Of course not. I apologise.' His expression softened. 'There is more talk about you than actual action.'

'Does it matter?'

'No. But do you think I don't know how much of the Bella Sanchez "story" is made up?'

'You don't want to know the truth?' She straightened, determined to defend her scarlet honour even when really she'd never been that 'scarlet'.

'I know it already. You give yourself away every time I touch you. Every time I come near you. You react differently to me.' He put his hands on her waist and drew her closer. 'You cannot hide how you react to me.'

'That's not fair,' she said huskily. 'As if you're all that experienced.'

He laughed appreciatively. 'I might be rusty, but I'm not ignorant. And you're not the sophisticated vamp you try to portray.'

If this was him 'rusty' then heaven help her when he hit his stride.

He ran his hand up and down her spine, partly soothing, mostly arousing. Every touch seemed designed to torment her.

'The other morning...' He paused and looked at her with concern. 'I saw you. I felt you. What happened, how I made you feel...was more than you expected.'

She flushed, embarrassed that he'd known her orgasm had come as a surprise.

'I want to make you feel that good again.' Intent darkened his eyes.

'It's not wise.' But her body yearned for it.

'Because I made you emotional?'

'You were too.'

He froze for a moment; his hands stopped those teasing touches. 'I like being able to make you feel good. And you do want me to kiss you again.' Deliberately, lightly he rubbed his finger across her lip. 'And I want to. Everywhere.' He suddenly pulled her hips against his. Hard. Letting her know exactly where else he intended to use his mouth.

'You always get what you want?' she asked breathlessly, the feel of his body against hers was so good. The promise in his eyes exquisite torment.

'I'm the Crown Prince—most people are pleased to do things for me.'

'So I should feel honoured?'

He shook her gently then pulled her to rest against him again. 'Stop trying to stall and just admit you feel the same.'

'The same?' She stiffened, trying to hold back the desire threatening to overwhelm her. Did he really feel this as intensely as she? Did he want her the way she wanted him this second?

'I like how good you make me feel,' he muttered.

'I didn't do anything. You wouldn't let me.' She'd been so hurt by that.

A wry smile curved his lips. 'You need me to prove it? Again. Untrusting creature.'

'Do you blame me?' she asked. 'You ask me to admit things when you rejected me so harshly. You wouldn't let me near you. You made me—' She broke off. 'And then you left. You couldn't get away quickly enough.'

His smile faded. 'I apologise. You took me by surprise. You were right and I was wrong. I shouldn't have walked out and I have regretted it every second since.'

'You're the Penitent Prince?' She couldn't breathe.

'I want you more than I've ever wanted anyone. I wouldn't be here now if I didn't.'

At his words that last little knot of anger disintegrated within her.

'Nor would I.' But she shivered because somehow his admission made *her* feel vulnerable.

He slid his hand beneath the hem of her thin tee, tracing his fingers up her spine. His touch warm and firm.

'Chemistry like this…I didn't think it happened,' she confessed.

'Nor did I.'

It was just physical, right?

'You don't like it,' she muttered, her thoughts derailed by the swirling pattern he was drawing over her skin with his fingertips.

'It's a distraction,' he answered evasively. He slid his hand up to cup the nape of her neck and pushed her back over his arm so her shirt pulled taut. He gazed down at the way the fabric rubbed against her nipples, emphasising their hard outline.

'So you think if we have what we want, then we'll no longer want it?' She arched uncontrollably against him as he sucked one tight nipple into his mouth, bra and tee and all.

'Yes.' He bent to give her other breast the same sinfully good treatment. 'This cannot be anything more than here and now. You wouldn't want it to be anything more.'

She arched against him again, unable to resist rocking her hips against his hard pelvis. He was right. She didn't want any of what would come with this if it became public. 'Will you allow me to touch you this time?'

'I don't know how I got the strength to stop you. I don't know how I walked away,' he muttered. 'I want to see you naked.' His glittering gaze raked down her body, felt like a force—drawing heat from her, making her want to move in a way she'd never wanted before.

'We each take off one layer at a time,' she suggested. 'It's only fair.'

'Life isn't fair.' He smiled wolfishly and pushed her tee shirt up.

'*This* time, it is going to be fair.' She demanded it.

He didn't answer, but there was a glint in his eye

as he straightened her up, stood back and held out his arms, letting her peel the perfectly tailored jacket from his shoulders. Slowly, savouring the moment, she tugged his tie free, then unbuttoned the pearl buttons of his starched white shirt.

'That's more than one layer already,' he noted, his breath stirring her hair as she moved in close.

She didn't care. She was too busy exposing his chest. Heat balled low in her belly. He was gorgeous. Nothing but lean muscle and bronzed skin and a faint line of dark hair arrowing down the centre of his rigid abs to his belt. For the first time she took real pleasure in just looking. And then kissing. Then touching.

She traced over his ridged muscles. 'You're beautiful.'

'That's a word to describe you, not me.'

'You exercise.' She unfastened his belt and fumbled with his fly.

He moved to help her, toeing out of his shoes before shoving down both his dress pants, his briefs and socks until he straightened and stood utterly bared before her. 'Every morning.'

She stared, her mouth dry as she gazed on his honed, immaculate body. His regime had to be intense to be this fit—as if he ran or swam for long periods at a time. 'You're disciplined.'

'I have to be. I have a lot to do.'

And he was going to use that discipline and self-control with her now; she could see the intent in his eyes.

'You keep everything contained in its place,' she muttered. Work, exercise, sleep. She was in the sex box for him. And that was just fine.

So fine.

Except her heart was thudding and there was an ache within her that had never been there before.

'You're the same.' He lifted her tee, and she wriggled to help him. He unclasped her bra and briefly cupped her full breasts in his hands before moving to tug her trousers down. 'You're sleek, strong.'

'It makes me feel better if I've moved.' She nodded, lifting one leg, then the other, so he could take her panties off too.

In that they were a match—both physically driven, both worked hard. Both couldn't afford this messiness, but now they were both naked.

She licked her lips. She wanted everything all at once, but she didn't know where to start.

'Bella.' He muttered her name harshly and stepped forward, pulling her into his arms to French-kiss her senseless.

They kissed, touched, kissed again until she was all but delirious and weak-kneed. But then he dropped to his knees and pressed his mouth to her *there*.

She gasped his name.

'I can't wait to hear you,' he muttered approvingly. 'Again and again.'

Oh, no, this wasn't happening that way. Not again. She pulled back and fell to her knees too. 'I want to hear *you*,' she said.

But he was stronger. He lifted and laid her down on her back and moved between her splayed thighs. 'I can't keep my hands off you. Or my mouth.' He moved down her body, trapping her hands at her sides as he licked and kissed from her navel, to her most intimate curve where she was embarrassingly wet already. Then he rose onto his knees to study how he'd spread her beneath him. 'I want to taste you as you come again. Now.'

That devilishly sexy look in his eyes almost sent her over the edge then and there. But she didn't want to come before him. Not this time.

'I want *you* to enjoy it,' she moaned as he ran his hand over her breasts, gently cupping, then teasing.

'You think I didn't?' He shook his head and stroked her again with his skilful fingers. 'There's no greater feeling than knowing I've pleased you.'

'It's the same for me.' She arched uncontrollably as his hands worked further south. 'Can't you understand that?'

'I do.' He bent to her again and kissed her most sensitive nub. 'You can please me, right now. Come for me, Bella. Let me taste it.'

His tongue was so wicked there was no way she couldn't. Groaning, she ran her hands through his thick hair, holding him to her as he pleasured her with his mouth and hands. She rocked as she rode the crest of her orgasm, no longer embarrassed about how wet she must be, because the way his fingers were thrusting was so divine and the words of approval and pleasure tumbling from his wicked mouth were making her orgasm last longer than she'd have thought possible.

He cradled her as she recovered, small aftershocks making her quiver every so often. The pleased expression in his eyes called forth her own competitive spirit.

'My turn.' Suddenly energised, she rolled and moved onto all fours.

'Turn?'

'To taste.' She slapped her hand in the centre of his

chest and pushed, making him stay where he was, flat on the floor.

'Bella—'

'Don't argue with me,' she said fiercely. 'Don't deny me. Not this time.'

But he cupped the nape of her neck and drew her down to him, kissing her deeply. Almost she submitted completely to the desire to simply roll back and let him do whatever he wished with her. But she needed this. Wanted it.

She pulled away and looked into his eyes. 'I'm going to kiss you,' she said. 'Everywhere.'

He didn't answer, but nor did he stop her. She took her time discovering his body. He was strong, but sensitive too and she took pleasure in teasing out those secret spots. What he liked. Where he liked. His neck. His nipples. His thighs.

And slowly she honed in on his enormous erection. Licking her lips, she glanced up at him to gauge his reaction as she moved, curling her hand around the thick base of him.

'Bella…'

She utterly disobeyed the implicit order and opened her mouth to draw him in.

'Bella.'

There was no ignoring him that time.

She released him to glance up into his stormy eyes. 'Please.'

For a long moment he held her gaze, his expression strained. She realised he was holding his breath.

Then he sighed and an almost tender light entered his eyes. 'I'm the one who should be saying please.'

Almost shyly she smiled at him. Then she looked

back down at his straining erection. The single, glossy bead at the tip of his shaft told her he was close. Feminine pleasure flooded her. She wanted to taste all of it.

She heard his long hiss as she took him as deep as she could into her mouth. She sucked hard as she pulled back, and she rubbed and took him deep again. Oh, she loved to rub him. Loved to lick and suck and feel every powerful tremble she could pull from him.

She didn't stop. Rubbing, kissing, sucking, she lost herself in her rhythm, in the pleasure of touching him. His hips bucked, bumping her as she straddled his thighs. She shivered at the power beneath her. His legs were so strong, she couldn't wait to feel the full force of his lovemaking.

As his breathing grew harsher, she gazed up the length of his body. His skin gleamed from a sheen of sweat. His arms were outstretched to the sides; she could see the veins popping as he grasped at the plush carpet beneath him. Every muscle in his body was strained as he tried to hold back. She didn't want him to hold back.

'I'm going to drink every last drop.' She smiled with carnal promise. 'I'm going to watch and taste and feel you as I make you come.'

His muttered oath was mostly indecipherable but it made her smile deepen. Then she returned to him. He was so beautiful and all she wanted was to make him—

'Bella!'

His shout echoed in her ears, so filled with raw relief that she felt as if she were riding that crest with him. As the spasms eased she kept sucking him as deep as she could, holding true to her words and loving it as he shook beneath her.

'Bella.' He released a long breath and his body went lax. 'Bella, Bella, Bella.'

Still astride him, she sat up and looked down his length to his handsome face, tracing her fingers down her neck, between her breasts and to her belly, following the heated path of his seed within her. She felt so femininely sensual. And so aroused.

With shadowed eyes he stared back up at her.

Undaunted, knowing he too was finally sated, she smiled.

Swiftly he sat up and flipped her. She was flat on her back and he was pressing her hard into the plush carpet, kissing her breathless before she could blink. His fingers were between her legs and he made a guttural sound in the back of his throat as he felt how wet and ready she was. She writhed, riding his hand for a moment, so unbelievably pleased.

'Temptress,' he muttered and nipped her lips with his teeth.

He shifted onto his knees, reaching beyond for his trousers on the floor near them. In a second he was ripping open the foil package and rolling the condom on.

She lifted up onto her elbows, in awe of his already rigid erection. He glanced over and caught her staring. He smiled, but she read the determination in his eyes, felt the dynamism in his tense body as he covered her, and knew her moment of dominance was past. He was back in control. He was going to make her pay and it was going to be a heavenly price.

'I don't know how gentle I can keep this,' he muttered, stroking her intimately again. His eyes widened as he felt her body's reaction to his words. 'You don't want gentle?'

'I just want you in me,' she muttered low and harsh and hungry, unable to hold back her darkest desires. She wanted him too much. Only he had made her feel this way. And if she only had him this once, then she was holding nothing back. 'As deep and as hard as you can.'

He kissed her. His tongue lashed the cavern of her mouth with exactly the kind of fierce strokes she was aching for.

For the first time in her life she truly wanted passion.

'You have a hot, sweet mouth and a hot, sweet body.' He looked into her eyes as his fingers probed her wet arousal. 'But you don't want it all that sweet.'

She whimpered at his tormenting rubbing. But he was right.

'Answer me,' he commanded, pushing fractionally deeper and then pulling out.

She moaned in disappointment. 'Yes,' she admitted, aching for his return. For *all* of him.

'You want it hard.'

'Yes.'

'Fast.'

'Yes.'

'Now.'

'*Yes.*' Her head fell back as her blood burned. She writhed under him, desperate to assuage the ache so deep within her. 'I want you in me. Please.'

He nudged her thighs further apart with his knee and settled over her. He was so hard, so masculine and he smelt so good and she could feel him, almost there.

Never had she wanted a man like this.

She held her breath as she stared into his gorgeous

pale blue eyes. She saw the determined fire in them and wanted to be consumed in it. She saw his jaw lock. Then he pushed forward.

'Oh, yes.' She tensed, locking him in as an orgasm rolled over her in a sharp burst of ecstasy. 'Oh, yes- sssssss.'

Her breath shuddered in the shock of it. He was finally there and he felt so good. She moaned again, convulsing in pleasure.

'What are you doing coming so quick?' He smiled tightly down at her as she gasped for breath. His expression was teasing. But strained too.

She didn't know. She'd never come during penetration before, let alone that quickly. But the amazing thing was, she wasn't far off coming again.

'What are you doing not moving?' she moaned breathlessly, stunned that she was on the edge again. If only he'd move. If only he'd give her everything. Oh, God, she never wanted this to end.

'Enjoying the view. You're so beautiful like this. I could watch you come all day.'

She shifted, wrapping her leg around his lower back, trying to pull him deeper.

'Don't tease.' She stroked his face and whispered what she wanted most of all. 'I want you to come with me. In me.'

'Oh, hell. Bella,' he muttered hoarsely. His wicked smile faded as he gazed at her. 'Then you might want to hold on, sweetheart.'

But he held onto her, sliding his hands under her back and gripping her shoulders to keep her with him as he pressed forward, deepening his possession of her.

Her breath hissed as he pushed to the hilt. She met

his gaze and knew she was in the eye of the storm. Hurricane Antonio was about to hit.

'Please,' she asked one more time. She wanted it all.

At last he moved, pulling back only to grind into her. Hard and deep he drilled into her, again and again and again. And it was so good. She met him thrust for thrust. Energy sizzled between them; their ride suddenly became frantic and wild. Their sweat-slicked bodies banged faster and faster.

'So good, so good,' she muttered over and over and over.

But then she could only moan in mindless pleasure each time he drove deeper. It was so carnal and so physical and so good. She kissed him everywhere she could with honest, unchecked abandonment. This wasn't sweet, this was decadently sensual and she had to curl her fingers into his muscled flesh to hang on as he forced his pace faster still.

'Come with me, Bella,' he commanded harshly, then kissed her.

His kiss held so much passion, it felt as if he were pouring his very soul into her. She felt him shaking against her even as he drove deeper still.

She arched, every muscle in her body straining. Her breaths were high-pitched moans as he pushed her nearer and nearer to that peak. She heard his breathing roughen, felt the rigidity in his whole body and revelled in it.

'Yes!' She managed to lock her arms around his back, fiercely holding him to her as she shattered beneath and about him, her screams unchecked and raw as that intense sensual tension exploded.

She heard him groan her name, then his hoarse

growl of intense pleasure as he thrust one last time, releasing long and hard into her.

When she could think again, she found he'd eased off her and was lying on his side facing her. Her heart thudded.

This time when he grabbed her wrist it was not to reject her. It was not to push her away. It was to demand the exact opposite.

'More,' he grated, his expression untamed. 'More now.' His passion was utterly off the leash now. 'You should have come as soon as you got my card.'

'I couldn't.' And she couldn't be more sorry about it.

'There is not enough time.' He moved over her, his body hard again. 'We didn't even make it to the damned bed.'

'This is all the time there is.' She parted her legs wider to accommodate his muscular strength. 'This is all there can be.'

She saw his reaction at the remembrance. Duty before desire.

'Then we'd better make the most of it,' he said, his jaw tight, his eyes savage.

His determination made her hot. His intensity made her tremble.

It was slower that time. And silent. There were not the hot, wickedly teasing words to start. He was careful not to bruise where she was most tender. But his gentleness was such exquisite torture. He made her feel so good tears welled in her eyes as she squeezed her muscles tight to lock him in place. She didn't want this to end. She didn't want him to stop holding her, looking at her. Didn't want him to stop ensuring she was out of her mind with pleasure. He could make her feel such unutterable, exquisite pleasure. She embraced him with all the fervour she could, yearning to return that favour. That was when it grew wild again. Loud and physical and fast.

But finally they lay slumped together, utterly spent. Silent again.

This time he was the first to move. This time he didn't meet her gaze. This time really was the end.

Quietly, carefully he left her, disappearing into another room. She sat up, curling her legs up and wrapping her arm around her knees. Dazed, she took in the discarded mess of clothing. He was right, they hadn't even made it from the lounge floor they'd been so eager and hurried. And it was all over already. Bittersweet melancholy filled her.

He walked back into the lounge. He'd swiftly dressed in jeans and a tee shirt. They might be casual wear for him, but he'd slipped back behind his reserve.

She wanted to kiss him. She wanted to fall back onto the floor and take him with her. She wanted that delicious feeling all over again. But she didn't dare.

'I am sorry, I must leave.' He glanced at his watch, his thoughts clearly elsewhere. 'I'm late already.'

'Of course.'

'Stay and sleep,' he instructed politely. 'The bed is through there…' He had the grace to look slightly sheepish.

'No, I have things I need to do as well.' She pulled her clothes nearer. 'I'll leave ten minutes after you. Will use a different exit from the building or something.'

He was silent. 'I would like Matteo to ensure you get home safely.'

That poor guy was still in the building ready for

service? 'That's not necessary.' Her skin burned anew with that all-over body-blush and she quickly pulled her tee shirt on, not bothering with her bra first. She just wanted to cover up. She just wanted him to leave already.

His jaw tightened but he didn't argue. He stood for another moment and she inwardly winced at the awkwardness.

'Goodbye,' he said stiffly, still frowning at her, looking as if he might say something more.

She didn't want him to.

'Goodbye, Prince Antonio.' She lifted her chin and threw him her most sophisticated 'Bella Sanchez' smile. 'It was a pleasure.'

CHAPTER FIVE

IT WAS ENOUGH. It *had* to be enough because he didn't deserve the pleasure she could give him and she didn't deserve the pain he would inevitably give her. He had to retain his control. She was out of bounds now. Once was a calculated risk. Once more could only be a disaster.

Antonio walked past the line-up of guests, greeting them as he went, determined to be as focused as ever. He was almost halfway through the continuous schedule of event after event in the festival fortnight. He'd been spared her presence at some occasions. But not this one. At his request she'd been sent an invitation and she had not refused. She was not stupid.

She wore a black dress that revealed nothing yet managed to imply everything. Her loose hair shone, the reddish strands glinting like threads of fire under the chandeliers. She stole his breath. And that was before she smiled. Or spoke.

If she spoke, he'd be lost.

But his desire for her wasn't the reason why he'd ensured she attend this particular function. It was in *her* interest to attend. It wasn't that he was desperate to see her again. He was simply helping her out, because he was in the position to be able to.

Salvatore Accardi was also a guest at this late afternoon's drinks, yet Antonio noticed the man didn't say hello to Bella. He was her father, Antonio was in no doubt of that, yet he didn't even acknowledge her presence with the politeness you'd afford a stranger. He acted as if she weren't there. Beyond rude.

But Bella was working the room with that bulletproof style of hers, refusing to let her father's ostracism daunt her. Antonio felt like cheering her. He understood social isolation and he didn't want her to feel the sharp edge of it. She'd done nothing to deserve it. He'd checked her out. Beyond that super-seductive façade, there was nothing. She'd not been caught lying or stealing or cheating…she was a woman—that was all. A woman who couldn't help who her parents were. A woman he still wanted.

He caught Matteo's eye.

'Ensure she's not left alone,' Antonio instructed as the aide came over. 'There are people here it would benefit her to meet and people who might give her a hard time.'

And then he decided to set the example for everyone. He deliberately walked over to talk to her; it would be too obvious if he didn't and he refused to be anything like her father.

'It is always a pleasure, Ms Sanchez.'

She didn't immediately reply but her eyes narrowed on him.

She wasn't appreciative of his efforts?

His focus changed, arrowing on the electricity arcing between them. He'd made a mistake. He'd thought he'd be lost if she spoke to him, but, really, it had taken only one look.

'It seems you have guests from every sector of San Felipe society here tonight,' Bella murmured, trying to regulate her racing pulse, but seeing him threw her balance completely. 'Business leaders, rally drivers, retired politicians…' Her voice trailed off. 'Even me.'

Antonio almost smiled. 'Why shouldn't you be here?'

'You know very well why.' She shifted, restless because of his nearness. 'You shouldn't have invited me. Our agreement was once only.'

She'd been a fool to think once would've been enough. The last few days since had been horrendous. And this invitation? It hadn't been in his hurried scrawl. It had been formal, printed and distant, yet she'd not hesitated for a second. The craving to see him had been too great. She'd applied her lipstick with a shaking hand, she'd been so full of anticipation. Now he was right with her and holding herself back was almost impossible.

But she hadn't slept properly in weeks because she'd been getting the club ready and now it was open she was frantically busy and the sleeplessness was affecting her more each day. So she didn't have the energy to build her defences; she couldn't control her own heated trembling.

'That wasn't why I invited you,' he answered impassively.

Bella's blood iced. It wasn't? Didn't he want her again? Had that one morning truly been enough for him?

'This is a reception for San Felipe's most successful local business leaders,' he continued with his customary distance. 'You are a businesswoman who's carving out a brand and a service that has seen unprecedented success already. That's why you're here.'

Rejection and bitterness bruised. 'To network with people who don't want my business in their town because I'm some kind of bad influence?' she asked acidly.

Salvatore Accardi had been sending hostile waves across the room since she'd walked in.

She curled her suddenly cold hands into fists. She wanted to leave. To escape Antonio more than anything.

'It's not like you're running a brothel,' Antonio drawled softly enough so only she heard. 'Entertainment is a large part of what San Felipe offers and you're drawing in large numbers of younger customers. We don't want the island to be famous for being the holiday destination of only the old and wealthy.'

'It's never been that. The old and wealthy men have always had their young and beautiful companions with them on San Felipe,' she mocked.

That was what her mother had been for Salvatore Accardi—the nubile young accessory. And in recent years with the two Princes in charge? Beautiful and ambitious and hopeful women had been visiting in droves. Bella was just giving them a place to display themselves.

Antonio's eyes gleamed but then he glanced over her shoulder and his expression became as remote as ever.

'You are not out of place here.' He bowed formally. 'I hope you enjoy your evening.'

That was *it*? No heat? No words with hidden meaning or secret smile? Nothing. Disappointment deepened as he walked away.

It *was* all over for him.

Well, she wasn't letting him see how that hurt. She'd stay, she'd 'schmooze' and show both Salvatore and Antonio she was made of stronger stuff than either of them realised.

To her surprise it wasn't dreadful. People talked to her. Complimented her on her past career and asked about the club. She became aware of Salvatore Accardi talking loudly on the other side of the room about the degeneration of inner-city San Felipe, but she wasn't going to engage. She knew people were watching.

Antonio was watching. But he needn't worry, she wasn't going to cause a scene. Despite what he thought, she'd not chosen to set up her business in San Felipe so she could exact some kind of patricidal revenge on Salvatore. Life wasn't that simple. She'd come here because it was the one place she could. And it was the one place she actually enjoyed being, other than the stage.

But Salvatore Accardi's voice was drowned out when a ruddy-cheeked older man arrived late and walked straight over to Prince Antonio and greeted him with an etiquette-breaching booming voice.

'Please pass on my congratulations to your brother Prince Eduardo on the birth of his daughter,' the man gushed loudly as he beamed at Antonio.

'Thank you.' Antonio nodded intently, seeming aware of the sudden interest from all those standing near. He lifted his head and spoke clearly. 'It is very exciting for us. I am informed she's very determined to maintain her own schedule and refuses to fall in with her parents' request that she sleep at *night*.' He paused as everyone chuckled, a small smile lightening his features. 'So I am confident she will make a wonderfully stubborn Crown Princess in the future.'

There was the tiniest silence before a woman ventured another question.

'Will we get to meet the little Princess soon?'

Antonio's expression tightened and he paused before replying. 'Princess Sapphire is very young and this time in her life is very precious and private for her parents. I'm sure you'll all agree.' He softened his words with another glimmer of that rare smile and absolutely everyone in the vicinity completely agreed.

But Bella watched as that small smile faded from his eyes and her heart smote. With masterful PR skills, he'd offered just a hint of something personal about the new baby Princess to satisfy public curiosity while protecting her privacy. But at the same time his words had underlined his own abdication from any family or personal life of his own. He had no intention or desire to marry and provide an heir of his own. His niece would one day take the throne.

Until then he would be alone. Because he was the Heartbroken Prince.

Her heart thumping unaccountably quickly, Bella turned towards a waiter to ask for a glass of sparkling water. But as she turned her gaze hit upon the man who didn't just deny his role in her existence, but who'd chosen to denigrate and torment her mother *and* her.

Salvatore Accardi was looking right at her with such undisguised loathing she stumbled. Her lungs malfunctioned. She straightened but couldn't turn away.

Salvatore Accardi could. With a final condescending appraisal, he muttered something indecipherable to the person next to him and deliberately turned his back on her.

It was the most public of rejections and yet probably—hopefully—no one would have noticed.

Except *she'd* noticed and she was so humiliated that not even years of experience controlling her emotions as she faced huge crowds could help her stop the blush from spreading like a sudden rash over her skin. She glanced at others in the group, unable to resist the curiosity—had anyone seen?

The person who stood next to Salvatore, a tall brunette, was staring. Her half-sister. Francesca. Beautiful and—with the way she too then turned her back—every inch her father's daughter.

Bella finally found the power to move. She walked almost blindly from the room. She didn't want to talk business and she definitely didn't want to banter or flirt or *be* Bella.

'Ms Sanchez.'

Bella blinked and paused. Matteo had materialised beside her looking bland, but he spoke with gentle courtesy.

'I thought I would introduce you to Tomas Mancini. He owns the island's most popular Michelin-starred restaurant here on San Felipe. He owns several others too, in mainland Europe.'

His lengthy explanation gave her a chance to breathe and as he slowly walked her to the other end of the vast reception room she had time to pull herself together properly.

Tomas was about seventy, accompanied by his elegant wife, also around seventy years old, and they were both charming, both talkative and standing with them was somehow soothing. She stood with her back to the rest of the room, relieved of feeling the pressure of vindictive, prying eyes.

'Tomas started out as a firefighter, you know. He was based at the station you have refurbished as your club,' Tomas' wife, Maria, informed her. 'That's when I met him. He rescued me, you know.'

'Did he?' Bella was diverted. 'From a fire?'

'A fire *alarm*. There was no danger but I was mortified.' Maria nodded in all seriousness. 'But I like to think of young people having fun there now.' She paused for a second then added quietly, 'I had fun there once.'

There was nothing in her tone, but Bella looked sharply into the older woman's eyes. There was the veriest hint of a wink. Bella finally smiled.

'Maria, Carlo has just arrived.' Tomas turned to Bella. 'He was our first chef who moved to an outer island to open a satellite restaurant for us last year. Would you like to join us?'

'Thank you, I will shortly,' she said, wanting to give them a chance to have some time alone with their friend. 'I'll freshen up first and then find you.'

'If you'll accompany me, I'll show you the way.' Matteo stepped alongside her again.

Bella glanced at him in surprise; she'd thought he'd been called away.

'Thank you,' she said, quietly appreciative of the way he walked between her and the group that Salvatore and Francesca stood in. Salvatore's voice still carried; she couldn't hear the words but just the tone oozed arrogance.

'It is in here.' Matteo paused by a discreet door out in the long corridor.

Bella stepped inside, drawing in a deep breath, but as she closed the door behind her someone loomed right in front of her. Just as she was about to scream she realised who it was.

'You gave me such a *fright*.' She clapped her hand on her chest, almost needing to thump it to get her heart started again.

Antonio stood a breath away, his customary reserved expression incinerated by the raw need in his eyes. But he said nothing.

Now her hurt heart raced—sending anticipation and hunger sparking around every one of her cells.

'What are you doing in here?' She licked her dried lips and watched that need in his eyes burn all the more intensely.

'I need to see you again. Alone. Tonight.'

Relief hit her like a tornado, blowing the roof off her tension. She released her breath in a shaky sigh. But just as relief hit, so did the impossibility of what he was saying. 'We *can't*—'

'Not now, no,' he agreed. But that didn't stop him taking the step nearer so he could pull her against him.

His hand smoothed down her back, as if he were trying to soothe her, but she felt the rigidity of his body and realised how tightly *he* was coiled. She rested her head against his shoulder, stifling her groan of sheer relief.

'I'm sorry I used Matteo again,' he muttered against her hair. 'But there are too many people—'

'It's okay,' she interrupted. 'I understand.'

She understood he was lonely and that for whatever

reason he wanted *her* to help him find physical release. That was okay; she wanted him for the same.

They were both hurt and lonely.

She placed her hand on his chest and looked up at him, willing to accept however it had to be, as long as it could happen again. Just the once more.

'Bella.'

She barely had a chance to hear his strained mutter before his lips were on hers.

Passion burst free at first chance. She wrapped her arms around his neck, wriggling closer for more heavenly contact. His arms tightened, lifting her clear off her feet, and she moaned. She never wanted this kiss to end. Always he made her feel so good, filling her with that incomparable bliss. Dangerously addictive and too good to deny. She rocked against him, using her body to blatantly offer him everything. Right here. Right now. She was beyond caring.

'Bella, we can't,' he muttered.

'We can,' she pleaded. 'Just quickly. So quick.'

He touched her, growling between his teeth as he felt her readiness. 'Without protection?'

She bit back her own moan and vehemently shook her head. 'You think I'd ever make the same mistake as my mother? Contraception is covered.'

He stared at her another second and then crushed her mouth with his. The kiss was nothing but raw frustration. But then he tore from her—lifting his head to look down at her, holding her in place so she couldn't rub against him any more. She felt his tension morphing back to that impenetrable self-control. He had no intention of having his way with her here and now.

The disappointment was appallingly deep. Again.

'I've missed you,' he said.

She melted. His completely. But she made herself pull back and stand on her own two feet. 'I'd better get back out there,' she replied, determined to be as strong as he.

'You'd better redo your lipstick first,' he replied, flashing a wicked smile.

'And you'd better remove it.' She eyed his pristine white collar meaningfully. 'Before you end up wearing more.'

His hands loosened from her waist and he stepped further into the beautiful powder room, allowing her space. 'I'm sorry Salvatore Accardi is here tonight. He is too loud.'

Bella shrugged as she opened up her small evening purse and stepped forward to check her make-up in the gold-framed mirror. Her fingers shook.

'Does he ever talk to you?' Antonio watched her carefully restore the glossy sheen to her lips.

'He only talks *about* me.' She grimaced at her reflection. 'He thinks all I want is money from him.'

'And do you?'

She turned and sent him a sharp glance. 'I'd rather starve.'

'I saw him look at you. Then blank you,' Antonio said.

Embarrassment burned through her again and she turned away, wishing Antonio couldn't still see her face in the mirror. 'The most cordial we've been in years.'

'Don't try to make light of it.'

'He doesn't hurt me.'

'Don't lie to me,' he said softly. 'Go ahead and give him a hard time. Just don't make a mess.'

She added a last swipe of gloss. 'I'm not here to give him a hard time. I want nothing to do with him. I don't care what he thinks or says or does.'

Antonio was silent a moment. 'I will make arrangements for tonight.'

She put her lipstick back in her small purse and then turned. 'I will deal only with you and Matteo. No one else.' But she would give him that.

'Thank you.' He cupped her face and gazed down at her for a long moment, as if reading her thoughts. But he resisted her silent request to kiss her again.

'I must go now,' he said apologetically and then swiftly left the room via another door.

Bella turned back to her reflection and tried to think calm thoughts to reduce the telltale colour in her cheeks. But flickers of excitement shot through her veins. She wanted him again. Couldn't and wouldn't say no to him or herself.

Maybe that made her his concubine. But she would take nothing else from him. Not a penny, a dress or a jewel, not a thing. And she was not his friend. Only his lover. And only for one more night.

CHAPTER SIX

THE HOURS THAT night stretched for ever. For the first time since she'd opened the club, she couldn't wait to close it. As soon as she'd seen off the last of her employees, she stood in the doorway. It was still dark, but in another hour or so the sky would lighten and the sun rise. A black car slowly cruised down the street towards her. Unmarked but opulent, it pulled in just by the main door, parking illegally. The driver's tinted window wound down a couple of inches. She'd expected Matteo, but it was Antonio.

Quickly she stepped forward and got into the passenger seat. He pulled away in seconds. She couldn't help but glance along the street, nervous that someone would have seen them. But the road was empty.

Silently he steered towards the very heart of San Felipe.

'You can actually drive?' She tried to make conversation with a tease, but her throat was dry and her voice tight.

'I am allowed, occasionally,' he replied in his formal way, but then he smiled. 'Ready?'

The giant gate before them opened without him hitting a button. She didn't see any guards or any officials as she stepped out in the internal garage that was bigger than the average-sized house and was filled with eye-wateringly expensive cars.

'This is the palace.' She whispered the obvious as he led her into the wide hallway. Even with the dim night lighting she could see the gilt-edged paintings lining the walls, the pedestals with priceless sculptures and the glass cabinets filled with antiquities and artefacts.

Her heart hammered. She'd never expected him to bring her to the palace. Wasn't it too risky?

The imposing building was incredibly silent and huge and she was paranoid there were security cameras everywhere snapping her with him.

'I know,' he whispered back. 'I want the comfort of my own bed.'

'But—'

'Be quiet.' He turned and quickly kissed her for emphasis. 'Someone might hear,' he whispered, then took her hand and led her through the maze.

Surprised, she glanced at him and saw the mischievous grin on his face.

He was Antonio, the ultra-serious Crown Prince, wasn't he? He owned this oversized, unbelievably opulent place and yet here he was sneaking around like a teenager.

He led her up some stairs, then more stairs and long corridors and finally came to a set of doors on the third or fourth floor—she'd lost count. He opened them and hung back to let her walk in first.

'This is your private apartment?' she asked, knowing the answer anyway, but feeling as if she needed to say *something*.

When he'd closed the doors she turned to face him.

But that gorgeous, elusive smile had faded and his expression was even more closed off than usual. Did he feel as awkward as she?

'When did you last have a…guest up here?' she asked.

That brought his smile back but he remained silent.

'You're just trying to make me feel special,' she joked lightly.

'You are special.'

She walked around the large room, mainly to hide the blush she could feel heating her cheeks. He didn't mean anything by it, but the gentle flirt was nice.

His apartment was a masterpiece of elegant understatement, the decor minimalist compared to the multitude of treasures in the cabinets lining the corridors. But it was so impersonal it made her heart ache for him again. Even she, with few truly personal possessions, had put her own stamp on her room. She had the flowers she loved to get from the early morning market, she had a small print from Paris to remind her of happier times with her mother, she had the ballerina jewellery box she'd won in her first ballet competition when she was barely five and had treasured ever since. But Antonio had a beautifully styled masculine lounge with nothing obviously personal that she could note. There were no paintings on the walls and no photos at all— not of him and his family and none of Alessia—which relieved her in one way, yet saddened her in another.

She turned to face him again and found he'd been slowly following her. Now he was only a pace away.

'You want to see all my rooms?' he asked, something veiled in his expression.

'I want to see everything,' she replied before thinking. She was so much more curious than she ought to be.

'There's not really that much to see.'

Well, there was beauty and incredible design and craftsmanship, but she wasn't here to admire an art gallery and she didn't want to treat him or his home as a museum exhibit. That was what his life must be like all the time and she wanted to understand more about him.

That was when she realised his place didn't matter; it was the *person* before her who held all the clues. If she wanted to understand him at all, she needed only to spend time with him. But they had only now. She gazed into his unfathomable eyes and wished she knew how to make him smile.

'I thought you wanted to see everything?' he finally prompted her.

'No.' She shook her head. 'Now I just want...' Her words faltered.

He took the last step towards her. 'Me.'

She nodded. 'Just you.'

She wanted to focus wholly on him, but they weren't here to talk. This was a clandestine convenience. A risky, stolen moment. Her heart tripped and thudded too fast. She waited, anticipating that burst of passion. They probably still wouldn't make it to his bed.

But he didn't kiss her. He took her by the hand. 'Let me show you one thing.' He walked down the hallway and opened the furthest door, waiting for her to walk in ahead of him.

'What's in here?' She summoned a tease. 'Your hidden den of iniquity?'

She walked in without waiting for an answer and stopped in surprise.

The room was large, its floor-to-ceiling windows protected by billowing drapes, protecting his privacy yet allowing the citrus-scented summer air to perfume the room. It was all but empty. Bella drank in the large expanse of polished wooden floor. And in the corner was a baby grand piano.

'You have your own dance studio?' That floor was begging to be danced on.

'Music room,' he corrected with a laugh.

'You're a musician?' She turned to look at him.

'You're surprised.' His rare smile flashed and stayed.

'You never seem to do anything other than serious "prince" things.'

'I appreciate many things. But especially music.' He walked over to the piano. 'It relaxes me. As dancing relaxes you.'

She was delighted to discover this and that he'd shared it with her. And she wanted him to share more. 'So will you play for me?'

He raised his brows at her.

'Please.'

'It would be my pleasure.' He sat down at the stool.

Bella crossed the floor and rested her hand on the smooth, glossy wood of the piano. It was beautiful to touch and she bet it would be an amazing sound. He glanced up at her for a moment then looked down to the keys. Intrigued, Bella leaned closer.

He began. After only a moment, Bella froze, unsure of how to react. He'd chosen an elementary piece and was literally banging it out. Two fingers smashed down on the wrong notes. He hit so *many* wrong notes, and it was so loud, Bella didn't know where to look.

But then a wicked smile spread over his face and his hand positioning changed. The melody changed. *Everything* changed.

'You tease.' She laughed, relieved, and moved closer to watch. He shifted on the piano stool, straightening.

'The look on your face.' He chuckled as he played, beautifully.

'Who knew solemn Prince Antonio would be a prankster?' She leaned over his shoulder, letting her hair brush against his cheek, aiming to distract him and make him hit a wrong note for real this time.

'You didn't know what to say.' He stopped playing and reached up to hold her in place near him, turning his head to press a kiss to her cheek. 'I was lowering your expectations. Now you think I'm better than I actually am…'

She pulled back to read his expression. 'My assessment of your performance matters to you that much?' She never would have thought he'd care.

'I've never played for anyone else.' He shrugged and glanced back to the black and white keys.

'I'm honoured.' And she was touched, that warmth in her soul that he'd let her into his secret life, just a little.

'Dance for me,' he softly requested as he began another piece. 'The way you were that morning I spied on you.'

'Okay.' Her heat soaring, she kissed *his* cheek in the lightest of caresses and stepped away from the piano. 'Barefoot, okay?' She kicked off her shoes.

'Don't feel the need to stop there.' He sent her a wicked look. 'Naked would be amazing.'

She laughed, pleased at his emerging playfulness. 'I never dance this way for just anyone, you know.'

He nodded, all seriousness again. 'I do know.'

She laughed again at the arrogance implicit in his reply but her heart fluttered, enjoying the lightness and liberty to just *be* with him.

He'd chosen a romantic melody and it was so easy to let go and lose herself in the streaming beauty of it. Smiling, she stretched her arms wide and simply moved, not showing any fancy steps, not needing to prove anything to him.

That was the thing, with him—physically, at least, she could simply enjoy the sensations, the moment. And now, the music.

But as the melody worked towards its crescendo she couldn't help looking at him to gauge his reaction. Her gaze meshed with his and was caught fast. His magnetism pulled her nearer. As the music grew softer, she danced closer. Softer and closer still until, as the last note died away, she slipped between the piano and him. He leaned back to let her straddle his muscular thighs. That wicked smile curved his lips and he began to play another piece, a teasing glint warming his ice-blue eyes.

She decided two could tease. She bent close and poured all the radiance she felt into her kiss. The notes of the piano continued to sound for only a moment. Then his magic fingers began to play her and she was so very glad she'd worn a dress.

He slipped the soft fabric up her thighs, exposing her to his touch. She wriggled and he slipped the silk right over her head.

'Antonio,' she breathed softly, so hot for him already.

'At your service,' he promised, leaning forward to kiss the crest of her breasts. 'I'm wondering if I can make you sound as good as my piano.'

'Play me and see.'

'I can already see,' he muttered in a pleased tone.

She felt his hardness beneath her and ached to free him from his clothing. She reached for him.

'Nu huh.' He shifted her above him with a laugh. 'I'm playing you, remember?'

'I was going for some harmony. Accompaniment.' She needed him with her. In her. Like now.

'Soon.' He soothed her with a kiss.

'No. Now.' She kissed him hard.

But he was ruthless. Relentless. He caressed, kissed, rubbed. Hard then soft, changing his stroke and rhythm, tormenting her until she banged the damn piano keys herself, trying to hurry him to get him to take her. When he finally relented and let her reach her release, she screamed long and loud until she slumped into his arms with a sigh.

'I can't take any more,' she begged. 'I need you. Please.'

He clasped her tightly and carried her through to another room. He set her on her feet and stood back from her.

'Take me, then,' he invited.

She noticed nothing at all about his bedroom. She was only focused on him. But he had to help her strip him out of his clothes. She was too frantic, too needy to get her fingers to work properly.

'Condoms. Pocket,' he muttered roughly.

She retrieved one and with a small smile set about ensuring he was sheathed. She took her time and used her mouth as much as her hands and when she'd finally finished he was swearing in a continuous stream beneath his breath.

She laughed and pushed him so he fell back on the bed. But the moment she knelt on the expansive mattress to join him he moved, as quick and powerful as a panther catching his prey. She rolled, letting him, welcoming him. She couldn't wait a second longer anyway.

'Hurry,' she called to him. 'Please.'

But he paused and smiled down at her and she knew what that wicked, gleaming smile meant.

Sheer, delightful torture.

'You're not going to do this fast, are you?' She shivered as her body geared up for more of his teasing onslaught.

He angled his head as if considering the plea in her words. 'It might end up that way. Eventually.'

She licked her lips and ran her hand down his rock-hard abs. 'I'm willing to fight dirty.' She'd do whatever she could to make him claim her sooner rather than later.

That challenge sharpened the edge in his expression. 'Go ahead, darling, do your worst. I intend to fight dirtier.'

Oh, Lord, she was in trouble. She yelped in laughter as he tugged her further up the mattress so he could claim the part of her most begging for his attention again.

And then she just gave in to his desire to see her soar again. He might be reserved, but when he was fully focused on *her*—it was wicked heaven.

That magical hour later she smiled as he lay sprawled, sweat slicked and breathless, at the opposite end of the bed. The coverings were on the floor, the dawn light warmed the room and she'd never been as relaxed in her life. And she'd never felt as close to anyone else either. Not just physically, but it was as if she was in tune with him and they'd made the most beautiful music together.

He rested his head on his hand and ran a finger along the jagged red scar than ran down her shin and to her ankle. 'Does it hurt?'

'No. It just tickles,' she murmured.

'What happened?'

'Glass in my shoe.' She stretched her foot languorously, unutterably relaxed.

He frowned. 'Glass?'

'In my pointe shoe,' she explained briefly. 'Not much. I didn't feel it until I was partway through the performance. But, you know, the show must go on.'

He shifted down to her foot and inspected her toes.

'Don't.' She tried to curl them away because they were so ugly and now she was self-conscious and regretted telling him that much.

'You kept dancing?' He released her foot and she pulled her legs from his reach.

'Of course. When you're in the zone, you feel invincible. You don't notice until it's almost too late. At first I thought it was just a bad blister or something. In the end I fell and landed badly and broke my ankle and shin.'

And when she'd looked later, there'd been blood seeping through her pointe shoe. The cut had been so deep it had severed nerves and the chunk of glass they'd struggled to remove had been viciously jagged.

'The show went on.' She shrugged, playing it down with a casual smile. 'The understudy stepped up. I went to hospital.'

One of the pins they'd put in was still there and during those months in plaster she'd lost flexibility, muscle tone. Confidence.

Everything.

'There was no way you could build up your strength again?' he asked. 'Retrain and get back out there?'

'Not to the level I want.' And it had been ruined for her. That someone in her own company had hated her that much to do something so horrific?

She'd thought the company had been her safe haven but she'd been wrong.

So she was determined to be independent now. Any success she had, she would own in its entirety. She wouldn't be vulnerable by being reliant on anyone else. She had to control her own destiny and haul herself out of any problems alone. It was the lesson her mother had never learned.

'How did the glass get in your shoe?' Antonio asked ominously.

She didn't want to answer but she knew that look in his eye. The wickedness had vanished and he was in 'ruthless ruler' mode. She shouldn't have answered so thoughtlessly in the first place. 'I guess some people didn't believe I deserved my position in the company. That I was there because of my profile, not talent. Sex appeal, not technique.'

He looked grim. 'Did they catch whoever did it?'

'I didn't want to cause a scandal and nor did company management.' Sebastian had asked her not to go to the police, arguing bad press would destroy the company. And she'd had her reasons for agreeing with his request.

'*What?*'

She flinched at the fury in Antonio's tone.

'I didn't want people to know I was a victim,' she defended herself hotly. 'I didn't want the world to know I had enemies who'd do something that mean. I didn't want to show that.' She hadn't wanted *anyone* to know how vulnerable she was. How isolated. So she'd left and played up the party queen. 'I fell. My leg broke. End of story.'

And she'd trust no one now. Not even a prince.

She reached out and ran her hand over the small silver elephant that she noticed sitting on the nightstand, wanting to distract them both. 'This is pretty.'

He glanced at the trinket, still frowning. 'Alessia gave it to me for my birthday.'

Silently she wondered which birthday, how long ago and what significance the elephant held. All she knew about elephants was that supposedly they never forgot anything.

Maybe that was what it was—for him to remember her. They'd been school sweethearts for years before getting engaged, hadn't they? Bella returned the trinket to the table and looked back down the bed to Antonio.

His expression had shut down, of course. Remote, reserved Prince Antonio had returned. He might be lying at her feet, but he couldn't be further removed and it couldn't be more obvious that he didn't want to discuss it with her. Of course he didn't.

That sense of intimacy she'd felt only moments before—that closeness beyond the physical—dissolved. He'd never let her into his life the way he'd let his fiancée. He'd never love like that again. He wouldn't let himself. And that was fair enough. She too knew how much it was possible to hurt.

She smiled, determined not to let it show that *she* hurt right now. She was the distraction, the secret lover, the light relief for the royal workaholic. And she'd keep this private and fun because *he* was her distraction too. He was the one man who'd finally made her feel *good* and enjoy her sensuality and she wasn't going to let anything ruin this last stolen moment she had with him. Certainly not any stupidly weak emotion.

But how did she forbid her heart from falling for him?

CHAPTER SEVEN

THE HOURS AND days stretched ahead, empty and frustrating, loaded with meetings from European delegations and civic duties. Nothing he could get out of.

He'd certainly been unable to decline this afternoon's invitation to tour the new addition to the cancer unit at the hospital. While there, the staff had taken him on a tour of Alessia's Garden. Amongst the beautiful roses and serene seating in the heart of the hospital grounds, he'd given his speech and thanked the committee for all the fundraising they'd done over the years, and continued to do, in his fiancée's name. Because of them her name lived on.

They didn't know that because of him, she'd died.

Not even his brother knew the truth.

Desperation curled around him as he read through the next day's timetable. He needed a break from it. For the first time since he'd been crowned he wanted a holiday and an escape from the weight he carried on his shoulders. He'd never had more than a few days away and even then he'd taken work with him. It had been the one constant in his life, the one thing he knew he *could* do right. It was his calling.

But now he craved another moment of escape—

from duty, from his past, from the lie he lived day in and out.

He didn't deserve it, but he hungered for a moment of selfishness—the time to laze, linger and laugh on a bed with Bella instead of stealing a too-quick liaison in the last hour of the night.

He wanted just a little more. A whole night. A whole day. Enough of a feast to cure him and help him forget.

Three days since he'd done the unthinkable and brought her home, he sat alone in the palace, watching the hands of the clock slowly tick by.

There was no escape from his unrelenting schedule. And even if there was, he couldn't go to the island: his brother, Eduardo, was there.

Eduardo.

The brother to whom he'd never told the truth. The brother who'd repeatedly asked him how he could serve him better. The brother who'd changed so much in the last year since finding happiness with his soldier wife.

Antonio stared at his desk and finally picked up his phone. His brother answered immediately.

'I need you to come to San Felipe,' Antonio said quietly. 'I need you to attend a couple of events for me.'

'You're not well?' The shock in Eduardo's voice burned.

'I'm fine.' He couldn't lie about that. 'I only need a day or so out.'

'I will come right away,' Eduardo answered, still obviously stunned, but he didn't question more.

'Thank you.' Antonio rubbed the back of his neck. 'It's nothing serious. I just need a little time.'

'It's fine. I'm glad you asked.' Eduardo sounded as if he was moving already. 'If I need to make contact—'

'I'll be on the water.' Antonio gazed out of the window to the inky black space where the Mediterranean ebbed and flowed. 'You can radio me on the boat.'

Because he wasn't completely reckless. But nor could he wait 'til dawn.

An hour later he stood in the landing just outside her office, looking over the narrow balcony railing to where she was in the middle of the dance floor. It had been a risk, but at this hour the club was mostly in darkness, the lights flashing, confusing, disguising.

Everyone present was too busy noticing her to notice him anyway. In white trousers and a slim white top she danced in the centre of the main floor. There was a space around her, like a halo, as if somehow everyone knew they were forbidden to get too close.

But they watched. They *all* watched. And Antonio watched as Matteo told her. She stiffened and swiftly walked off the dance floor. Antonio stepped back into her office, anticipating.

'You shouldn't be here,' she said, striding in only moments later and slamming the door behind her.

'And yet here I am.' And he couldn't help but be aroused and amused as he drank in her energy. This was exactly what he wanted. Bella looking strong and fierce and crackling with fire.

'This is my club.'

'This is my country.' He crossed his arms, forcing himself to wait for her comeback.

'And you want to be seen here?'

'I thought this was the place to be seen. Am I going to inhibit your guests' pleasure?'

'They'll be thrilled to be in your presence. I'm sure they'll bust out their best moves for you. Especially our female guests. Will you be joining them on the dance floor or just *watching*?' Her eyes glinted.

He breathed in carefully, cooling his blood. But he was looking forward to the next twenty-four hours too damn much. It was all he could do not to reach for her now but if he did that, they'd never leave.

'Or is this another snap compliance inspection?' Bella smirked.

'Actually, this is an abduction.' He smiled back, hugely appreciating her not so subtle bite.

Her eyes widened. 'I'm sorry?'

'I'm taking you with me.'

'Pardon?'

'You don't need to pack. We're leaving now.'

'I can't leave *now*.'

Satisfaction thrummed. It was only timing she was concerned with? She wanted to come with him. 'Either you come quietly and right away, or I have the whole place shut down.'

Her gaze met his. Her face flamed at the double entendre he'd intended. He shifted on his feet, releasing the tension that was streaming through his body.

'Nothing like abuse of power, Antonio,' she finally responded.

'I have your best interests at heart.'

'Really.'

'Seriously.' He admired her independence but it irritated the hell out of him at the same time. 'We can leave quietly. Everyone is interested in the other celebrities on the dance floor.'

'Getting good at plotting, aren't you?'

'You look tired.' He frowned, because she did. And she looked paler than usual.

'Way to make me feel attractive.'

'When did you last get to bed before midnight?' he asked.

'What concern is it of yours?' She shook her head at him. 'You're not supposed to start caring, Antonio. That's not what you're about.'

It wasn't about *caring*. It was about having a very little more time for just the two of them. 'You work too hard and sleep too little.'

'So do you.' She shrugged. 'But that's not the point. It's no business of yours and I am not here waiting for your beck and call. I don't live for your summons. I have my own life to get on with.'

'Yes, you're right.' Every word she spoke was true. But there was something else equally true. He strolled up to her, framing her face in his hands and tilting her head so he could see right into her eyes. 'But you want this as much as I do.'

Her expression altered, the defiance drained and disappointment brought those shadows back.

'What I want doesn't really matter, though,' she admitted, a hint of sadness colouring her soft tone. 'I can't leave.' She gestured to her laptop open on her desk. 'Because I need to run the business. I need to understand it. I'm more than the face for it. I need to be the brains behind it. I need to make it work.'

Bella wasn't about to admit it, but Antonio was right: she was so tired and in need of a break. And that he was *here*, that he'd come to her once more?

That stunned her. Delighted her. *Distracted* her.

But if she could stay focused for just a little while she could pull her life back on track, *without* relying on anyone else. No one was taking her career from her again. No one was taking anything. 'I can't go with you.'

His eyes lasered into her, branding her even as she tried to resist him. She lifted her chin. It wasn't her problem if he didn't like hearing the word 'no' for the first time in his life. But after a moment her heart starting skipping.

'Don't look at me like that,' she whispered.

'Like what?'

'You know.' She shook her head. 'It's not fair.'

His smile appeared. 'You look at me like that.'

Her resistance wavered. 'Antonio, please,' she asked, determined not to let him dictate her world in this way. She needed to keep this on her own terms. She *wasn't* a plaything—for all that manufactured media representation. She had concrete goals and she had to meet them. He couldn't derail her long-term plans. 'Don't make me change my mind.'

But she was tempted. And he knew it.

'Bella,' he whispered. 'It's just for a little while. Little more than a day. Don't you think you deserve that? Don't I? Matteo will ensure the club is closed and secure. There's only another hour to go anyway. It will be taken care of.'

He was so high-handed and arrogant and confident. And kind.

'What do you want more?' he asked. 'To put me in my place or take just a moment for yourself?'

In truth her reluctance wasn't about making him pay, it was about giving herself the time to draw strength to cope with him. He was so overpowering, she couldn't let him tear down every last defence and get a foothold in her heart. She couldn't be that weak over him. But she couldn't say 'no' any more than she could stop breathing.

He smiled. He knew he'd won.

He took her hand. She curled her fingers around his and walked with him. He already had his phone in his other hand and was sending a message, presumably to Matteo.

'We need to go up to the roof.' He led her to the emergency exit door.

'Why?'

It became clear in only a moment.

'You landed a helicopter on the roof of my building?'

'And picked the lock on the door.' He chuckled. 'It was fun. But you need to install a better security alarm'

'It was *crazy*.' She walked up the stairs with him. 'Is it safe to fly at night?'

'I have the best pilot on duty, don't worry,' Antonio answered. 'And the sun is going to rise soon enough.'

He was right: the sky was lightening.

Suddenly shy, Bella didn't even look at the man in position behind the controls.

'Are we going to Secrete Reale?' It was the smallest island of the San Felipe archipelago, the Princes' private haven. It was the place his brother had taken countless women, if those rumours were to be believed.

'We can't. Eduardo's family is there,' Antonio answered briefly.

She watched as they flew low and fast over the water. It was only a twenty-minute trip and as the sun rose she saw the gleaming white jewel waiting on the water.

Her blood ran cold.

It wasn't a boat. It was a gargantuan palace. From

the air she could see the large pool and spa on deck, the surrounding plush furniture scattered with bright white cushions and, on one side, the helipad that they were now descending towards. It was the ultimate example of ostentatious wealth and luxury.

Cold horror slid down her spine as she realised that history was repeating itself in the most tasteless of ways.

She was his mistress and being 'treated' to a little more than a few stolen hours. Just as her mother had been so many times.

Her nerves jangled but she could say nothing under the noise of the engine. Antonio opened the door as soon as they'd landed and jumped out, turning to help her.

'I can't stay here. I can't be seen on here.' She wrung her hands, anxiously watching as the helicopter lifted off again within seconds of their disembarking.

'If you prefer, you do not have to leave the cabin at all.' He grinned wolfishly.

That humour tore the last of her control.

'You have no idea,' she turned to rage at him. 'How spoilt can you be?' She glared. Wounded and angry with herself for being so weak and willing. 'I don't want to be here with you.'

He visibly recoiled at the venom in her tone. 'I apologise.' His expression shuttered. 'We will return to town immediately.'

She met his gaze. The stiffness in his stance didn't hide the tiredness in his eyes. He was trying to do something nice. He'd just gone about it in princely fashion, arrogant as hell. And he didn't know or he would never have chosen this as their destination.

She sighed and sat down in the nearest seat, literally unable to stand any more. 'Antonio.'

His eyebrow flickered. 'Something you want to tell me?'

She rested her aching head in her hands. 'My mother went on a boat like this once.' More than once. Her mother had loved this kind of lavish holiday. 'With Salvatore Accardi.'

Antonio squatted in front of her so he could see up into her face. She couldn't hide from him.

'They took photos from a helicopter,' she said.

'There will be no helicopters other than the one we just arrived in,' he said.

'You don't understand,' she mumbled, her cheeks scarlet with shame. 'My mother and her lover were photographed on the deck of the boat. It was the moment of my conception.' Or so the papers had speculated at the time. That image—of her mother naked on her back with her married lover between her legs—had been one of the most scandalous images of the decade. The flaunting of an affair that had only hurt all the women involved.

Accardi had denied the dark-haired man in the picture was him.

Deny, deny, deny, was all he ever did.

'I should have talked with you first,' Antonio said quietly. 'I thought you would like it.'

'Anyone normal would,' she admitted. She closed her eyes. 'I'm sorry.'

Here she was on the same kind of symbol of opulence and wealth and corruption, with a man who could have anything—and any*one*—he wanted.

'I'm sorry too.' He caressed her cheek with his

thumb. 'But you're not her. And I'm not him.' Standing, he reached forward and scooped her into his arms. 'What we both are is very tired. You've been burning the candle at both ends. You need a rest.'

She half smiled at the stiff way he expressed the old saying. She rested her head on his chest, feeling his heart beating, suddenly unbearably tired. 'Yes.'

'Then let's get you to bed.'

She wanted to touch him and feel the mindless relief that he could bring, but the waves of exhaustion rolling over her were too strong and in his arms she relaxed completely. Her eyes closed as she felt him descend the steps into the body of the boat.

She felt him place her on the soft bed, felt his lips on hers. Too gently. Too briefly. But she couldn't win the fight to open her eyes again.

'Stay,' she murmured, at least she tried to say it but it might have only been a moan.

'I'm right here.'

And he was. Curled up beside her, drawing a soft blanket over them both.

CHAPTER EIGHT

BELLA HAD NO idea what the time was when she woke, but, given light was streaming through the beautiful window, she figured it had to be late in the afternoon.

'I didn't realise you were going to sleep for hours.'

She turned at the sound of Antonio's drawl.

'Hours.' He threw her a mock chagrined look.

With a sleepy smile she rolled onto her back and stretched her toes. 'Sorry.' She glanced back at him. *'Not* sorry.'

Silently he regarded her, his reserved expression more pronounced, when suddenly his solemnity broke and the sexiest smile spread across his face. He crooked his little finger at her. 'Maybe you'd better come here and show me how "not sorry" you are.'

Her body hummed in anticipation, but she couldn't resist attempting another tease. 'I can't make it all the way over there...' She stretched lazily again.

'Going to make me do all the work?'

'You seem to like to be in charge.' She shrugged, sending him a look from under her lashes.

'You like choosing not to do what I ask.'

'Maybe it's all in the *way* you ask...' She let her voice trail suggestively.

'How should I ask?' he asked. The ominous tone made her tingle all the more.

'With kisses, of course.'

He reached out and grabbed her foot, hauling her down the bed towards him. 'Good thing I know how and where you like to be kissed.'

Bella could only arch up on the bed and let him.

Slowly the sky turned from blue to a burnished gold as the sun seemed to sink into the water.

'Come up on deck,' Antonio invited gently. 'It's almost dark. No one is there to see us.'

He was right, there was no one there. He must employ incredibly diligent and discreet staff—because while she and he had slept, they'd worked hard to create a sheltered lounge area on the deck that had silk walls and sofas surrounding a sensual plunge pool. Silver platters were scattered on the low table, laden with freshly prepared treats. It was private and beautiful and *safe*. She wrapped herself in the robe he'd handed her and curled on the plush cushions. She bit into a strawberry, relishing the burst of flavour.

'Do you often come away on this boat?' she asked, watching in amusement—and unashamed appreciation—as he slipped into the warm splash pool.

'Not as often as I'd like,' he admitted, sweeping his wet hair from his brow and looking too sexy for comfort. 'I usually bring work with me.' He angled his head and eyed her wickedly. 'I guess I brought manual labour with me this time.'

'Manual?' She arched her brows.

He held up his hands, then wiggled his fingers. 'Hours and hours of hard, physical labour.' He sighed theatrically. 'Except you slept away so *many* hours...'

'I woke once or twice,' she informed him primly. 'And found you fast asleep beside me.' He'd been utterly gorgeous too—handsome and relaxed and not at all reserved. 'Admit it,' she dared him. 'It wasn't so bad.'

'I think we both feel better for it.' He rubbed his jaw with a grin.

She certainly felt better. She couldn't stop smiling. The more she was with him, the less she could believe this was real. That quiet, reserved, emotionally distant Prince Antonio was warm and funny and kind when relaxed. When alone with her and away from the rest of the world he was charming and witty. And so gloriously sensual.

It was better than any fantasy. She just had to remember it wasn't for ever.

He'd fallen silent. She realised he was studying her as much as she was studying him but that the laughter in his eyes had faded, replaced by a frown.

'What's wrong?' she asked before thinking better of it.

A shadow flickered in his eyes before he spoke. 'It's weird not to be working.'

She felt certain that wasn't what he'd been thinking, but she didn't challenge him on it. 'You're allowed a break. That's what you told me, remember?'

'You know what it is like to devote your life to your career. It would feel strange to miss a day of training for you, right? It's a calling more than a career.'

'I chose mine. You were born to yours.'

'It's in the blood, I guess.' He reached out to take her foot, rubbing her scarred skin. 'When did you choose ballet?'

'I got my first personal trainer just before I turned two. And a ballet coach.'

His hands stopped the delicious massage. 'A personal trainer when you were *two*?'

She chuckled at his outraged expression. 'I was my mother's cute accessory that she toted around until I grew too big for her to carry.' She'd been the pretty little girl. Until she started to attract comment that she was more attractive than her mother. 'I won a scholarship to study at a dance academy in England when I was ten and eventually she let me go. I loved it. There were no boyfriends, no cameras, no scandal. I could just get on with doing the thing I loved.'

'But you were away from your mother?'

'That wasn't a problem,' she said wryly. Keeping her mother's secrets had been a burden she'd been too young for. And she hadn't liked the vulnerability she'd felt as a teenager with those men around.

He hoisted himself out of the water to sit on the deck and reached for a towel. 'So you weren't close.'

'It was complicated.' Bella frowned. 'I loved her very much, but she had a lot going on in her life.'

'By a lot going on, you mean a lot of men.'

'Yes.' Bella refused to deny it. 'She spent a large part of her life looking for love and she never found it.'

She'd been used and had used lovers herself.

'Are you looking for love?' Antonio asked.

Bella laughed. 'I know what I'm not looking for.' She gazed out at the darkening water. 'Before I went home to Mother for a holiday one summer Matron at school taught me some self-defence moves. Ways to try to get away and a few lines to spin to get some distance if I needed them.'

'Did you need to use them?'

She shrugged. 'Fortunately I spent most of the holidays at other ballet summer schools or camps. I'd only see Mother for long weekends at the most. And when I did, there were lots of cameras. Cameras can actually make things safer.'

He inclined his head questioningly.

'People are more aware of their own behaviour when they know they're being recorded.' She stretched her foot. 'And I think my mother knew there was a safety net in having a boyfriend. It means you're taken.' She smiled. 'It keeps others at a distance. Mostly.'

'But you don't do that too—there's no safe boyfriend?'

'Only the one when I was young and thought I was in love.' She wrinkled her nose at her naïveté.

'But you weren't really in love with him?'

'I wanted to be.' She'd wanted to be loved. To feel secure. To be held and cared for. To be safe. To have someone want her—*all* of her—and just her.

'What happened?'

'I thought he was honest and strong. He wasn't. He let me down.'

'How?'

She didn't like the thundercloud that had appeared on Antonio's face. 'He didn't really want me. He wanted the…fame…of being with me. I was the prize.' She rubbed her arm. 'But he expected more from me. What with my family history…'

'More?'

'A sexpot between the sheets,' she said bitterly. 'Like my siren of a mother. The famous lover of all those powerful men…'

'And you're not a sexpot.' He leant forward and cupped her cheek. 'Not for just anyone.'

She felt her flush rising. 'Don't tease...' she whispered.

He gazed at her, his expression utterly solemn. 'I'm not a sexpot for just anyone either.' And then he smiled.

She laughed a little, as he'd intended her to. 'He was seeing someone else on the side.'

'Because he was a jerk,' Antonio stated simply. 'Not because of anything you did or didn't do.' He reached out and lit one of the candles in the table, casting a small glow in the darkness. 'And since then?'

She shrugged. 'There hasn't been anyone serious.'

'You don't like trading on your sex appeal.'

She paused. 'I don't want to be ungrateful. I know how incredibly lucky I am compared to so many other people—to live on San Felipe, to have secured the financial backing for my business, to have access to all those clothes...some women would love that. But I want to be able to do what I really *want* to do. So all this "show" is only 'til the club becomes a commercial success. I need to earn for a couple of years, then I intend to step back and do something else.'

'But you must love it in part—no one can fake it for that long. All those photos. All that dancing.'

'I adore dancing.' She leaned forward. 'And I guess I do quite like the clothes.' She chuckled. 'I like feeling like I look okay—it's the way I was raised and old habits die hard—it's a weird paradox. But I don't want that to be *all* I'm known for. When I was dancing, I had that as well.'

'So what is going to replace it?' He looked at her

curiously. 'You must have some ideas if it's not the club.'

'No, that's a means to an end. I couldn't get the backing I needed for what I really want to do.' It wasn't going to be a money spinner, but she needed only enough for herself to live on.

'And that is?'

She paused, then laughed at her own self-consciousness. What did it matter if he knew? 'I want to establish my own ballet school. I want to have my own academy and teach.' She felt her flush rising again. 'I know it won't exactly make me a fortune, but it's what I love and I want to share it.'

'You want to teach ballet?' Surprise glinted in his eyes.

'Yes.'

He nodded but then frowned again. 'Why San Felipe? If not to taunt Salvatore?'

'I came for some holidays here with my mother. She had another friend here, for a time.' She knew he'd understand she meant another lover. 'I always loved it here. The beaches are beautiful, the city old and majestic.' She shrugged with a soft smile. 'You know it has a magic about it.'

'And your mother's friend?'

'The relationship didn't last, of course. He passed away a few years ago.' She sighed. 'So there you have it, why I'm here. It's not that exciting at all, you see.'

Silent, he ran his fingers along her scarred shin as if he could somehow smooth it away. 'Why did you never ask for an investigation or press charges?'

'About the glass?' She faltered, but then pressed on. She'd worked hard to reconcile her decision. 'I didn't want them to see how much they'd hurt me. They'd win if they saw that. I'll never let them see how much they got to me,' she said in a low tone, keeping her head high.

'You're not bulletproof,' he said.

'It doesn't matter.' She tried to shrug it off.

'It matters immensely. You had the thing you love most stolen from you. You were stolen from us—the audience.'

She smiled softly at his support of her. 'It just is what it is. I've accepted it and I'm moving on. I'm a survivor.' She was determined, and proud to be.

The sun had vanished but now the stars had come out to shine. And the moonlight glittered over the water. He fetched one of the blankets that were folded on one of the sofas and brought it back to where she was nestled in the cushions.

He paused at the solitary candle flickering on the low table. 'You want to stay out here with me tonight?'

She nodded and watched him blow the candle out.

The dreadful thing was she'd stay with him wherever he asked, for as long as he wanted. Yes, she was falling for him, but she also agreed because he shouldn't be out here alone.

He'd been on the front page of today's paper, standing in the hospital garden that honoured Alessia. In his midnight-blue suit with his pale, emotionless eyes he'd looked so isolated. She wished he wouldn't shut himself away so completely. She wished he'd open up like this even more. There was a warm, funny, compassionate guy locked away in there and someone—never her—should help him be happy.

He should be happy.

But she wasn't the woman who could make that happen for him. She was the woman who had him only for now.

CHAPTER NINE

SHE WAS WOKEN with a kiss. She smiled—how could she not when he looked at her like that? He was tousled and stubbled and tired about the eyes and so very sexy.

She'd told herself she wasn't going to sleep at all during their night on deck under the stars, but he'd teased her so long and made her come so hard her body had waved the white flag not long before dawn.

'What time is it?' she asked him.

'Stupidly early,' he admitted apologetically. 'But there's something I wanted you to see.'

Holding the soft blanket to her, she sat up on the deck and realised he was in nothing but swimming trunks and a life jacket and was dangling a bikini from his hand.

'You think I'm going to wear that?'

'Or just the life jacket, I don't mind.'

She snatched the bikini from his hand and wriggled into it as he laughed.

The sky was pale blue from the first fingers of sunlight, the ocean still and beautiful and fresh and nothing could mar its beauty. She snuggled against his waist as he rode the jet ski, laughing at his show of speed and control. But he suddenly slowed right down and all but cut the engine. Then she saw what was swimming towards them in a joyous streak of energy.

'Dolphins,' she breathed.

'A whole pod.' He nodded, turning to see her face. 'They're often out this way to feed.'

And *play*. The creatures leapt and somersaulted as if it were the dolphin Olympics.

'There are hundreds of them.' She laughed in delighted awe. She'd never seen anything as beautiful or exhilarating in her life.

'You want to swim with them?' He was smiling at her, looking the most carefree and vital it made her heart flip in her chest.

'Can we?'

'Sing to them,' he said, handing her a dive mask he'd stowed in his vest. 'They'll come check you out.'

'Sing?'

'Anything.' He chuckled at her look.

But she slipped into the water and tried what he suggested. To her amazement three of the curious creatures swiftly circled around and around her. She floated face-down, eyeing the beautiful animals until she had to lift her head and gasp for breath. Antonio surfaced next to her, smiling triumphantly.

'Antonio.' She breathed hard. 'They're amazing.'

'I know.' He hauled himself back onto the jet ski and leaned down to give her a hand. 'You know they're one of the few creatures to mate just for the fun of it?' He chuckled. 'They feed and play and make love all day. Not such a bad life, is it?'

'Not bad at all.'

She watched as he looked out over the beautiful waters again and that carefree expression slowly faded from his eyes. He glanced at her ruefully. 'We'd better get back to the boat. Breakfast will be waiting.'

Their time was almost up.

Back on board, she showered, disappointed when he didn't join her in there. In the bedroom the clothes she'd arrived in were somehow cleaned and pressed and waiting for her. She blushed at the thought of those nameless, invisible servants knowing she was here and no doubt knowing why. She dressed then went to the lounge. Antonio sat at the laden table, already showered and dressed and waiting for her.

'I'll never forget that, thank you so much.' She smiled across at him.

He had been so kind to her, she'd never forget any of it.

For a split second he looked as happy as she felt, but then that reserve smoothed his features and that was when she couldn't hold back any more. She didn't want to see the vibrant man of the night return to that frozen state now they were about to leave.

'You shouldn't be alone,' she said softly.

Antonio carefully put his tumbler of juice back down on the table. 'Pardon?'

'I said, you shouldn't be alone. You should laugh more often. You deserve more happiness in your life.'

His blood iced.

'Do you feel sorry for me?' he asked quietly, but he was so close to the edge of anger.

Last night hadn't lasted long enough. While she'd slept, he'd watched, like some sick stalker. But he'd been unable to rest any more, too conscious of time ticking. And now?

It wasn't a clock but a bomb ticking. He did *not*

want her to go there with him. He didn't want to hear that lie the world believed. Not from *her* lips. He didn't want her to believe that damn pious story. He was unworthy of her empathy and her generosity. He was unworthy of *her*.

'Of course I do,' she replied simply. 'I'm very sorry you lost her.'

Alessia.

His gut clenched.

'Is that why you're here now, because you pity me?' He stood up from the table and walked away so he couldn't see her face. 'You've been willing to let me do whatever I want with you because you want to make me feel better?'

He heard her small gasp of shock.

'Why are you so angry?' She stood too, following him to the centre of the room, standing defiantly straight and in his face as always. 'I understand you don't want to be hurt again—'

'You understand nothing.' It wasn't about *him* getting hurt. 'It isn't about me. It isn't fair to ask anyone to share the kind of life I lead.'

'That's just an excuse.' She actually rolled her eyes at him. 'Your kind of life can be managed. Media can be managed.'

'Like how that worked out for you and your mother?'

She flinched but the cut didn't stop her. 'Look, I know I'm not the right woman for you, but she's out there. You're just too afraid to find her.'

Hearing her say that infuriated him. Did she really think she was somehow not worthy of him? She had no idea who the worthy one in this room was. It sure as hell wasn't him.

He wanted to shut her up. He should kiss her. Have her. Fast and physical so he could feel the best he'd ever felt in his life for a few minutes again…but he couldn't because she was looking up at him all sincere and sweet and kind and *that* was what wasn't right.

Her eyes were so luminous, so genuine. 'You deserve to find love again.'

No, he didn't. And there was the killer—he'd never found love in the first place.

Bu she misread his silence. 'You do, Antonio. You're a good man. You deserve—'

'I deserve *nothing*,' he snarled in guilt-drenched fury. 'I *destroyed* her.'

Finally Bella was silenced.

And he was aghast at his slip and so, so angry. 'You think you know what happened? You think you know me?'

'Antonio—'

'Stop,' he said, wildly raising his hand. 'Stop and just let me say it. You want the damned, bloody ugly truth?'

For once in his life someone would see him as he really was and it might as well be her. It might as well be the one woman he couldn't stop wanting. And that was good, because she wouldn't want him once she knew. And this would be over.

'I broke up with her before she went away to university. The engagement thing had been more my parents' wish than my own and I was young and didn't want to be tied down. But Alessia was devastated. She begged me not to tell anyone. Wanted to keep it a secret until after she'd gone to England. And we'd let the press know we were no longer together after she'd been there a few months. I agreed. I could see she needed some time to compose herself...' But in his mind he'd been free and he'd been so damned relieved.

'A month or so later I went to see her when Eduardo first went over to study.' He dragged in a desperate breath and carried on fiercely, frantic to get the bitter truth out. 'She'd changed. She'd lost weight and was pale. She was nervy and wanted to get back together.' He paused again, clenching his fist as he remembered how he'd treated her that day. 'I told her that starving herself wasn't going to win me back. I told her to get a grip on herself and stop the drama-queen crap. I was *so* hard on her.' He'd told her he wasn't in love with her and that that wasn't changing no matter what she did.

He'd thought he was doing the right thing to make her pull herself together. Being cruel to be kind.

It had just been cruel.

He made himself look at Bella, made himself ignore the tears building in her beautiful eyes. 'Apparently she didn't see a doctor until another month or so later. She'd thought the weight loss and sore throat was just anxiety and heartache. Instead it was because of a fast-growing mass in her stomach. The kind of cancer that grows so fast, every day before detection matters. Every day missed meant she was closer to death.'

If found in time, treatment could work well. But if not found in time?

Too late already.

'Antonio—'

'My parents were killed the weekend she got the diagnosis. Her prognosis was dreadful. She decided I had enough to be getting on with, so she didn't tell me. Her parents didn't tell me. Eduardo didn't tell me.'

Because he'd been so arrogant to think he could handle the coronation and transfer of power all on his own. He'd refused to allow Eduardo to return to help. In his own grief for his parents he'd wanted just to *work* his way through it.

But he hadn't realised how much that decision would hurt those around him. And ultimately haunt him too.

'Not long after, I found out through the press, as the world knows. But the world still thought we were engaged…' He released a shuddering, painful breath. 'I saw her once more before she died.' He paused, hating that memory more than any other in his life. 'And the worst of it was, *she* apologised to *me*.'

When he'd been the one to break her. He had never regretted anything as much in all his life.

Bella walked over to him. But he was too on edge and he didn't want her compassion. He didn't want that caring. He didn't want anything from her. Not now. He held up his hand again. Desperate to control his damned emotions. *'Don't touch me.'*

Bella flinched at the raw agony in that command. But this time she was ignoring his rejection of her. She had to. She wrapped her arms around his waist.

'Don't.' This time it was a whisper. 'I don't…'

She held him in the gentlest, smallest of embraces.

'You didn't kill her,' Bella said softly. '*Cancer* killed her.'

'If she'd seen a doctor sooner…if she hadn't been stressed and heartbroken…if she'd fought harder…so many ifs. So many mistakes that were my fault.'

But as he spoke his voice went from emotional to expressionless.

He put his hands on her arms and lifted them so he

could step back, free from her. She gazed up into his shadowed face but she could see the determination glinting in his eyes. Goosebumps peppered her skin. He was so used to controlling himself. Even now, he could pull himself together. A cold fear rose within her.

'I will not hurt another person the way I hurt her,' he said softly, intently looking down into her eyes. 'Do you understand?'

'And you think keeping yourself isolated is the way to do that?' It was hard to talk past the giant lump that had formed in her throat. 'You think living only half a life is going to somehow make up for the loss of hers?'

'I lie,' he said harshly, his hold slipping for a second again. 'I live a lie. Every. Damned. Day.' He slammed his fist on the wall behind him. 'I'm not some heart-broken hero. I'm a cold-hearted bastard.'

'You're not that at all.' A tear spilt down her cheek. 'Because you *do* lie. You're protecting her memory. You're caring about her parents and her.'

'It doesn't make it okay,' he said roughly. 'It will *never* make it okay.'

CHAPTER TEN

HE NEVER, EVER should have told her. Because now it *was* pity in her eyes when she looked at him. And he didn't want that. He forced himself to walk away from her. It was over. There was no going back to their lovers-go-lightly affair now.

But she was more beautiful than he'd ever seen her. Her skin glowed, her hair hung in a long, glossy swathe, she smelt of sea and sun and when she'd first got back to the boat after the dolphins she'd looked supremely happy and relaxed. And he was arrogant and egotistical enough to take pleasure in that it was because of something he'd done. But now, the truth was out and she was in tears and their escape was up.

'The helicopter will be here in twenty minutes,' he said formally, determined to recover his equilibrium. 'We have to go back.'

'Of course. I'm ready now.' When he turned back to face her she'd dried her eyes and her back was straight.

He wanted to bring her glow back. That unadulterated happiness that for once had had nothing to do with sex. He wanted to know she was going to be happy *beyond* this moment. He hated the thought of her returning to that club and its exhausting demands.

He wanted to know she was going to be happy in her future.

'I want to give you the funds to establish your ballet school,' he said without thinking.

She stared at him fixedly.

'As an investment,' he clarified quickly. 'San Felipe is a cultural capital of Europe and we don't have a ballet school that could train dancers to professional level...' He trailed off as her expression hardened.

'It's a poor investment,' she said. 'You won't get the return that you would for almost anything else.'

He didn't want a damn return on his investment. 'Is that what that backer told you? He doesn't know what you're capable of.'

She would make it a success, he knew, because she would work herself to the bone to ensure she did. She was more determined than anyone he'd ever met.

'I appreciate what you want to do, but I can't accept it.' She was very, very polite.

'Why not?'

She paused, picking her words with care. 'I want to do it myself.'

'You don't have to do everything on your own,' he argued grimly. 'You want the academy, it's yours. No one will ever know where you got the backing from.'

Her eyes flashed fire. 'Are you trying to buy my silence? Are you worried I'm going to go back to shore and suddenly sell my story?' She paced across the room, turning back to berate him in a furious whisper. 'I will never tell a soul what you told me about Alessia. Not a word. Nothing about this trip. Nothing about us. Not *ever.*'

'I never for a second thought you would.' That

wasn't why he'd mentioned this at all. He knew he could trust her. She understood too well how it was to be judged.

'I don't want to be dependent on a lover for my lifestyle. I don't want to be my mother.'

'This isn't like that.'

'It's exactly like that,' she snapped back.

He paused as the *whomp-whomp-whomp* sound of the helicopter echoed. The boat's interior had amazing soundproofing, which meant that the helicopter had to have arrived for them to be able to hear it at all. Sure enough, within another second the whirring began to fade as the pilot powered the engine down. They wouldn't leave until Antonio gave the word.

He wasn't ready to do that yet. He walked towards where Bella stood glaring at him. 'I just want to help you.'

'Why? You won't let me help you.'

That was different. This was an easy kind of help. This was just money. 'Bella—'

'I'm not a prostitute, Antonio. I'm not your concubine or courtesan. Don't treat me like one.'

He drew up short, feeling out of his depth now. 'You're a *friend*. Friends help each other.'

'Not like this they don't,' she said. 'We're not friends. And I'm not using you for this, Antonio.'

'You won't be using me.'

Why did she look so wounded? His anger boiled over. He should have known she'd reject his offer. He'd never put himself out for anyone. Never offered another woman what he'd offered her. Couldn't she appreciate that? She was so damn stubborn and independent and now acting as if he'd somehow insulted her?

'Why can't you accept I'm just trying to help you?' he asked.

'Why can't you accept that that kind of help isn't something I can ever be comfortable with?'

'Then pay me back,' he exploded back at her. 'We can make it a loan. Just as you have a loan from the backer of BURN. He's not as nice a guy as I am and yet you're happy to accept his assistance.'

'Ours is a strictly professional relationship. Always has been, always will be.'

'And our relationship?'

'We don't have a relationship. We *can't* have a relationship.'

He knew she was right but her refusal angered him anyway. He loathed being told what he could or couldn't do. 'No?'

'Of course not.' She turned and walked towards the nearest door. 'We need to get on that helicopter. We need to stop this.'

'Stop?' He strode over to her. 'What do you mean "stop"?'

She paused and glared up into his eyes. 'You know exactly what I mean. It was fun while it lasted—'

'You're saying we're over?'

'I think that's for the best, yes.'

'Because I offered to help you?'

'It's really nice you wanted to help, but it's not appropriate.'

'What am I supposed to do?' he asked her in frustration.

'I've never asked you to do anything for me.'

No. She hadn't. And that angered him even more.

She didn't want anything from him. Other than hours in his bed.

Which was all he wanted too, right? Because as he'd told her just moments ago, he was never hurting *anyone* the way he had Alessia. Yet here he was, feeling as if he'd just hurt Bella. Badly.

'You're not ending this.' He turned her towards him, then backed her up two paces to the wall. 'This isn't finished. You know it. I know it.'

'Antonio—'

'Shut up and kiss me.'

He needed to vent the frustration rushing along his veins. Sex would help. Sex right now would help a lot. And he knew it would help her too.

'We're supposed to be leaving,' she argued, but her flush deepened.

'I don't care.' He didn't give a damn about his timetable. He needed her soft in his arms, looking upon him with sparkling, sleepy-eyed pleasure, not this hurt and annoyance.

He didn't want to feel guilt where Bella was concerned. Only pleasure. She'd only brought him a sense of well-being and that was the least he could do for her.

He couldn't make her accept his offer. He, who could make decisions that affected every one of the people in his country with the stroke of a pen, had no power over her. Not even to damn well help her. She would never forgive him for it even if he tried to force her. He couldn't make her do anything—except in this one area.

'In this you won't say no,' he said, aching for her sexual submission. Frustrated despite her warm willingness as he pressed against her. 'You will not deny me the permission to pleasure you. You'll come. Over and over.'

'Egotist.' Her eyelids were heavy but she kept those green jewels tightly focused on him.

'You want it too.' He sighed in gut-wrenching relief when she sighed and turned towards his touch. 'More than anything.' He leaned close. 'Isn't that right? Say yes.'

He needed to hear the words as well as see the willingness in her eyes and feel the hot softness of her body.

'Only to this,' she whispered back, her lips brushing his as she answered, her gaze still locked on his.

Oh, he knew that. He knew it and he hated it. Her slender body was hot and wet and tight as he pushed his finger into her sweetly slippery curve.

'We're not done,' he promised with another rough kiss as he pressed close.

'I know.'

But they were. And they both knew it. They were both lying now.

'Antonio,' Bella muttered as he pressed tiny little kisses over and over her mouth and his wicked hands tormented her and all the while he watched her. He watched and he *knew*.

Because she'd caught sight of the determination glinting in *his* eyes and knew he made all the rules as he pleased. And he was damn well going to please her now.

And she could no more deny him than she could deny her lungs air. She wanted to embrace him. Wanted him to feel as good as she. She was so hurt for him— more now she knew the truth of his past, than before. The guilt he felt? The burden he carried?

He'd denied it, but he punished himself so much—how could she deny him this last pleasure? How could she deny herself?

But it was too much.

'It wasn't supposed to be like this,' she groaned harshly as he made her come. So quickly. So intensely. And she was so hungry for more.

It was supposed to have only been a physical relief. A one-night stand to boost her sexual confidence, to make her smile, to be her secret. But it had become more. She *wanted* more. But *not* his money. Not his condescension.

And he wouldn't let her in where she really wanted to be. He'd made that clear. This had become too emotional for him. And for her.

Dazed, she leaned back against the wall, watching as he quickly shed his clothes all the while watching her, his ruthless expression so easy to read. He was ready to test her erotic limits again. And heaven help her she wanted him to already. Because that was the thing: she ached to be with him on so many levels—and she wanted to comfort and be comforted by him even if it could only be in this most basic of ways.

'You're sure you're covered?' he roughly asked, pausing just before taking her.

It took her a moment to realise he meant contraception. 'I am,' she assured him. 'But is it too much of a risk for you?'

'Everything about you is a risk.' He pushed her legs further apart and claimed her with a powerful thrust that made them both groan. 'But worth it,' he muttered hotly before kissing her. 'Worth it.'

This one last time.

Their hands locked together, their bodies locked, their gazes locked. He started, a searing, slow, devastating drill. He held her to him, teasing all her most sensitive parts with that skill and determination she'd come to accept was his strength. She couldn't stop herself muttering his name in a broken whisper over and over as he ruthlessly thrust her to that agonising, tense peak.

She didn't want to read all those conflicting emotions in his pale blue eyes. She wanted this to be the carnal affair it had begun as: they were here for orgasms only. Not for opening up emotionally and admitting old hurts that couldn't be healed.

But she couldn't look away, couldn't break the physical bonds shackling her to him. She should. She knew she should. But she couldn't. Because he held more than her body in his hands now. He held her heart.

And he was about to crush it.

CHAPTER ELEVEN

THE CONJECTURE ABOUT Antonio's twenty-four-hour absence was subdued, thanks to the valiant efforts of Eduardo, who'd surpassed his own legendary ability to charm an entire nation with his smile and good humour. He'd done that by simply bringing his wife and new baby to the event. As it was the first formal photo opportunity with the baby Princess, and was wholly unexpected, the press had a field day. Sure, there were questions about Antonio's whereabouts, but Eduardo had simply told them he was working on an important matter in the palace and had wanted Eduardo and Stella to have their moment.

'It went well. I appreciate your effort.' Antonio stood by the helicopter. Eduardo's wife and daughter were already safely strapped inside.

'There's nothing else you need me to do?' Eduardo asked, his gaze keen. 'I can stay longer...'

Antonio shook his head. 'Go back to the island with your girls. I'm in control here now.'

'You're never not in control,' Eduardo teased, but it was barely a joke.

Thing was, Antonio had never felt less in control. 'Thanks for coming,' he said gruffly.

'Thanks for asking me to.' Eduardo flashed the smile that had made millions swoon. 'See you in a few more weeks.'

The next couple of days passed in a blur of meetings and events, greetings and parties. As they rolled into one Antonio attended on auto. Too much of his mental energy was taken up with trying to forget. Trying not to want more time with her.

Trying not to miss her.

But at every event he couldn't help but cast his eye over the crowd feeling both the dread and hope of seeing her. Bitter disappointment flooded him every time.

But the San Felipe festival fortnight was almost over and his schedule would return to normal busy, not insanely busy. For the most part from now on, he ought to be able to avoid her. He ought to be able to stay in control.

Except the final event loomed tonight. There was no way Bella Sanchez would miss the annual San Felipe Masquerade Ball. Not when she was the nation's club queen. She'd be there in all her sensual beauty.

He buttoned up his starched shirt and fastened his tie. Each guest would hold a delicate mask, but he didn't bother. Everyone knew who he was; there was no escaping it.

He knew there was no escaping that public attention for Bella either. Not yet. But she didn't really want to be in this fishbowl world with a camera in her face every second and the press writing stories about every aspect of her life. She wanted to be free of it and once she'd funded her business she'd retreat into a normal life that had privacy.

That was what she wanted and it was best for her. So

she'd been right on the boat: it *had* to be over between them. No more stolen moments. No more kisses. No more laughter. And that was right for him too—he'd had his time.

He gritted his teeth as he fought back the wave of physical longing. God, he missed her.

The only way of getting through tonight was with no *looking*. Tonight he was going to have to avoid her completely.

Bella applied a final dab of mascara. She'd barely been able to eat a thing all day, and now the moment had finally arrived she was tempted to strip out of her glamorous dress and hide at home in her pyjamas.

She'd made a massive mistake in getting involved with Antonio. Why had she ever thought it would only be a simple, sinful moment of pleasure? It had become all-consuming and her heart *ached*. For him and for her. That he blamed himself so bitterly over Alessia's illness? That he isolated himself so completely?

And that he hadn't made any kind of contact with her since they'd left the boat?

Those last few moments together had been so intense, so profound but the memory of them was now so painful. Because despite his imperious argument at the time, it *was* over.

And she was devastated.

But she couldn't let her emotions get the better of her. She had to move forward. She'd long known how it felt not to be wanted or needed or loved, but she'd never let that stop her from doing what she needed to before. She'd go to the ball, hold her head high and continue building that swelling interest in her business. She might not have succeeded in many things in her life, but she was *not* failing at that. She had her gilt-edged invitation card, she had her dress and she had her years of standing on stage and being stared at. This would be easy.

As long as she kept her distance from the Crown Prince.

But when the liveried guards waved her in to the grand ballroom of San Felipe palace an hour later, she stood a second in the doorway and took in the sight before her. There was grand, and there was opulent, and there was majestic. This was more than all those things, but it wasn't the dazzling venue making her dizzy.

It was anticipation and fear and deep-buried desire. She *ached* to see him.

Her heart thundered as she greeted a few people. Several society faces were now familiar to her and they welcomed her. She knew it was only because of her club's success and her social-media status, but she'd take it.

The first time she saw him, he was only a few yards from her but a crowd separated them. His immaculately tailored tuxedo emphasised his height and proud stance, and she saw he was intently listening to a tall brunette in a form-flattering black gown. Bella froze as she recognised the woman. At that exact moment Francesca Accardi glanced over at her. Time halted as she looked right at Bella, her eyes widening slightly, only then she turned to smile coyly again at Antonio, her face animated.

But she'd offered no nod or smile or any outward sign of recognition towards Bella.

That old rejection stung, but most especially because

Francesca was her own blood. Her half-sister was their father's favourite and now she was with Antonio?

Feeling cold, Bella stared at him. He'd turned to see what had caught Francesca's attention. Now his eyes remained on Bella even as Francesca tried to talk with him. But only for a moment. Then he too glanced away as he muttered something in response to the brunette.

There'd been no smile. No polite inclination of his head. No sign of recognition whatsoever. There was only a callous blanking. He'd seen her, but chosen to pretend he hadn't.

He hadn't acknowledged her at all.

Blinking, Bella turned, blindly moving towards the back of the ballroom. She would never, ever let him know just how much he'd hurt her in that moment.

And she would never, ever forgive him.

She spoke to more people. Made herself take a glass of champagne. She'd have a few sips and then she'd leave. But she wouldn't run immediately. She wouldn't give him that satisfaction. So she smiled. Talked. And the hurt morphed into an anger that grew bigger and hotter with every moment. She smiled more. Talked more. Laughed more.

She wouldn't show any of them any weakness.

Ten minutes later she glanced from the group of young businessmen she was talking to to find his fiery gaze on her.

Still no smile. No inclination of his head. But she read *his* anger this time. Adrenalin surged through her blood.

This time she was the one to turn her back.

She kept talking, but her awareness of him was more acute than ever. She sensed him near, looking icy, but she could feel the simmering fury coming towards her in waves.

She sent her own angry vibes right back at him.

As her smile brightened and her laughter rang her tension mounted. He stood nearer still, but still didn't speak. There was only the look, only the sharpness in the atmosphere and only the two of them felt it.

Finally he passed close enough to speak to her.

'You shouldn't be here,' he said in leashed, low tones.

'You're ordering me to leave?'

'As if you would if I did.' He kept walking past her but his quick glance back was rapier-sharp.

She answered with a death look. But her body felt charged. It didn't care whether it was anger or lust, her body just craved his attention. And she had it now—his gaze on her, his eyes watching as she talked with other guests.

For the next half-hour she talked and laughed and acted like the social butterfly she was supposed to be and it came easy. Every few minutes she glanced at him, their gazes clashed, held, *fought* until she turned away.

Still no smile. No nod.

She turned back, registering how crowded the massive ballroom had become. It was filled with people—women—craving time with Crown Prince Antonio. That tipped her tension from anticipation to unbearable.

She didn't want all these others to be here. She wanted to be alone with him. Fiercely, privately, intimately alone. And that wasn't going to happen. This was only a game, only for tonight. She wasn't going to get what she wanted. Not ever.

Her emotions crashed.

She turned, finally ready to leave. She shouldn't have come. She should have proudly kept her distance and encouraged her customers to come to her club earlier.

She'd miscalculated completely. She took the first door out of the ballroom that she could find. So many people, beautifully dressed, lined the corridor, laughing and talking. She brushed past them, following her instinct to get away. She'd got along its length and had just turned right towards the heavy doors when she heard him.

'Bella.'

She paused, but she didn't turn around.

'Second door on the left.'

It was a command. All her antagonism reared in a passion. But despite knowing better, she couldn't resist. She opened the door he'd meant and stalked into the room. It was a comparatively small meeting room—decorated with more gilt-framed paintings and opulent over-stuffed furniture.

He didn't slam the door behind him. But though he closed it quietly, he locked it, then stood with his back to it. Blocking her exit.

'You shouldn't have come here tonight.' He glared at her, all icy-eyed handsome magnificence in that onyx-black suit.

Despite the fact that she completely agreed with him, she wasn't about to admit it. 'You might be the Prince but this isn't some feudal village in the Middle Ages. There's such a thing as freedom of movement and freedom of speech and it's important to me to be here for my business and you *can't* stop me.' She glared at him, unable to hide her hurt or anger. 'You were so rude when I arrived. You didn't even say hello or nod or anything.' It had been the most pointed, painful dismissal of her life.

'You were the one who said it would be best if we kept this discreet,' he argued.

'You were the one who then kidnapped me for a night on your boat.'

'It was still discreet.'

'And hauling me in here is discreet?'

'I didn't haul you in here.'

No. He hadn't. She hadn't felt his hands on her at all.

'So because I didn't speak to you soon enough, you retaliate by parading round the ballroom in that dress.' He gestured wildly at her body.

'What is wrong with this dress?' She tossed her head and glared at him. 'It's a beautiful dress. And, not that it matters, it's a hell of a lot less revealing than the red one I wore at the ballet.' And she hadn't been parading. 'And what would be wrong with speaking to me?'

'I'm trying to protect you.' His teeth snapped. 'Do you really want those headlines—all the "The scandalous dancer and the Prince" stuff? All that rubbish they'll print on endless pages? Your life won't be your own if they find out.'

'I don't need your protection,' she argued. 'You think I don't know how to handle those headlines? You think I haven't been handling them all my life?'

'I didn't want you to have to handle more.'

'No. You just didn't want to acknowledge me at all.' Always she was denied. As if she were somehow shameful. Not good enough.

'I couldn't—' He broke off with a frustrated growl and then stepped closer, his whisper hoarse with absolute exasperation. 'I couldn't bear to even *look* at you because I cannot concentrate on anything else when you are in the room.'

'You're more of a man than that.' She shook her head, even more incensed by that lame excuse. 'You're the head of a country and have had to perform in way more difficult challenges than—'

'All I wanted to do is sneak you somewhere private and—'

'You're not an animal.' And he was hardly all over her now.

Only then he was, standing so close and squeezing her shoulders so she looked up into his face. And what she saw there made her gasp.

'All I wanted to do was sneak you in here so I could strip you bare,' he finished furiously.

The fire in his eyes made her so reckless. 'Then why don't you?'

She bared herself in that one sentence—bringing that desire right into fore.

He smiled. A small mocking smile. 'Always the provocation.' Swiftly he released her shoulders only to bend and pick her up. 'How much proof do you need?'

'All of it,' she demanded roughly as she felt his arms tighten still. 'I need all of it.'

He took three steps to the plump sofa near the wall. She hooked her legs around his waist just before he sat, so she then straddled him. He released her only to grasp her hair and tug so she lifted her chin and met his kiss. Hard and passionate and endless.

She writhed above him, aching to feel him there. Right there. Centring her, anchoring her. Completing her.

Their hands tangled as they sought to touch more intimately. His hands pressed against her curves, teasing, frustrating. She hated her beautiful dress, she wanted to feel his skin on hers. She wanted them both to be naked.

Neither were.

But their passion was utterly bared.

They moved quickly, angrily. He shoved her dress up to her waist with a jerky hand while unfastening his trousers with the other. She lifted herself off him only long enough for him to free his straining erection. And then she gave in again to the delight of rubbing against him. Of fighting to get closer, closer, closer still.

Their eyes met in a moment of frustration and desperation. She felt him move, his hand fisted around the crotch of her panties and he tugged hard. The silk and lace ripped. A moment later she sank onto him—fast and hard and utterly complete.

His hand squeezed her thigh almost painfully. His groan sent a shiver of raw delight down her spine. Now she was happy. Now she was with him. Now time could stop.

But it didn't. It couldn't. Nor could they stop.

He bucked beneath her, powerfully thrusting up, as if he could possibly get deeper within her. Desire for him burned—for more of how good he felt inside her. She pressed down to meet him, wanting more of him. Always more.

They fought to get closer, wild and desperate and so quick yet not quickly enough. And it wasn't slow enough either. She wanted him so much, *all* of him, but she didn't want it to end.

Except it was about to. She felt it coming—that unstoppable wave of pleasure that only he had ever brought forth from her. She arched back, whimpering as he bore it upon her. He thrust faster still until it was a frantic final coupling as frustrating as it was ecstatic.

'One last time,' he commanded. 'I need to see you come one last time.'

She stared at him in blissful agony, then closed her eyes against the despair in his. Bittersweet torture wracked her body as her orgasm hit. It was so good, but it tore her heart. Because this *was* the last time. Her mouth parted, but his hand pressed hard on her lips. In that final moment of release, he silenced her.

'I'm sorry,' he choked as he stiffened beneath her. 'I am so sorry,' he groaned in a harsh whisper as he too hit climax.

Bella dared not open her eyes. She didn't want to face this end. Through the door and walls, she could hear the ball in full swing but the silence between them in the private room was horrendous. She slipped from his knee, turning her back as she adjusted her dress.

'I didn't mean to be rude when you first arrived,' he said quietly, his voice still tinged with infinite regret. 'But I am not able to hide how I feel about you.'

'Is that so terrible?' She braced herself and faced him to ask, 'Would it really be so awful for people to know you'd finally moved on?'

He didn't answer. He didn't have to. Because for once his expression was so easy to read.

To her horror, her eyes filled with tears. He didn't want anyone to know how much he wanted her. Which basically meant he didn't *want* to want her. He didn't want to move on. He *hadn't* moved on.

She turned and ran, just getting to the door and

turning the key in the lock. But he must have run too because he reached above her head and pushed hard, so she couldn't open it.

'You're not leaving now,' he said.

'You're not stopping me.'

'I am. This time I am.' He turned her to face him. 'You can't go out there looking like that.'

'Looking like what? A slut?' With no underwear and kiss-swollen lips and the blush of orgasm still on her skin?

'I'm sorry.' He apologised again as he retreated into that damn formal reserve. 'This shouldn't have happened.'

She didn't want him to turn all princely polite. She didn't want him to regret what had happened. She just wanted him to want more the same way she did. But he didn't. She cared more for him than he did her. And she was heartbroken. She looked at the floor, unable to bear looking into that emotionless face of his.

'Forgive me.'

Angered, she lifted her head. '*I'm* not the one who needs to forgive you. *You* need to forgive *yourself.* You're a coward, Antonio De Santis.'

He actually lost colour.

'You think you're so damn noble, burying yourself in duty. You think you're protecting Alessia's name? You're only protecting yourself. You think you can keep yourself safe by not bothering to participate in life?' She shook her head, so angry with him for shutting her out. 'It doesn't work that way. Who's hurting now, Antonio? *Who* is hurting?'

'I'm sorry,' he said tonelessly. 'I cannot be the man you want me to be. I cannot be the man for you.'

It was the most humiliating moment of her life.

And he wouldn't admit that *he* was hurting either. 'I will control myself better in future. This won't happen again.'

'No.' She nodded painfully. 'It won't. I don't expect you to say hello or anything—you're absolved from any duty to be polite to me.' She half laughed bitterly at the heartbreaking mess she was in. He only wanted her for sex, whereas she? She'd gone fully in love. 'This can only be all or nothing. You can't give me *all*. So it has to be nothing.' For her own sanity it had to be nothing. But she was so, so hurt.

He didn't argue with her. 'I can have you escorted discreetly—'

'I'll go out the door I came in.' She straightened and pulled together the last shred of pride that she could. 'But I need five minutes alone first.'

He stared down at her, as if he could somehow break her and make her change her mind. But he couldn't. Her dignity was the one thing she'd leave this room with.

He had the intelligence not to apologise again, though she knew he wanted to. She could see that in his eyes. But she didn't want his pity. What she really wanted was the one thing he couldn't give her. He didn't want to give her.

And that wasn't his fault.

'Leave, Antonio.'

And then he did.

She locked the door again right away and took deep breaths to recover her equilibrium. She was not crying here. She was holding her head high and walking out of there.

No one would ever know how she'd been so crushed.

It took ten minutes before she was ready. Then she unlocked the door, squared her shoulders and walked back down the corridor and around the corner to where the people were thronging and still laughing, oblivious to the cataclysmic encounter in that room so close by. She got into the ballroom and began her trek along the edge to the exit at the end. She was walking so quickly, and with such concentration, she almost crashed into the broad-shouldered man who suddenly stepped in front of her.

'Do you really think you can ever belong here?'

She stared blankly for a second before realising who it was.

Salvatore Accardi. Her father. For the first time in her life he'd addressed her directly. And he wasn't being conciliatory.

Frantically she processed his words, wondering at what he'd meant.

'Look at you,' he snarled. 'You think it isn't obvious what you've been doing?' Salvatore sent her a scathing look. 'Like mother, like daughter. Giving it all to anyone who asks. No doubt you're aiming to get pregnant as quickly as possible and you'll blame it on the nearest wealthy man.' He stepped closer. 'You're the daughter of a whore and you're a whore.'

Oh, God, did he know? Had he seen? She glanced to the side, wondering if everyone here knew. How was that possible?

'You need to leave San Felipe,' Salvatore added.

She couldn't cope with this onslaught right now. Not after Antonio's rejection.

But as she stared at Salvatore, aghast and unable

to speak, she saw his eyes widen at something over her shoulder.

'Is there some kind of problem, Salvatore?' Crown Prince Antonio walked up behind her.

Salvatore's expression tightened.

Antonio took her hand, holding it tight. It was the smallest, but most pointed, of gestures and she was so shocked she still could say nothing.

'Bella and I are very close,' he said. 'So I'm glad to see you talking. I'm sure you want to make her welcome. But if you'll excuse us, we're going to dance now.'

Bella gazed at Antonio in utter astonishment. Why had he reappeared? Why had he taken her hand? And what on earth did he mean by dance?

She looked up at him to see, but he wasn't looking at her. He was coolly looking into her father's eyes.

For a single second there was complete stillness in the ballroom. The glittering guests were motionless, all looking at them, like a tableau at the start of an Ancient Greek play—though whether it was to be a tragedy or not was yet to be determined. Even the orchestra was silent. He'd chosen to move in that small gap between pieces.

Then everyone moved at once. Voices heightened, laughter rang. The excitement that had been palpable before was incandescent now.

San Felipe society was on fire.

Salvatore was now the speechless one. Everyone else surrounding her seemed to melt away. And then Antonio walked her away from him, holding her hand as if it were the most everyday thing in the world, when in fact it was the most intimate, most public display imaginable.

'What are you doing?' she asked as he led her through the crowd.

'As I said. I'm making my way to the dance floor.'

She stumbled and he paused, to put his arm around her waist and draw her nearer to him. Her heart thudded. *Why* was he doing this? Why when in private he had just ended *everything*?

He turned to face her and pulled her even closer to dance with him. His hold on her wasn't polite; it was the hold of a man who knew the woman in his arms intimately.

And the whole world was watching.

'Why did you say that to him?' Why tell him they were close? She stared up at Antonio. He was watching her mouth in all the noise—not the way he did when he wanted to kiss her, but with intent concentration. That was when she figured it out. 'You *lip-read* what he said to me.'

He'd heard that abusive 'whore' slur and he'd come running to the rescue.

But Antonio didn't answer her now.

'Antonio,' she prompted him.

She saw the muscle working in his jaw and knew she'd guessed right.

'Can you at least try to dance?' he said shortly. 'People are looking.'

Finally she understood. It was all about the *appearance*. Of course it was.

'You don't have to do this,' she choked.

'Do what?'

'Give me a Cinderella moment so you can control whatever scandal Salvatore might try to unleash. You're trying to protect my name, like what you did with Alessia.' And it was unbearable.

'This is different.' His words were clipped.

'I know.' She felt a blush burn her cheeks. 'This is far less serious. And far less tragic...far less...everything,' she whispered. 'But you're still trying to protect someone, and painting yourself into a corner. This time you don't have to.'

'What do you mean I don't have to?'

'I don't want you feeling obligated to. You've been through that once before and it affected years of your life. I won't be the reason for that happening again.'

'Bella—'

'You know, just because someone cares about you, it doesn't mean you're obligated to return those feelings. You don't owe that person anything.' He owed *her* nothing.

'You're wrong,' he said. 'You are always obligated to do no harm.'

Oh, God, he was trying to protect her. He was trying to be honourable. Even when she already knew he didn't want to be that man for her.

'Okay.' She struggled to keep breathing steadily and not scream at him. 'But you're to do no harm to *yourself* either.' She gave up on attempting to dance. 'This is harming you. This is not what you want.'

He'd just told her so in that private room when he'd promised that mad lust wouldn't happen again and broken her heart in the process. He'd wanted *nothing*, not *all*.

She knew he was protective of those he cared about, or those he felt he owed or who he felt responsible for.

She didn't want him doing that for her. She didn't want to trap him into something he didn't really want because he felt *sorry* for her. Not even for a short time.

The tears flooded her eyes and the lump blocked her throat. She could hardly see and she definitely couldn't speak.

'Bella—'

She forced back the burn in her chest. But the overwhelming heartache threatened to drown her. She wrenched her hand from his, turned and ran, forcing her way through the staring crowd, leaving him white-lipped and alone in the middle of the ballroom.

CHAPTER TWELVE

ANTONIO WORKED OUT in the early morning in the palace gym for the first time in days. A couple of times this hour had been Bella's and his whole body ached at the thought of her. Annoyed, he pushed himself harder, choosing to run on the treadmill to cool down instead of his customary walk through the pre-dawn darkened city streets. He both smiled and grimaced as he flicked the switch to increase the pace. No one had dared mention her—or the ball—to him but he'd not thought of anything since.

The look on Accardi's face when Antonio had taken Bella's hand? That naked fury? Antonio had revelled in it. He still did. But his smile faded when he remembered how she'd looked at him in that same moment. And when he'd hurt her so badly.

'Your Highness?' His valet ventured into the gym apologetically. 'You might need to get ready.'

Antonio glanced at the time and frowned. How had an hour gone by?

He stalked through to the shower. He had only two formal appearances this morning. Once they were done, he'd finally have the time to work out how to manage the intense media and public interest in Bella.

He was still livid that she'd walked out on him at the ball. Never had he met someone so determined to disagree with him and refuse his assistance. Independence was one thing. Pig-headedness another.

What had happened with Alessia was different. She had *died*. It was her parents and her memory he'd been protecting in the aftermath. And, he finally admitted, he'd been protecting himself.

He'd once told Eduardo that he would have married for love. Indeed it was the only thing he *would* marry for. But the way he'd treated Alessia? He couldn't risk doing that to someone else. He couldn't bear the thought of causing more pain and carrying more guilt. He didn't deserve happiness when he'd felt responsible for cutting her life short. He should have encouraged Alessia to seek help; time would have been the best chance she could have had.

But he'd failed her and he'd then chosen work. Bella had been right: it had been the easier option. He'd told himself that the constraints on him and the scrutiny he lived under meant there'd been no chance for love to develop with anyone else.

That had been an excuse too.

But then she'd danced into his life and challenged him on every level, hitting him hard and quick. With lust, certainly, but then there was everything else about her—honesty, strength, humour. She'd made him want to tease and laugh and live.

But in the moment when she'd needed him most, in that private room at the ball, he'd failed her. And when he'd put himself out for her in a way he'd never done for anyone else a few minutes later, she'd then questioned his motives. Of course she had. She'd rejected him. She was *angry* with him.

Well, he was *furious* with himself.

He slung a towel round his waist and stalked to his private music room only to find it now haunted by the memory of her dancing there for him. He sat at the piano and tried not to remember the way she'd straddled him on the stool. But all he could see in his mind's eye instead was the sweetness of her smile as she'd swum and sung with the dolphins.

He'd never felt as content as he had in that moment. Only he'd been too dumb to recognise why that was. And it wasn't about knowing he'd disarmed Accardi at the ball that had made him smile.

It was all about Bella—about making *her* happy.

This wasn't anger he was feeling now. It was *hurt*. He was hurt that she hadn't stayed, that she hadn't wanted him to help her. And it was fear, that maybe she'd hadn't really wanted *him* at all.

Yeah, he was terrified, because he was helplessly, utterly in love with her and he had no idea how to handle it. How could he get her to believe in him? She trusted no one. Now least of all him. And he didn't blame her. He was such an arrogant, ignorant idiot, who'd been so wrapped up in his own self-sacrificing, he'd not realised that he was sacrificing *Bella's* happiness too.

He picked up a phone and sent a message to his aide to cancel all his appointments for the day.

Because finally he'd figured out that his most important job of all was to love her.

CHAPTER THIRTEEN

NEEDLESS TO SAY the club was more popular than ever. Bella was reduced to barricading herself in her upstairs office. The number of people watching, wanting to get close to her, was terrifying. She was effectively a prisoner but she refused to call on Antonio to help her deal with them. He'd not made contact since she'd left the ball two days ago. It was over.

She'd employed extra security staff at short notice, enforced a strict entry policy and she'd hidden out at the top of the old fire station.

Coming to San Felipe had been a massive mistake. The paradise principality, all beauty and history, with its hint of pirate and sniff of Mediterranean magic, was supposed to have been the scene for her fresh start, but she hadn't even managed a couple of months before monumentally stuffing up by falling in love with the most impossible of men.

It wasn't because he was the Prince of the nation, but because he was so *principled*. He put duty before himself, put the needs of others before his own, and protected others regardless of the price to his own freedom, needs and desires.

She refused to let him do that for her. He didn't love her.

She also refused to give in to her weakest urge and run away. She couldn't. She was locked into the lease. She wasn't going to let the club's backer down. No quitting, no matter what. In a few weeks all the interest in her personal life would die down. The world would think they'd had a fling and that it was now over. Antonio had shaken free of her. And really, that was the truth.

She just had to grit her teeth and put up with the extra intrusion during that time.

But it wasn't that intense public interest that she wanted to run from. It was the heartbreak. She'd truly, totally, fallen for him but while she'd been the object of his lust, the only other emotion she inspired in him was pity. She had his courtesy, his misguided sense of responsibility. And that was almost worse than anything.

Energy—frustration, anger, futility—surged within her. She kicked the leg of her desk. But heat coursed through her rather than pain—he'd pushed her onto that wide expanse of wood and teased her to her first orgasm.

She didn't want to have it in her office any more. She might have to stay in his city for a couple of years but she didn't need this reminder of his sensual power over her in her home. She'd move the desk out this second. No matter that it was almost midnight and her club was full of patrons. She'd push the wretched thing out onto the landing and get the bar staff to take it away in the morning.

She shoved the paperwork to the floor behind her. Then she tried to shove the thing towards the door. It was so heavy, it took ten minutes to move it even two inches and even then it scraped a deep scratch in the wooden floor and she was furious enough to scream.

'Need some help?'

She jerked upright. Antonio was leaning in the now open doorway, watching with a soft smile curving the edge of his usually firm mouth. He was in jeans and tee, with stubble on his jaw, and his usually impeccable hair looked as if he'd been ruffling it with both hands for two hours. He had dark rings under his eyes as if he'd not slept in days and his pale eyes just burned right through to her vulnerable soul.

He looked *gorgeous*.

Her muscles liquefied. So not what she wanted when she was trying to shift a desk heavier than Stonehenge's largest rock.

'What are you trying to do?' he asked when she failed to respond to his first question.

'What does it look like I'm trying to do?' she answered heatedly. 'I'm moving this desk.'

His eyebrows shot up. 'It looks heavy.'

'Clearly.' She straightened and glared at him. 'And you're in the way.'

She didn't want him here at all—not looking like that. And looking at *her* like that.

It wasn't fair.

'How do you think you're going to get it through the door?' He didn't budge as she fruitlessly tried to move the behemoth another few inches. 'Ask me for help.'

For a split second she gaped. Then she snapped her jaw shut and stood upright to glare at him. 'No.'

He stepped into the room and kicked the door shut

behind him. Folding his arms across his chest, he mirrored her defiance.

'Ask me,' he dared, glaring back at her.

Something shifted deep within her when she saw that flickering expression in his eyes. Something she really didn't want to shift. He couldn't break down her resistance with just that *look*.

'I don't need to move it tonight,' she murmured weakly.

He leaned forward, planting both hands on the desk that stood between them. 'I need to know I can help you,' he said huskily, still pinning her in place with that unwavering, intense gaze. 'That you feel you can count on me. That I'll be there for you.'

Bella breathed gently, trying to stave off the emotion swirling too close to her surface. He still didn't get it, did he?

'I don't want to have to count on you,' she said. 'I don't want to use you in that way.'

She didn't want him to 'rescue' her. She didn't want to be any kind of 'duty' to him. She tore her gaze away, frowning down at the desk.

'It's not using me.' His spread hands snapped into fists, his knuckles whitening. 'I ache for you to need me. Because *I* need *you*.'

Stunned, she glanced back up to his face.

'It's okay to ask for help and it's okay to want to be loved,' he argued roughly. 'That desire doesn't weaken you in any way.'

'Have you been reading self-help memes on the Internet?' she croaked.

'Stop trying to push me away. I'm not going anywhere.' An expression crossed his face—one she hadn't seen in him before. 'I've spent the last two days racking my brains trying to come up with some elaborate way in which I can convince you. Considering what happened at the ball I figured a grand public gesture wasn't it. In the end I decided it comes down to just you and me. No audience. No performance. Just truth.'

At that vulnerable intensity in his eyes, her grip on her emotions slipped. Anguished, she broke. 'What do you want from me?'

'Everything,' he whispered. 'I want everything from you. Everything *with* you.'

'No, you don't.' She shook her head, haunted by all the constraints on them. 'Kings have flings with dancers. They date them. They don't—' She broke off, embarrassed at where she'd been heading. At her *presumption*.

'Don't what—' he smiled a little crookedly '—marry them?' He waggled his eyebrows. 'Isn't it a good thing I'm not a king?'

'You know what I mean,' she mumbled, mortified and unable to think further than her next breath. 'And you're a king in every other way.'

'You think I wouldn't marry you?'

'I think you *can't*.' She burned. He couldn't possibly be serious.

'Have you been reading the papers?' His gaze narrowed. 'You know what they say isn't true.'

'I haven't been reading them,' she answered his lecturing tone scornfully. 'I'm not stupid. I *never* read them. I don't need to read them to know what they say.'

And from his one comment she was glad she hadn't. It had taken sheer willpower and strategic unplugging of the Internet to resist the temptation. But she'd done it. She'd made herself focus on nothing but the club these last two days. She'd caught up on her accounts, her business studies and she'd paced for hours, alone and inconsolable. 'I'm not suitable for you.'

'You're the one declaring that you don't want to be defined by your past, or by the reputation others have foisted on you, yet you're the one saying that you can't be with me because of what others might think,' he said. 'I don't care what they think so why should you?'

'I care about what they say about *you*,' she said fiercely. 'I'm trying to protect *you*.'

'Why?' he shot back at her. 'Because you care about me?'

There was a moment of pulsing silence. In that one moment she was bereft of more than words, but everything.

'This isn't the Dark Ages.' He softened his approach and that wicked smile suddenly flashed across his face. 'There are no scarlet letters in my country. It's not like you have a sex tape.'

'My mother's one is still doing the rounds—' she interrupted, cringing inside.

'And you're not your mother,' he interrupted her back. 'Even if you did, I wouldn't care.' He leaned forward, pressing his fists harder on the desk. 'No more roadblocks. *I* choose *you*, Bella. If my people don't want you as their Crown Princess then I'll abdicate. You're more important to me than anything.'

'You can't do that.'

'I can. And I would. But the truth is I won't have to. Screw the scandal. They'll get over it.'

'No.' There was no way that would happen. 'I don't

think so. I think you should leave.' She needed him to go. Now.

His eyes narrowed on her. 'Do you know what I think?' he asked, bitterness sharpening his soft-spoken words. 'I think that no matter what I do, no matter what I say, I can't win this. You will still say no to me.' He blew out a harsh breath. 'You don't want me enough to fight for this. For us. For me.'

That tore her heart in two.

'Don't,' she begged him. 'Please don't.' Because it wasn't true. It wasn't fair.

She was trying to do what was *right*.

Large tears welled in her eyes, her breathing came uneven and quick and she wanted to run. But there was a huge desk and an immovable man in front of her.

And he wasn't going to let her run.

He watched her for a long moment, seeming to see right through her.

'This is fear,' he told her firmly. 'Pure and simple. You're afraid to believe in me. You're afraid to trust that I'm really here for you, because no one has ever been there for you before.'

Hot tears now scalded her cheeks. She couldn't stop them, couldn't stop him. She couldn't bear to look at him, yet nor could she tear her gaze from his.

'That changes, Bella. Tonight,' he promised her. 'I'm here for you now. And I have enough fight for the both of us.'

She blinked, spilling more tears, but she still couldn't get her voice to work. She still couldn't get her body to move. She still couldn't get her brain to believe.

'I have been such a coward,' he said quietly. 'I was a pompous jerk, believing that my "duty" was more important than anything when really it was an excuse not to let anyone get close. I have felt so guilty about Alessia and blamed myself for a long time. I felt like I didn't deserve this kind of happiness because of what happened. But you were right that I needed to forgive myself. To move on. And now I think maybe the way to make amends is to love a woman the way *she* deserves to be loved. To love *you* more than life itself.'

Bella closed her eyes, but he kept speaking and she couldn't block him out.

'It's very easy to love someone when she's the right person for you,' he added softly. 'I know you're scared to believe in this. In me. I know you don't trust me. Not yet.'

She wanted to hide because her skin was burning with pain and vulnerability.

'Give me time,' he added. 'We can work on that together, Bella.'

The sincerity in his voice compelled her to look him in the eye again. Hope did more than shift within her, it unfurled.

'You're not just saying this because you feel somehow responsible for me?' she asked. 'Because I'm okay. I'll be okay. I can survive—'

'Well, good for you, but I can't,' he snapped, his smile vanishing. 'I won't be happy without you. And I won't stop until you're at my side.' He growled at her. 'I never understood what love really was until I met you. Be brave. Trust me. Turn to me. Need me the way I need you. Love me the way I love you. Like nothing else matters. Because nothing else does.'

He was too compelling. Too honest. And nothing else did matter except that he was standing miles from her and while she'd heard everything he'd said, she needed to *feel* it too. She needed to experience that certainty in his strong embrace.

He'd fallen silent, watching her process everything, but his smile had returned. She realised he was waiting for her to come to him. Waiting for her to be as brave as he'd asked her to be. And she wanted to be, but her legs trembled as anticipation and ecstatic relief surged through her.

He met her halfway around the stupid desk. Reaching out, he framed her face with both hands and looked down at her for a long moment.

'Don't you want to kiss me?' She gripped his wrists hard, *dying* at his hesitation.

'More than anything this whole freaking time,' he muttered. 'But I was determined to *talk* to you. I knew you'd say yes if I made love to you first, but I didn't want to seduce you that way. I wanted to be sure you listened. And heard. You need to believe in me.'

He kissed her then—a soft, sweet kiss that breathed love and laughter into her once forlorn heart. Oh, Lord, was it possible to die from happiness?

She rose on tiptoe, refusing to let him pull back too far. She needed him near. She needed his touch. 'You thought you could seduce me into saying yes?'

'I can seduce you into saying anything.' He played up his wicked tease, his eyes dancing. 'Into saying yes, into saying how much you want me…but I wanted you to mean it.'

'Seduce me anyway,' she invited. 'I'll say it. And I'll still mean it.'

'What will you say?'

His question was barely audible, but she read the hunger in his eyes. Suddenly it was easy to be brave.

'That I love you.'

He too was so very easy to love.

'I do love you,' she repeated, no longer caring that she was crying again.

His kisses smothered her words but she kept on chanting them—in her heart, in her touch. And he met her, promise for promise, kiss for kiss, touch for touch.

He pulled her close. She'd missed him so much. They worked frantically, undoing buttons, pushing fabric aside, eager for skin, sensation, surety.

'No more secrecy,' he muttered. 'No more stolen moments.' He swiftly moved, spinning and lifting her onto the broad desk, his smile both tender and outrageous, his eyes filled with love. She parted her legs and pulled him to her, equally teasing and true.

'Love me,' she begged as he kissed his way down the length of her body and back up again.

'Already do. Always will,' he answered roughly, grabbing her leg and wrapping it higher around his hip so he could rub tantalisingly harder against her core, almost claiming her, but not quite. 'You're mine. I'm yours. Love me back.'

The pleasure was so exquisite she could barely comprehend his words. 'Yes.'

'Keep. Saying. Yes.' He thrust into her with each word, but not all the way, only teasing, arousing her beyond sanity.

'Yes. Yes. Yes.' She never wanted him to stop this torture—but at the same time she wanted it all. Now.

'Marry me,' he demanded as he thrust into her to the hilt.

She gasped and stared up at him, registering the brutally satisfied look on his face as he pinned her hot, willing body with his.

'You bully,' she breathed as she saw the laughing, loving determination within him.

'Not bullying,' he corrected with another devastating thrust. 'Seducing.'

'It's too soon.'

'Always you need convincing,' he teased. But he smiled tenderly at her and gently kissed away the tears falling fresh from her eyes. 'No matter. I'll seduce you every day until you say yes to this. To everything. To me.'

She gasped as he pushed closer still.

He looked into her eyes, his own revealing exquisite torment as he paused. 'We'll get there together, darling. You can count on it.'

He reached down between them to touch her. Merciless. Relentless. Utterly loving. Determination hardened his face as she trembled, shaking in his arms. There was more than an orgasm coming. There was bliss of the for-ever kind.

'Yes,' she sobbed. 'Yes, yes, yes.'

EPILOGUE

Two years later

'YOU'RE NOT A good accompanist for my beginner classes,' Bella admonished her laughing husband once the last of her students had left the studio.

'I thought I did pretty well.' Crown Prince Antonio spread his hands in an innocent gesture as he left the piano and sauntered over to where she stood in the middle of the wooden floor.

Bella tried not to be swayed by his gorgeous casual jeans and tee combo but she just loved seeing him this relaxed. 'Breaking into Happy Birthday in the middle of the warm-up was not helpful.'

'But it is your birthday and they loved singing it to you.'

It was his smile that was her undoing—that wickedly tempting glint that flashed from behind that formal reserve and hit her like sensual lightning.

'I've cancelled the rest of your classes for today.' He walked past to lock the studio door and turned back to face her with an arrogant wink.

'You haven't,' she breathed, outraged and delighted at the same time.

Two years in and he was still stealing moments for them alone.

'I have,' he confirmed with zero apology. 'Not only is it your birthday, it's our first wedding anniversary and I'm in charge of all celebrations. Especially the private ones.'

'You do love to be in charge, don't you?' she murmured as he came close enough to kiss.

'I've had a lifetime of experience.' He nodded as he brushed his lips over hers. 'Don't hold it against me.'

Laughing, she curled her arms around his neck and snuggled close. She'd never have thought she could feel so happy and so secure.

Salvatore Accardi had sold his property on San Felipe, loudly declaring he preferred Sardinia. Which was more than fine as far as Bella was concerned because Antonio had been muttering about banishing him from San Felipe for ever on some pretext and that would have only caused scandal and pain, neither of which she was interested in.

Antonio's brother Eduardo had welcomed her with rakish charm and she'd bonded with his wife Stella over her beautiful baby daughter Sapphire.

But the best thing of all was the man in front of her. That her Prince had become so playful still amused her. When the crowds weren't around he was filled with warmth and laughter, but it had spilled over into his public persona as well. The press headlines gushed over the transformation in the Prince—he smiled, he laughed, he was so obviously happy, they seemed to think she was Wonder Woman... So to her absolute amazement, the people of San Felipe had welcomed her completely. Speculation about Princess Bella's possible pregnancy was rife. But that was the one thing she wanted to share with him alone.

She looked up into his beautiful eyes, unable to keep her secret a second longer. 'I have an anniversary present for you.' Even though she was so excited, she was suddenly shy and couldn't get her voice above little more than a whisper.

But he could lip-read and, besides, he knew already, didn't he?

Her eyes filled as he dropped to his knees before her.

'Tell me it's true,' he muttered roughly, wrapping his arms around her legs so tightly she almost toppled.

'I thought we didn't read the papers.' She couldn't resist a final tease as she ruffled his hair gently.

'I haven't read the papers. I've read here.' He placed his hand on the very gentle swell of her stomach. 'And here.' He cupped her breast. 'And here.' He cupped the side of her face, wiping the tear from under her eye with the gentlest finger and then tracing the full curve of her lips. 'So tell me it's true.'

She smiled a watery smile. He groaned, a raw sound of heartfelt longing and wonder. She bent to kiss him quiet, pouring her heart and happiness into it, into him. She could never give him enough—not when he'd given her so much.

'Dance with me,' he whispered against her mouth, pulling her down to the floor with him.

'Any time,' she promised.

Because the music between them played for ever.

* * * * *

*In case you missed it,
the first story in Natalie Anderson's*
THE THRONE OF SAN FELIPE
series is available now!
THE SECRET THAT SHOCKED DE SANTIS

MILLS & BOON®

EXCLUSIVE EXCERPT

Dario Di Sione's triumph in retrieving his family's
earrings is marred by the discovery that his traitorous
wife Anais has kept their child a secret! But Anais's
return to his side casts a new light on past events,
and now it's not the child he just wants to claim…

Read on for a sneak preview of
THE RETURN OF THE DI SIONE WIFE
the fourth in the unmissable new eight book Modern series
THE BILLIONAIRE'S LEGACY

Dario froze.

For a stunned moment he thought he was imagining
her.

Because it couldn't be *her*.

Inky black hair that fell straight to her shoulders, as
sleekly perfect as he remembered it. That lithe body,
unmistakably gorgeous in the chic black maxidress she
wore that nodded to the tropical climate as it poured
all the way down her long, long legs to scrape the
ground. And her face. *Her face.* That perfect oval with
her dark eyes tipped up in the corners, her elegant
cheekbones and that lush mouth of hers that still had
the power to make his whole body tense in uncontrolled,
unreasonable, *unacceptable* reaction.

He stared. He was a grown man, a powerful man
by any measure, and he simply stood there and *stared—*

as if she was as much a ghost as that Hawaiian wind that was still toying with him. As if she might blow away as easily.

But she didn't.

"Hello, Dare," she said with that same self-possessed, infuriating calm of hers he remembered too well, using the name only she had ever called him—the name only she had ever gotten away with calling him.

Only Anais.

His wife.

His treacherous, betraying wife, who he'd never planned to lay eyes on again in this lifetime. And who he'd never quite gotten around to divorcing, either, because he'd liked the idea that she had to stay shackled to the man she'd betrayed six years ago, like he was an albatross wrapped tight around her slim, elegant neck.

Here, now, with her standing right there in front of him like a slap straight from his memory, that seemed less like an unforgivable oversight. And a whole lot more like a terrible mistake.

Don't miss
THE RETURN OF THE DI SIONE WIFE
by Caitlin Crews

Available October 2016

www.millsandboon.co.uk

MILLS & BOON®

18 bundles of joy from your favourite authors!

Get 2 books free when you buy the complete collection only at
www.millsandboon.co.uk/greatoffers